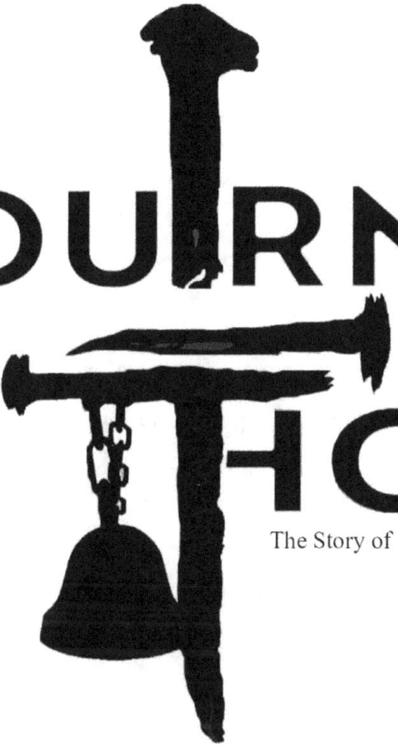

JOURNEY OF HOPE

The Story of Father Joseph Albrecht

BOB RIEPE

Gotham Books
30 N Gould St.
Ste. 20820, Sheridan, WY 82801
https://gothambooksinc.com/
Phone: 1 (307) 464-7800

© 2022 Bob Riepe. All rights reserved.
No part of this book may be reproduced, stored in a retrieval system, or transmitted by any means without the written permission of the author.

Published by Gotham Books (August 26, 2022)

ISBN: 979-8-88775-033-0 P
ISBN: 979-8-88775-034-7 E
ISBN: 979-8-88775-035-4 H

Any people depicted in stock imagery provided by iStock are models, and such images are being used for illustrative purposes only.

Certain stock imagery © iStock.

Because of the dynamic nature of the Internet, any web addresses, or links contained in this book may have changed since publication and may no longer be valid. The views expressed in this work are solely those of the author and do not necessarily reflect the views of the publisher, and the publisher hereby disclaims any responsibility for them.

Scripture texts used in this work are taken from the NEW AMERICAN BIBLE, copyright © 1970, by the Confraternity of Christian Doctrine, Washington, D.C., and are used by permission of copyright owner. All rights reserved.

Several quotes made by Father Willibald Willi and Mother Brunner were taken from FOUR UNPUBLISHED BOOKS, by Father Francis Brunner. Messenger Press has copyright. Used by permission of coypright owner. All rights reserved.

Dedication

This book is dedicated to:

MY DAUGHTER
BRENDA

MY DAUGHTER
TAMMY

MY SON
ROBERT

About The Author

Bob Riepe was born in Perham, Minnesota, December 4, 1948. He was raised on a farm near Perham, and a graduate from Perham High School in 1966. He graduated from Moorhead State in 1970, with a B.S. Degree in Secondary Education, with a major in History. He is married and the father of three children. After serving over ten years in the U.S. Navy as an Arab linguist, and then as a Russian linguist, he returned to Perham, where he is presently a District Sales Manager for Barrel O' Fun Snack Foods. He has an avid interest in family geneologies, which led to the creation of 'Journey of Hope.'

It is a very interesting account of his amazing life. You handled a delicate life story with great skill and understanding.

-Rev. Robert C. Harren Chancellor St. Cloud Diocese

You are to be commended on your ability to take the vast amount of material you found and put it into an organized, readable account. Congratulations on an excellent piece of research.

-Sister Mary Linus, C.PP.S. Archivist, C.PP.S.

It is the result of intense research, long hours of decision making and excellent writing. You have handled the delicate situation with gentleness and integrity.

-Sister Alice Doll, O.S.B. Director of Education, St. Cloud Diocese

Acknowledgments

The following people, societies, and organizations have been extremely helpful in providing information and insights on various topics, covered in this book: Sister Charlene Herinckx, S.S.M.O., Beaverton, OR; Rev. Ralph Bushell, C.PP.S., Liberty, MO, who so kindly allowed me the use of his books concerning the C.PP.S. history and that of Father Brunner; Rev. Dominic Gerlach, C.PP.S., St. Joseph's College, Rennselaer, IN; Rev. Vincent Tegeder, O.S.B., St. Johns Archives, Collegeville, MN; Rev. Milton Bailor, C.PP.S., St. Charles Seminary, Carthagena, OH; Msgr. Alphonse Kremer, St. Cloud Chancery Office, St. Cloud, MN; Sr. Teresita Kittell, O.S.F., Manitowac, WI; Rev. Bernard Neumann, Scio, OR; Rev. Martin Pollard, Rev. Ray Donnay, Rev. Charles Meyer, Rev. Martin Cawley, Ed Foltz, Dave Huebsch, Alois Gerber, Rose Strecker, Zeno Jutte, Ed Friedsam, Catharine Drahmann, Agnes Welter, Ottertail County Historical Society, Fergus Falls, MN; Pam Brunfelt; Perham Public Library; Viking Library System, Fergus Falls, MN; Seneca County Historical Society, Tiffin, OH; Montana Historical Society, Helena, MT; Oregon Historical Society, Portland, OR; Heart 0 Lakes Genealogical Society, Clare Gibbons, LDS Research Library, (Cay Merriman), Fargo, ND; Portland Diocese Chancery Office, Portland, OR; Cleveland Diocese Chancery Office, Cleveland, OH; St. Paul Diocese Chancery Office, St. Paul MN; and Sister Betty Bender, S.S.M.O., Beaverton, OR. There are many others who gave of their time and I want to thank all of them.

A special thanks to Sister Mary Linus, C.PP.S., who graciously and unselfishly, supplied me with countless pages of information. She is the archivist of the C.PP.S. community and is very knowledgable in the field of C.PP.S. history. She spent many hours of proofreading, as did Mr. Joe Thomas of Perham, Fr. William Doll, Sister Alice Doll, and Ron Miller. I greatly appreciate their efforts.

Preface

When I began this project in 1982, I had no idea of what was all involved. The more I researched Father Joseph, the more interesting and sometimes, controversial facts came up. I have heard many different stories about this man and his life. What I have tried to do is correct some of the erroneous information that has been passed down over the years.

There still may be errors in what I have written, but, to the best of my knowledge, I have tried to stay on the right track. All facts in this book are based on the truth, and all names are real. My goal in this book is to take a sad story and give it a happy ending, for all of the characters involved, deserved a happy ending.

There are so many points of religion which were pertinent 100 years ago, and still pertinent today. My only hope is that once the reader has completed this book, he or she will have a better understanding, not only of Father Joseph M. Albrecht, and what he stood for, but also a better understanding of their individual religious beliefs.

Contents

CHAPTER	TITLE	PAGE
I	In The Beginning	1
II	Wedding Bells	9
III	Free Thy Right Hand	13
IV	Preparing The Way	23
V	Never Again	27
VI	Duchess of Orleans	37
VII	Arrival in New York	64
VIII	Life in Thompson	81
IX	Ordinations	93
X	Cholera Epidemic	104
XI	Father Willi	108
XII	Himmelgarten	113
XIII	Mary's Home	125
XIV	A Visit With Father Brunner	133
XV	Liverpool	139
XVI	Return to Himmelgarten	143
XVII	Crinolines	157
XVIII	Preparations For Departure	162
XIX	Trip to Minnesota	176
XX	Early Life at Rush Lake	200
XXI	The Summer of '67	223
XXII	Return to St. Nazianz	233
XXIII	Lightning Strikes	248
XXIV	Music To Their Ears	253
XXV	More Settlers Arrive	257
XXVI	A Letter To The Pope	268
XXVII	Construction Of St. Joseph's	274
XXVIII	Dedication And Excommunication	281
XXIX	Assault On The Nunnery	296
XXX	A Hunting Accident	309
XXXI	Life At Rush Lake 1874-78	319
XXXII	Church Fire	330
XXXIII	Death Of Father Joseph	345
XXXIV	Preparations For Departure From Minnesota	354
XXXV	Trip To Oregon	361
XXXVI	Life In Oregon	371

EPILOGUE

In The Beginning

CHAPTER I

"Joseph Albrecht, I baptize thee in the Name of the Father, and of the Son, and of the Holy Ghost," stated the elderly priest, as he administered the baptismal ceremony on this particular afternoon of March 15, 1801.

The newborn baby, wrapped in a beautiful hand-made, white, blanket, was being held by his godmother, with the godfather beside her. Next to him were the parents: John and Anna Albrecht. John, a tall, husky man of six feet, like many of the other men, wore a full-length beard. He had on a modest brown suit jacket over a white shirt and brown tie. His wife, Anna, had on a very colorful dress, with frills running down the side, and ruffles in the sleeves. Everyone was smiling on this joyful occasion, for Albrecht's first-born child was being entered into the Holy Church.

Anna Ernst Albrecht had just given birth, earlier that morning, at her small village home in Neuhauser, and was still very weak. Almost immediately after the birth, John had taken his wife and child, to the Catholic priest, at Kirchzarten, for baptism. As soon as the priest finished his ceremonial duties, the child was handed to John, who gently took and wrapped him in another blanket. After handing him to his wife, they departed the church.

It was a short distance from the Catholic Church in Kirchzarten to the small village of Neuhauser, a path which Joseph Albrecht would, over the course of the next 48 years, learn by heart. His home, a small two-story village hut, had a main floor consisting of a livery stable and barn, which housed a few cows, chickens, and pigs.

The family living quarters were situated on the upper level. It was a modest home — nothing fancy, but, compared to many of their neighbors, it was luxurious. John Albrecht, like most of the other villagers, was a farmer. He would walk to his fields each morning, and return in the evening, just like his father before him. Altogether, he owned 40 acres, but the parcels were divided up, with a few acres here and a few there. Nevertheless, John was considered by many as well-to-do, for being a landowner in the Austrian district ol' Breisgau, meant power and influence. Life in the village had been improving over the past few years, mainly due to the reforms of the Austrian ruler, Joseph II. To better, the lot of the peasants was his main goal, and he emphasized this in many of his reform measures. The influence of this ruler was to have a lasting effect upon the lives of all the people in Breisgau, in- including young Joseph Albrecht.

Joseph II had become Emperor of the Austrian Empire in 1765. In the course of ten years, the son of the famous Maria Theresa, had ordered over 6000 edicts. Many of these edicts dealt with the Catholic Church. He felt that his Empire was being influenced too much by the Roman Pope, so, in order to break all ties with Rome, he set up a number of rules and regulations. He wanted priests and bishops to be useful to him and not to an Italian Emperor. He placed all monastic orders, in his provinces, under the supervision of bishops, whom he had appointed. These monasteries then became devoted to contemplation. Priests and bishops simply became pawns of Joseph II. They would carry out his wishes, for they knew that if they did not, they would probably be without a job. Such was the condition of the Church in which Joseph Albrecht entered. Upon arrival at the house, the Albrecht family was greeted by a group of friends, anxiously awaiting the arrival of the newest addition to the village.

"Congratulations," they exclaimed. "Thank you," replied John.

"Anna, let us see the new Mr. Albrecht," requested one of the elderly ladies.

"Of course," replied Anna, as she took the child from John, "but we must go inside first. It is much too cold out here."

The ladies proceeded into the house, being led by Mrs. Albrecht, while the men stayed outside.

"Well John, you now have a son," stated one of the men. "You must be very proud?"

"Oh, I am. Hopefully, it will be the beginning of a large family, which I've always wanted. Come now! Let's go upstairs. I think I may have little wine to celebrate with."

Joyfully, the men followed John up the stairs. Upon entering, they noticed the women all sitting near the fireplace, admiring the new baby. John led the men over to the other side of the room and proceeded to get a bottle of homemade wine out from under his coat. He walked over to the kitchen, took out a glass for each of the men, poured a small amount of red wine into each glass, and handed them out.

"Enjoy it, my friends," stated John, "this is some of last years' crop. One of the best we've had in a long time."

Baden Map

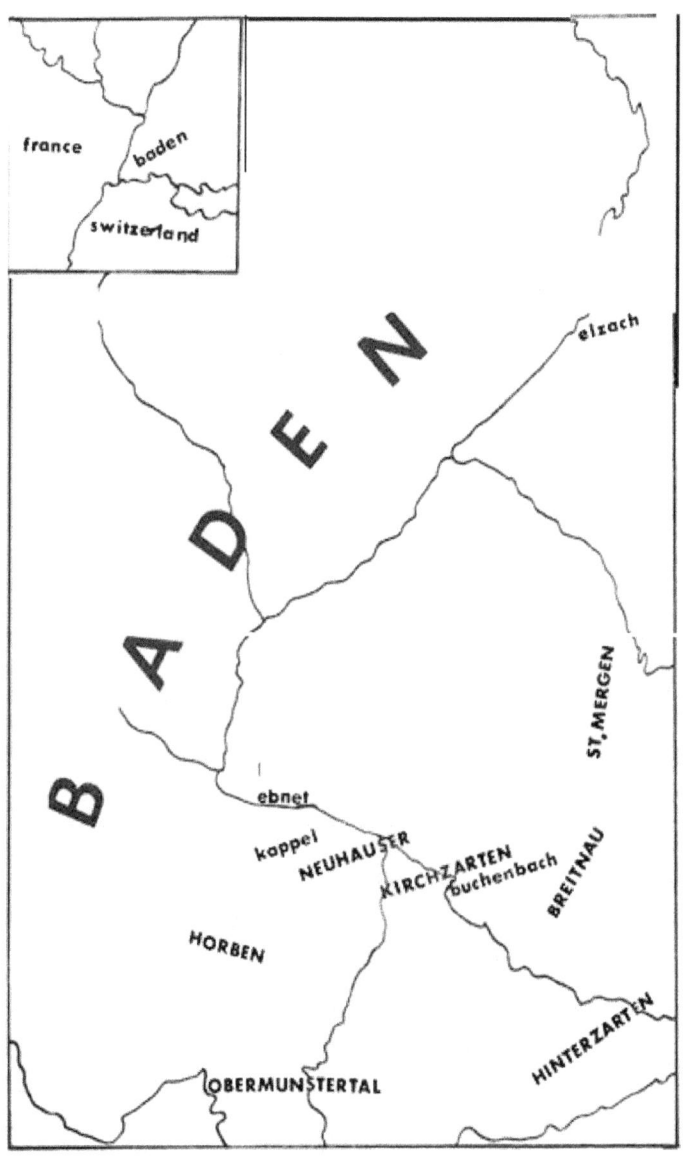

"To Joseph Albrecht, the pride of Neuhauser," exclaimed one of the elderly men, as they toasted each other and drank up.

As the years passed, Joseph Albrecht did make his mark in Neuhauser. At a very early age, it was already noticed that he held a deep interest in religion, probably due to the influence of his parents, for, whenever possible, they would all take the short walk to the church at Kirchzarten and spend much time in prayer.

Along this path to the church, was a monastery. As his father and he were passing by one day, Joseph asked: "Father, what are they doing in there?"

John Albrecht looked through the gates and noticed something strange taking place. "It looks like they are closing the place," he stated, as he watched men taking furniture and other items from the buildings. There were no priests or brothers to be seen in the area. "It probably is another one of the government's ideas," noted John. "Ever since Joseph II, these people have done much damage to the Catholic religion and its institutions around here. I don't know why they have to do such things. They are continually taking away and never giving anything in return. These people just enter and help themselves, having no regard to the fact that they are stealing from God."

Joseph could see that his father was quite irate, so he tried to change the subject. "You know, father, I have seen many soldiers traveling throughout this area, lately. What are they doing?"

"The French Emperor, Napoleon, is on the rampage, he thinks he should rule the world. Thank God there are people who don't agree with him. The soldiers you have seen are ours. There is rumor that the French will be coming through this area soon, so our men are getting prepared."

"Will you have to be a soldier?"

"It is quite possible, my son," replied John, looking somewhat disgruntled. "Only time will tell. Come now! It is time for us to move on. We must get back home."

Little did Joseph know, that a few weeks later, his father would be drafted into the Austrian army. One morning, John walked over to his son, who was in the barn, feeding the animals. "I must leave home for a while, Joseph, the French are getting very close. We must put up a fight. Napoleon al- ready has troops up by Ansbach, and it looks like he is going to- wards Ulm. I must get there and help General Mack."

"What are we going to do, while you are gone?" queried Joseph. "Your Uncle Frederick will come over and make sure every-thing is alright," replied John. He then turned to his wife, Anna, who was busy milking the cow, and said: "Anna, you take care of the garden. Frederick will tend the fields. Joseph can help both of you. I don't know when I'll be back, but I'm sure it won't be very long. The men are gathering down in the courtyard, so I better get going." After hugging his wife and 4-year-old son, he silently departed.

END OF OCTOBER - 1805

The scene was at the Catholic Church, in Kirchzarten, where Joseph and his mother were sitting in the front pew. The priest, a short heavy-set young man of about 25, with glasses in hand, was at the pulpit, delivering a sermon.

"I have heard that the French has won at Ulm. I do not know if any of our men have been hurt or killed, but we must continue to pray for their safe return. We must continue to pray for the defeat of the French. They must be stopped. They are spreading their atheistic beliefs wherever they go. We must be leary of these people. They have been influenced by the devil and we must do our best to destroy this satanic invasion. These revolutionaries are attempting to usurp the powers of God. They believe that paradise can be found on earth. There is no way that this is possible. God put us here for other reasons. If there was paradise here now, what good would the hereafter be? No, we must await for the day when we can enter paradise. These invaders must be destroyed."

Joseph was sitting in his pew, fervently listening to what the priest was saying. This sermon was to stick in his mind for many years to come.

The next year saw the District of Breisgau overtaken by the French troops. It seemed that wherever Joseph walked, there were French troops. One afternoon, Joseph and two of his friends were playing near the communal woods. It was here that Joseph, and the other children, would go and get their supply of wood for their fire-places. It so happened that on this particular day these three boys noticed a large concentration of French troops. What a rough-looking group! They were all drinking and raising havoc. Several of them had gone into the village, earlier, and brought several young ladies back with them. The three boys sat behind some trees, at a short distance, and watched in amazement. Joseph did not like what he saw, for he knew that it was not right. "Come, Fritz, let's get out of here," he begged.

"No Joseph, not yet" replied Fritz. "Let's watch a little longer.

I've never seen anything like this before."

Just then, one of the soldiers noticed the boys. "Hey, you kids," he shouted, "what are you doing here?"

The boys jumped up and attempted to make an escape. The man came running after them. Joseph was caught, while the others got away.

"What do you think you are doing?" shouted the man, in a rough voice, as he grabbed Joseph by the arm and began to drag him back to the camp.

"Nothing," replied the scared Joseph.

" Nothing?" returned the soldier. "You've been spying on me. Why you little scoundrel, you want to watch what I do? Come! I'll show you."

As the man brought little Joseph into the camp, he continued: "Look what I have here. A little spy. What do you think I should do with him?"

"Take him to the wagon," shouted one of the drunken soldiers, as he took another drink out of his bottle. "Show him the fun soldiers can have."

Joseph was now getting very frightened. What was he to do? If only his father were here.

"Good idea," replied the captor, as he grabbed Joseph, again, and took him over to a nearby cart, placing him inside. "Now, sit here," he demanded, "I have something to show you."

The man went over to the campfire and grabbed a young 18-year-old girl and brought her back to the wagon, taking her inside. He then proceeded to tear off the top half of her dress.

"See young man? See what beauty there is hidden under clothes?" noted the man.

Joseph was shocked. Never before in his life had he seen such a sight. He was becoming nauseated as the man began to rape the young girl. Joseph had to escape. He waited for the right moment, and then made his exit. He jumped up and out of the wagon, running full speed from the camp. The soldiers just stood there and laughed. It may have been funny to them, but to Joseph, it had been a night-mare. He ran home as fast as he could, and never had anything to do with the French soldiers again. In July of 1806, the Confederation of the Rhine was proposed by Napoleon. It consisted of 16 states, with Napoleon as the self-pro- claimed protector. Although Neuhauser was included as part of Baden, and part of the Confederation, very few of the villagers had to remain in the army. Therefore, by fall, John had returned home and was able to do the farm work.

Over the next few years, Joseph noticed several items of importance. Many French ideas and institutions were being actively received by the Germans. Many of the customs and laws, which had been developed and carried on over the years, were being ruthlessly discarded.

State control of the Church affairs was at the forefront. The Church organization was reestablished but was not very powerful. It was only a matter of time before the clergy, and even the people, began looking for strength and guidance from the Pope in Rome. With the fall of the Holy Roman Empire and subsequent French influence, fears were expressed that the Catholic Church would not survive. These were trying times for John and Anna Albrecht, and the other German peasants. These were times when they did not know which way to turn. Prayer had to be the answer. Surely, God would put everything into its correct order!

By 1815 the conditions of the Church were desperate. The Catholic Church was still the prevailing religion of the masses but was heavily influenced by outside interference. With the defeat of Napoleon, Baden was in a precarious situation. The land was ravaged by war. The internal government was in a floundering shamble. The economy was in turmoil. Confusion reigned everywhere. Joseph, now age 14, was a witness to all of this. He could see first-hand what was going on in the countryside. The people were rejecting the romantic ideas of the French and returning to the old forms and expressions of their religion.

"What a welcome sight," thought Joseph. "At last, the people are realizing how wrong the French were."

Although drastic changes were made in Neuhauser during these years, many of the old ways remained. The communal way of living continued. Everything was based on the fact that the community came first. The surrounding woodlands were held in common, for the betterment of the village inhabitants. Logs, fur, deer, and wild boar, from these forests, were, normally, strictly regulated and this became the main job of John Albrecht. During the past few years, he had inherited several pieces of land, which he now rented to other farmers in the area. This gave him more time for other things, namely, being elected to the village council and being put in charge of the supervision of the forest lands. Rich people were few and far between in Neuhauser, but John Albrecht was setting a path that led in that direction. He wanted to make sure that his son would be better off than he had been.

"Joseph, my son, when you grow up, I want you to marry into the Schutterle family. I already have my eyes on a girl for you. Her name is Mary Strub. She is in line to inherit a great fortune and I would like to see you get some of it," stated John.

"But father, I don't need money. I would rather study for the priesthood."

"Yes Joseph, but you need to have money in order to make it in this world. Why it even takes money to become a priest. With money comes influence. With influence comes power. With power comes success. Only then will you be able to get whatever you want," continued John.

"I find that hard to believe," noted Joseph, "but, I've never doubted your word before, father, so I guess that must be true. When I grow up, I want to change all of that. Money should be used for the common good of man, not for temporal things, but strictly for survival."

"There are things in this world that money cannot buy, such as love, happiness, and salvation. But it still plays an important role in being able to survive," continued John.

"You know father," added Joseph, "if I ever get the chance, I will use money as a means to save people. Then, I wouldn't have to worry about saving myself."

"I am glad you feel that way," replied John. "Hopefully, you will get your chance. I plan on talking to Mr. Strub very shortly. If he consents to my request, then you shall be married."

Wedding Bells

CHAPTER II

November 29, 1826-Kirchzarten

The day had arrived when Joseph decided to bow to the wishes of his father. This was the day he was to be married. The bride, Mary Ann Strub, had been born on May 8, 1080, in Kirchzarten, to Joseph and Magdalena Strub. She had gone to the same church that Joseph had, so they had known each other for many years.

The weather on this particular Wednesday, in Kirchzarten, was very harsh. Cold winds were blowing in from the north, accompanied by snow flurries. The sky was covered with slow-moving gray clouds.

Joseph was standing in the sacristy of the church, with his best man, 25-year-old Michael Bussel. Both were nervously waiting for the organist to begin playing, while the priest was busily preparing for the Mass.

In the back of the church, people were entering, while Mary Ann and her maid of honor, Andreas Vogt, were in the entryway, anxiously pacing the floor. Mary Ann, a short slender girl of 18, wore a beautiful white floor-length gown, with a white veil that extended to the floor. Around her forehead, she wore a garland of flowers.

Soon the music commenced. The maid of honor began marching down the aisle of the crowded church, followed by Mary Ann. Upon reaching the altar, they were met by the best man and Joseph. As father Anton Schmidt stood in front of the altar, flanked on each side by a server, Joseph presented his left arm for Mary to take. Together, they proceeded up to the altar, and to the awaiting priest.

They were both very happy. Although neither has many choices in this marriage of convenience, both were willing to accept the fact and make the best of it. The wedding ceremony went smoothly. After the vows were exchanged, the Mass completed, and the wedding blessed by Father Schmidt, the wedding party made their glorious exit from the church. Joseph and Mary Albrecht now stood at the church entrance and were congratulated by the people, as they left.
"What a lovely couple!" exclaimed a certain elderly Mrs. Ernst, as she took Joseph's hand. "You look just fine."

"Thank you, Aunt Clara," replied Joseph. "I am glad you could make it."

"I wouldn't have missed this," continued Mrs. Ernst. "I'm sure you have made your father happy. God rest his soul."

" I only wish he could have been here today," stated Joseph.

"I'm sure he us here in spirit," replied Mrs. Ernst.

The reception line continued to progress. Afterwards, a large celebration was held with many friends and relatives partaking in a joyful scence of merriment and folic. These were people from the surrounding villages of Leitenweiler, Kappel, Horben, Neuhauser, Ebnet, Breitnau, Buchenbach, Hinterzarten, Kirchzarten, and Freiburg. All of them had come to wish Joseph and Mary the best of luck.

Joseph and Mary lived their married life in the same house that Joseph had been born in, 25 years earlier. His father had passed away shortly before the wedding and left everything to him and his mother. Mary had recently inherited a large sum of money and a vast amount of land. Joseph took control of these holdings. Combined with what he had inherited, he now was one of the richest people in the entire area. Because of this, Joseph became a powerful landlord and owner of the Schutterlehof Estate. Another name for it was the 'Albrecht Castle'.

The first year of their marriage was quite uneventful. There were two things, however, that did occur. Shortly after the wedding, Anna Albrecht died. This greatly affected Joseph, as he had been very close to her. The other was that Mary became pregnant.

On September 6, 1827, a daughter was born to Joseph and Mary. She was baptized at Kirchzarten and given the name of Rosina. This was a joyous occasion for Joseph and Mary, for it brought them closer together.

As time went by, the Albrecht family grew in spiritual life. They spent much of their time either at church, in Kirchzarten, or in their home, holding family prayers.

One day the family was seated by the dining room table. Little Rosina, commonly called Rosalie, was busy playing with her dolls. Joseph and Mary were involved in a conversation. "You know, Mary, God has been good to us," began Joseph. "He has blessed us with a beautiful daughter and has allowed us to have all the necessities of life. We haven't had to worry from day to day where our next meal was going to come from, like some of the other families around here. We have been blessed with an abundance of harvests."

"Yes, Joseph, we have been very fortunate," agreed Mary. "I have always wanted to be able to help other people," continued Joseph. "Being that we have more than we need, I think we should share with our neighbors. I am going to set up a fund for those in need."

"Next Sunday," suggested Mary, "there will be a Trappist priest coming to the church. His name is Father Francis de Sales Brunner. Father Schmidt said that he is from the Qelenberg monastery and will be looking for aid. Maybe you could talk to him."

"That is a very good idea," replied Joseph. "I think I will do just that."

The following Sunday, Joseph, Mary, and Rosalie went to church in Kirchzarten. It was there that they met Father Brunner, for the first time.

Father Francis de Sales Brunner, C. PP. S.

Father Brunner had been born on January 1O, 1795, at Muemliswil, in Switzerland. In 1809, he entered the Mariastein monastery. In 1819, he was ordained to the priesthood. In 1829, during his annual retreat, he had severed connections with the Benedictines, and joined the Trappists, at Oelenberg. Now, in 1830, he was on his way back to Switzerland to find a new home for his 'Trappist brethren.

"Hella Father," greeted Joseph, as he was coming out of the church. "My name is Joseph Albrecht, and this is my wife, Mary Ann, and daughter, Rosalie. We are from Neuhauser."

"Hello," answered Father Brunner.

"That was an excellent sermon you gave today," continued Joseph. "Very inspiring."

"Thank you," politely replied Father Brunner.

"Say, you are more than welcomed to come to my house, for the night," suggested Joseph.

"Why. thank-you Mr. Albrecht" noted Father Brunner. "I must continue my journey to my homeland, but I will lake you up on your offer."

As they headed for Joseph's wagon, Father Brunner continued:

"Father Schmidt has mentioned your name several times to me this morning, Mr. Albrecht."

"Please Father, call me Joseph," stated Joseph.

"Alright Joseph," continued Father Brunner, "anyway, I have heard about you from others, also. They all speak very highly of you."

"Oh, it's nothing special," replied Joseph. "Tam only trying to help those who need it."

"I admire you for that, Joseph," stated Father Brunner. "Lord knows What a job you have. I have seen much suffering throughout my travels. Many people are simply giving up. There are many out there that need our help. We need more priests and brothers and sisters, to go out and reach these souls. We need people, like you and Mary, who give their time and money for the betterment of the less fortunate."

'Yes, Father, it has always been my desire to become a priest, but my father wished for me to marry, as I was an only child." replied Joseph. "Mary has been good for me, though. She has been a great help. She is an excellent example of the perfect wife and mother."

"Have you ever thought of leaving the married life?" queried Father Brunner.

"Why no," replied Joseph. "Our wedding vows stated till death do us part."

"You could get special dispensation from the Bishop," suggested Father Brunner.

"You mean we could become unmarried, just like that," queried Joseph, as he snapped his fingers.

"It is a possibility," replied Father Brunner.

"That is something to think about," noted Joseph, "For now, what can I do to help you?"

"I am on my way to find a new home for the Trappist brothers in Oelenberg," replied Father Brunner. "Because of the Revolution, we are being kicked out of our home. I could use some financial help to make this move easier. I could also use some money to obtain food. I have been begging of late and have been ridiculed and mocked."

"Before you leave Father, I will help you," promised Joseph, as the wagon, carrying the four passengers, continued slowly down the trail towards Neuhauser.

Free Thy Right Hand

CHAPTER III

"Follow the Bible. There you will find truth and salvation. Pay particular attention to the Acts of the Apostles. Do as they did, and you shall be saved," noted Father Brunner, as he continued giving his talk at the local schoolhouse in Boedigheim, a small village not too far from Kirchzarten, in the fall of 1835.

There were several families present at the informal gathering, including the Albrechts, who were sitting in the front row. They listened intently as Father Brunner continued: "According to Paul, in his letter to the Corinthians, the time is short. From now on those with wives should live as though they had none; those who weep should live as though they were not weeping; and those who rejoice as though they were not rejoicing. The unmarried man is busy with the Lord's affairs, concerned with pleasing the Lord; but the married man is busy with this world's demands and occupied with pleasing his wife. This means he is divided. We are living in a time of moral corruption, a time of indifference, a time of religious contempt, a time of radical change, a time of laxity. Our schools and seminaries are being influenced by indifferent and liberal-minded governments. What can we do about it? We must give up our temporal lifestyle and prepare for the next world. We must fight off the devil. Then we can enjoy the fruits of our harvest. Then we can reach our goal."

Father Brunner's voice was very dominating. Every word seemed to embed in the minds of the people, especially Joseph and Mary, a feeling of wanting to do whatever he told them to do.

"Free thy right hand from the cross and sprinkle a drop of Thy Precious Blood upon the countenance of every hearer, that he may know the truth," continued Father Brunner, as he took his right hand away from his cross. "You who have followed me, in the regeneration when the Son of Man takes his seat upon a throne benefiting his glory, you who have followed me shall likewise take your places on twelve thrones to judge the twelve tribes of Israel. Moreover, everyone who has given up home, brothers, or sisters, father or mother, wife or children or property for my sake will receive many times as much and inherit everlasting life."

"My mother and I have a place in Switzerland, called Loewenberg Castle. You are all welcome to come and visit, anytime. We are preparing women for the sisterhood and have an orphanage for young girls. If any of you are interested, please see me after this meeting. Now, I must leave," noted Father Brunner, as he prepared to depart.

As Joseph, Mary and Rosalie were preparing to return to their Wagon, a very close friend of Joseph's, Mr. Andrew Spiegelhalter walked up beside Joseph, and stated: "That man is an excellent speaker."

"Yes Andrew, there is a lot of truth in what he says," noted Joseph. "The time has come for Mary and me to make a decision. Next week we are going to travel to Loewenberg."

"What do you mean?" queried Andrew.
"We are separating. We have already received a special dispensation from the Bishop. In the eyes of the Church, we are no longer married. I am taking Mary and Rosalie to Loewenberg. Then I'll return to Neuhauser."

"Is that all right with you?" queried Andrew, as he looked directly at Mary.
"Of course," replied Mary. "It is God's will"
"But Rosalie is only eight years old," objected Andrew,
"We are running out of time." continued Joseph. "It will be the perfect setting for her. It is never too early to give one's self to the Church. How about Crescentia? She is 15 now. Maybe I should take her along."
"No, not yet" replied Andrew. "My daughter is going to stay at home, I need her there."

NOVEMBER 19, 1835

The wagon pulled up to the Loewenberg Castle. Joseph Albrecht was driving, with his wife, daughter, and another small girl, named Maria Schmicil, as passengers. Father Brunner was standing' by the entrance with his elderly mother.

The magnificent five-story castle was situated on a hill, overlooking the Rhine Valley and the small village of Schleuis, in the Canton of Graubunden, Switzerland. The building was truly a sight of splendor to the eyes of the travelers.

"Welcome to Loewenberg."
"Hello Father," replied Joseph. "It was quite a trip, but we finally made it."
"Joseph, I would like you to meet my mother. Mother, this is Joseph Albrecht, the man I've been telling you so much about. This is his wife, Mary, and their daughter, Rosalie," stated Father Brunner.

"And who is this young lady?" he queried, as he approached young Maria Schmidt.
"This is Maria Schmidt," answered Joseph. "She lost her parents and has been staying with us."

"You are all welcome," continued Father Brunner. "Joseph, please come with me. We have so much to talk about."

"Yes, and the rest of you, please come with me," interrupted Mother Brunner, a short, elderly lady of 67, with gray hair and a robust shape. She was wearing a floor-length gray skirt with a white, puffed sleeve blouse, under a black vest, which had five golden eyelets running down the front, on each side. A black string crisscrossed through the eyelets, and upward. Around her neck, she had on a large golden cross pendant. Over her head was a black bonnet. Her wrinkled face was showing signs of age, yet her simple smile brought out serenity and piety, two characteristics that would symbolize the Sisters of the Most Precious Blood.

"We have only a small group here," noted Mother Brunner, but it is a beginning. I will introduce you to the women when we get in the chapel."

As they walked towards the chapel, Mother Brunner continued: "We lead a very simple life here. Much of our time is devoted to the adoration of the Most Precious Blood. We place much emphasis on the Blessed Virgin Mary and on the passion and death of Jesus. We observe the rule of poverty, chastity, and obedience. When we aren't working in the fields or doing household chores, we spend our time in prayer. This room here is where I live," she continued, as she pointed to a small room, to her left. "And this is the chapel," she added, as she pointed to the entryway.

The four entered the small chapel, where five ladies were kneeling near the small altar. All of them were dressed in black, but their attire was really not much different than what the typical woman in that area wore. These women included: Elizabeth Maisen, Salome Wasmer, Franciska Kuhn, Mary Ann Denz, and Dorothy Meier. All of them were in their middle thirties. "Much time is spent here in prayer," quietly continued Mother Brunner, as they approached the altar. "We place much emphasis on the rule of silence. In the fields, the women silently say the rosary. In the chapel, the women silently pray for the devotion of the Precious Blood. It is a simple life, and we are all content with what the Lord has in store for us. Come, let us kneel and pray."

Meanwhile, back in Father Brunner's room, Joseph and Father Brunner were involved in a discussion. "What do you plan on doing?" asked Father Brunner.

"I have to return to Neuhauser and take care of my personal affairs," replied Joseph. "There is a lot of work to be done. Many people need my help. I will sorely miss Mary and Rosalie, but I feel content that they will be leading perfect lives here."

"Have you given much thought to the idea of becoming a priest?" queried Father Brunner.

"Yes, I have, but the time is not right. There are other things I must accomplish first."

"Perhaps you could be of some assistance to me," suggested Father Brunner. "My desire is to build up a large army of priests, brothers, and sisters. Maybe you could recruit for me, back in the Breisgau. I'm sure you could convince many to join the missions."

Yes, Father, I'll keep that in mind," replied Joseph. "Now, I must leave."

"Already?" objected Father Brunner. "You just got here. Besides, aren't you going to say goodbye to Mary and Rosalie?"

"No, I think it would be better this way," noted Joseph. "It would be too hard on Rosalie."

The two men got up from their chairs and headed for the wagon. As Joseph got aboard, he turned toward Father Brunner, and said: "I'll keep in touch."

"Yes, you do that," replied Father Brunner. "Goodbye, dear Joseph."

"Goodbye Father," stated Joseph, as he began to depart the castle grounds.

As Joseph was returning to Neuhauser he stopped at the small village of Breitnau and paid a visit to a certain Mr. Hog. It was at this time that he obtained the services of Mr. Hog's 15-year-old daughter, Barbara, who was to become his maid.

Upon his return to Neuhauser, several men were standing in front of his house, awaiting his arrival. "Welcome back Joseph," they stated. One of the men added: "While you were gone, the burghers held an election for mayor, and you were chosen."

"What?" exclaimed Joseph. "How am I going to find the time for that?"

"Surely, you will have the time now that Mary and Rosalie are gone," stated one of the other men.

"Yes, but I had other plans," interrupted Joseph. "Now I don't know what I'm going to do."

"We were supposed to tell you to come down to the courthouse, as soon as you can," continued one of the men.

"Very well," answered Joseph. "Tell them that 1 will be down there tomorrow morning."

As the men left, Joseph took young Barbara Hog into the house and showed her the new home she would be in charge of.

"My! My!" she exclaimed, as she looked around at the roams.
"This should be easy to keep clean."

"I would like for it to be kept just as Mary had it," requested Joseph.

"Your room will be over here," he continued, as he led her to a small room, at one corner of the house. "It isn't much, but it'll have to do."

Barbara walked into the room, which was no more than six feet by six feet. As she placed her bag on the bed, which was the only piece of furniture in the room, she exclaimed:

"This will do just fine."

Meanwhile, back at Loewenberg, Mary and Rosalie were quickly becoming accustomed to the religious life. Their pattern was basically the same each day. Up at five, for common prayers, then the Holy Mass, fieldwork, dinner, Way of the Cross, work, supper, rosary, benediction, general examination of conscience, and nightly vigils.

On January 8, 1836, the entire group of women started a novena in preparation for the feast of the Holy Name of Jesus. As the women were all kneeling in the chapel, Mother Brunner, who was in the front pew, said: "Oh Lord, I beg you for the necessary graces for my daughters. For myself, all I ask is a happy death. I realize my time is short here on earth." Just then, something happened. She sat back in the pew. A fever was raging through her body, Mary, who was kneeling beside her, helped her sit down. With a small handkerchief, she wiped off Mother's forehead.

"Oh my God." exclaimed Mother Brunner, "if a little fever can cause a person such anxiety and dread, how will it be with me when I must appear before the terrible judgment seat of God? Until now I have led a tepid life, and much good that I could have done, I have omitted out of sloth. Now I am no longer worthy to do it."

"Please don't talk like that," begged Mary.

"It seems the gracious Lord would wish to begin to take from me the little that I still have. His will be done, if only He be merciful to me." continued Mother Brunner.

"Francesca," shouted Mary, "come, help me take Mother back to her room."

"Maybe we should call for the doctor," suggested Francesca.

"No! No! Nonsense," exclaimed Mother Brunner. "I have no need for a doctor, All I need is some blessed articles from the chapel, to set beside my bed."

The two women helped Mother Brunner to her room and then into her bed.

"Thank you, my children," noted Mother Brunner. "Now, I shall be fine. You can go back to the chapel."

The two women turned and departed the room. Once outside, Mary turned to Francesca and said: "I'm very worried. She does not look very good. You better run over and advise Father Brunner on what has happened."

As they were talking, Sister Clara Meisen approached them, and asked: "How is she?"

"She is preparing herself for the long-awaited journey," replied Mary. "I don't think she is going to make it this time."

"Go back to the chapel, and have everyone pray for her," requested Sister Clara.

On Wednesday, January 13, Father Brunner was standing beside his mother's bed, offering Holy Communion.

For the past few days, Mother Brunner seemed to be in better health, but shortly after receiving Communion, she again began suffering chills, high fever, and a plaguing cough.

"Oh, my Jesus!" she exclaimed, as she grasped her crucifix and looked towards the picture of the Sacred Heart, that hung opposite her bed. "I do love Thee. Oh Jesus! Have mercy on me.

Oh Jesus! My Lord and my God. Grant me faith, hope, love, humility, meekness, and patience. Give me a new heart, a heart entirely according to Thy divine Heart! Oh, Precious Blood, cleanse, strengthen, and protect me. I do not regret leaving anything in this world. I wish only that before my death, I could have assisted in causing the Sacred Heart and the Precious Blood of Jesus in the Most Blessed Sacrament to be specially honored by perpetual adoration in a number of places. For this cause, I would have given not only my last farthing but also the last drop of my blood. If, however, I shall find mercy before God, I hope to contribute toward this good work even in eternity."

The other sisters were all kneeling beside her bed. Mary was next to Clara. They looked at each other. They knew that she was dying, and they could not help but show their emotions with tears.

"My children, this is not a time of sadness," exclaimed Mother Brunner. "This should be a time of joy. Just pray that I am able to enter Heaven when the time comes."

On Friday, January 15, Mother Brunner died. Although Mary had only known her for a few years, a lasting impression of purity and beauty was instilled in her. The same held true for the other sisters. She had been a prime example of saintliness to follow. She would be dearly missed at the castle.

As time went by in Neuhauser, Joseph, the new mayor, had become accustomed to his job and title. No matter how busy he was, however, he still found time to aid in the affairs of Father Brunner.

By 1839, he had become the closest confidant of Father Brunner and was made his financial adviser.

One morning, in September 1839, Joseph was standing in his flower garden. The sun was shining brightly as he was inspecting his flowers. At that time, a young man approached him.

"Why, Stephen Wehrle, is that you!"

"Yes Joseph," replied the young man.

"How is everything in Loewenbers? Why do I have the honor of your presence?"
"Father Salesius sent us out on a begging tour. We are having financial problems and he is hoping that we will be able to provide him with some assistance. I am among the first

seminarians at the castle and Father Salesius could use the extra help to provide for our welfare. He suggested that I come back here and look up some of our old friends. You were the first on my list."

"What can I do for you?"

"Is it possible that you could give some money or food? In return, I have a list of prayers drawn up by Father Salesius, himself. They will be offered for all benefactors, by the sisters and students and Loewenberg."

"Of course, please come in." noted Joseph, as the two men entered the house, "Barbara," continued Joseph, "please make our guest something to eat. He has made a long hard journey, and I'm sure he must be hungry."

"Yes sir," obediently replied Barbara.

"Here, sit down," offered Joseph, as he motioned to a chair by the table. "I'll be right back."

"Tell me, Mr. Wehrle, how is everything at the castle?" asked Barbara.

"Tell me, Mr. Wehrle, how is everything at the castle?" asked Barbara.

"Things could be better, there are nine men there now, studying for the priesthood. Father Salesius is our instructor. The Latin is very hard, but with perseverance, I think we'll make it."

"Do you ever see Mary or Rosalie?"

"Yes, they are doing fine. There are twelve women there. If it weren't for the sisters, we would never accomplish any of our goals," answered Stephen.

"Joseph has never come out and said it," continued Barbara, "but, I'm sure he misses them."

Just then, Joseph returned, "Here you are, Stephen. Take this back to Father Salesius, and give him my regards," he stated, as he handed him a large bag.

As Stephen took the bag, he said: "Thank you, Joseph. Surely, Father will be very happy with this."

"Here," noted Barbara, as she handed him a plate of food. "This should take care of your appetite for a while."

"Thank you, Barbara." replied Stephen, as he quickly began to eat, After several seconds, Stephen continued: "Uh, this is excellent," as he raised his fork of food. "Joseph, you are a very lucky man to have such a good cook,"

"I know." replied Joseph, "Tell me, Stephen, where are you going from here?"

"Up to St. Mergen, to see my parents," stated Stephen. "After that, I'm heading back to Loewenberg."

"How is Father Salesius?" asked Joseph.

"He is doing fine," noted Stephen. "He still has a problem with his leg. but other than that, everything is fine."

After several minutes of virtual silence, Stephen got up from his chair and said: "Thank you very much for everything," As he wiped his mouth, he continued: "Now, I should be on my way."

"Must you leave so soon?" queried Joseph.

"Yes, I would like to get home before dark."

Joseph and Barbara escorted the young man out. Once outside, farewells were exchanged, and Stephen was on his way up the street.

"There goes a fine young man," stated Joseph, as he watched him depart. Barbara stood there and nodded in agreement.

"Well," continued Joseph, "I have got to get down to that meeting, I'll be back in a couple of hours. I'm sure the men are already waiting for me."

Several minutes later, Joseph had arrived at the small meeting place. It was a one-room, wooden storage building, located about one block from his home. The only furniture in the building was small wooden chairs and one large wooden table. The walls were completely barren, except for a large crucifix, positioned in the center of one wall, between two windows.

As Joseph entered, he noticed the men were already seated. There was 34-year-old Joseph Marder, from Weilheim, 43-year-old Joseph Dufner, from Elzach; Joseph Ernst, from Leitenweiler; Andrew Spiegelhalter, from Breilnau; John Steiert, from Horben; Mr. Goldschmidt, from Kirchzarten; John Ruh, from Neuhauser, and

Father Ambrose Oschwald.

For the past several years, this motley group of farmers had been holding these meetings at various locations throughout the area. It so happened that this month it was held in Neuhauser.

The leader of the group was Father Ambrose Oschwald, born March 14, 1801, one day before Joseph, at Mundelfingen, in Baden. He was ordained to the priesthood on August 1, 1833, and since then, had been serving various parishes in the Freiburg diocese.

"Welcome Joseph," noted Father Oschwald, as he noticed his arrival. "Please be seated. We are just beginning."

"Today, my brothers, we're going to discuss part of the Book of Acts," continued Father Oschwald, as he opened his Bible. "In the Book of Acts, chapter four, verses 32 through 36, it is said: "The community of believers were of one heart and one mind. None of them ever claimed anything as his own, rather, everything was held in common. With power, the apostles bore witness to the resurrection of the Lord Jesus, and great respect was paid to them all; nor was there anyone needy among them, for all who owned property or houses, sold them, and donated the proceeds. They used to lay them at the feet of the apostles to be distributed to everyone according to his need."

As he put the Bible down, Father Oschwald looked around the table, and asked: "Does anyone have a comment on these words?"

"I do," quickly replied Joseph, as he raised his hand. "If we follow in the footsteps of the apostles, we would all be saved. In this day and age when we see moral decadence and atheism wherever we turn, it would be an excellent idea to set up a communal society,
preferably in America, where we could put this practice to use. The way everything is going here, the future of the family structure is very questionable. I have read quite a bit about that new country and have been very impressed. The communal way of living in the perfect setup, just as it was for the apostles. Father Salesius Brunner has been talking about going to America and setting up a Church Order. I think we should be offering any assistance that we can, in this endeavor, and if possible, to put the communal living aspect at the forefront."

"Yes Joseph, I agree with you," replied Father Oschwald. "But, until the time comes, we should follow the lives of the apostles, here in Baden. If Father Brunner needs help, you can assist him. I think we should continue to have these meetings and set up plans for aiding the destitute people around here, and not plan to leave, yet."

"Yes, but father," objected Joseph, "every time I try and set up some kind of aid program, here in Neuhauser, the government officials step in and put a stop to it. It's as if they didn't care at all about the welfare of their people."

"We must have patience, Joseph," continued Father Oschwald. "Our diligent effort will one day be recognized. Maybe not right away, but someday, people will look back and say that surely, those men were saints."

Several of the men could not help but laugh at those words, but Joseph was not one of them. He was serious when it came to matters of religion and looking out for his fellow man. He looked at the other men, in disgust, and finally said: "You speak the truth, Father. I agree with you. Let us hope that one day we will all meet our just reward in Heaven."

"How do you expect to enter the Gates of Heaven, when you lead such a sinful life on earth?" queried Mr. Spiegelhalter.

"Andrew," continued Joseph, "you know, as well as I, that God has sympathy for us sinners. He will forgive us for our sins if we express a deep desire for Him to do so. There are three things that we must avoid. They are pride, vanity, and lust. If we do not fall
into these bad habits, we have a very good chance of success. If we put our neighbor before ourselves and look out for his welfare, before we look out for our own, that too will help us attain our final goal."

Preparing The Way

CHAPTER IV

"Sister Mary, pray for us," stated the short, jovial, 26-year-old Father Anton Meyer, as he placed his baggage on the wagon, on this particularly cold day of Friday, September 29, 1843. "We are ready to leave."

"Yes Father, we shall pray every day for your safe journey," replied Sister Mary, who was standing beside the wagon.

The first group of missionaries were ready to depart Loewenberg, for America. Besides Father Meyer, there was Martin Bobst, Jacob Ringele, Carl Margaretelli, Peter Capeder, John Jacomet, John Van den Broeck, Peter Homburger, Henry Buesser, Aloysius Castrishcher, Peter Kreusch, Mathias Kreusch, Stephen Geshwind, and Fridolin Baumgartner. Jacomet, Van den Broeck, Meyer, Bobst, Ringele, Margaretelli, and Capeder were already ordained priests, while the others were students. All of them, in their 20's or 30's, were wearing black cassocks, with the priests wearing their distinctive cross over their left breast. As they were boarding the wagons, which were to transport them, they all showed signs of jubilation and excitement at the thought of going to America.

"I have written to Joseph, and he plans on meeting us at Mulhouse," continued Father Meyer, as he boarded the front seat of the wagon.

"Give him my regards," stated Sister Mary.

"Certainly," answered Father Meyer.

As he sat down beside Father Capeder, the driver, Father Meyer turned to 32-year-old Father Joseph Butz, who had been standing on the other side of the wagon, and said: "Joseph, take care of this place now. I will have Father Salesius write to you as soon ag he can. We're supposed to meet him and Father John in Basle."

"Yes Father," replied the shy, quiet priest. "Good luck and God be with you."

As the gracious sisters completed their task of loading the two wagons with the necessary articles of clothing and food, Father Meyer looked at them, and then at Sister Mary, and said:

"Remember to always be obedient to Sister Clara. Do not be saddened at the fact that Father Salesius is going with us to America, for he has said several times: 'I go to prepare a place for you.'"

With those words, the wagons began to pull away from the Loewenberg Castle. With the good-byes said and done, Father Butz and the good sisters returned into the castle.

The men were on their first leg of a journey that was to take them to Basle, by way of Zurich, then to Havre, France, and across the Atlantic, to America.

Meanwhile, Joseph Albrecht was patiently waiting for the arrival of the group, at a hotel in the city of Mulhouse. It now was the 10th of October, and still no sign of his friends. He had arrived here on the 5th and was beginning to wonder what had gone wrong. He was pacing back and forth near the reception desk. Every once in a while, he would take out his gold pocket watch, and check the time. He then would put it back into his pocket and continue to pace. "What could have happened?" he would ask himself, "They should have been here long ago."

Finally, late in the evening of the 10th, the group arrived. Father Salesius was the first to enter, followed closely behind by the others. Upon seeing him, Joseph went over to the door and greeted him.

"Hello Father," stated Joseph, as he gave him a friendly hug.
"Hello Joseph," replied Father Salesius. "We had some difficulties in Basle and the men left some of our baggage in Zurich. It took
four days before we finally got it. That is why we are so late."
"16," answered Father Salesius. "I left Father Butz at Loewenberg, with the sisters. Ackermann, Job, Capaul, and Haefele are at Drei Aehren."

"This trip must be costing you quite an amount?"
"It cost 65 francs per person to get to Havre. Once we get there, we'll find out what it'll cost to cross over."

"Do you have enough to make the trip?"
"It is quite possible that I could come up short," bluntly replied Father Salesius.

"Well, you mentioned in your last letter, that I should bring some along," noted Joseph. "Here," he stated, as he handed him a small brown bag. "Included in this are the collections you had earlier sent me, plus a small token from me. It should be more than
enough to get you and the others to Ohio."

"Thank-you Joseph, I shall see to it that you get repaid."
"No need for that," shrugged Joseph.

"You have been a great help to us," continued Father Salesius.

"Someday you will receive your just reward."

"Tell me, Father, how has your trip been progressing?"

"Travelling in priests' garb is not the best way to go, I have heard more cursing and profanity than I care to mention. Here, nothing is holy, nothing spiritual, or respectable, or safe. Everything is insulted, ridiculed, laughed at, spoken of in an insulting manner,

cursed and idly sworn upon. I only hope it is not like this for the entire journey."

"Yes, it is like that around Neuhauser too," noted Joseph. "It almost makes you wonder if it's worth fighting. One wonders how the battle will end."

Just then, a young man came running into the hotel. He approached the reception desk. "Is there a Father Brunner here?" he shouted.

"Yes, here I am, replied Father Salesius, as he raised his hand.

"Sir," continued the young man, as he walked over to Father Salesius, "there has been a mix-up in the baggage. It was inadvertently put on another stage, which has left for Freiburg. We sent a rider to stop it, but it looks like we won't be able to leave for Belfort

until tomorrow morning."

"Thank-you for telling me, my son, we'll just have to stay here for the night."

"John," continued Father Salesius, as he turned and looked directly at Father John Wittmer, "go up and see if we can get a room for the night."

As Father Wittmer obediently turned and went to the reception desk, Father Salesius turned back to Joseph, and asked: "How has everything been for you over at Neuhauser?"

"Fine, every couple of weeks our group meets for discussions. It is too bad you have never been able to be with us. There are some truly fine gentlemen there, Father Ambrose is still our spiritual leader, and he is a remarkable man."

"Good," replied Father Salesius. "I hope you continue this practice. Maybe someday you will be able to come to America and join me in Ohio. Lord knows how much I could use you."

"I don't feel that it is time yet, Father, I still have much work to do here."
"You know, Joseph, our Society, founded by Gaspar del Bufalo, is not a religious order in the strict canonical sense. It is a loose organization of secular priests living a common life. We are dedicated to the task of giving missions. Gaspar hoped that his priests could be

models for the secular priests. The only bond of union among us is that of fraternal love. Any member who no longer feels himself attracted to this mode of common life, or to the giving of missions, is free to leave at will. Our primary objective is the devotion to the Precious Blood."

"Yes, | know Father. T would very much like to follow you, but I still must complete my tasks here, first."

"I understand," replied Father Salesius.

"Well, I'm sure you are all very tired, and would like to get some rest, so I think I'm going to leave," stated Joseph, as he prepared to depart. "I would like to get back home as soon as possible.

I do hope you have a safe trip, and when you get there, please write and tell me all about your journey."

"Of course," noted Father Salesius, "but, must you leave so soon? It is dark out, and travel will be very difficult at this time. Can't you stay until morning?"

"No, I really must be leaving, I know this area very well, and am not afraid of traveling through it in the dark."

"Good-bye dear Joseph," stated Father Salesius, as he walked Joseph toward the exit. "I will surely miss you," he continued, as the two hugged each other.

'Some day we will be together," noted Joseph. "I know that I will be coming to America. I just don't know when."

Never Again

CHAPTER V

"Sister Mary," shouted Father Butz. "I have just received a letter from Father Salesius. "He says they are doing fine in Ohio. There is a hermitess, by the name of Francesca Bauer, who would like to share her house and lands with some of you sisters. Father also added that the men are having difficulty with the washing and mending. It is basically the same letter that I received last week, but he adds that the climate is excellent. He has a small horse that he would give to you if you came. I am supposed to hurry and sell part of the estate and send several of you to the States. Would you and Rosalie like to go?" asked Father Butz, as he put the letter down, on this beautiful morning in May of 1844.

"Why, of course," replied Sister Mary.

"Good," continued Father Butz. "I'll set up the travel plans as soon as possible. Maybe, you will be able to stop over at Neuhauser on your way. Go tell Rosalie and Martina to prepare for a long trip. I'll go talk with Sister Clara," continued Father Butz, as he put the
letter in his pocket and began to walk toward the chapel.

Mary, hurriedly went in search of her daughter, finding both her and Martina in the garden. As she approached them, she said: "Rosalie, Father Brunner wants us three to come to America."

"America!" exclaimed Rosalie. "When?"

"As soon as Father Butz gets the travel plans together," answered Sister Mary. "Perhaps in a few days. He said that we should be able to see Joseph on our way. Come! We must begin our preparations."

The three of them promptly headed for their rooms, in order to get ready for their departure.

The next morning, Father Butz was holding a discussion with Mary, Rosalie, Martina, Maximilian Homburger, and two other brothers.

"Several months ago, I received a letter from Father Salesius, in which he wrote the following resolutions: 1) to adhere to the Society until death, despite disturbances, scandals, and disaffection, 2) to be circumspect regarding the admission of candidates and not readily to advance them to orders. The candidate should be tried for a long time. Every means should be used to break down pride and self-will. If the candidate would not part with them, then he or she should be dismissed, 3) no one will be accepted who comes with the sole purpose of studying for the priesthood and sisterhood. We will accept only such young men and women as are eager to sanctify themselves and willing to spend their lives in the service of the Society. We must obey blindly as children. Keeping these three items in mind, I have decided to send you all to America. You are all perfect examples of the type of person that Father Salesius wants in America."

Turning towards Maximilian, Father Butz continued: "Max, I am putting you in charge. This is a copy of your travel itinerary." After handing Max several papers, he continued: "You are to proceed from here to Basle, Freiburg, Rotterdam, and then to New York. Father Salesius had gone from Havre to New Orleans, but he suggests that it would be cheaper and easier to go to New York."

"When are we to leave?" queried Max.

"As soon as possible," replied Father Butz. "I have some money here for you, but when you stop at Neuhauser, you are to see if Joseph can help out. Sister Clara and Sister Nothburga have packed some food for you to take along, so it should not cost much. Father Salesius will be looking forward to seeing you, and I, someday, also hope to see you again. God be with you on your journey. My prayers, and those of everyone else in the Society will be for you."

"Good-bye," exclaimed Max, as the group quietly got up and left. None of them knew what was in store, but all were willing to move forward, simply because that is the way Father Brunner wanted it.

Two days later, the small group arrived in Neuhauser, at the home of Joseph Albrecht. As they approached the house, Barbara noticed them.

"Joseph, Joseph," she excitedly exclaimed, "look who is here!" Joseph, who was sitting in a chair, reading, jumped up and went over to the window, to see. "Why, it's Mary and Rosalie," he exclaimed, in a very surprised tone.

They both ran to greet the visitors. "Hello," exclaimed Joseph, as he met the travelers by the outside door.

"Hello Joseph," greeted Mary, with a big smile. "Mary, welcome back," continued Joseph. "Lord knows how much I have missed you and Rosalie. Rosalie, just look at you. My! How you have grown! You must be what? 17 now?" "Yes," answered Rosalie, "almost 17." "Well, what brings you here?" queried Joseph.

"We are on our way to America," answered Mary. "We have come to say good-bye and get some financial help," added Max.
"To America?" questioned Joseph. "Are you going where Father Salesius is?"
"Yes," replied Mary. "He needs our help so we must go. We cannot stay here very long, as we have to be in Freiburg very shortly."
"Come inside, please," begged Joseph, as he motioned for the group to enter his home. "You must have time for a little something to eat."

"We have a few minutes," stated Max, as they entered.

"Barbara, would you please make something for our guests?" requested Joseph.

"Of course," obediently replied Barbara, as she scurried up the stairs, ahead of the rest.

As the group was walking up the steps, Joseph had more questions for the group. "What has it been like in Loewenberg?"

"Fine," answered Mary. "We are getting more and more candidates. Truly, Mother Brunner started something wonderful!"

"I am glad," replied Joseph. "And, how about you, Rosalie?" "Everything is fine," she exclaimed. "I am very content with the lifestyle that you and mother have chosen for me."

As they entered the house, Joseph stated: "Please, have a seat. I will be back in a minute." He went into his bedroom, and, before everyone was seated by the table, he had returned. "Here is what you need, Max. This should be enough to get you to Ohio. Whatever you have left, give to Father Salesius. I'm sure he could use it."

"Thank-you," replied Max, as he took the small bag from Joseph.

"I also have a letter in there for Father Salesius," added Joseph. "You can take it to him. Now eat up," he continued, as he took the plates of fruit and bread from Barbara and began to pass them around the table.

"I am building a new house," he continued. "I have sold some of the lands up by Schutterthal and have decided to use some of the money for myself. The place is only about a mile from here, out in the country. If you would like, we could go out and see it."

"I don't think we have the time," remarked Max, "but why are you doing this when there is only you and Barbara?"

"We need more room," answered Joseph, "and I'm getting tired of the smell of cows in my house. The new place has everything separated. Also, I will be able to use it as a meeting place, for our religious meetings."

After a brief visit, the time came for the group to continue on the journey. A tear came to his eyes as Joseph watched Mary, Rosalie, and the others depart. He looked at Barbara, and said: "Someday, Barbara, we will be together again. Some day."

On July 22, 1844, the group arrived at St. Alphonse, in Peru, Ohio. It was a most welcomed sight for Father Salesius Brunner and his associates. As time went by, the Precious Blood Society was asked to take care of more and more new German settlements that were springing up throughout Ohio. Convents were begun at Wolfscreek, Thompson, and Maria Stein. Because of the dire need for more help, early in 1847, Father Salesius sent Sister Mary back to Europe, with the sole purpose of gathering recruits for these missions.

One day, while Joseph was sitting by his desk, in his new home. Reading there was a knock at the door. Barbara, who was busy preparing supper, went to see who was there.
"Joseph," stated Barbara, as she opened the door, "it's Mary." "Joseph got up from his desk and hurriedly went to the door.

"Mary, what are you doing here?" he asked. "Father Salesius sent me back to get recruits. For the next year, or so, I will be traveling throughout the area."
"Excellent," exclaimed Joseph. "You can stay here. I'll even help you."
"Oh, thank-you Joseph, but I don't think I should do that," objected Mary.
"Nonsense," blurted back Joseph. "You are to stay here and that's final."

"How is everything in America?" he continued.

"We desperately need help," exclaimed Mary. 'There are just too many people to take care of. The priests cannot handle it. There are more and more settlers coming all the time. Ohio is a very big area, and it takes some time for our few priests to cover all that territory."

"Please tell me about your trip over and what you have been doing there," insisted Joseph.

"We had some difficulty on our trip over." continued Mary. "We were delayed for several days in Rotterdam. When we did make it to New York, after a terribly rough trip across the ocean, we didn't know where to go. A certain Father Kunze spotted us at the harbor
and helped us out greatly. We finally got to see Father Brunner towards the end of July. Soon we moved to Wolfscreek, or as it is becoming known now as New Riegel. In "45, I was sent over to Thompson, which is located midway between St. Alphonse and New
Riegel. We have an eighty-acre farm there, with a convent and chapel."

"How was Rosalie been?" queried Joseph.

"She has been doing much better of late," replied Mary. "When we first got there, she had been quite sick, but she got over that. She keeps herself busy with the children at St. Alphonse's, plus her other chores. I talked to her shortly before I left, and she told me that you are always in her prayers."

"How was the trip back?" continued Joseph.

"Everything went smoothly, I traveled with Archbishop Purcell, as far as Freiburg. He went to visit the Bishop, while I came here."

"What are your immediate plans?" asked Joseph.

"I want to tour the surrounding countryside and see if I can convince anyone to give up their worldly life here, and travel to America" noted Mary.

"Excellent!" exclaimed Joseph, "Tomorrow we shall begin our search. I have been holding meetings over the past few years and know some good candidates. Did you have any trouble finding my place?"

"No," replied Mary, "when I got to town, I asked your cousin, John Wilderle, and he gave me the directions."

"What do you think of it?" queried Joseph, as he looked around.

"Quite impressive!" remarked Mary

"I have hired men who do all of the farm work and yardwork." continued Joseph, "That gives me more time to handle the financial affairs. Barbara is my only maid. She has a lot more to clean, but she is one never to complain, Would you like to see the rest of the house?"

"Yes, that would be fine," replied Mary.

As Joseph led Mary through each room of the two-story mansion, he continued: "We have four bedrooms upstairs. One for me, one for Barbara, one for Carl Birkenmeier, my new chore man, and one for guests."

"You mean your godchild is working for you?" asked Mary.

"Yes, he takes care of all the chores around the yard. He milks the cows, feeds the animals, gets the wood, and does anything else I want him to do. He is a very good worker. My cousins, John, and Agatha, should be very proud of their son."

"How old is Carl?" queried Mary.

"Let's see, he was born April 30, 1830, so he is 17 now," replied Joseph, after he thought for several seconds.

"My! How fast they grow!" remarked Mary.

"Let me take you upstairs and show you where you will be staying." continued Joseph, as he led her up the long open staircase.

Within several weeks, Joseph and Mary had enlisted a large group of people to their cause. This list included: John Siewert, John Hummel, Sebastian Ganther, Joseph Rieslerer, and Leopold Eberle — all young men who had taken part in several of Joseph's meetings.

Also signed up were a group of girls: Maria Ernst, Maria Weibel, Theresa Wellman, Crescentia Geri, Ursula Stegg, Elizabeth Kaminer, Maria Flam, Elizabeth Meyer, Rigitta Meyer, Cenovieve Beckert, Crescentia Naper, Rosalic Beyerli, and Maria Eva Thoma.

Mary at the Crib, Wolfscreek — 1844

Mary of the Angels, Thompson — 1845

Joseph provided for their passage and soon, this group was on its way to America.

Meanwhile, Joseph and Mary continued their search. They went from Neuhauser to Kirchzarten, Leilenweiler to Brietnau, Hinterzarten to Schutterthal, St. Mergen to Elzach, Berenthal to Glotterthal, Horben to Kappel. Not a village was missed. At each stop, Mary would tell of the dilemma facing the Precious Blood Society in Ohio, and Joseph, who was becoming an excellent speaker, would tell how things could be so much better for them.

"Many of our German friends are leaving this disease-infested, heavily populated land and venturing out across the sea to a new promised land. A place where a farmer can get free land. A place where he can earn a decent living and raise a perfect Christian family. But these people need priests to look out for them. They need sisters to properly instruct their children. They need brothers Lo help build these Christian communities," stated Joseph, at one of these informal meetings held at the Catholic church in Hinterzarten. "America is a land that practices freedom of religion. It is a place where we will not have to worry about the government interfering, not only in matters of our daily lives, but also in matters of religion. It is a place where we don't have to worry from day to day where our next meal will come from, for there is an abundance of wild game and fruits. It is virtually a paradise on earth."

"I have been mayor of Neuhauser for several years now. I have seen the economy going from bad to worse. I have seen crop failure after crop failure. I have seen the morality of the entire area go downward; I have seen paupers everywhere. I have seen the pubkeepers drawing in young men, feeding them beer and wine, and encouraging them to waste their time by playing sinful games of cards. I have seen idiotic styles of new clothing appear. I have seen enough."

"Soon, Sister Mary will be going to America. I have decided to go with her. I am giving up my life here. I am giving up my job as mayor. I have had enough; I have had enough degradation. It is time to set out for the New World. That is where our future lies, not
here in Europe. Won't you please come with us? Thank you."

Joseph stepped back from the table and wiped his brow. He had not only worked himself into a frenzy but also had stirred the crowd up.

Mary, who was standing beside him, had a big smile, as she took his hand. "That was beautiful, Joseph." she stated, "It was as if Jesus was talking through you. It was very inspiring."

"Thank you, Mary," replied Joseph.

"When will you be taking off?" queried one of the bystanders.

"We are scheduled to leave Freiburg on the sixteenth of March," replied Mary.

"What do I need to do?" asked a young woman, as she walked forward, along with several others.

"What is your name, dear child?" asked Joseph.

"Magdalena Helzinger." replied the young girl,

"How old are you?"

"16."

"Are your parents here?"

"No, but that is alright. I don't live with them anymore."

"Just fill out these papers," stated Mary, as she handed her two small pieces of white paper, "And then we'll get in touch with you."

"Next" shouted Joseph, "What is your name?"

"Rebeeca Hirseher," replied the lady.

"Age"

"34"

"Please fill out these forms," stated Joseph, as he gave her two pieces of paper.

That evening, while Joseph and Mary were returning to Neuhauser, Mary stated:

"I think we have enough recruits for now. As soon as Sister Kunigunda gets here from Loewenbers, I think we should inform everyone of our departure. If she followed the schedule, she should have left the castle yesterday."
"Andrew is supposed to come over tomorrow," noted Joseph.

"Then we'll get all of the legal matters out of the way."

"One of his daughters is coming with us, isn't she?" asked Mary.

"Yes. Crescentia" replied Joseph. "Andrew has already given his consent."
As this conversation continued, they entered the yard of Joseph Albrecht. Just as they were getting out of the wagon, a young man came running up to them.

"Mr. Albrecht," the 20-year-old shouted, "Have you heard the news? There have been Catholic revolts in many of the larger cities and they have been suppressed by the soldiers. Now the government is placing even stricter measures against us. Things don't look good."

"They were asking for freedom of the press, abolition of religious restrictions to political rights, independence of judges, popular participation in government administration, and the abolition of feudal elements. They were screaming for jury trials and a popular militia."

"Those fools," noted Joseph. "How stupid can they be? Don't they know how futile that is? Now, we'll definitely have to get out of here."

The next day, final preparations were made. Andrew arrived early that morning and was given all of Joseph's personal papers.

"You are to hold these papers, for safekeeping, Andrew," noted Joseph. "I have kept enough money to get us all to America, plus enough to get us started once we get there. The remainder, I have in a bank. Only you and I can withdraw it. I have the papers here, to show what property I own. For now, do nothing with it. Father Brunner does not like for his people to have money, but I have plans for some of it, I'm sure he won't mind."

While Andrew and Joseph were sitting by the table, more visitors arrived. Among them were Sister Kunigunda Wehrle and Barbara's younger sister, Theresa.

The short, jovial, heavy-set. 37-year-old, Kunigunda went into the kitchen with Barbara and Theresa. "How many are going to be in your group?" she asked, after greeting Mary, who had been sitting on a chair, near a window. 35," replied Mary. "27 women and 8 men. There is another group of about 200 that will be leaving in a few days, and we all will meet in Havre."

"All of them going to Ohio?" queried Kunigunda.

"Yes, to the best of my knowledge," answered Mary.

Just then, there was another knock on the door. Barbara turned and went to see who it was. It was Mary Ann Rub, the slender, 35-year-old neighbor of Joseph.
"Mary Ann," stated Barbara, "please come in."

"Hello Barbara," replied Mary Ann, as she entered. "Has Joseph started yet?"

"No." replied Barbara. "he is still waiting for Crescentia."

"Good," noted Mary Ann, as she took off her long shawl, and folded it up as she walked over to where the other women had gathered.

Just then Joseph and Andrew walked into the kitchen and sat down by the table.

"We will have to start without Crescentia," noted Joseph, as he looked around at the other women. "Our plans are finalized. We will all meet here on the 15th. I have a list made up here for each of you. I need you to go out and inform the others about the exact plans."

As he handed each of the women a piece of paper, he continued: "Behind your name are the names of people I want you to each contact. Do it as soon as possible. We don't have much time left here. Make sure they are all here by the morning of the 15th. Have them bring whatever money they can. It is alright if they have none. I will gladly take care of their needs. That is all I have to say for now.

MARCH 15, 1848

The cold northerly winds were blowing very strongly down upon the Albrecht Castle this particular morning, as the motley group of men and women were gathering. It had snowed the previous night but had now diminished to flurries.

Joseph and Andrew were sitting by the kitchen table, having a conversation. Barbara and Mary were busily packing up their few belongings. Sister Kunigunda was standing near the entrance, greeting the arrivals as they came in.

"We're supposed to meet at the Cathedral, in Freiburg, this afternoon," stated Joseph, as he nervously looked at his pocket watch.

"Where is your daughter?"

"I don't know," replied Andrew, "She should be here any minute."

Just as he had finished speaking, 28-year-old Crescentia Spiegelhalter entered.

"There, now we can leave," stated Joseph, as he got up from his chair.

Andrew also got up and he walked over to his daughter and said: "My dear child, I wish you the best on your trip. Pay close attention to what Joseph and Mary tell you. They are wise and know what is best for you."

"I know Father," replied the shy Crescentia.

As Joseph looked out the window, he continued: "It looks like the wagon is ready. All we have to do is get aboard."

Slowly, the group went down to the awaiting wagon. Many of the local townspeople were gathered around the wagon, preparing a send-off for their friends.

"Joseph, I hope you write to me when things get settled in America," noted Andrew.

"Of course, I will," replied Joseph, as he shook Andrew's hand.

"You make sure you take good care of my holdings here. It will mean a great deal to me, as I have many plans and will need your assistance."

"You can depend on me, Joseph," assuredly replied Andrew.

With that, the wagon took off. Everyone was waving goodbye. Each of them knew that they probably would never see each other again.

After a short tedious trip, the wagon pulled up in front of the Cathedral at Freiburg, where there was already a large crowd gathered.

"Ah, Father Ambrose," stated Joseph, as he got down from the wagon.

"Hello Joseph, my dear friend," noted Father Oschwald, as they hugged one another. "You are truly going to be missed around here."

"Well, you could come with us," suggested Joseph.

"Maybe, someday I will go to America," replied Father Oschwald. "Maybe someday."

Duchess of Orleans

CHAPTER VI

s Mary pulled out a piece of paper from her pocket, she stated: "Listen, everyone. I am going to read off the list of names. When you hear your name, please answer."

Immediately, she began to read. After each name was called, the word "here" was heard. The following is the complete list of people who were preparing for the journey: Joseph Albrecht, Joseph Dufner, Michael Homburger, Rochus Schueli, Joseph Hog, Urs Haener, John Butz, Joseph Marder, Mary Ann Albrecht, Crescentia Zipfel, Kunigunda Wehrle, Barbara Hog, Theresa Hog, Maria Kleiser, Afra Kleiser, Theresa Goldschmidt, Maria Holt, Ursula Ernst, Susanna Schueli, Rebecea Hirscher, Brigitta Stoll, Mary Ann Ruh, Crescentia Spiegelhalter, Anna Helzinger, Salome Wasmer, Cecelia Stohr, JoAnna Winterhalter, JoAnna Dangler, Theresa Ganther, Mary Ann Beyerli, Anna Maria Haener, Magdalena Helzinger, Maria Wangler, Maria Heitzler, and Crescentia Schultheis.

All were present and ready to depart. Some, already, had friends living in America. Some had known Father Salesius Brunner and desired to follow him. All were influenced by Joseph Albrecht, and it was primarily his convincing speeches that made them decide to leave their homeland and head for the unknown.

After completing the roll call, Mary turned to Joseph and asked: "Is there anything you want to tell them?"

Joseph nodded his head and stated: "We have 5 wagons here. We will be traveling from here to Strasbourg. Once there, we are to load our wagons with supplies, to be delivered to Paris. Until then, the sisters and the young girls can ride in the wagons. The men will
have to walk besides, I will drive the lead wagon. Dufner, you drive the second. Barbara, you drive the third. Mary, you drive the fourth, and Urs, you drive the last. We still have a lot of daylight, so we should take off as soon as possible."

Everyone went to the wagons. In a matter of a few minutes, everything was set. Joseph got aboard the first wagon, grabbed the reins, turned around, and said: "Let's be on our way."

"God be with you," shouted Father Oschwald, as he waved at Joseph.

"Goodbye Ambrose," replied Joseph.

As the small wagon train slowly began to depart, Father Oschwald turned to Andrew Spicegelhalter and said: "There goes a magnificent person. I am honored to be his friend."

"I' m sure you two will meet again," noted Andrew, as he watched the wagons go out of sight.

The weather was quite a biller. The cold March winds came blowing in from the north, sending chills through everyone. With dark, gray-lined clouds building up in the distance, it looked as if it were going to start snowing.

Most of the travelers were dressed appropriately, except for 30-year Crescentia Zipfel, of Neuhauser, who was wearing a small black shawl over her black dress. Everyone else was wearing heavy black coats and gloves. Several of the women were also wrapped up in blankets, Soon, Crescentia had on a blanket, also.

Joseph was dressed like the other men, except that his clothes were all very worn, He had a tear in his coat, several holes in his gloves, and a small hole in his hat.

"It seems to be getting colder," noted back to 54-year-old, Joseph Dufner.

"Yes, maybe we should stop for the night and set up campfires," suggested the short, gray-haired Mr. Dufner.

"Yes, maybe we should stop for the night and set up campfires," suggested the short, gray-haired Mr. Dufner.

"Soon Joseph, soon," replied Joseph. "I'd like to get across the river before nightfall. It should only be about a half-mile down the road."

The wagons continued along the trail. Soon, they arrived at the river. There was a large ferry boat setting along the shore, which Joseph drove right up onto. The rest of the drivers did likewise. After tying the reins, Joseph got down. While walking over to the man in charge, he took a batch of papers out of his bag, which he had been carrying over his left shoulder. He showed the papers to the tall middle-aged man, who took them and glanced over them.

"The trip across will cost 30 florins," stated the man, as he handed the papers back. "What?" queried Joseph. "50 florins. That's outrageous!"

"Pay it or leave." returned the man.

"What a choice!" exclaimed Joseph, as he reached into his coat pocket and pulled out the correct amount and handed it to the man.

"Thank you, sir," politely replied the man, "We will be leaving immediately."

The man took the rope and placed it across one end of the ferry. The boat, slowly, proceeded on its short journey across the magnificent Rhine River.

"Take a good look back, Joseph," stated Mary. "It will probably be the last time you ever see your homeland."

"Yes Mary, I'm sure I'll never return," noted Joseph, as he stared back across the water. "I'll miss it. I'll miss being around my friends and being able to help them out in times of need. But I won't miss the government officials."

A tear came to his eyes, as he quietly stared back to the land, he had lived on for the first 47 years of his life.

"Try not to think too much about it," suggested Mary. "Just think of the future. Think of the help you'll be able to provide for the poor German folk in Ohio, Think of all the help you'll be able to give to Father Salesius."

"Yes, I suppose you're right, Mary, as usual, I should be praying to God, asking him to give me the power and strength necessary for the new tasks ahead."

"I'm sure you already have those powers," commented Mary, as she held his hand.

"Tell me," continued Joseph, "when we get to Ohio, where do you suppose you will be going?"

"Either Wolfsereek or St. Alphonse."

"Where will I go?"

"Probably Thompson Seminary, Father Salesius will want to get you studying for the priesthood, as soon as you can."

"I'm not sure if I want to be a priest," continued Joseph, "It seems like that involves a lot of responsibilities. I don't know if I could handle that."

"It is not in your hands now; it is up to God. If he wants you to become a priest, you will. If he wants you to become a brother, you will. I, for one, know that you would make an excellent priest. You have all of the ideal qualities necessary."

"If only I had as much faith in me as you do," stated Joseph.

Just then, the ferry landed on the other side of the river. The man took the rope off, as Mary went back to her wagon. Several minutes later, the wagons were driven ashore.

Once they were a short distance from the ferry, Joseph turned around and shouted to Mr. Dufner: "This looks like a good place to camp for the night."

"Rochus," continued Joseph, as he turned his attention to the 19-year-old boy who had been walking beside Joseph's wagon, "You and Michael, go get some firewood."

"Yes Mr. Albrecht," replied Rochus, as he and 28-year-old Michael Homburger quickly headed into the nearby woods.

As the wagons were parked, everyone got out of the wagons and prepared for the night. Some of the men began to feed the horses, while the women prepared the supper.

After Rochus and Michael returned with a large bundle of kindling wood, several campfires were started.

As the sun disappeared from the sky, the air became colder, causing everyone to scurry tor a choice spot around one of the fires. Joseph's hands were really hurting, but he knew that he would have to wait till Rochus and Michael returned with more wood. While patiently waiting, he kept rubbing his hands. As he walked over lo where Mary was already sitting, he handed her a wool blanket. "Here Mary. Here is an extra blanket for you," he stated.

"No Joseph. If I take it, then you won't have one."

"That is alright, I don't need one."

"You are always so considerate. Always thinking of others and never of yourself. Some day you will get your just reward," noted Mary, as she took the blanket.

Soon, Rochus and Michael again reappeared with more kindling. Within a matter of minutes, there were five large fires going, all being enjoyed by the 35 travelers.

Joseph sat down close to one of the fires and said to Urs: "I hope the weather gets better. Otherwise, it could get very rough."

"I hope so too," replied the 42-year-old Urs Haener.

"Barbara," shouted Joseph, as he looked over towards Miss Hog, "how about singing a song for us? We would surely enjoy listening to some good music."

Barbara blushed as she slowly got up in front of everyone. She paused for a few moments, looked around at her friends, placed the guitar, which she had set beside her, on her knee, and began to sing. Everyone seemed to enjoy her beautiful voice. Upon completion, she put down the guitar and crawled back under her blanket, at which time Joseph said to her:

"Excellent, Barbara, excellent. Perhaps someday you will sing in the choir at my church."

"In your church?" queried Barbara, with a smile.

Joseph just looked at Barbara and returned the smile. He then reached into his pocket and pulled out his long black rosary, and silently began to pray.

The next morning, everyone was up and about very early. The sky was clear and the air brisk. It had been quite cold the previous night, so everyone was glad to see the sun coming up. Each person was putting their blankets and personal things back into the wagons. Several of the men were busy putting out the fires, while several others hitched up the horses, while Joseph was looking over a map, with Mary.

"If we have any luck at all, we should make it to Strasbourg by nightfall," noted Joseph, as he pointed at the map.

"That seems quite far," replied Mary, as she looked at where Joseph was pointing.

"Yes, but the road along the river is in excellent shape," added Joseph.

Slowly, the group departed, following the river, northward. By evening they did reach their goal of Strasbourg, a highly congested city, teeming with a strong musty odor. As the group entered the city, they could not help but notice the desperate situation of many of the inhabitants. Abject poverty was prevalent everywhere they looked. Men, women, and children, all in ragged clothing, were situated at various points along the roadside. They were seen huddling up to makeshift campfires. Many at the houses along the road were no more than huts, put together by whatever materials were available in the area. The entire area was a scene that Joseph would remember for a long time. The group proceeded to set up camp in a small open field at the edge of town.

"Tomorrow morning," stated Joseph, as he looked at Urs, "we'll have to send a couple of men downtown, to find that place where we are supposed to pick up that freight."

"Yes," agreed Urs, "Marder says that he has been here before and that he thinks he knows where that place is. I'll have him and Homburger go down there first thing in the morning."

"Good idea," replied Joseph, as he grabbed a plate of hot food, which had just been handed to him by Mary. After making the sign of the cross and silently saying a prayer, and again making the sign of the cross, he began to eat.

The next morning, after Joseph Marder and Michael Homburger returned from downtown, the group again prepared to leave. Young Michael Homburger now droves the first wagon, with Joseph sitting beside him. Upon arrival at the freight house, the men hurriedly went about the task of loading the freight. Once this was completed, the caravan was again on its way. Paris was now the next destination.

"We'll follow the Marne River, right to Paris," stated Joseph, as he looked at Mary, who was seated right behind him. "I'm going to have to switch with one of the other men that are walking."

"You should stay right there," replied Mary. "Those men are much younger than you. They can take the walking better."

"I should be treated no different than the rest," noted Joseph.

"You always were that way," stated Mary, in somewhat of a disgusted tone.

Joseph just shrugged his shoulders and stopped the wagon. As he was getting down, he hollered: "John!"

28-year-old John Butz, who was walking alongside the second wagon, ran up to Joseph and said: "Yes?"

"You drive for a while. I would like to walk."

"But Joseph. Don't you think the walking will harm you?"

"Nonsense. The good Lord has a job for me in America. A little walking surely can't harm me. He'll see to that."

John got up on the wagon, sat down, took the reins, and started the wagon moving again, while Joseph walked alongside. As they were going along the river, they often met caravans going in the opposite direction, returning from Paris, loaded down with cotton.

"Where are you headed for?" queried Joseph, to a middle-aged man, who was driving one of the wagons.

"Strasbourg," replied the man.

"How long did it take you to get this far from Paris?"

"Two days," answered the man. "It would have been faster, but we were having problems with the government officials. Ever since that changeover, they have really clamped down."

"Yes, I've been expecting to be checked any day now," replied Joseph.

"When you do, be careful," warned the man. "They will try and take you for whatever they can."

"Thank you for warning us," stated Joseph, as each continued on their separate way.

As the group got closer to Paris, they noticed more and more soldiers stationed alongside the road. At one of these stops, two French soldiers blocked the road, forcing the wagons to come to a halt.

"Who's in charge here?" queried one of the men, as he looked at John.

"I am," interrupted Joseph, as he stepped forward.

"Where are you headed for?" continued the soldier.

"America," replied Joseph. "We are going to get a boat at LeHavre. We have to deliver these goods to a certain Mr. Pierre DeVoe, in Paris, and then we are heading for LeHavre."

"Then what?"

"Why are you asking so many questions?" objected Joseph.

"We are meeting very many of your kind," continued the soldier. "All of you say that you are going to America, but many of you end up in LeHavre, without any money and no means to get back home."

"Don't worry about us," assured Joseph, "We already have friends in America and have been told about each step of the way, where to go, and what to do."

"Are you carrying much money with you?" queried the other man.
"Enough," replied Joseph.

"How many are in your group?"

"35"

"All of you going to the same place?"

"That's correct."

"What's your occupation?"

"I am going to become a priest," said Joseph. "The same with the other men. The women are either nuns already or are going to become nuns."

"Well, well," noted the soldier, "then you probably are hauling all sorts of gold?"

"Sorry, but you are wrong. You are welcome to check the freight," continued Joseph, as he motioned for them to look into the wagons.

The two men walked behind the first wagon and opened it up. They looked for several seconds at some of the boxes which were stored along the inside. The women, who were sitting on these boxes, got up and allowed the men to open them up.

"There is nothing in this box, except for a bell," remarked one of the soldiers, as he closed the lid.

"What's in this box?" asked the other soldier, as he looked at Joseph, who was now standing right behind him.

"Relics," bluntly replied Joseph. "Relics of St. Candidus."

"Come on Jacque," stated the soldier, in disgust, "they have nothing here that would interest us."
The two men got back out of the wagon and allowed the group to continue onward.

"What did you do with that box of gold?" queried Mary, as she looked at Joseph.

43

" I had it under the relics," answered Joseph, as he laughed.

Upon arrival in Paris, the caravan went immediately to the address where they were to deliver the goods. When they completed that task, they went to an area along the Seine River, and proceeded to set up camp.

"Urs, come with me," requested Joseph. "We have to find out where we can sell these horses and wagons."

The two men departed camp. What they saw along the way was exactly what they had seen in Strasbourg, earlier. Signs of poverty were everywhere. Children were rummaging through the garbage piles, looking for scraps of food. There were old men sitting alongside the road. Some were sleeping, some drinking, and some just lying around talking. All of them were unshaven and dressed in ragged clothing.

"What a sight!" exclaimed Joseph.

"It makes me wonder why God would allow such a condition to exist," stated Urs.

"He has plans for these people," answered Joseph. "They are living their hell on earth. They are paying their dues now, just like those in Strasbourg."

"There must be something we can do," exclaimed Urs.

"There is," replied Joseph. "Pray for them. Pray that they have the courage and willpower to survive. Pray that they get what they deserve in the next world."

The two men continued to walk. Soon, they arrived at a huge barn, where there was a large group standing, As Joseph and Urs approached, they noticed that most of the people were of German descent. They were busy trying to sell their horses and wagons to a couple of Frenchmen, who were eyeing the horses over very closely, and offering bids on them.

"This is the place," exclaimed Joseph. "Get back to camp and have the men help you bring all the horses and wagons here as soon as you can. Hurry! We have no time to waste."

"Yes." replied Urs. as he turned and began walking back to where they had just come from. Meanwhile, Joseph got closer to the Frenchmen.

"Are they giving a fair price?" asked Joseph, as he looked at one of the Germans that was standing nearby.

"Not really," shrugged the German, "but, we don't have much choice. They know we have to get rid of them"

"I suppose," continued Joseph. "Tell me, where are you headed for?*

"LeHavre," answered the German, "We are supposed to have reservations there for a boat to America."

"Oh!" exclaimed Joseph. "Where in America?"

"We have relatives in Pennsylvania." replied the German,

"How about you?"

"We are going to Ohio, by way of Lellavre and New York," stated Joseph.

"There are barges that travel the Seine daily," continued the German, "I've been told that it should be very easy to catch a ride on one of them. There also is a stagecoach line, but they are very expensive,"

"Do you know where to go to find out about these barges?"

"Yes," replied the German, "it is only a short distance from here." As he pointed in an easterly direction and locked that way, he continued: "Over there."

"Ah, yes," noted Joseph, "I see."

Knowing that Urs would probably net return for another half hour or so, Joseph decided to go over to the river and see what he could find out.

As he was leaving, he exclaimed to the German: "Thank you for your help. Maybe, we shall meet again."

Joseph now headed in the direction of the river. Soon, he was at the dock. There were people everywhere. Various barges and small boats were being loaded and unloaded.

"Excuse me," noted Joseph, as he addressed a young French dockworker, "Could you tell me whom I should see, concerning a ride to LeHavre?"

"Over there." exclaimed the man, as he pointed in the direction of a large 3-story building, located next to the waterfront.

"Thank you," replied Joseph, as he began to walk in that direction.

Once inside the building, he looked around until he noticed a sign which read: LEHAVRE FRIEGHTLINES LIMITED — INFORMATION, He walked up to the desk of an elderly man, and exclaimed: "Excuse me sir, can you tell me how we can get a ride to LeHavre?"

"How many?" questioned the man, as he put down his cigar.
"35."
"H'mm," noted the man, as he looked at some papers, lying on the desk. "We have a barge leaving this afternoon. If you don't mind riding on the deck, we could put you all on there."
"How much will it cost?"
"Let's see," replied the man, as he did some figuring on a piece of scratch paper. "70 florins."
"When do I pay?" asked Joseph.
"Right before you go aboard."
"Excellent!" exclaimed Joseph. "I'll be back in a few hours with the entire group."

45

Joseph, hurriedly, returned to the horse fair. While he had been down at the riverfront, Urs, and several other men, had arrived with the horses and wagons.

"Michael," shouted Joseph, as he walked up to the men,
"get back to the group and bring them over here, right away. I have found transportation to LeHavre, but we don't have much time, so be as fast as you can."
Michael immediately turned and departed.
"Urs," continued Joseph, "help me take these horses over to those two guys."
"Tell me, sir," began Joseph, as he and Urs brought the ten horses up to the two Frenchmen,
"what will you give me for these fine-looking animals?"
The man slowly looked over the animals, one at a time. After several minutes, he turned and looked at Joseph, and said: "ten francs a piece."
Joseph couldn't believe what he heard. "Ten francs! Why they're worth ten times that."
"I'm sorry, but that is the best I can offer," continued the man, knowing full well that Joseph had no choice but to accept it.

"Alright. I'll take it."

The man reached into his pocket and counted out the money, and handed it to Joseph, who, immediately, put it into his pocket.

After looking to see what time it was, Joseph walked over to a large shade tree and sat down underneath. He pulled out his rosary from his pocket, and silently began to pray. While he was still praying, Michael returned with the group. Noticing their arrival, Joseph got up, and said:

"Good. Now that we have everyone here, let's go straight to the docks. Follow me."
With Joseph in the lead, the others quietly followed. Each was carrying their own personal belongings, as well as the belongings of Joseph.

As they were walking to the barge, Joseph looked at Mary, and said:

"It probably won't be a very comfortable ride. We have to ride on the top deck. Fortunately, it shouldn't take too long."

"I'm sure we'll manage," noted Mary, as the group arrived at the dock.

"Pick out a spot," noted Joseph, as the group began to board the river barge. "Try and make the best of it. Stay close together. This will be your transportation for the next day, or so."

The group obediently listened to Joseph, and they were all, soon, situated aboard, patiently awaiting their departure. As Joseph looked around, he noticed that they were all huddling together, and wrapping themselves up in blankets. He glanced over at Mary, and said:
"They are being put to the test already. I hope they have the stamina and determination to make it."

"Everyone seems to be doing fine," remarked Mary.

"All except Crescentia Zipfel. She has been complaining of a chest cold and nausea, but, with proper care, she should get better."

"Maybe I should go see her," suggested Joseph.

"That would be a good idea," replied Mary.

After looking around and seeing where young Crescentia was sitting, he walked over to her, and said: "Crescentia, my dear, how are you feeling?"

"Not so good, Mr. Albrecht," replied the sickly young lady. "I'm not sure if I'm going to be able to go much further."

"I will pray for you," replied Joseph. "Be sure to wrap yourself up very warmly and don't over-exert yourself."

"As long as I have Maria and Joanna taking care of me, I will be all right," assured Crescentia, as she took the hand of 39-year-old Maria Wangler, who had been sitting beside her.

"Fine," continued Joseph. "You must get better. Father Salesius has a great need for you in Ohio."

"I hope so," noted Crescentia, "I hope so."

Joseph now returned to his original spot and sat down next to Mary. "I am afraid that we may have a problem," he stated. "I don't think Crescentia is in very good shape."

"Maybe we should leave her at LeHavre," suggested Mary.

"No, I will leave it in the hands of the Lord. If he wants her in America, he will find a way for her to get there."

"Is that really fair to her?"

"She is the one that desires to continue on," answered Joseph.

"Who am I to stop her?"

"When we get to LeHavre, we should have the Ursuline sisters take care of her. When she gets better, then she could continue on," suggested Mary.

"We'll see," noted Joseph. "Now, I think I'm going to try and take a nap."

As he wrapped himself up in a blanket, it began to rain. The boat trip down the Seine River went very slowly for the passengers. Hours passed with the same monotony. The rains continued to come down, making it miserable for everyone. After a short nap, Joseph again got up and went over to where Crescentia Zipfel was lying. Her coughing seemed to be getting worse, but Joseph did not know what to do for her. As he sat down beside her, he grabbed her hand and smiled. Crescentia looked up and returned his smile.

"I sure wish your brother, Fridolin would have come along," noted Joseph.

"He could probably take much better care of you than we can."

"He says he will be coming over shortly," replied Crescentia.

"Besides, someone had to stay and take care of the house, until we can get it sold."

"You know," Joseph continued, "him and I always seemed to get along quite well. I will miss him."

"Yes, he talked about you often," noted Crescentia. "He has nothing but admiration for you."

"Perhaps we shall meet again, some day," stated Joseph, as he stared out over the side of the barge.

"Joanna," continued Joseph, as he turned his attention to the 21-year-old lady who was lying on the other side of Maria Wangler,

"perhaps you should take over for Maria, it looks like she could use a rest."

The petite young lady quietly got up and exchanged positions with Maria.

"Well, my child," added Joseph, as he looked back at Crescentia, while getting up, "let us hope for the best. We should be arriving at LeHavre shortly. Perhaps then we can get you to a doctor."

"Thank-you," quietly stated Crescentia, as she grabbed at Joseph's left hand.

Within an hour the barge arrived at the harbor.

"What a nice sight! " exclaimed Joseph, as he got up from under his blanket and looked out at the harbor. "Now we can finally get off this barge."

Everyone, including Joseph, began to pick up their personal belongings and headed for the exit ramp.

"Where do we go from here?" Joseph asked Mary.

"When I came through, the women stayed with the Ursuline Sisters and the men went with a certain Robert Marzion, the head of the St. Vincent dePaul Society."

"Good. Will you show us where to go?"

"Of course."

As they departed the barge, the group noticed, immediately, that there were many German innkeepers and dockworkers in the area.

"Why?" queried Joseph. "Why are there so many Germans here?"

"Many of them have traveled to this city, with the hope of finding passage to America. Many came with very little money, if any, and after finding out that they couldn't afford the passage, they decided to stay until they could save enough. Others have come to take advantage of the travelers and others have come to make the trip easier for others," replied Mary.

"Who do we see about tickets?" continued Joseph.

"Hopefully, Mr. Marzion will take care of that. I was hoping he would be here to meet us, but he really didn't know when we would be arriving. Come! Follow me! He doesn't live too far from here."

The group remained together and silently followed Joseph and Mary down a side-street to the home of Mr. Marzion. As they approached, they noticed how extraordinarily beautiful the three-story stone building of Mr. Marzion's was. The large house was entirely surrounded by a beautiful garden. One could imagine what the yard would look like in full bloom. The entire area was enclosed with a tall, black, metal fence. Joseph and Mary entered through the gate while the others stayed on the street. When they reached the doorway, Mary knocked.

"Why Mary!" exclaimed Robert, as he opened the door,

"What a surprise! I wasn't expecting you people for another day or so."

"Hello Robert," returned Mary.

"Come in, please," noted Robert.

"Robert, I would like you to meet Joseph Albrecht, my ex-husband," continued Mary.

"Hello Joseph," replied Robert, as he shook his hand.

"Hello," replied Joseph.

"Tell me, Mary, do you know when you are going across?"

"I was hoping that you could get us on board one of the ships," answered Mary.

"I see," said Robert. "Well, it's too late this evening, but, tomorrow, I shall see what I can do. For now, we must find you a place for the night. How many of you are there?"

"35," replied Mary. "8 men and 27 women."

"Maybe you should take the women over to the convent. They will be able to provide lodging. I have room here for the men."

"That'll be fine," noted Mary. "I'll go back out and tell the men to come in."

"Come back tomorrow afternoon," noted Robert. "I should know the situation by then."

"Good night, Mary," offered Joseph.

"Good night," replied Mary, as she left the house.

As Joseph and Robert watched Mary depart, Robert looked at Joseph and asked:

"Do you regret getting your marriage annulled?"

"Definitely not! I will always have a certain feeling for Mary, but we both believe we made the right decision. God has a plan for both of us and we must carry out those plans."

"How do you know that?"

"It is written in the Bible," answered Joseph, as he stepped aside, to let the other seven men enter.

"Welcome to my humble abode," stated Robert, as he greeted the men. "Please, come in."

"Pierre," shouted Robert, to his butler, "take these men to their rooms, upstairs."

"Yes sir," replied the butler, as he headed for the staircase, being closely followed by the seven men, while Joseph remained behind with Robert.

"What are your plans?" asked Robert.

"I hope to be accepted by Father Salesius to become a Precious Blood priest."

"Aren't you too old for that?"

"Too old for what?"

"Too old to be a priest."

"One is never too old to dedicate his life for God and his sheep," Joseph sternly replied. "I am 47. I'm sure I have many good years left."

"What makes you think that?"

"Many times, I have talked with God. He has told me to prepare myself for a mission. It is to be a mission of saving souls. It will take me to three places in America. He called it a trinitarian mission."

"What do you mean by that?"

"My life evolves around the Trinity — the Father, the Son, and the Holy Ghost. It is because of them that the mission must be carried out. I must dedicate my life to the fulfillment of their commands. I must do what they demand. In order to do that, I must be a priest. Mary has been asked to do the same. She, therefore, became a nun. Our daughter, Rosalie, too, has been called upon. She is already in America. We are both longing to see her once again."

"Yes, I met Rosalie," interrupted Robert.

"It has been four long years since I've seen her," noted Joseph, as he stared into space.

"Tell me, Joseph," continued Robert, "what do you think of Father Brunner?"

"He is my idol. He is a living saint. The perfect example of what a man should be. His ideals are excellent. Every day I pray that I will someday arise to his standards."

"I also think very highly of him. When you get to Ohio, give him my regards."

"Of course," replied Joseph. "Now, I must get some sleep. Where do I go?"

"Take the first room on the left, at the top of the stairs.",

"Thank-you," replied Joseph, as he got up from the chair and began walking up the stairs.

50

"Good night," offered Robert.

"Good night."

The next morning, the men were up very early. One by one they came downstairs, taking a seat by the dining table. Joseph and Robert were the first ones there.

"Good morning, Joseph," noted Robert. "Did you sleep well?"

"Not too good," replied Joseph. "I had a terrible dream. I dreamt that Rosalie had died, and then, I found out that I would not be allowed to become a priest."

"Well, luckily it was just a dream," consoled Robert.

"Yes, fortunately," replied Joseph, as he sat down by the table, next to Robert.

"Shall we pray?" queried Joseph, as the butler was serving breakfast.

As everyone bowed their heads, Joseph began:

"In the name of the Father, and of the Son, and of the Holy Ghost. Lord, Bless this food which we are about to receive from Thy bounty, through Christ, our Lord. Amen. In the name of the Father, and of the Son, and of the Holy Ghost. Amen."

All of the other men replied: "Amen," as they finished making the sign of the Cross and began to eat.
"Tell me Robert," asked Joseph, "what are your plans for the day?"

"You and I will go down to the harbor, this morning," replied Robert.
"I'll talk to a few people. They'll know what's available for transportation. Then, we should be able to set up some plans."

"Hopefully, we won't have to stay here for too many days,"
noted Joseph. "The Lord knows how anxious we are in getting to our final destination."
"It is hard to say. Sometimes there is plenty of room on these ships and, sometimes, not. It will all depend on the weather. Mother Nature can be very nasty sometimes."

"This was an excellent breakfast," commented Joseph, as he pushed himself away from the table.

"Thank-you," replied Robert, as he too finished.

Before the men got up, Joseph led them in a prayer of thanksgiving, after which Robert asked: "Would anyone like to smoke?", as he lit up his pipe.

"No thank-you," replied Joseph. "That is one habit, none of us indulge in."

"Say Joseph, wasn't there another group coming?"

"Yes, they were supposed to leave shortly after we did."

"Who's in charge?"

"Peter Arnold and George Allgiers. They are supposed to meet us at the docks."

"How many are in that group?"

"About 215."

"All from the same area?"

"Yes, and there are hundreds more who have expressed a desire to come, but, I think, most will wait till Father Oschwald leaves."

"Times must really be tough there?"

"Yes, it was getting to the point that it was almost unbearable."

"Well, we better be on our way," suggested Robert, as he got up from his chair. Joseph did likewise, and the two men walked to the door. As Joseph was about to go out, he turned and looked at Joseph Marder, and said:

"Stay here until we return. We shouldn't be gone too long."

"Yes Joseph," replied Mr. Marder, as he, along with the other men, watched Joseph and Robert depart.

The weather in LeHavre this particular day was excellent. Clear skies and a warm sun. The air was somewhat crisp, but yet, very soothing. A cool breeze was coming in from the ocean, but it was still warm enough to be without a coat. The streets seemed to be overly crowded with people. Many of them were travelers from various parts of the German States. Many of the others seemed to be preying upon these travelers. They were each trying to offer deals to the weary travelers, as they went by. Joseph and Robert walked directly to the docks, where there were a countless number of ships moored in the bay. Intermingled among these, were barges and boats of various sizes, seemingly going in every direction. There were several large ships being unloaded and several others being loaded. Joseph watched in amazement at all of the activity. "Is it always like this?" he asked.

"Sometimes, it is even busier."

"Who are we supposed to see down here?"

"Come, we'll enter here," replied Robert, as he pointed to an entryway of an old, dilapidated building.

As they entered, they were noticed by a heavy-set elderly man, sitting by a desk, near the door. He put down his cigar and arose.

"Robert," he exclaimed, "what brings you in here?"

"Hello Rene," stated Robert. "I need your help again."

"Joseph, I'd like for you to meet Rene Boudreau. Rene, this is Joseph Albrecht. He is one of the leaders of a group of Germans, who are seeking passage to America."

"Hello," greeted Rene, as he shook hands with Joseph.

"Hello," replied Joseph.

"How many in the group?" queried Rene.

"250," answered Joseph.

"Huh, that is a very large number. Where are you planning to go?"

"We need transportation to New York," noted Joseph. "Our final destination is Ohio."

"I see," replied Rene. "Let me take a look at the ship lists."

He began paging through a pile of papers. Within a matter of seconds, he abruptly stopped, and said:

"Here we are. There is a ship coming in the day after tomorrow, with a load of cotton. They will be hauling freight back to New York. As of now, there are no passengers signed up. Leave it to me, Robert, I'll have everything set. I'll make sure I get the group on this ship."

"What's the name of the ship?" asked Joseph.

"The Duchess of Orleans," replied Rene.

"Ah," remarked Joseph, "now I know our trip will be a success. We'll be under the protection of a lady. Like the Blessed Virgin Mary helping us in our times of difficulty, so will the Duchess."

"Thank-you Rene," stated Robert. "I'll be back tomorrow, to make sure everything is set."

"That will give me time to find out the costs too," agreed Rene.

"Very well," continued Robert. "Have a good day."

"Good-bye my dear friend," replied Rene. "Nice meeting you, Joseph."

"The same here," answered Joseph. "Good-bye."

As they left the building, Joseph noticed Mr. Arnold and Mr. Allgiers standing nearby.

"Peter! George!" exclaimed Joseph, in a loud voice, as he ran towards the two men.

The two men looked over at Joseph and were equally excited upon recognizing the caller.

"When did you get here?" asked Joseph.

"We just arrived," replied Peter, as he hugged Joseph. "Good to see you again."

"Where are the rest?" asked Joseph, as he looked around.

"We left them down by the mouth of the river," replied George.

"Many of them are quite tired from the trip. We decided it wasn't necessary for everyone to come looking for you. Is everything set?"

"We should know for sure in a day or two."

"Good," exclaimed Peter. "The sooner the better."

"How is everyone doing?" continued Joseph.

"Most of them have been doing fine," replied Peter. "John Frey's wife Christina, has become very sick. Some of the older folks are getting tired, but a day of rest should help them."

"Robert, I would like to go with Peter and George, and see the
others," noted Joseph. "I'll return to your house, shortly."

"Of course," replied Robert, as he turned and began to walk away. "I will see you then."

The three remaining men began to walk in the opposite direction. Soon, they arrived at the bustling campsite.

"Greetings, my friends," exclaimed Joseph, as he walked amongst the group. "Everything is just about set for the trip across. In a few days we will be heading for America. I'm staying with a certain Mr. Marzion, who has been a great help. As soon as he finds out the details, he will let me know. Then, I'll pass the information on to you."

Walking over to one of the younger men, 31-year-old John Frey, Joseph noted:
"John, my dear cousin, how is your wife?"
"Much better, thank-you," replied Mr. Frey.
"That's good to hear. Do you think she would mind having a visitor?"
"I'm sure she would enjoy seeing you, Joseph," replied John.
"Come! I'll take you to her."

The two men proceeded over to a makeshift hut and entered. Inside, was a 29-year-old woman, wrapped up very tightly in a large winter coat, and sitting next to a large box. She was awake and when she noticed her husband and Joseph, she attempted to sit up.

"Joseph! What a surprise!"
"Hello Christina. I hear you are feeling better."
"Yes. I still have a fever, but the cough is gone."
Grabbing her hand, Joseph quietly said a short prayer, after
which he stated: "I know God will take care of you. It is our destiny to get to America. God will see to it that we get there."
"Oh Joseph. If only I had the faith you have. It always seems that God is listening to you. I hope you are right."
"You take care of yourself, Christina. In a few days we should be on the boat. I will pray for you."

"Thank-you Joseph. You are most kind."
"Tell me, John, how long has she been like this?"
"Ever since we left Kirchzarten," replied John. "We were seriously thinking about staying there, but she insisted that we all leave together.

"Everything will work out fine," assured Joseph, as he began departing.

"I'll return as soon as I find out when we're leaving," noted Joseph.

"Until then, you will all have to stay here and make the best of it. I'll send some of the Ursuline Sisters down to check on Christina, and on anyone else who may need special attention."

"Very well," replied John.

"By the way, Peter," continued Joseph, as he turned to Mr. Arnold, "do you have a complete list of all the people in your group?"

"Yes," answered Peter. "I have it here in my bag."

He searched in one of the small bags and soon came up with a large piece of paper. "Here it is," he noted, as he picked it out of the bag, and handed it to Joseph.

"Let me use it. That way I'll know exactly how many will 'be traveling."

As he took the piece of paper and put it in his pocket, he continued: "I'll be back soon."

Joseph now returned to the home of Mr. Marzion, where he stayed for the next two days. On the end of the second day, a messenger arrived at the house.

"Yes, what would you like?" asked Robert, as he greeted the boy.

"Mr. Boudreau sent me, to tell you that the Duchess of Orleans is in port and that it was to be leaving for New York in two days and that your entire group can board tomorrow."

"Excellent!" interrupted Joseph, who was standing beside Robert.

"Did he say anything about the costs?"

"No sir."

"We'll have to find that out when we go back down there," stated Robert.

"Thank-you my son," replied Joseph, as he handed the messenger a small coin, and watched him leave.

"Let's go right away," stated Joseph, as he looked at Robert.

"I must find out the cost, to make sure that everyone can afford it."

"It is getting rather late," objected Robert. "Couldn't we wait till tomorrow morning?"

"No, we must get down there today," insisted Joseph. "I'd never be able to sleep tonight if we put it off."

"All right," agreed Robert. "Let's get our coats."

The two men put on their coats and walked out the door, heading, once more, for the docks.

As they approached the dock, they noticed the huge ship "Duchess of Orleans" being unloaded.

"What a beautiful vessel!" exclaimed Joseph. "It looks very sturdy."

While Rene was standing in front of his office, with another man, he spotted Robert and Joseph standing near the ship, so he walked over to greet them.

"Ah my friends," stated Rene, "I would like you to meet Captain Richardson. He is the captain of the Duchess."

"Hello," replied Robert, as he shook hands with the unshaven, middle-aged man who was wearing an old worn-out winter coat, along with a black scarf, and a baggy pair of trousers. He had on a large captains' hat, that was supposed to be white, but was just as dirty as the rest of his clothes. Just by looking at him, one could tell that he had been out to sea for quite some time.

"Greetings, mate," answered the captain. "Please to meet you."

"This here is Joseph Albrecht," continued Rene. "He is the man in charge of the passengers which you will be carrying."

"Hello Joseph," commented the captain.

"Hello."

"We'll be pulling out the day after tomorrow," noted the captain. "The winds are just right now. The air is still very cold out there, but if everyone is dressed well, we should have no problems."

"How long do you think it'll take to get to New York?" queried Joseph.

"Well," thought the captain, as he pulled on his beard, "if everything works out, we should be there by the end of April. It'll depend on how things are at Liverpool. We have to stop there to pick up some extra cargo."

"End of April," noted Joseph. "That sounds like a long time to be on the water, but I suppose we don't have much choice in the matter. Then we should be able to get to Ohio in time for the spring fieldwork."

"Your group contains mostly farmers?" asked the captain. "Yes. As well as quite a few religious or, at least, people who are studying to be, or planning on being, priests or nuns."

"Well, have everyone boarded by tomorrow evening. I have my crew unloading now. Tomorrow morning they will be loading. I hope to be out of LeHavre by the next morning."

"How much will it cost?"

"That depends. Are you bringing your own food, or do you want to be fed with the crew?"

"We have our own provisions. We would never be able to afford it otherwise. We are just a bunch of poor peasants."

"Very well. We will write up our passenger list as you come aboard. We'll need that list anyway when we get to New York."

"I'm going over to my people right after I leave here," stated Joseph.

"I'll make sure they are down here in plenty of time. Most of them should be able to pay their own way. I'll be responsible for the religious group. I'll be the first one on, so I can check when they board."

"Alright. That will be fine. Meanwhile, I'll figure out what the costs will be," noted the captain.

"I shall see you tomorrow then," continued Joseph, as he again shook hands with the captain.

"Robert," stated Joseph, as he looked at Mr. Marzion.

"Do you want to come along with me?"

"No, Joseph, I think I'll go over to the convent and let the girls know about tomorrow."

"Excellent idea, I'll return to your house as soon as I can."

Joseph now hurriedly departed for the camp. He could hardly wait to tell them the good news. The short distance was quickly covered, and he was soon in camp.

"Peter, I have good news," shouted Joseph, as he approached Mr. Arnold. "We have a ship. Have everyone down by the docks tomorrow morning. I'll meet you down there bright and early."

"What's the name of the ship?" asked Mr. Arnold.

"The Duchess of Orleans. It's located near where we met earlier. You won't miss it."

"Very well. I'll pass the word."

The next morning came quickly. During the night, fog had set in, and with it, came a cold biting breeze from the ocean. The scene along the docks was one of frantic bustle. Heavily clad dockworkers were busily doing their jobs. Joseph had arrived early with his group of men, who were all content on watching the dockworkers do their work. Mr. Marzion accompanied Joseph, and the others, to make sure everything went as planned.

In a very short time, the women arrived from the Ursuline Convent and, almost immediately after that, the remaining large group of travelers arrived.

"Good morning, Mary," noted Joseph, as the group of women approached.

"Good morning, Joseph."

"Not very good weather to be traveling in, is it?"

"No, but it could be worse."

"Shortly, we will be boarding. I would like it very much if we all stayed close together. It would be nice if you stayed by my side."

"Of course."

As Joseph and Mary walked over towards the ship, they were met by Captain Richardson.

"Good morning," stated the captain, as he looked at Joseph and Mary.

"Good morning," replied Joseph. "When can we board?"

"You can come aboard now. I'll give you a short tour of the boat and show you where everyone will be berthed during the voyage."

"Good," noted Joseph, as the two men began boarding the ship.

"We normally carry about 200 passengers on each trip, but this time we have less cargo, so it will be all right to carry more passengers."

As the two men walked across the gangplank onto the vessel itself, Joseph stated: "This is an excellent vessel."

"Thank-you," replied the captain. "I am very proud of it. Come over here. Follow me down this ladder. I'll show you the sleeping quarters."

Once below, Joseph immediately noticed how dark it was.

"This is the main sleeping area, for your people. This is where they will eat, sleep, and live during this voyage. It will probably be somewhat crowded, but they'll have to make do the best they can."

"It does not take much to please my people," retorted Joseph.

"I have had some firewood put onboard. They can use that for heat and for cooking. When we're out on the open ocean, everyone must stay below, unless we are at a standstill. Every once in a while, we encounter a storm or two, so it would be safer for your people if they did not venture up the ladder. It is very dark down here, but there are portholes that can be opened, plus there are several torches and candles that can be lit."

"I'm sure it will be satisfactory with my people," noted Joseph.

"Have your people start boarding as soon as they can. It will probably take them some time to get situated and comfortable," continued the captain.

The two men climbed back up the ladder to the main deck. As they approached the gangplank, the captain continued:

"I will have a table and chairs here. This is where everyone will board and register."

"Very well," replied Joseph, as he began departing the vessel.

"I shall return shortly with the entire group."

After Joseph hurriedly walked back to Mary and the others, he stated:

"Have everyone get their belongings together, Mary. We can board now."

"Yes Joseph," replied Mary, as she turned and began spreading the word.

The entire group was anxious to leave, and shortly, they were all lining up alongside the Duchess.

"Follow me," requested Joseph, as he walked the gangplank, onto the vessel. He then sat down beside the captain, who was filling out a large sheet of paper.

Slowly, the group began to embark. Each was asked their name, age, where they came from and where they were going. The process was very time-consuming. Every age group was involved, from new-born children to grandparents. Each of them, excluding the real young children, were loaded down with personal belongings and food supplies. Everyone already had a tired look on their faces. Each was thinking about the long journey still lying ahead, and of the possible dangers and experiences that could occur. The line continued to move at a snail's pace. Mary approached the table, finally. Ahead of her were Anna and Magdalena Helzinger. Behind her was Anton Dufner and John Butz.

"Put my name on the list here," interjected Joseph. "Once everyone gets aboard, I'd like to be with Mary."

"All right," replied the captain, as he began to write. "Your age?"

"47."

"Your name?" queried the captain, as he looked over at Mary.

"Anna Maria Albrecht, age 38," replied Mary. "Most people call me Mary, but you can write Anna."
"Next?"
"Antonio Dufner, age 53," stated Mr. Dufner.
As the captain was writing, Joseph turned to Mary, and said:
"Mary, just follow the group below deck. Save some room for me, and I'll be down afterwards."

Without saying a word, Mary nodded her head, as she picked up her small bundle of personal effects and proceeded towards the stairwell.

The fog was now changing to a heavy mist. The damp air caused Joseph to wrap a blanket around himself, in an attempt to be more comfortable.

"I sure hope it gets better," stated the captain. "If it stays like this, we won't be going anywhere."
"Don't worry," noted Joseph. "Many of my people are praying for good weather."
"Do you think that will really change it?"
"Why, captain, I'm surprised of you! Don't you know God is always listening?"

"Really!" exclaimed the captain, in utter disbelief.
"Just wait and see," continued Joseph. "I'll say a special prayer this evening and I'm sure we will be leaving right on schedule."
"I hope you're right. I don't care to spend too much time in this harbor."
The heavy mist was now turning into a steady rain. The deck of the ship was getting wet and slippery. Extra precautions were made by everyone to assure their safety.

"Be sure to hold onto your kids, Mrs. Beichenbach," advised Joseph, as he looked at 27-year-old Maria, and her 28-year-old husband, Peter. They had three children with them: Carl, age 5; Elizabeth, age 2; and a new-born daughter, Catharine. "Yes Joseph/' replied Maria, as she grabbed young Carl by the hand. She already was holding Catharine in her other arm. With Peter holding on to Eliza, the family slowly moved forward. After everyone was registered and aboard, Joseph climbed down the ladder, followed by the captain. Once reaching the lower deck, Joseph looked around and was aghast at what he saw.

"How are we going to be able to live under these conditions for three or four weeks?" he asked, as he looked at the captain.

"I realize that it is not the greatest, but it is the best I can offer. Many a poor soul has traveled in these confines. Most of them make it to their final destination. Why, on some of my trips, we've had twice as many in here."

As Joseph continued to look around, he added: "Well, I suppose the good Lord is just putting us to another test."

He spotted Mary in the crowd, and proceeded to slowly move towards her, comforting his fellow passengers, as he went. The younger children always loved to talk to Joseph, and this time was no exception. They could sense a feeling of sincerity generating from this man. They knew he had a devout interest in their welfare and that he would be there to console them in times of trouble. The adults too, had a distinct adoration for this saintly man. They knew that he was a special person, sent probably by divine providence to help guide them in their daily life, always seeming to say and do the right thing at the right time. As he moved through the crowd, he could see all the gratitude they held for him. Finally, Joseph arrived beside Mary.

"Well, I see you have found the choice seat in the house," stated Joseph, as he looked out the porthole, and sat down along the wall, next to her. "Is this what it was like the other times you traveled?"

"Yes," replied Mary, "except for when I went with Father Salesius, we were more crowded."
"I'm hoping that you will be a great help on our way over," continued Joseph.

"I'll try. I can help the women and show them how to get along with the bare necessities, if they don't already know."

"I knew you would be willing to help. You always have. I'm sure there are going to be problems arising, but since you've already experienced one of these trips, you should know what to do."
Joseph now turned and tried to get the attention of the crowd.

"My friends," he shouted. "I realize that the conditions here are somewhat primitive, but God is testing you. He wants to see if you can persevere. He wants to find out if you really want to get to the promised land. You know, that if you really want something good, you usually have to work hard for it, as well as suffer for it. Have patience and we will make it. Say a rosary every day while on the voyage and everything will turn out for the best. If you do have any problems, feel free to ask me, or Mary, for help. Just remember to treat your neighbor as yourself. Share with them, but most of all, have patience. Don't let vanity and pride interfere. Always remember the suffering Jesus went through. Then, you will realize that you don't have it so bad."

The entire group was listening very closely to what Joseph was saying. All of them had known him for many years and they respected him for what he had to say.
"Now, my dear friends," he continued, "take out your rosaries, and I shall lead you in prayer."
The next morning came and, with it, clear sunny skies, a calm breeze, and warm air. Joseph awoke early and made his way up the ladder, to the main deck.
Captain Richardson was making final preparations with his crew when he noticed the arrival of Joseph.
"Good morning, Joseph,"
he shouted. "I see your prayers were answered. Look at this beautiful weather."
"Yes, isn't it excellent? I just knew the good Lord wanted us to leave today."
"Well, we should be leaving very shortly."
"Good. I'll go back below and tell everyone," noted Joseph, as he turned and began to descend the ladder.

Within a matter of minutes, the Duchess was beginning to move. It slowly left the dock area, heading for the open sea. Down below, there were people standing by the portholes, looking out at the scenery they were passing. All of them were wearing faces of anxiety, for they knew they were beginning a journey into the unknown. None of them, except for Mary, really knew what to expect. Many of them got down on their knees, rosary in hand, and began to pray.

Some of the younger children were joyfully playing, not knowing what was taking place. Joseph was standing beside Mary, looking out a porthole. After staring for several minutes, he turned to Mary, and said:

"Our fate is now in God's hands. We have no control of our destiny. It is up to him, whether we make it to New York, or not."

The next several weeks went by slowly. As each day passed, the living conditions aboard seemed to worsen. The heavy odor of excrement and bodily smell was getting almost unbearable. The food supplies were dwindling to the point where rationing was necessary. The unending sway of the vessel caused many to become seasick. After several days, most of them were able to adjust, but, for a few, the sickness became worse.

"Joseph," exclaimed Mary, one morning, as she was preparing breakfast, "I think you should go see Crescentia again. I was up with her almost all night. She is very sick."
"All right, Mary. I'll go over and see her right away."
He walked through the crowd, to the other side of the ship. There, lying on a mat of straw, was the young Crescentia Zipfel. She was wrapped up in several blankets. Another young lady was kneeling beside her, wiping her forehead.
"My dear Crescentia," noted Joseph. "What is the matter?"
"Oh Joseph," she weakly replied, "I have lost all of my strength. I cannot eat and I have a burning fever."
"Let me say a prayer for you," offered Joseph, as he knelt down beside her and took her hand. Looking upward, he quietly said a short prayer. Just as he finished, Crescentia smiled, and looked upward.
"I think it is time," she exclaimed.

With those words, she closed her eyes forever. Joseph squeezed her hand tightly. Tears came to his eyes. "Oh, Lord, take good care of this young innocent child. She wanted to dedicate her life for you, but you had other plans for her. She has now come to be with you," noted Joseph.
Word of Crescentia's death spread rapidly. Everyone was saddened. Several of the older men helped Joseph take the lifeless body over to a small storage room. As Joseph quietly said some prayers, he gently wrapped a white sheet around her, and placed her in a long wooden box.

"This should suffice, until we get to New York," he noted.

"We should be arriving very soon. It is already the 18th of April, and the captain figured we'd be there by the 20th or 21st."

"Anton," he continued, as he looked at Mr. Dufner, "please tell the captain to have this room locked up. We won't need to get in it until we reach port."

"Yes sir," replied Anton, as he departed.

Joseph walked back over to Mary, who was kneeling amongst a large group of women. They were in the middle of praying the rosary, so he pulled out his, knelt down beside Mary, and joined in.

While the group was praying, the ship began to sway back and forth, seemingly becoming more viscious with each roll. Back and forth, back, and forth. Thunder could be heard, getting louder and louder, with each passing minute. The sound of rain, beating down on the deck, caused everyone to stop what they were doing and move closer together. Not only the children, but the adults too, were showing signs of being scared.

"Put the fires out," shouted Joseph, to several of the men, as he fought his way along the side of the vessel. He gradually made his way towards the front of the ship, in an attempt to secure the port-holes. Upon completion of this task, he slowly made his way back to where Mary was sitting. She was holding on tightly to the wooden handrail, in an attempt to keep from sliding with the sway of the ship. As he got near her, he slipped and fell to the floor, rolled over several times, and bumped into some of the baggage. He slowly got back up on his hands and knees and crawled over to Mary. Grabbing on to the handrail, he sighed:

"Whew! I'm not sure if this old body can take much more of this."

As he looked around, he could see several people becoming sick. Some of them were vomiting, others were in a state of fever.

"Oh, Lord," he shouted, "why are you testing us like this? Haven't we been through enough already?"

He then got up and looked out one of the nearby portholes. He could hardly believe what he saw. The waves were very high. The strong winds were blowing the heavy rains in an almost horizontal direction. He noticed that the water was gradually seeping through the porthole, so he quickly shut it. Turning around, he shouted to Mary:

"Grab another blanket. It looks like it could get very wet in here."

As Mary crawled over to her baggage, and picked out another blanket, she heard Joseph begin coughing.

"It sounds like you are getting a bad cold," she exclaimed.

"It is nothing," replied Joseph, as he wiped his mouth.

"You must pay more attention to yourself, rather than everyone else," begged Mary.

"I have been put on this earth for one reason," shot back Joseph. "It is my job to help as many people as I can. If I do that, then I will not have to worry about myself. Through them, I will receive my just reward."

As he sat down beside Mary, once again, he wrapped himself tightly in a blanket and laid down for a rest. He continued to cough intermittently, with sweat beginning to run down his forehead. Mary crawled over to him and gently took part of her shawl and wiped his forehead, as she quietly murmured: "Joseph, Joseph, you'll never learn."

Arrival in New York

CHAPTER VII

On the morning of April 21, the Duchess of Orleans came within sight of New York harbor, slowly making its way closer and closer to its final destination.

As word passed that they would soon be on land again, the attitudes of the passengers changed drastically. It soon became apparent that they were tremendously relieved at the thought of being able to leave the rancid odors and unhealthy conditions and exchange them for fresh air and solid ground. Their journey of weeks seemed to have been one of months and now this nightmare was about to end. Once realizing this, they began to smile and shout for joy. They quickly began scurrying about, putting all their personal belongings together, for their final departure. Many of them continued to look out the portholes, in an attempt to catch a glimpse of the American soil. However, heavy, overcast skies, with gently rolling fog, prevented them from seeing much of anything.

Joseph, who was standing beside Mary, watched as the crowd went from a miserable state to one of ecstasy. He too, began to smile, for it was a pleasure for him to see such happiness on the faces of so many people. After several minutes, he attempted to get their attention. "My friends," he shouted, "this would be a good time for a silent prayer of thanks, and to ask God for guidance for the rest of the trip."

Everyone bowed their heads and stood silently for a minute. As they were doing this, one of the ships' crewmembers came down the ladder and walked over to Joseph.

"Mr. Albrecht," stated the rough-looking middle-aged man, "the captain would like to see you." "Tell him, I'll be up in a few minutes." "Very well," noted the sailor, as he went back up the ladder. "Mary, make sure everyone has all of their belongings together.
It won't be long, and we'll be out of this living hell," suggested Joseph. "I'm going up to talk to the captain. By the way, who did you say that priest was, that lives here?"

"Father Kunze."

"I'll see if I can get in touch with him and get a proper burial for Crescentia. I'll be back down soon." Up on the main deck, the crewmembers were busily working to get the vessel prepared for docking. Joseph cautiously walked to the navigators' room, where Captain Richardson was busily giving instructions.

"We are to berth at number 17968. According to the chart, we should be approaching that area very soon. Turn 45 degrees, Smitty," commanded the captain, as he turned and noticed Joseph.

"Hello Joseph," continued the captain.

"Good morning."

"In about an hour, we should be ready to unload. Make sure everyone is ready."

"All right," answered Joseph, "Say, when we get off, where could I find a Catholic priest?"

"There is a Catholic church only a few blocks from where we pull in. You should have no problem finding it."

"Fine."

"Say, I would like you to take that body off, as soon as possible."

"Of course. As soon as I find a priest. If there is nothing else, I'm going back down. If I don't see you again, I want to thank you for the help you have provided."

"I just hope everything turns out for the best," stated the captain, as he watched Joseph go towards the stairwell.

After Joseph returned to the lower deck, he went over to Mary, who was busy packing several bags. "Do you have everything?" he asked.

"Yes, these are my things and that one there is yours," replied Mary, as she pointed at the bags.

"The captain says we can get off in about an hour, so we'll just have to wait. I'm going to walk around and see if there is anything I can do for our friends."

Joseph walked slowly amongst the crowd, talking with them as he went. He would pat the little children on their head, and tell them words of comfort, and then continue on. He walked over to where Urs Haener, Joseph Marder, and Anton Dufner were conversing.

"Gentlemen," he noted, as he interrupted their conversation.

"And what are we discussing?"

"We were just talking about what we were going to do, once we got to Ohio," replied Urs.

"And what may that be?"

"Hopefully, Father Salesius will accept us all. But, if he doesn't, we were thinking about what else we could do."

"I'm sure he will gladly take you under his wing," assured Joseph.

"Rather than spend time in idle talk, you should be contemplating on what day it is. We must not forget that today is Holy Saturday, and that we should prepare ourselves for the meditation of the death of Jesus, and what it means to us. One of the lessons in today's Mass deals with Moses, the man who led the Israelites to the promised land. Think of yourselves as Moses. We are leading our friends to the promised land. We are taking them from slavery and giving them freedom. We are responsible for them. It is going to be up to us, not only to guide these people, but also, the others that we will come in contact with, once we get to Ohio. Always remember that it will be our job to act as Moses did, and we then shall receive our just reward in the next world."

"We have our doubts, Joseph," interrupted Mr. Dufner. "Surely, you could do the task, but we do not think we are capable. You are the one with the strength and the willpower. You are the one that has the strong voice and the ability to use that voice in a persuasive manner. We are but humble men, shy in our ways, and with weak voice."

"What little faith you have in yourselves," continued Joseph. "Perhaps you have not received your calling yet. Perhaps you never will, but I know that I have. The Lord put me on this earth for one thing, and that is to save as many souls as I can, so that when we go to the next world, which will be soon, we can all sit at the table of the Lord and celebrate together. It is then, that I will have accomplished my task."

"Is that not an impossible task?" queried Mr. Marder. "Mr. Marder, don't talk that way. No task is impossible. If your faith is strong enough; you have all the necessary powers to be able to accomplish anything you set out to do."

"I have always admired you, Joseph," continued Urs. "You always seem to be able to say the right things at the right time. But I am not like that. I always seem to have to think so long before I can say something, and then, it never comes out right."

"That's not true, Urs. You will make a good priest. Your beliefs in the Catholic faith are excellent. Your desire to help your fellow man is admirable. You must remember that, according to the Bible, it will not be long, and the end will come. What better way is there for preparing yourself for that final day of judgement, than by preparing others?"

"Oh Joseph, if only I had half of the strength you have. I would be so overjoyed." "I'm sure you do, Urs. You just haven't realized it yet."

Joseph now took his watch out of his pocket and checked the time. "Well, let us be on our way," he suggested, as he looked around at the others. He now walked back over to Mary, picked up his bag, and proceeded up the ladder, being followed by Mary and the others.

What a joyful feeling they had when they finally were able to leave the vessel! As they touched land, many of the travelers knelt down and made the sign of the cross. Others touched the soil with their hands and shouted: "Thank-you dear Lord!"

Everyone felt good. The men were hugging their wives and children. The religious were carrying their small bags in one hand and a rosary in the other, with big smiles on their faces.

Joseph grabbed Mary's hand, looked straight in her eyes, and said: "We've made it!" He then turned to Mr. Dufner, and continued: "Anton, you and Marder, and Butz, go back and get Crescentia. Bring her over here. Mary and I are going to find Father Kunze and see if he will bury her."

As Mr. Dufner left, Joseph again turned to Mary, and continued: "Come with me."

"The church is over this way," offered Mary, as she began walking in that direction, being closely followed by Joseph.

Within a short time, Joseph and Mary returned with the elderly Father Kunze. The thin, bald priest, dressed in his black cassock and biretta, was taken directly to the small pine box, which contained the remains of Crescentia. Upon arrival, he quietly said a short prayer.

"Rochus," stated Joseph, "Father Kunze is going to be kind enough to say a funeral Mass for Crescentia. She will be buried here in New York. Pass the word. Anyone who wants to come along, may follow us. The church is only a few blocks from here."

19-year-old Rochus Schueli quickly walked amongst the crowd, passing the word.

Soon, the procession to the church began. Crescentia was on her way to her final resting place. She was never to see the lands which she had heard so much about. Only the memories of her poor innocent life would travel westward.

Father Kunze led the procession, followed by John Butz, Urs Haener, Joseph Albrecht, and Mary Albrecht. Behind them was the wooden pine box, being carried by six men. They were followed by many of the others. As they headed towards the church, the priest led in the singing of a hymn.

Several of the men remained at the docks, to keep an eye on the personal belongings that were left behind.

Because it was Holy Saturday, Father Kunze had the casket placed in the sacristy. A small service was held, but the funeral Mass and burial would not be conducted until the following Monday.

After the services were done, the group remained at the church, for some rest. Joseph and Mary, along with 36-year-old Ursula Ernst and 27-year-old Crescentia Spiegelhalter, were sitting near the back, quietly talking.

"I can hardly wait to see Rosalie again," exclaimed Joseph.

"Yes, I miss her too!" remarked Mary.

"I can't remember the last time I seen her," noted Ursula. "It will be nice to meet my cousin again."

"Crescentia, have you written to your father yet telling him of our arrival?" queried Joseph.

"Yes, last night," replied Crescentia. "But I don't know where to take the letter."

"Give it to me. I'll send it to Captain Richardson. I'm sure he'll take it back with him."

"Very well," answered Crescentia, as she reached into her coat pocket and pulled out a crumpled piece of paper and handed it to Joseph.

As Joseph put the letter in his pocket he said: "I've written several letters, so I'll send mine along with yours. I'll have one of the men take it back to the ship."

"Father Salesius has provided us with the itinerary," continued Joseph. "We are to travel by barge up the Hudson River to Albany and then, by wagon to Buffalo. From there, we take a boat to Sandusky City, Ohio. Then, all we have left is the short trip to

Wolf screek."

"How long do you think it will take?" asked Ursula.

"We should be at our new home within a month. Sometime in

May."

"Oh Lord! I hope I have the endurance to last," added Crescentia.

"We'll make it," comforted Joseph, as he patted Crescentia on the back.

Just as this conversation was being held, Mr. Dufner came into the church, from the side entrance, and walked straight over to Joseph. "Joseph," he noted, "I just talked to the barge captain, down on the waterfront, and he wants to leave this noon, or sooner.

He told me to tell you to bring everyone down there right away."

"All right," stated Joseph. "Spread the word. We better get everything together and leave immediately."

Within a matter of minutes, the group was on its way back to the docks. As they were leaving, Joseph turned to Father Kunze and said: "Thank-you Father, for your kindness and generous hospitality. I wish we could stay for Mass and Easter services tonight, but we must be moving on. Good-bye."

"It has been my pleasure," replied Father Kunze. The group slowly walked to the waterfront, picked up their belongings, and boarded a small barge, not too far away. They were about to begin their next leg of the trip.

The uneventful trip up the Hudson River, to Albany, was miserable for the travelers. The spring rains had arrived and fell continually, for the entire trip. Many of the passengers caught colds.

Joseph's health, which had already been deteriorating, worsened. His cough was becoming more and more persistent. Mary tried to sooth it, but without much success. She wrapped blankets around him, and rags around his throat, but even that did not seem to help. The rains kept soaking in.

By the time the barge pulled into Albany, everyone was relieved. It was still raining, but now they could at least seek cover, until it was over. As they disembarked, signs of weariness were on everyone's faces. The long journey was beginning to take its toll on the health of everyone. Even the children were less active now, than before. The religious women continued to carry a rosary in one hand and their belongings in the other, but they too, now were becoming very tired.

Joseph led the group down the wharf, to a nearby hotel. Leaving them outside, he entered the lobby.
"Good evening, sir," stated Joseph.
"Hello," answered the bald, middle-aged innkeeper. "May I help you?"

"My name is Joseph Albrecht. I have a large group of travelers with me. We are on our way to Ohio. Several of them are quite tired and sick. Could I get a couple of rooms for the night?"
"I'm sorry, sir, but we are filled up."
"Well then; could you tell me where 250 people can find shelter for the night?"

"250?" wondered the innkeeper, as he paused for several seconds, and then said: "Why, yes, I can. About a block from here, there is a large boathouse. Take them down there. Here, I'll show you.

The innkeeper grabbed Joseph, by the arm, and took him back out the front door. Outside, he pointed to his left, and continued: "See that big building down there? Go, and enter at the main door. It is a public building, so you shouldn't be thrown out."

"Thank-you," politely noted Joseph, as he turned and walked back over to the others. As he reached Mary, he said: "Just like Joseph and Mary, on their way to Bethlehem, they don't have room in the inn. He did tell me where we could go though."

He then looked at the others and said: "Come! Follow me!" As they were heading for the boathouse, Joseph looked at Mary, and said: "My people have been through a lot. I pray that they don't give up now."

"Don't worry about that, Joseph. Their faith is strong enough to get them through this ordeal."

Upon entering the huge building, Joseph exclaimed: "What a relief! Maybe we'll have a chance to dry out."

A sign of appreciation was showing on everyone's face as they came in, out of the rain. They proceeded to take off their wet coats and blankets, and find a place to sit down, for a much-needed rest. While Joseph was sitting down beside Mary, he reached into his small bag and pulled out his little black book. He opened it up and, silently, began to read. Mary, already in the midst of praying the rosary, looked at him, and smiled.

Urs Haener walked over and sat down beside Joseph. "Excuse me," he stated, as he crawled under a blanket. "I don't want to interrupt you from your reading, but I would like to talk to you."

"Sure," noted Joseph, as he set his book down. "What can I do for you?"
"What are you reading?"
"Since tonight is the Easter Vigil, I thought I'd read the gospel."
"We could find a Catholic church somewhere, here in Albany, in time for midnight Mass," suggested Urs.

"No, that would be too hard on these people. Besides, we don't really need to attend Mass if it is too inconvenient. As long as we lead a good life, we shouldn't have anything to worry about."

But it says that we are supposed to attend Mass every Sunday, as well as all Holy Days of Obligation."

"Yes, but only if it is possible, and within reach," interjected Joseph. "The Lord is not going to keep us out of the gates of Heaven because we missed Mass on Sunday or didn't fulfill our Easter obligation. He is keeping a close eye on each of us, and he knows how we live. We can fool the people here on earth, but we cannot fool him. We can go to church on Sundays and live a life of sin the other six days, and most people would probably only notice us in church and think to themselves: 'My! He will surely get to Heaven!', but you can't fool the Lord. He knows how we live the rest of the week. We can go to church every day of our life, and yet, if we don't lead a good Christian life, we will never be able to enjoy the hereafter. We will never receive our just reward."

"You mean to tell me; you don't think it is necessary to go to church on Sundays?"

"No. That is not what I am saying. Surely, it is good if a person can go to church every Sunday, but that is not the important thing. The important thing is what you do with the rest of your time. You do as God dictates, and not what bishops say. You use your own good judgement. Remember, God gave you a free will for you to use. He is testing you every day to see if you will follow his rules, or if you will make up your own, or follow someone elses. That is the key to salvation."

The next morning, the group again was on the move. The rains had stopped during the night, much to the pleasure of everyone. The skies had cleared, and the sun was now brightly shining.

Joseph had hired a wagon master and rented six wagons for the journey to Buffalo. These wagons were now parked in front of the boathouse, and the people were beginning to load their belongings into them. Some of the older people were able to secure a place for themselves in the wagons, but the majority had to walk.

As final preparations were being made, Joseph stood by the lead wagon with the wagon master, a tall lanky thirty-year old man, dressed in buckskins.

"Well, is everyone ready?" queried the wagon master. "It looks like it," replied Joseph, as he looked down at the line of loaded-down wagons.
"Are you going to be walking?"
"Yes, of course."
"There must be room in one of the wagons for an old man like you?"

"Never mind that," insisted Joseph. "I prefer to walk."

"Then, let us begin," stated the man, as he mounted his horse, and led the small wagon train out of town, towards their next destination, Buffalo.

It so happened that, earlier, Father Anton Schmidt had brought a group of immigrants from Kirchzarten, and the surrounding area, and settled near Buffalo. Joseph was now anxious to see him again, for he had been the priest that married him. Joseph had sent a letter several months earlier, advising him of the planned trip, and approximate time of arrival. He was now patiently awaiting for the day to arrive when they would meet again.

The wagons slowly made their way across the State of New York. Finally, one week later, they arrived in Buffalo.

After several inquiries, they were able to find the church of Father Schmidt. Joseph, still walking alongside the lead wagon, noticed Father Schmidt, near the church entrance. He immediately hastened ahead of everyone else, up to the surprised priest.

Father Schmidt, an elderly gray-haired man, dressed in his usual priestly garb, recognized Joseph, and came down to the street to greet him. "Mr. Albrecht," he exclaimed, "What a joy to see you! I have been patiently waiting and praying for you."

"Hello Father," replied Joseph, as he gave him a big hug.

"Good to see you."

"How has the trip been?"

"We lost Crescentia Zipfel right before our arrival in New York. Several of the people are somewhat sick, but, other than that, all has gone quite well."

"Sorry to hear about Crescentia," consoled Father Schmidt. "It sounds like you are getting a cold."

"Yes, but once I get to Ohio, I will get better."

"It is still too early for the ships to be traveling on Lake Erie," continued Father Schmidt. "I have been down to get transportation for you, but the earliest will be in about a week."

Joseph was disappointed. "I was hoping to be at Thompson, within a week."

"You are more than welcome to stay here."

"Yes Father, but there are at least 250 in our group."

"My people know many of you, and I'm sure many of your group would like to see their friends and relatives who live here. This week will give them a chance to rest up and visit."

"Nicholas," shouted Father Schmidt, as he looked at a young man of 25, who had just arrived on the scene. "Come here!"

"Joseph, this is Nicholas Gales," continued Father Schmidt. "Nicholas, this is Joseph Albrecht. He has just arrived from the homeland. He is with a large group who are on their way to the missions in Ohio."

"Hello Nicholas," stated Joseph, as he extended his right arm, and shook hands.

"Glad to meet you sir," replied Nicholas.

"Nicholas has been a big help to me," continued Father Schmidt. "He has been studying diligently to become a priest."

"Is that right?" queried Joseph. "Excellent! I too have been studying. I am going to Thompson Seminary, in Ohio, and, with the help and guidance of God, I will be able to become a Precious Blood priest."

"Precious Blood?" asked Nicholas. "Then, you must know Father Brunner?"

"Of course. He is my best friend. If there is one man in this world that has had influence on me, it is Father Salesius."

"What must I do to join your Society?" asked Nicholas.

"When I get to Ohio, I'll talk to Father Salesius. If he gives his approval, I will write to Father Schmidt and advise him."

"Nicholas, could you ring the church bell? I would like to tell the people of your arrival," stated Father Schmidt, as he looked, first at

Nicholas, and then at Joseph.

"Yes Father," replied Nicholas, as he obediently headed into the church.

As the church bells were being rung, almost immediately, people began congregating at the church. As they arrived, they noticed the new group of visitors, and were soon reacquainting themselves with each other. Barbara, Theresa, and Joseph Hog, once again, were able to meet their family, for the first time in several years. Besides their mother and father, they talked with their sister, Agatha, and their brother, Aloysius.

Campfires were started near the church. Everyone seemed to be in a very good mood, as they went about preparing for the evening.

"It won't be long before your ship will be ready to go to Sandusky City," assured Father Schmidt, to Joseph, as they were walking along the street, in front of the church.

"I have prayed for God's intervention to send us as soon as possible," noted Joseph. "Only time will tell."

"You know," continued Father Schmidt. "I have many young girls and boys who have expressed a desire for Holy Orders."

"Fine. I'm sure Father Salesius could use all the help he can get. He has told me, on several occasions, that the job in Ohio is huge and that he needs, not only financial assistance, but also men and women to help in his fight to save souls. The next time Father goes to Europe, I'll have him stop here and talk to you."

"Please do. Now, I must leave you for the night. It is getting rather late, and I must still finish my breviary." "Good night, dear Father," stated Joseph, as he began to head towards the wagons. "I'll see you in the morning, for church." "Good night, Joseph," noted Father Schmidt, as he headed for his small abode, behind the church.

Many of the women, led by Mary, were praying the rosary aloud, beside the campfire. Joseph went over to where Mary was kneeling. He took two blankets out of the wagon, spread them on the ground, next to the fire, and crawled in between them. Another day had come to an end.

TWO WEEKS LATER

The cold north winds were blowing briskly, causing the waves on Lake Erie to be quite turbulent. The small vessel was bobbing up and down, like a toy boat in a bathtub. It was slowly progressing towards its destination of Sandusky City. On board, the large group
of immigrants were anxiously awaiting the sight of land. Many of them were standing on the left side, keeping a watchful eye into the distance. The winds did not bother them now. They knew that their long journey was soon to be over. They knew that once they got to Sandusky City, they would soon be at their final destinations of Wolfscreek and Thompson.

Joseph and Mary were among those standing along the side. Next to Joseph, was Urs Haener. Beside Mary, was 35-year-old Mary Ann Ruh.

"It won't be long now!" exclaimed Joseph. "We should be seeing Rosalie very soon."
"Once we get to Sandusky City, we should be at Wolfscreek within a day," offered Mary.
"How far is Thompson from there?" asked Joseph.

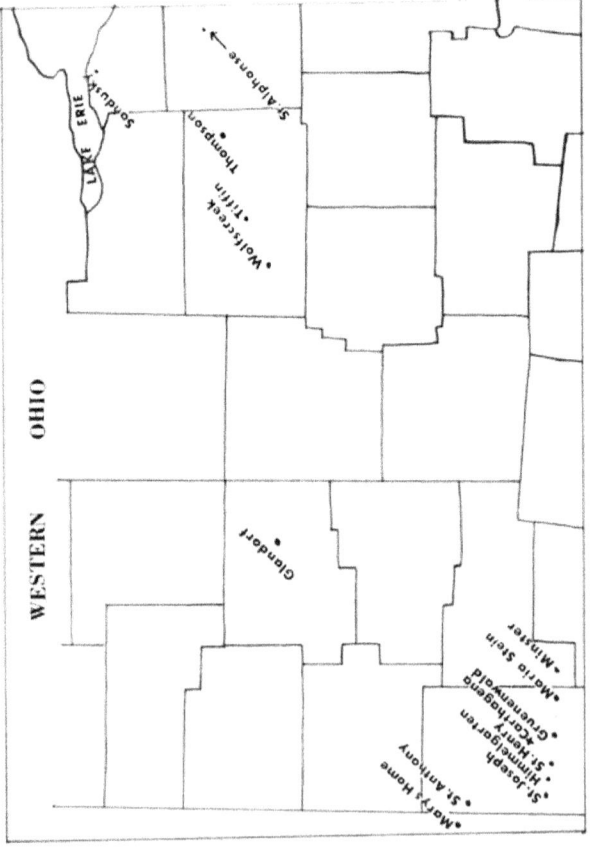

"About 40 miles."

As this conversation was being held, land was sighted. Everyone scurried to get their belongings and try to be the first ones in Ohio soil.

The ship slowly pulled up to the long wharf. Within a matter of minutes, it was ready to rid itself of its cargo and passengers. Joseph and Mary were the first ones to get off. As Joseph reached over and touched the Ohio soil, he exclaimed: "Alleluia!" He got down on his knees and made the sign of the cross, saying a short prayer. Mary did, likewise, as did many others. "I was hoping Father Salesius would have had wagons here for us," exclaimed Mary.

"Wagons?" queried Joseph. "We don't need wagons now. We can walk to Wolfscreek."
"Walk!" exclaimed Mary. "That's too far!"
"Just show me the way."
"All right," replied Mary, as the two began to walk southward.
Joseph turned around and shouted at the group: "Follow me!"

The large group slowly headed for Wolfscreek. Their bodies were tired, yet their spirits strong. Along the way, they were able to enjoy the beautiful Ohio scenery. The trees and flowers were in full bloom. Deer, squirrel, and chipmunks stood at a distance, and watched the newcomers invading their domain.

After a short time, the group approached the small mission of Thompson. Upon their arrival, they were greeted in front of 'Mary of the Angels' chapel, by Father John Wittmer, a short stocky young man, with bushy eyebrows.

"Welcome to 'Mary of the Angels'," he stated to Joseph.

"Hello Sister Mary Ann," he continued, as he looked at Mary.

"Hello Father," answered Joseph.

"So, this is Thompson?" noted Joseph, as he looked around at the surrounding buildings.

"Yes, this is where you will be staying," continued Father John.

"We have a small seminary behind the chapel. That is where you will live and study. To your left, is St. Michael's church, small but sufficient."

"Where is Father Salesius?"

"He is on a small errand at Wolfscreek. He should be back in a day or so."

"Fine. Mary and I will go to Wolfscreek. We want to see Rosalie anyway. Please see to it that the girls get a place to sleep."

"Of course."

"I shall be back in two days."

"Mary," continued Joseph, as he turned towards her, "get your things."

"Urs," continued Joseph, as he turned to Mr. Haener. "Take my things over to the seminary. Father John will show you where to put them. Mary and I are going to Wolfscreek."

"What about the others?" asked Urs, as he pointed towards the group.

"They know where they're going. They don't need our help anymore."

Joseph and Mary quickly said good-bye to many of their close friends, and soon were on their way to Wolfscreek.

As they were walking along the path, Joseph turned to Mary and said: "Aren't you excited? We are finally going to see Rosalie again."

"Yes, I really have missed her."

"What should I say to her, when we meet?"

"Oh, I'm sure you'll find the right words. You always do."

Soon, they arrived at Wolfscreek. Several sisters, out in the field, noticed the two approaching, and ran towards them. "Mary!" exclaimed one of them.

"Welcome back!"

"It is good to be back," replied Mary. "Tell me, where is Sister Rosalie?"

The two sisters looked at each other. Several seconds passed and then one of them spoke up: "Didn't you know that Sister Rosalie passed away?"

"What!" exclaimed Joseph, in utter disbelief. "When?"

"Last October. October 17th, to be exact. Father Brunner buried her over there in the cemetery."

"Oh my God!" stammered Joseph, as he sat down by a tree. "I can't believe it! My little Rosalie! Why, Lord? Why? She was so young. She had so much she wanted to do. Why?"

"I thought Father Brunner would have sent you a letter," stated one of the nuns.

"No, he didn't," noted Mary, as tears came to her eyes.

"Come Mary," continued Joseph. "We must still visit her."

Turning back to the nun, he asked: "Where do we go?"

"Follow me."

The three of them went towards the cemetery. They walked down a path that led past the small mission house of 'Mary at the Crib.' The three-story log building, which housed the nuns and postulants, was to their right. Almost immediately beside that, and to the rear, was the three-story chapel.

"How did you come up with the name 'Mary at the Crib'?" queried Joseph, as they walked by the chapel.

"When the first solemn Mass was held here, back on Christmas of '44, there was a beautiful small crib set up. The residents gathered around this nativity scene, and this gave us the idea to call it 'Mary at the Crib,' " replied Mary.

As they continued walking, the nun pointed to a small two-story building, to their right. "This is where Sister Rosalie taught school.

"She was helped by Sister Salesia Weisenberger."

"Is that Maria Francesca?" asked Joseph.

"Why, yes," replied the nun.

"We know her. Is she still here?"

"Yes, she is."

"Good. I'd like to see her later."

"Here is the cemetery," noted the nun, as she pointed to her left.

"Thank-you," replied Joseph, as he and Mary walked into the small plot.

They walked around and read the names on the several tombstones. When they found their daughter's grave, they stopped. Both of them knelt down by the small wooden cross, and began to pray, silently.

What a sad time for Joseph and Mary! For such a long time they were thinking how wonderful it would be to see their child again, only to find out that she had died seven months ago. Joseph tried very hard to hold the tears back. He clenched his fist, looked around, seemingly in a daze. Then, he glanced upwards and smiled. He realized that his young daughter must be in heaven.

"The Lord works in mysterious ways," he exclaimed, as he looked at Mary. "I'm sure she is at peace with God."

Joseph and Mary got up. Holding each other, they departed the cemetery. As they were returning to the convent, 24-year-old sister Salesia Weisenberger approached them.

"Hello, dear Sister," stated Mary.

"Hello, Mother Superior," greeted Sister Salesia, as she genuflected and kissed the right hand of Mary.

"Welcome Mr. Albrecht," she continued.

"Hello, my dear child," replied Joseph. "Tell me Sister Salesia, what happened to Sister Rosalie?"

"She had been quite weak ever since her arrival here. She tired very easily, but she never complained. She worked as hard as anyone else. Her health seemed to have improved greatly after she took over as Superioress here, but it did not last. She had a relapse. She died at 6:30, on Saturday morning, October 17th. I'll never forget that. I was at her side those last hours. She was a perfect example of a saint. One of the last things she said to me was to tell you that she loved you and thought of you often. She had only hoped that she could have seen you once more. Father Brunner said the funeral Mass for her. He had an excellent sermon, mentioning how she loved to pray to St. Joseph and St. Aloysius. How she dedicated her life, completely, for the betterment of mankind. Yes, I'll never forget that.

"Thank-you for telling us," offered Joseph, as the three now began walking back over to the convent, where they were greeted by Father Salesius.

"It looks like my prayers have been answered," stated Father Salesius, as he greeted the arrivals. "How many candidates did you bring along?"

"35," replied Mary. "And there were more that wanted to come."

"Excellent! We can use everyone. There are more and more Catholic families arriving each day."

"It is good to see you again," stated Joseph, as he gave a hug to Father Salesius.

"Likewise," replied Father Salesius.

"Tell me the names, Mary. I must put them in my registry."

Father Salesius pulled out a small black notebook and pencil from inside his cassock. He turned a few pages and exclaimed:

"There. We must get everyone's name and age. I have to decide where to put them all."

"Wait a second!" interrupted Joseph. "Why the hurry? We just got here."

"Excuse me, Joseph, but you must realize how excited your arrival has made me. I have been waiting, patiently for days, to see you."

"Why didn't you tell us about Rosalie?"

"Rosalie? But I did. Didn't you get the letter?"

"No."

"I wrote to you immediately after her burial. The letter must've gotten lost. You mean, you just found out today?"

"Yes. We just came from her grave."

"I am sorry. Of course, you must realize that she is in heaven. She was a precious sister. Perfect in every way."

"I only wish I could have had more time with her," Joseph sadly noted.

"She did a wonderful job. Right up to the time of her death. She has been dearly missed by all of us, especially the children, whom she taught."

"Yes, she always loved the children," added Mary.

"I did write to you, right after the funeral. I really thought you knew."

"Well, perhaps it's better this way," noted Joseph, as he reached into his pocket, and pulled out a small black bag.

"Here," he continued as he handed the bag to Father Salesius,

"here is a little something for you."

As Father Salesius took the bag, he asked: "Does anyone have any extra money left over?"

"I haven't made a collection yet," answered Joseph.

"Of course, you realize that no member of our Society is allowed to have money without my expressed permission. But you, Joseph, are an exception. You may keep yours, as long as you use it wisely. I do have a need for some now, though. I have been making plans to expand our missions."

"Is Mr. Spiegelhalter taking care of your financial affairs back in Kirchzarten?" continued Father Salesius.

"Yes, he is. It is a very messy situation, though. The government is getting very greedy, so I don't have any idea of what will happen, nor when. It will probably take years before he can get all my lands sold."

"Did you bring quite a bit with you?"

"Enough. I have several small chests, that I left at Thompson. In one of them, I have a full-sized relic of St. Candidus. In the others, I have gold."

"Well, use it to the best of your ability."

Where are we going to be living?"

"All of the men will be going to Thompson. I'm not sure about the women. I'll have to figure that out. One thing though, Mary will be here at Wolfscreek. She will once again be the Mother Superior."

"Tell me, what has everything been like around here?" queried Joseph.

"We are really in need of people," answered Father Salesius. "I only have a few priests and there are so many parishes to take care of. Some of them, we can only get to about once every two months. That is not good. It gives the devil a chance to work on the human

weaknesses."

"How long do you think it'll take me?"

"Hopefully, in about a year. The Bishop doesn't like to hurry these things, but I can convince him, considering the circumstances."

"When do you plan on going back to Thompson?"

"As soon as I have a private meeting with Sister Mary. I would like to get a complete list of the new arrivals."

"Come Mary," continued Father Salesius. "Let's go over to the convent. Joseph, please have patience. Find something to do for about a half hour."

"I'll go over to the church," replied Joseph, as he pointed towards St. Micahel's.

With that, Father Salesius and Sister Mary began to walk towards the convent, while Joseph turned and slowly headed for the small church, coughing very heavily all the way.

As Joseph entered the church, he noticed the beautiful interior. The hand-carved altar was truly splendid. He could see that many hours of labor were put into the intricate designs. The three statues of Jesus, Mary, and Joseph were the domineering features. Here was a statue of St. Michael but was located to the side of the main altar. As Joseph approached the altar, he noticed the small wooden benches on each side. They were all hand-made. They were primitive, yet very beautiful.

Upon reaching the front of the church, he knelt down in the first pew. Looking up, he silently began to pray. As Joseph finished praying, several men entered the church, and walked straight up to him.

"Are you Mr. Albrecht?" queried one of the men.

"Yes."

"Father Brunner would like to see you. He is in front of the convent."

Joseph made the sign of the cross, got up off his knees, and departed the church.

Father Salesius, who was standing with Sister Mary, in front of the convent, noticed Joseph approaching, and said: "Joseph, when you get back to Thompson, Father Wittmer will be your Superior. He'll decide what you must study, and do, while there. I will be staying there, but you must listen to him. He is younger than you, but he is good. He has been a great help to me."

"Of course," replied Joseph.

"Are you ready to return?"

"Whenever you are."

"It is one of my stipulations," continued Father Salesius, "that relatives should not be at the same mission. Since you and Mary have chosen the religious life, I must demand of you that you should have nothing to do with each other. It is God you will be serving, and not each other."

"Yes, Father."

"Come and let us be on our way."

Joseph looked at Mary. Without saying a word, he turned and departed with Father Salesius.

Life in Thompson

CHAPTER VIII

Joseph and Father Salesius grabbed their small bags and departed for Thompson. The trip took several hours, but it was enjoyed by both. This time gave the two men an atmosphere of pleasure to talk in. It gave them time to talk, time to discuss the past, present, and future. It gave them time to contemplate on the plans that Father Salesius had for Joseph, as well as the Precious Blood Society. It gave them time to discuss the roles of the sisters, brothers, and the priests. It gave them time to reacquaint themselves with each other.

"Each of my missions should be self-supporting," suggested Father Salesius. "Each will have at least one priest, several brothers, and several sisters. The priests will look after the souls, not only of the mission, but of the surrounding area. The brothers will mainly be used for field work and building projects. The sisters will take care of the churches, vestments, garden work, field work, schools, orphanages, and nightly adoration. Each mission will have a Sister Superior. She will be responsible for all finances. The priest will give her the collections, and he must go to her for any monetary assistance."

"That is ridiculous!" replied Joseph. "No woman will ever take care of my money."

"But it will not be your money. It will work out better this way. I have noticed that money can do evil things to a person. I do not want priests to become too powerful. I do not want them to use money to influence others. They will have enough to do, besides handling the money."

"How much of an area are we responsible for?"

"All of Ohio. We only have a few missions now, but, in a few years, I hope to have many more. There are a lot of Catholics down by Minster, and I'd like to set up missions down there. For now, all I want you to think about is becoming a priest."

The two men now entered the grounds of the Thompson Seminary. They noticed the nuns, busily working in the garden. Not too far from them were several brothers, in the process of building a small shed, with Father John Wittmer, standing nearby, supervising.

"Is this the building we were discussing last week?" queried Father Salesius, as he approached Father John of the Cross. Father John Wittmer, C.PP.S.

"Yes Father," replied Father John. "I thought we'd get it done before the crops were ready."

"Good idea."

"Joseph," continued Father Salesius, "Father John here, is not only an excellent carpenter, but he also knows Latin very well, and is an authority on the church history and the Bible. It will do you well to listen to what he has to say."

"Greetings, again," stated Joseph.

"Hello Joseph," countered Father John, as they shook hands.

"Get him started on studying right away," requested Father Salesius. "I have plans for him, but he must receive Holy Orders first. Take him over to the house and find him a place to stay."

"Of course. Come with me," demanded Father John, as he looked at Joseph.

The two men walked a short distance to the small seminary building that was used as a sleeping quarter for the men, as well as a school for the students. Meanwhile, Father Salesius turned and went to his small room behind the church.

"This is where you will be living," stated Father John, as he showed Joseph a small room, not much more than eight feet square. There was a small table and chair, with a candle, in one corner. In another corner was a short wooden bed, extending from the wall.

There were no decorations on the walls, except for a small wooden cross directly above the table.

"My new home!" exclaimed Joseph, as he walked around the room.

"I realize the bed will be too small for you, but you are about a foot taller than anybody else," exclaimed Father John: As Joseph laid down on the bed and put his feet over the end, he stated: "That's alright. I am used to small beds. This will do just fine."

Father John reached into the closet and pulled out several books. "You can start reading these when you have the time. You must realize though, that you will have to work hard around here, just like everybody else. Just because you are much older than the rest, that will not matter when it comes to doing the chores."

Joseph looked at him in astonishment. "I have come to America to become a priest and help the poor souls attain their goals. Not to dig in the fields, like a commoner."

"For now, you are a commoner. Your main priority will be for the betterment of the missions. Studying will be done in your spare time. I don't care if you are a close friend of Father Salesius, or not. Here, I am in charge, and you will do what I tell you."

Joseph glanced over the three books that he had just been handed. Looking up, he asked: "Will we be holding classes to discuss these books?"

"Yes, when we find the time. There are several other men here studying, just like you. This evening you shall meet them. We eat supper at seven o'clock, downstairs in the main dining room. You are expected to be there on time. If not, you don't get to eat. The sisters prepare the meals, making the best of what we have. You are not to talk to any of them. If you want to tell one of them something, tell me, and I'll pass it on to the Mother Superior. We have no time for freeloaders around here. There is no need to converse with others, unless told to. We have too much work to be done."

"The Lord has guided me for 48 years, John. He knows what's in store for me. I have prepared myself to accept whatever he wants."

"Tomorrow, I shall take you over to see the Mother Superior," continued Father John. "At that time, I'll also get you some new clothes. The rags you have on are not becoming to a future priest,"

"What's wrong with my clothes?" blurted Joseph, as he glanced down at his clothes.

"They're rags," shouted back Father John.

"How dare you!" exclaimed Joseph. "You may tell me what to do and when to do it, but you have no right telling me what to wear."

"Father Salesius has told me about you. I didn't believe it was possible, but I see that he was right. He said that, at times, you could be stubborn. Oh well, do as you like. I must leave now. Remember, supper at seven. Good day."

Joseph remained lying on the bed. After placing the three books under his bed, he put his arms behind his head, looked up, and quietly said: "Oh Lord, what have you done to me?"

Just then, he heard a knock on the door.

"Come in!" he shouted.

The door opened and in came Joseph Kaltenbach, who was a short stocky man with a receeding hairline of gray. He looked rather young for his age of 55.

"Hello, Mr. Kaltenbach," greeted Joseph. "Please come in."

"I heard that you had just arrived," stated Mr. Kaltenbach, as he entered and shook hands with Joseph. "I couldn't wait to see you again."

"It's good to see you."

"How was your trip?"

"Slow and boring."

"Sounds like ours."

"When did you get here?"

"We arrived on the 6th of April."

"Then, you made good time. It took us over two months to get here."

As the two men were talking, they were interrupted by another knock on the door, and the entry of Urs Haener, carrying a small wooden cot.

"Excuse me Joseph, but I was told by Father John to move in with you," stated Urs, with a smile.

"Come in. Put the cot down there," stated Joseph, as he pointed to the empty corner.

After Urs set the cot down in the appointed location, he said:

"There."

"Hello Joseph," he continued, as he looked at Mr. Kaltenbach.

"Hello Urs. Welcome to Thompson."

"Thank-you."

"You men will soon find out that there are a lot of younger men here who are somewhat lax. They have a lot of ideas that I don't agree with, and if you or Joseph heard about them, you too, would be disgusted."

"I think that is why Father Salesius wanted to get some older blood over here," stated Mr. Albrecht. "It'll be our responsibility to straighten these guys out. It'll be our job to provide the perfect example for them to follow."

"Yes, but Joseph, we won't have any say until we become priests," stated Urs.

"That's why we'll have to study hard. Maybe, within a year, we can take that step."

"What is your impression of Father Wittmer?" asked Mr. Kaltenbach.

"I'm not very impressed," replied Joseph. "I think his power has gone to his head, just like the Bishop, I knew back in Freiburg."

Just then, the sound of bells could be heard in the background.

"Ah," exclaimed Mr. Kaltenbach, "that means that it's time to eat. Come! I'll show you where to go."

The three men left the room, walked down the center hallway, down the stairs, and into the small eating room. They were joined by many of the other men from the mission.

Once inside, Joseph noticed the long roughly hewn wooden table, with benches on each side. The table had already been set, with a small amount of food on each plate. There were no signs of any sisters in the room, but they were there, hiding in a small room, off to the rear. Their normal procedure was to set the table, serve the food, and then ring the bell. While the men were eating, they would remain in the refectory.

"Take any place you wish, except at the ends," suggested Mr. Kaltenbach, "but do not sit down until Father Salesius and Father John come in."

As Joseph and Urs picked out a place, Father Salesius and Father John entered.

When everyone arrived, Father Salesius offered a prayer of grace: "Oh Lord, bless this food which we are about to partake. Thank-you dear Lord, for providing us with this food. It shall always be remembered that it is because of you that we are succeeding in

our efforts of caring for your flock. Amen." He then looked around and said: "Please be seated."

As the men sat down, and began to eat, Joseph noticed many familiar faces. Many of them came from the same area of Baden, as he did. Most of them were much younger than he was, and that bothered him. How was he to influence these men, he thought to himself. "Just give me time," he added, as he smiled and continued to eat.

After completion of the supper, Father Salesius said a prayer of thanksgiving, after which he said: "Now, it is time for everyone to go to their rooms and study and examine their conscience. Ask yourselves if you had a fulfilling day; if you accomplished your goals; if you acted the way God would want you to act. If you decide you are weak in some areas, try and strengthen yourself tomorrow. Ask God for his help. Always remember that the devil is out there, tempting everyone — yourselves included. Be aware of pride, vanity, and lust. Guard yourselves against them. Live the life of a saint. Remember, it will not be long and all of us will be gone from this earth. Time is of the essence. Good night."

All of the men got up from the table, at the same time, and departed for their rooms.

Upon arriving in their room, Urs sat down on his bed, while Joseph lit the candle, and then walked over and picked out the three books from under the bed. As he glanced over them, he remarked:

"This is ridiculous! I don't see why we have to learn some of this. I think I already know more than a lot of these young priests."

"I agree with you," replied Urs, "but, we will have to play their silly game."

The two men began reading silently. Several hours passed. Urs had fallen asleep as Joseph rubbed his eyes. Soon, he decided it was time to also quit. He put his book down, walked over to the candle, and blew the flame out.

The next morning Joseph and Urs were awakened very early, by the ringing bells. Joseph slowly got up and looked out the window. "It's still dark!" he exclaimed. "I suppose that means it is time for breakfast."

"What time is it?" queried Urs, as he yawned and rolled over in his bed.

Joseph fumbled for his pocket watch, and then exclaimed: "Six o'clock."

"It seems like I just got to bed," continued Urs, as he got up into a sitting position. He scratched the back of his head and again yawned.

Both had slept in their regular clothes. As a matter of fact, Joseph even slept with his boots on. Therefore, it did not take long for either of them to be on their way to the dining area.

"Good morning, Joseph," greeted Father Andrew Kunkler, the high-spirited gangly young priest of 24.

"Good morning," replied Joseph. "It is good to see you again. I see that you have already become a priest."

"Yes, I was given the tonsure last January 26th, in Tiffin, along with Max Homburger, Engelbert Ruf, and Andreas Herbstritt. On February 23rd, we were ordained by Bishop Rappe."

"What are you doing here?"

"I had to see Father Salesius. I just got here late last night and will be leaving this morning, for Maria Stein."

"Maria Stein, where is that?"

"Quite a way from here. In western Ohio. In due time, you will be going down there. Father Salesius has big plans for that area."

As the three men continued to walk towards the dining area, Joseph asked questions. "Tell me, that beautiful chapel over there,

`Mary of the Angels,' who lives upstairs?"

"The nuns."

"How much land do we have here?"

"In early 1845, Father Salesius, with the help of a certain Mr. Gerhardstein, purchased 80 acres. We have been gradually clearing it. In a few more years, we should have most of it cleared. Father Salesius has really been working the priests, brothers, and sisters, to accomplish that goal. He has been getting a lot of recruits, but many of them don't stay very long. He always stresses hard work. He constantly reminds them how ignorant they are, yet after such a hard days' work, no one feels like studying. He easily accepted the recruits, but he would always reserve the right to decide whether they would become priests or brothers. Many of the men did not like this and, consequently, they left. You see, Joseph, it takes a certain type of person to belong to our Society. Father Salesius is very stingy. He is constantly counting his money. He is always trying to find ways of getting more. He doesn't like to see money in the hands of the priests and brothers. He would rather have complete control of the purse strings."

"I know what you mean," interrupted Joseph. "I sometimes think that is why he has been after me for so long to come over. He is always asking about my financial situation."

"Yes, but you must realize his situation," continued Andrew.

"He does have a lot of responsibility. He set his goals high, and tries to obtain them, as soon as possible. He almost always accomplishes what he sets out to do."

"That's true. That's why I admire the man so much."

Just then, the men walked into the dining room and went directly over to the table. Father Salesius was already standing at one end.

"Joseph," he exclaimed. "Would you please sit here next to me?"

Joseph took up a position, immediately to the left of Father Salesius, with Father Kunkler on the other side of him. Urs was to the right of Joseph.

"I have a few things I would like to talk to you about, after breakfast," noted Father Salesius, as he looked at Joseph.

The routine for breakfast was the same as any other meal. Father Salesius said the prayer, everyone sat down and ate. Upon completion, Father Salesius said the prayer of thanksgiving, after which he said:

"Check with Father John, to see what he wants you to do. Joseph, please stay here."

One by one, the men went to Father John. He had a list which he was checking off, as he handed out the daily assignments. Father Salesius reached into his pocket and pulled out a small, folded piece of paper. As he unfolded it, he said:

"I have a note here, Joseph, that I wrote when your daughter died. As you know, I said the funeral Mass for her. It grieved me very much when she passed away. Here, you keep this."

Joseph took the piece of paper and read to himself : "He who does the will of my Father who is in heaven, he is my brother, my sister, and my mother. Here from the grave, she exhorts you, Sister, Brother, pray for me. Life is short, death is sure. The hour of death,

God only knows. One soul you have, and only one. If you lose it, see what you can do."

"How true!" exclaimed Joseph. "I shall always remember these words," he continued, as he folded the paper and put it in his pocket.

"How is your cold?"

"It's getting better. I still get headaches when I get up in the morning, though."

"You should try and take better care of yourself," suggested Father Salesius. "The climate here, you will find, is quite like back home, so you'll have to be careful. I am going on a short trip today, with Mr. Lange, over to Glandorf. Back in March, we bought 120 acres there, and now I hope to build a new education center for the men. Bishop Rappe wants us to be apart from the nuns, and I agree with him. Here at Thompson, people are already talking about nuns and priests living together. This is one thing I never like to hear.

There are 70 acres of land cleared, plus a house, barn, and orchard already there. So, you see, it would be an ideal place for some of the priests and brothers. However, yesterday I received a letter from some of the residents of Glandorf, and they want me to send them

some nuns, for their school. I should be back in about a week. While I'm gone, I hope you get accustomed to our lifestyle. Be sure to listen to Father John of the Cross. He may be younger, but he is very wise."

"Yes, Father."

"There was one more thing I was going to ask you. Did you bring that bell along, that we were talking about?"

"Yes, I did. I have it packed in one of the crates, along with the relic of St. Candidus."

"Excellent! You will always have the responsibility for its care.

Some day we shall have a need for them. Now, I must leave. Go see what Father John has for you."

Both men arose from the table and walked to the other end, where Father John was sitting.

"John," started Father Salesius, "what do you have for Joseph?"

"Joseph, let's see," replied John, as he fingered down the list.

"Ah, here we are. Let's see, Joseph, I want you to go with Brothers John Steiert and Joseph Riesterer. They are in the garden out back. They are putting up a fence to keep the animals out. After that, you men will be pulling weeds."

"Very well," replied Joseph. "I'll go right away."

Father Salesius and Joseph began walking out the door.

"I see that you are still having problems with that foot," observed Joseph.

"Yes, from time to time it acts up. Lately, it has really bothered me."

"Sounds like you should take better care of yourself," suggested Joseph.

"I have no time. Too many things to do!"

"You know John and Joseph, don't you?" continued Father Salesius.

"Yes. I met John in Horben, and Joseph, I've known him all of his life."

"Well, there is the garden and there are the brothers. Join them and have a good day. I must talk to Father Andrew before he leaves, and then, I must be on my way."

"Good-bye Father."

"Good-bye Joseph."

Joseph walked right past several nuns, who were already weeding the new garden, and went directly to where John and Joseph were busily putting up a fence.

"Hello, my friends," stated Joseph, as he approached the two men.

"Father John said that I was supposed to help you."

"Here," noted John, as he wiped his forehead. "Take this," he continued, as he handed him a saw. "Those logs over there need to be cut into six-foot sections."

Joseph grabbed the saw, and obediently walked over to the pile of freshly cut poles. He took a long look at them, glanced back at John and Joseph, grabbed one of the poles, measured off six feet, and began to saw.

Soon, he had a large pile of six-foot logs, lying beside him. Every few minutes he would have to stop and catch his breath. Once that was accomplished, he would wipe the sweat from his brow, and proceed to the next pole.

Brother Joseph walked over and sat down near Joseph, and stated:

"You are working much too fast. You should slow down. If we get done too soon, we'll have to weed the garden."

"If that is what Father John wants us to do, then that is what we should be capable of doing."

"I can tell you just got here," retorted Brother Joseph. "Once you've been here, you'll realize that the more you do, the more he will want you to do."

"That is a very good philosophy, Brother Joseph. There is much work to be done. Idleness is sinful. A person who has idle time, is a dangerous person. This work is for the betterment of all of us. Be grateful for the chance to serve the Lord. Be thankful that he has chosen you to do his work here on earth. Always remember, the end is fast approaching. You must do all you can. There is no time to waste. No time to spend in idleness. Everyone must work and pray. On Sundays you can rest. The other six days are for work."

"Ah, Joseph," stated Brother Joseph, as he got up, "you speak beautiful words. Someday you'll make a good priest. As for me, I don't think Father Salesius has much planned for me."

"Why do you say that?"

"He never lets me study. Whenever he, or Father John, see me reading, they tell me something else to do. Father John says that studying is not necessary right now, and that there are more important things to be doing."

"Never give up hope. The Lord has plans for each of us. If he wants you to become a priest, you'll become a priest. If he wants you to marry, you will marry. You have very little to say in the matter. His plans for you are already prepared. Whatever will be, will be."

"Now," continued Joseph, "let's get these poles over to John."

The lifestyle for Joseph, over the next year, quickly became routine. He would use every free second, for study. Many a night was spent by the table, using a lighted candle, to read and study his Bible and missal.

On one particular evening, August 15, 1848, eight men gathered in Joseph's room. There was Joseph Riesterer, Urs Haener, Joseph Marder, Rochus Schueli, Joseph Hog, Anton Dufner, 18-year-old Patrick Henneberry, and Joseph Albrecht.

Joseph and Urs sat in their chairs by the table, while the others either sat on the beds or on the floor. Each of them had two small books with them.

Before any discussion could begin, there was a knock on the door.

"Come in," shouted Joseph.

The door opened and in walked Father Salesius, closely followed by Father John.

"Good evening, gentlemen," noted Father Salesius, as he walked toward Joseph, who was now getting up from his chair.

"Good evening," replied the men.

"How are my students doing?"

"We just don't seem to have enough time," replied Urs.

"We have so much work to do during the day that, when evening comes, we are all too tired to do much studying."

"I realize there is much to be done around here. But, in time, everything will work out. Soon, we will have more candidates arriving. Then, maybe, you will have more free time for study. By next summer, I'm hoping that some of you will be ready for the priesthood. I have talked with Bishop Rappe, of Cleveland, and he is of the same opinion as I, that study is not the primary necessity right now.

Lead a good life, set a good example, give all you can to the Lord, and you will make good priests."

"Joseph," continued Father Salesius, as he turned his attention to Mr. Albrecht. "I just received word from Wolfscreek, that Sister Ludwina Crescentia Spiegelhalter died last night. She was buried today. Would you please write to Andrew and tell him the news?"

"Why, yes," replied Joseph. "Poor Andrew. He so loved his daughter. She was what? Only 29 years old. Yes Father, I will write tonight."

"Very well."

"What did she die of?"

"The messenger told me that she had trouble breathing, but I don't exactly know what the actual cause was."

"I'll tell Andrew."

"Joseph, I'm going over to Glandorf tomorrow, with Father John. Would you like to come along?"

"Why, yes. When?"

"At sun-up. Right after Mass. It is about 55 miles so we would like to get going as early as possible. We bought some land over there. Several days ago, I received a letter from some of the citizens concerning a request for some of our sisters to teach school there.

I'd like to check it out. Be at my room at 6:30. We wouldn't be gone for more than two days."

Turning his attention to Father John, he continued: "Well John, let us be on our way."

Father John nodded his head, in agreement, and walked to the door. Opening the door, he turned and said: "Good night, everyone."

The men replied: "Good night, as they watched the two priests depart.

Joseph closed the door behind them and returned to his original seat. "Now, gentlemen, let us begin our studies.

Today was the Feast of the Assumption. What does this feast mean to you?" he asked, as he glanced at each of the men.

Outside, Father Salesius and Father John were walking.

"What do you think of Joseph?" asked Father Salesius.

"He is very set in his ways. He is sincere, devout, and pious," noted Father John.

"He is an eloquent and influential speaker. He is very religious. Someday, he could make a good priest."

"Have you noticed any faults?"

"I think his main fault is that he is stubborn. He has his religious views and when someone doesn't go by his views, he gets mad.

Some of the younger students don't hold the same opinions, as he does, and that bothers him."

"I have known Joseph for many years. You know, of course, that he still has much property in Baden. He is still a very wealthy man. He could be a tremendous help to our Society."

"I realize that. But we must be very careful. Money could be his downfall. Several times I have noticed him in deep thought, with a very angry look on his face. Something is bothering him, but I haven't the slightest idea what."

"Maybe we can find out tomorrow," suggested Father Salesius.

Ordinations

CHAPTER IX

The next morning came quickly for Joseph. After spending several hours in group discussion, the previous night, he was able to enjoy several hours of sleep before he had to get up once more.

It had clouded over during the night, and it now looked like it would rain any minute. As he walked over towards the residence of Father Salesius, he noticed a horse-drawn buggy standing in front of the doorway, with Father John sitting in the front seat. Father Salesius was just closing the door to his residence.

"Good morning, Joseph," greeted Father Salesius, as he noticed him approaching.

"Good morning, Father."

As Father Salesius boarded the two-seat buggy, he asked Joseph: "Are you ready?"

"Yes," answered Joseph. "I think I would rather walk, than ride."

"Really?" queried Father Salesius, in a tone of utter amazement. "As you wish."

Father John grabbed the reins, and the three men were off on their excursion.

"I hope it doesn't rain too much today," noted Father John.

"The grain is ready for the harvest. It should be a good crop."

"Just keep praying," suggested Father Salesius.

"Well, Joseph, you've been here three months now. How do you like it?" queried Father Salesius, as he turned towards Joseph.

"There is so much to be done. I don't know if I will ever be able to do my share."

"I'm hoping that by next summer you'll be able to receive Holy Orders. Then, your work will really become difficult."

"I'm not sure that I would be worthy enough to become a Precious Blood priest."

"Why do you say that?" queried Father John.

"I have my doubts. I've been trying to learn Latin, but it is too difficult. It's as if someone up there is trying to tell me something."

"Ah, Joseph," interrupted Father Salesius, "perseverance, my friend. You need perseverance.

Joseph looked at Father Salesius and shook his head. Changing the subject, he continued: "Tell me, why did you want me to come along today?"

"I wanted your opinion on some land over there," answered Father Salesius. "Since you are good in money matters, I wanted to find out what you think the land is worth. I also wanted to give you a chance to see all the beautiful scenery in this area. And, finally, this trip will give me a chance to see how you have progressed in your studies."

"I know everything necessary to becoming a priest, except for Latin. Although, I can't really see why we need to know that anyway. If I can read the Mass, and understand what I'm reading, then that should suffice."

"Not quite, my dear Joseph," shot back Father Salesius. "There is a lot more to being a priest than you think. If you have a sound foundation in Latin, you will not only understand the Mass, but also the breviary, the administering of the Sacraments, and above all, you will understand Church history much better."

"Nonsense! The apostles didn't know Latin. They got by."

"Is it?" queried Joseph. "What is a priest? Isn't he an apostle?

Isn't his job exactly the same as the disciples of Christ? Isn't it his job to go out and spread the truth and save souls? Isn't it his job to look out after the sheep of the Master?"

"You speak the truth, Joseph," noted Father Salesius. "What you say is correct, but there is more. Studying never hurt anyone.

Bishop Rappe believes that Latin is a basic necessity."

"Who is Bishop Rappe?"

"He is the Bishop of Cleveland, my Superior," replied Father Salesius.

"Superior? My superior is the Pope."

"It is different here, Joseph, then back in Baden," stated Father John.

"Yes, Joseph, the bishops here are selected by the Pope. There is no politics involved. It is so much better here," added Father Salesius.

"That is hard to believe. I have gotten so used to the fact that a bishop is nothing more than a pawn for the government, being used as a ploy to keep the Catholics in line."

"You will find out that it is entirely different here," blurted Father John, with a shrug.

"I'll have to wait and see," replied Joseph, as he began to cough.

Onward, the three men journeyed. The rain clouds broke up, giving way to a warm August sun, which was now in mid-air, making it a perfect day for traveling through the beautiful, wooded area of Ohio.

By evening the men arrived in the small village of Glandorf, which consisted of a few log houses, scattered here and there.

"This area is getting more and more German Catholic immigrants every month," noted Father Salesius, as he looked at the abundance of new construction going on. "When Father Engelbert was here for two months this past spring, he had nothing but good words to say about the people who live here. They have had minor problems, but that has been straightened out."

"Over there," continued Father Salesius, as he pointed to the west, "is our land. As of now, 70 acres are cleared. I think I'll try and send some of the brothers over here, after harvest, to clear more of it."

As the wagon came to a stop in front of a small run-down two-story log cabin, Father Salesius continued: "This is it. You can see the barn and orchard over there. What do you think, Joseph?"

"It needs a lot of work. How much did you pay for it?"

"$1200.00."

"It's well worth that."

"I was hoping you'd say that. Several people have said that I paid too much. Hopefully, by next spring, we can start construction. I think this would be an ideal place for a seminary."

"Where is the school?"

"That is on the other side of town. We'll go there next." Father John turned the wagon around and the three men proceeded back across town. Soon, they approached a two-story building, located next to the small Catholic church. They were greeted by two elderly men, who were standing in front of the school. One of them was short, bald, and quite heavy. He wore glasses and was smoking a pipe. The other was gray-haired, quite tall, and very skinny.

"Welcome to Glandorf," stated the heavy-set man.

"Hello," replied Father Salesius. "Are you in charge of the school?"

"Yes, we are."

"Is this where the sisters would be teaching if I decide to send them here?"

"Yes, this is it. The small house to the right, there, could be used as their residence."

"Tell me, sir, does the church own this land around here?"

"No, but I'm sure you could get it very cheap, if you asked the owner."

"And who may that be?"

"Mr. Blackman."

"All we would need is about 5 or 10 acres. That way, we could bring the sisters here and they could support themselves, while teaching."

"Henry," stated the one man, "go and get Mr. Blackman. Have him come down here and talk to these men."

"Yes Karl," obediently replied to Henry, as he turned and headed up the road.

"Who teaches here now?" asked Father Salesius.

"We have several women doing that task, but that is not the same as having sisters. Our children need more religious instruction. If we had nuns here, the children would be well-trained. Father

Ruf, while here, suggested that we try and secure some Precious Blood Sisters."

"Well, I think we can help you. This would be an excellent place for a convent. If I can buy the land, I will see to it that you get several sisters here, right away, in time for the start of school."

"That would be most appreciated," humbly replied Karl, as Henry returned with Mr. Blackman, a middle-aged black-haired man.

"My name is Father Francis deSales Brunner," greeted Father Salesius, as he shook hands with Mr. Blackman. "I am in charge of the Precious Blood Society in Ohio. We would like to send several sisters here, to teach school, but I'd like to have about five acres of land for them. I understand you own this land. How much would it cost me?"

"Five acres," noted Mr. Blackman. "Let's see," he stated, as he paused for several seconds, while rubbing his chin, with his right hand. "Four hundred dollars."

"Joseph, what do you think?"

"Take it."

"Very well. I'll buy it. I shall return to Thompson and get Mr.

Lange, my lawyer. Have the necessary papers drawn up. On my return trip I'll bring my lawyer, and the money. I will also stop at

Wolfscreek and have the Mother Superior send six nuns here right away."

Henry and Karl had smiles on their faces. They were overjoyed at the thought of having religious women for their school. It would not be long, and their school would be run by six nuns of the Precious Blood.

The fall and winter of '48 went by with very little notice. Joseph spent much of his time in study, as well as getting to know everything and everybody involved with the Society. When spring arrived, Father Salesius had many plans, not only for his people, but also for building construction. Work was beginning at Glandorf, Maria Stein, and Wolfscreek.

One morning at Thompson, while everyone was going about their chores, Father Salesius came over to Joseph and Clement Schweitzer, who were busy cleaning the stable.

"Joseph, Clement," shouted Father Salesius, "I have good news for you."

Joseph and Clement stopped working and listened intently while Father Salesius continued: "I have just received a letter from

Bishop Rappe. He says he has decided to ordain you two and Sebastian. When he was here several weeks ago, he said he was satisfied with your progress. He realizes that you are still weak in some areas, but that you should be able to strengthen them with experience."

"When?" queried Joseph.

"June 5th, here at Thompson. He will be here next week to issue the diaconate. This couldn't come at a better time. What with all the cholera going on, my priests are becoming exhausted. With you three, the load will be somewhat lighter for the rest. Tell me, where can I find Mr. Ganther?"

"He went with Father John, over to Wolfscreek this morning," replied Clement, "but they should be back by this evening."

"Then, I'll just have to wait to tell him."

Joseph and Clement put their forks down and shouted with joy, after Father Salesius departed. "That's the best news I've heard in a long time," shouted Joseph, as he hugged Clement.

JUNE 5, 1849 — Thompson — Joseph arose very early this particular morning. He was so nervous that he had barely been able to sleep during the night. He got up from his bed and paced the floor, glancing up, occasionally, at the small picture of the Blessed Virgin

Mary, hanging above his bed. He nervously walked over to the table, opened his black book, and slowly began to read: "In Nomine Patris et Filii, et Spiritus Sancti. Amen." He abruptly laid the book back down on the table and exclaimed: "What's the use!"

Urs Haener, sleeping quietly, heard Joseph, and sat up in his bed. "Ah, today is your day, huh?"

"Yes, and I'm not sure if I'm going to be able to go through with it."

"Oh, everything will turn out for the best."

"I've always had trouble with that Latin," continued Joseph, in a disgusted mood.

"Just don't let it bother you," stated Urs, as he got out of bed.

"Just think about what you will be after the ceremony is over. Father Joseph Maria Albrecht, a priest of the Precious Blood."

"Ah, yes," thought Joseph aloud, "Father Albrecht. Yes, that sounds good."

Just then, there was a knock on the door.

"Come in," requested Joseph.

The door opened, and in walked Father John of the Cross.

"Good morning, Joseph, Urs," he noted.

"Good morning," replied the two men.

"Are you about ready to go over to the church?"

"Is it time already?"

"Father Salesius and the Reverend Bishop are ready. We need to go to the sacristy first, and get you dressed."

"Are there going to be quite a few people there?"

"I suspect the church will be filled."

"Did the sisters from Wolfscreek arrive?"

"Yes, I saw them just a few minutes ago. They already went into the church."

"Is Sister Mary amongst them?"

"Yes, she is."

As Joseph sighed in approval, he added: "Fine, I'm ready."

The two men left for the church. It was a short distance away, to the side entrance, where they entered. There was at least a half dozen men milling around in the small sacristy. Father Salesius, all decked out in his finest Mass vestments, was standing near the door-way. Beside him was Bishop Amadeus Rappe, a short slender man of 48, only one month older than Joseph. He had a gently receding hairline of white. Just by looking at him, one could tell that life had been rough on him. He looked more like 68 than 48. He was attired in a magnificent wardrobe of colorful vestments. Over on the other side of the room were Clement Schweitzer and Sebastian Ganther.

Both were dressed in a long white alb. This plain vestment, a symbol of innocence and purity, was a gift from the sisters, who had made one for each of the three candidates. Clement and Sebastian were talking with Father Kunkler and Father John Van den Broeck.

"Good morning, Joseph," noted Father Salesius, as he saw

Joseph entering.

"Good morning."

"Here is your alb," continued Father Salesius, as he handed the vestment to him. "Go by the others and put it on. Mass will begin shortly."

As Joseph walked over to the others, the church bells could be heard ringing.

"When we have the procession into the church, you three will sit in the front row and wait for the appropriate time, till the Bishop is ready for you," stated Father John, as he looked at the three men. Joseph quickly slipped the alb over his head and let it fall to the floor. At least, that is where it was supposed to fall, but, since he was so much taller than everyone else, the alb only came down halfway between his knees and ankles.

"Oh well," he exclaimed, "I guess that will have to do."

"Gentlemen, are we ready?" queried Father Salesius, as he grabbed his biretta and placed it on his head, looking at the three men.

The three looked at each other, as if each was waiting for the other to nod their head. Finally, Joseph looked at Father Salesius and said: "Let us begin."

The procession from outside the sacristy, around to the front of the church began. First to go was Father Kunkler, then Father Vanden Broeck, Clement Schweitzer, Sebastian Ganther, Joseph Albrecht, Father John, Father Salesius, and finally, Bishop Rappe.

As the church bells continued to ring, the air was filled with singing, from the men's choir, inside the church. Upon entering, the group of men joined in the singing. On the left side were seated the sisters, and on the right, were the priests and brothers. The scene was one of beauty, as the choir chanted 'SALVE REGINA'.

The procession slowly moved towards the front of the church. Joseph, Clement, and Sebastian genuflected, and went into the front pew. The remainder proceeded to the main altar. There was Father Kunkler and Father John on the right side, with Father Salesius on the left. In the center was Bishop Rappe.

Once the singing was completed, everyone genuflected, and Bishop Rappe began the High Mass.

Joseph, Clement, and Sebastian nervously sat waiting for their time to come. Joseph was thinking about how it had just been a little over a year since his arrival in America, and here he was, ready to become a priest. He gazed over towards the nuns. How unusual this was, he thought, for very seldom were the nuns allowed to partake in the Holy Mass, in full view of the men. He continued glancing around until he found what he was looking for — Sister Mary.

She was kneeling at the end of the pew, in the middle of the church. She immediately noticed that he was looking at her. She politely smiled, showing him her approval of what was occurring. That is all Joseph needed. As soon as she smiled, he turned back toward the front. He felt much better now. He knew that he now had the necessary courage.

Bishop Rappe, with his loud strong voice, continued with the Mass. After chanting the 'GLORIA', he kissed the altar, turned to the people, and said: "Dominus vobiscum," with the choir replying:

"Et cum spiritu tuo."

"Oremus."

At this time, Father Salesius walked over to the epistle side. Picking up a small black book, and opening it, he began to read:

"Oh Lord, we beseech you, graciously hear the prayers of your suppliant people, and keep under your perpetual protection those who, with devout hearts, serve you, that we may not be hindered by any trouble, but may always freely serve you. Through our Lord.

Amen. The Epistle today is taken from the Romans, chapter five, verses one through five. Brethren: Having been justified by faith, let us have peace with God through our Lord Jesus Christ, through whom we also have access by faith unto that grace in which we stand, and exult in the hope of the glory of the sons of God. And not only this, but we exult in tribulations also, knowing that tribulation works out endurance, and endurance tried virtue, and tried virtue hope. And hope does not disappoint, because the charity of God is poured forth in our hearts by the Holy Spirit, who has been given to US.)

The other priests replied: "Thanks be to God."

Now, Bishop Rappe walked over to the communion rail, where a

tall chair was placed. Setting his mitre beside the chair, he sat down. Father Van den Broeck, carrying two candles, and Father Kunkler, carrying the large book, accompanied him.

Father Brunner, still standing on the epistle side, stated: "Let those who are to be ordained, approach to the rank of Presbyter. Clement Schweitzer, Joseph Albrecht, Sebastian Ganther."

The three men approached the Bishop. They were handed a white cloth for their left arm, and a long candle for their right hand, by Father Kunkler. The men knelt down in the shape of a crown, around and in front of the Bishop, with Joseph in the center, Clement to the left, and Sebastian to the right.

"Most Reverend Father," continued Father Salesius, "the holy Mother Catholic Church asks that you ordain these deacons, present, to the order of priest."

"Do you feel that they are worthy?" queried Bishop Rappe.

"As much as human weakness allows, I feel and testify these men to be worthy of the charge of this office," replied Father Salesius.

"Thanks be to God," continued Bishop Rappe.

Once the High Mass was completed, the three new priests were escorted out of the church. They stood side by side and were congratulated by everyone as they came out. Bishop Rappe and Father Salesius returned to the sacristy. As they began disrobing Father Salesius asked: "I am overjoyed at the thought of those three men being priests. They will help us out very much. Nevertheless, I've been thinking that I should return to Europe, for more recruits. I would like to get your permission. I would like, not only to get more recruits, but also to check on the affairs at Loewenberg, get assistance from several missionary houses, check with Mr. Spiegelhalter on the financial situation of Albrecht's estate, and to get the necessary books and materials we so desperately need here."

"When would you like to go?"

"By next month."

Father John Van den Broeck, C.PP.S.

"Who will you leave in charge?"

"Father Wittmer. I recently received a letter from the prior at Mariastein. He gave me a very discouraging picture of the conditions in Europe. The revolution of the past year is really causing havoc. I would like to see for myself what is happening."

"You have my permission. Be sure that Father Wittmer keeps a close eye on our new priests. All three of them are very weak in some areas and will need a lot of guidance."

"I am keeping Ganther and Albrecht here at Thompson, for mission work. I am sending Schweitzer up to Sandusky City, to help Father Machebeuf."

"Who is going to assist Wittmer?"

"Father Obermueller."

"You have my blessings. You should also let Bishop Purcell know what your plans are."

"I plan on writing him shortly."

"Who are you going with?"

"I would like to take Van den Broeck with me."

As this conversation was taking place, the two men had completed taking off their vestments, and left the sacristy, heading for the front of the church, where several people were still standing around.

"I see my coach is waiting," noted Bishop Rappe. "Thank-you for the hospitality. I should be on my way back to Cleveland."

"I appreciate your coming," noted Father Salesius, as he helped him into the beautiful gold-colored coach, which was drawn by two huge white horses.

After waving farewell, as the coach departed the grounds, Father Salesius turned and walked back over to where Joseph, Sebastian, and Clement were standing.

"Well Joseph," he stated, as he walked up beside him, "this Sunday you will hold your first Mass here. I am so happy for you."

"Thank-you. Without your help, I would never have made it this far."

"Sebastian, you will say your first Mass over at .Glandorf, as you requested. Clement, you will be up in Sandusky City. I am so proud of all three of you. I have just received permission from the Bishop to return to Europe. I should be leaving in a month, or so.

While I'm gone, Father John of the Cross will be the acting Superior. I feel that I must return and visit the shrines of the Blessed Virgin Mary. Maybe that will help my poor health. I'm also going to bring back more recruits. But, for now, I must go get some rest. Have a good day."

"Good day Father," noted the three men, as Father Salesius departed.

Joseph stood there in a daze, wondering what it was going to be like being a priest. Finally, he was actually going to be able to do all the priestly functions that he had longed to do.

He was soon to find out that the road of a priest was very rough, for when he returned to his room and began preparing for the Sunday sermon, he could not write. He would sit by his table and contemplate on what to say, but he was unable to put it down on paper.

After an hour, he decided to call it quits for the day, and retire. Thus ended the fifth day of June 1849, a day which Joseph would remember for the rest of his life.

Cholera Epidemic

CHAPTER X

Father John and Father Joseph were riding along in their horse drawn carriage. They had been on the road all day and were anxiously awaiting the sight of Minster. It was close to the middle of July and the hot summer sun was beginning to take its toll on the two men.

"This is beautiful country," stated Father Joseph, as he wiped his forehead. "One day, I hope to be stationed down here."

"I'm sure you'll get your chance," noted Father John. "Father Salesius has big plans for this area."

"Here we are," continued Father John, as the sight of the small town of Minster came into view. "We should be there in a few minutes."

The wagon slowly made its way into the small prospering town. What Father John and Father Joseph saw was unbelievable. There were several wagons busily hauling cholera victims to their final resting place.

As they arrived in front of the church, they were greeted by Father Maximilian Homburger, who had just come out of the church.

"Hello, my friends," stated Father Max, as he extended his right hand. "Welcome."

"Greetings," answered Father John.

"Hello Max," noted Father Joseph.

"How is everything here?" asked Father John.

"Not so good. That cholera is really starting to have its effects."

"Is that why there isn't anyone on the streets?" asked Father Joseph.

"Yes, I'm afraid everyone thinks it is safer if they stay inside and away from everybody else."

"Do you know what is causing it?" asked Father Joseph.

"Not really, but it has something to do with the unsanitary conditions around here. Many of these people came here, thinking that it was an ideal place to live, but are now finding out that it is no more than a frontier town and the living conditions are still rather primitive. "

"What are its symptoms?" asked Father John.

"I'm getting ready to go on my rounds now. Why don't you come along and see for yourself?

"I'm sure Father Joseph would like to go, but I think I'll stay here at the church," replied Father John.

"Very well. Let's go Joseph."

Father Joseph got down from the wagon and began walking down the street with Father Max, while Father John got down and unhitched the horses.

"Aren't you worried about catching that disease?" asked Father Joseph.

"No, not really."

"There is another one of those wagons," pointed out Father Joseph. "Where are they going?"

"They are taking the bodies to the cemetery."

"No funeral? No procession?"

"That's right. They are simply wrapped in a black shroud, put in a pine box, and buried in mass graves."

"That sounds terrible!"

"What else can we do?"

As the two men approached a small one-story log cabin, Father Max continued: "Here we are. This is our first stop."

Father Max knocked on the door. After opening it himself, the two men entered. What Father Joseph saw was something he would never forget. There were four people inside. A man, about the age of 40, was lying on a small couch. Nearby, lay his wife. In a small side room were two children, ages 7 and 5. All of them were very sick.

"Tell me, Nicholas, how are you doing today?" asked Father Max.

"Not so good, Father," weakly replied the man. "It sounds as if the children are getting worse. They were doing a lot of vomiting last night."

"And, how about you?" queried Father Max, as he took a wet towel and wiped the man's forehead.

"I have this terrible thirst."

"Here is a glass of water," offered Father Joseph.

"Thank-you," replied Nicholas, as he took the glass from Joseph's hand and quickly drank it.

"How is the pain?" continued Father Max.

"Much better, but it's still there. Don't worry about me. Father. Please try and take care of my wife and children."

"Very well, Nicholas. I will keep you in my prayers," Father Max continued, as he walked over to the wife.

"I don't think she is breathing," exclaimed Father Joseph, as he looked at the lifeless body.

Father Max checked her pulse. After several seconds, he replied: "You're right, Joseph. She is gone. There is no more we can do for her. I'm going over to the children. Would you please give her the final Rites, and then, put her personal clothing in this sack, and set them outside. Afterwards, we will soak them in grease and burn them."

Father Joseph now took out his small black book and began to quietly pray. After this task was completed, he collected all of her clothes, and placed them in a gunny sack, which had been given to him earlier.

Soon, Father Max returned. "Take this red kerchief and tie it on the outside door," he requested. "'The wagon men will know to stop here on their next round."

"This all sounds so unreal," exclaimed Father Joseph. "I can't believe that I'm seeing this actually happen."

Father Joseph picked up her clothes and carried them outside. He tied the red kerchief on the doorknob, just like Father Max had told him to do. Upon completing this, he returned inside, and walked over to Father Max.

"The kids don't look very good either," stated Father Max.

"There must be something more that we can do for them."

"I'm afraid not. I wish there were, but I don't know what else it could be." As the two men departed the house, Father Joseph asked:

"Why would God give this disease to innocent children?"

"I don't know, Joseph. I just don't know."

The two men continued making the rounds throughout the town and countryside. There were sick people in almost all of the houses they visited. Some were getting better, some worse. By the time they returned to the church, they were both exhausted.

"This is too much for two men to do," suggested Father Joseph.

"Father John, when we get back to Thompson, I think we should tell

Father Salesius to send more help down here."

"Yes, I agree with you. Father Max could definitely use more help. Hopefully, when Father Salesius goes back to Europe, he will be able to find many recruits. Then Father Max will have extra help."

"Well," interrupted Father Joseph, as he looked at his pocket watch, "we better get going, if you are going to take me over to St. Joseph and St Henry yet, today."

"Must you leave so soon?" asked Father Max.

"Yes," replied Father Joseph. "We do have a lot to do yet before we return to Thompson."

After the good-byes were said, the wagon slowly departed the church property, winding its way westward, into the countryside, a countryside that would soon become very familiar to Father Joseph, for in a matter of several years, he would return to this area, carrying on his crusade. It was in this area that he would develop lasting personal relationships with new-found friends.

CHAPTER XI

AUGUST 25, 1849

Thompson —— The morning sun was still below the horizon, as the men began going about their daily routines.

Father Joseph was making preparations for Holy Mass at the convent chapel. Father Salesius had completed his travel plans and was now ready to depart. Several men had congregated in his small room. There was Father John, Father Van den Broeck, Father Capeder, and Father Obermueller. They were joined by Father Joseph, as soon as he had made his preparations.

"Good morning, Joseph," exclaimed Father Salesius. "Why are you running?"

"I was afraid you'd take off before I got here," stated Father Joseph, as he leaned against the table, trying to catch his breath.

"I wouldn't leave without saying good—bye to you," assured Father Salesius, as he walked over and put his hand on his shoulder.
"Besides, I have some papers here that I need to give you."

As Father Salesius picked up several papers off the table, he continued: "Please see to it that this letter gets to Bishop Purcell."

Father Joseph took the letter and placed it inside his cassock.

"I have a document here that was written last February," continued Father Salesius. "It is a copy which incorporates our Society as an Institution Benevolent. I want you to read it when you get a chance. It will give you an idea of how things should be run within our community. Here is a personal note to you that I jotted down last night. I want you to read it after I'm gone."

Father Joseph took both sheets and gently folded them, and placed them, also, inside his cassock.

"When I go to Freiburg, I'm going to see Andrew. I'm hoping we can get your financial affairs straightened out."

"I hope so too. It sure has been a long-drawn-out affair."

"There has been a lot of turmoil over there in the past few years, and I don't know if we are going to be able to get anything done or not."

"Well, good luck. I'll keep praying for your success. When will you be back?"

"I don't know. It should be within a year. Father Van den Broeck has a lot of things to do too, so I don't know how long it will take. Father John and Father Capeder will be traveling with me as far as Sandusky City. Father Obermueller has to go over to Glandorf, for a few days, so you will be in charge. That is part of the reason I want you to read those two notes."

"Well, good-bye then, and may God be with you on your trip," noted Father Joseph.

As the men boarded the wagon, Father Salesius looked at Father Joseph, and said: "Peace be With you, dear Joseph."

Father Joseph stood and waved good-bye, as the wagon carrying the four priests, slowly departed the seminary grounds. Once they were out of sight, he immediately took the two pieces of paper out of his pocket and began to read aloud: "The Society of the Precious Blood is hereby legally declared 'Institution Benevolent.' All property, be it movable or immovable, belongs to the Society. Should an individual decide to leave the Society, or be dismissed, he cannot and will not be allowed to lay claim against the Society. With the permission of the Superior, any member who possesses property may retain a portion or all of it. In case of death, this property will then fall into the hands of the Society, regardless of personal wills or testimonials."

"Huh," thought Father Joseph, as he folded the sheet, "I wonder why he wanted me to read this."

He then proceeded to read the next note aloud: "Dear Joseph, I'm writing you this note, to be read after I leave, because I did not want anyone else to hear what I have to say. I wanted to talk to you last night, but I did not get the chance. I'm not sure if I'll ever make it back to Thompson. My health, as you know, has not been very good. If something should happen to me, I want you to know that I will always hold a very high regard of you. I have always admired your religious zeal. You have been a perfect example of a Precious Blood priest. I only wish that all of the candidates were built of your quality. You must understand that I elected Father John and Father Obermueller to be in charge during my absence, simply because of their seniority. Father John of the Cross has been a great help to me, so I hope you will obediently listen to him. As soon as possible, I hope to have you placed in charge of the area down by Minster, but for now, I want you to continue your missions around Thompson. I have talked to several people in the neighboring towns, and they have had nothing but good words about you. I want you to know that I'm very pleased with your actions. I realize that some of the younger priests and brothers hold different views than you or I, but we'll just have to continue to pray for them. Maybe then, they will see how wrong they are. I will always remember you in my prayers.

Sincerely, Father Salesius."

Father Joseph folded the letters up, and placed them back into his pocket, as he began walking back towards the chapel, with a smile on his face.

During the absence of Father Salesius, everything went normal at Thompson. Father Joseph vigorously continued his task of giving missions to various communities, in the surrounding area. It was during this time that he developed an excellent talent for giving sermons. Every mission he gave would attract large crowds. When these people would leave, they would go home as different people. He had a way of making an individual seriously think about their lives and how they could change for the better.

Among other tasks that Father Joseph so willingly did were to visit the nuns, as their confessor. He also would spend much of his time visiting the sick.

On October 13, 1850, Father Salesius returned to Thompson. In his company were three priests: Peter Weber, Joseph Schelbert, and Lawrence Feger, as well as eight brothers and seventeen sisters and novices. The brothers were Christian Casanova, Julien Jobert, Anton Caminada, Joseph Jetzer, Erhard Glueck, Carl Fetz, Andrew Danbacher, and Willibald Willi. Of these, young Willibald Willi, born in 1825, in Canton Graubunden, became very attached to Father Joseph.

Immediately upon his arrival, Willibald devoutly spent countless hours in study. Many an evening would pass when he and Father Joseph would sit by candlelight and read and discuss religious thought and practices.

One evening, in January of 1851, a discussion was being held in the small classroom at Thompson. At this meeting were: Father Salesius, Father Joseph, Nicholas Gales, Peter Wilhelmi, Patrick Henneberry, and Willibald Willi. Patrick Henneberry, age 20, had arrived at Thompson in June of 1849, coming from Wisconsin. Nicholas Gales came in 1849 from Buffalo. Peter Wilhelmi had joined the Society in '49. These men, along with Willibald, had just been chosen by Father Salesius to devote their time and energy in the preparation for the priesthood.

"Bishop Rappe is coming tomorrow," noted Father Salesius. "We should expect him some time in the morning. He will give minor orders, sub-diaconate, and diaconate to those he thinks are ready. I realize none of you have put much time in study but I'm hoping the Reverend Bishop will realize the necessity. We are making plans for expanding our mission work and I need all of you. I have been looking at some land in Indiana, and I would like to find some more property down by St. Joseph. I hope you all give a good impression tomorrow, then maybe I'll have some candidates for the new area."

Turning his attention directly to Willibald, Father Salesius continued: "Willibald, I know you have only been studying here for about four months, and I realize that your health hasn't been that good, but I have watched you progress, and I see you have that certain desire to want to succeed. Given the circumstances, I'm sure the Bishop will want to elevate you to the priesthood. Father Joseph has told me much about you. If all goes well, I want to send you over to Glandorf and put you in charge. I'm sure you will be able to handle it."

Father Salesius now turned his attention to all four candidates, and said: "As you all know, we still do not have vows. Soon, I hope to have that changed. You must all pray that whoever does become a priest has the willpower and stamina to be a good priest and do whatever is asked of him. Always remember the chain of command, from God to the Pope, to the Bishop, and to me. You must remember that we are indirectly representing God here on earth.

"I don't completely agree with you," interjected Father Joseph. "The Pope is the true representative of Christ, here on earth. I have seen many bishops who have misrepresented Christ. They were elected into office and have used the influence of their post for personal gains. I have seen this happen so often in Europe that I have come to the conclusion that we have no need for Bishops."

"Nonsense," replied Father Salesius. "This is America. Things are different here."

"From what I've seen, it is the same here."

"No Joseph, that is not true. Both Bishop Rappe and Bishop Purcell have led devout, Christian lives. Both have spent much time in the betterment of the everyday life of the common man. Surely, you must see that."

"I will never trust a Bishop," answered Father Joseph. "The Pope should be the one to answer to."

"I sometimes wonder about you," stated Father Salesius, in disgust.

As Father Joseph and Willibald got up, Father Joseph stated:
"Come Willibald, it is time for us to do our self-examin and study."

As the two men were walking back to Father Joseph's room, Father Joseph noted: "I admire Father Salesius for many things, but he has a few ideas that I don't agree with, especially concerning bishops."

"Is it really that bad?"

"Yes. Always be on guard when there is a bishop involved. Just heed my words. Also, don't worry about when the bishop comes. Just remember the words of St. James: 'If any of you is wanting in Wisdom, let him ask it of God, and it will be given him abundantly.'"

The next day, Bishop Rappe arrived at Thompson, and examined the four candidates. All four received minor orders, subdiaconate, and diaconate. The following week, on Monday, January 27, three of the men were ordained. Patrick Henneberry's ordination
was delayed, because of his age.

After the ordination, Father Willi went to Glandorf, where, on

the following Sunday, he gave his first Mass.

As the year went by, the health of Father Willi gradually worsened. He had a severe painful cough, and often found himself spitting up blood. More and more, he was confined to bed.

In the spring of 1852, Father Joseph decided to pay a visit to his young friend. Arriving early one afternoon, he found Father Willi in bed.

"Hello, my dear friend," greeted Father Willi, as Father Joseph entered the small room.

"Hello Willibald," replied Father Joseph. "What are you doing in bed at this time of day?"

"I'm having problems. The pain has moved from my chest to my thigh. I have been able to eat some, but I still can't walk."

"That will come in time."

"I don't know. One must die, whether sooner or later matters little, if only one dies well."

"Ask God to give you your full health. He would surely grant it."

"There are others who pray sufficiently for this. I certainly cannot know what the best for me is. I would gladly want that which is the best for me, but at the same time, I can do nothing but leave all entirely to God. Let him dispose of me in such a way as to obtain his
greater honor and to accomplish his most holy Will."

"Father Salesius is going down to St. Joseph, in Mercer County, next week. He is looking for a new site for another convent. I'm hoping he will be successful because I'm about due to leave Thompson.

Maybe, if I get transferred down there, I'll try and get Father Salesius to approve for you to come there too."

"That would be nice."

"It is beautiful country down there. I'm sure you would like it."

Himmelgarten

CHAPTER XII

Father Salesius was riding along with the short elderly Ted Hemmelgarn, in a one-seat wagon.

"All of this land is included, Father," stated Mr. Hemmelgarn. "520 acres."

"It is beautiful," exclaimed Father Salesius, as he looked at the snow-covered landscape. "The gently rolling hills, the trees, the fields, everything is just excellent."

"It is good land. Ideally located, right between St. Joseph and St. Henry."

"Yes, that it is."

The wagon pulled up to the homestead. There, situated under several huge oak trees, stood two blockhouses. The wealthy Mr. Hemmelgarn had built them several years ago and they were larger than any other houses in the area.

"This is the house and barn," continued Mr. Hemmelgarn.

"They would be perfect for your brothers and sisters."

As the two men got off the wagon and walked toward the cabin, Mr. Hemmelgarn continued: "As you know, Father, I have been unable to live in this house. I kept hearing strange noises, and just about went crazy. I have no peace by day or night, but I am sure if a family of religious, such as has been established in the convent

Grunenwald, will make this their home, they will not be disturbed because of the many prayers they offer."

"This will do just fine. I will have to go up to Thompson, for the money. I'll return and then we can take care of this matter."

"Very well. You know, Father, an excellent name for this place could be Himmelgarten, the Garden of Heaven."

"Yes, that sounds very good. I could call it Himmelgarten, and dedicate the convent to Mary, Mother of Mercy."

The next day, Father Salesius returned to Thompson. He immediately went in search of Father Joseph, whom he found in the
church.

"Joseph, I need your help."

"Hello Father. What can I do for you?"

"I have found an excellent piece of land down by Grunenwald. It's 520 acres and would be an ideal spot for another convent. We need it desperately. Could I get the money from here, to help pay for it?"

"Of course. I'll get Sister Lucretia. I'm sure she has no objection."

"Good. Bring her here. I would like to talk to her."

Father Joseph left and soon, returned with Sister Lucretia (formerly Barbara Hog). She was wearing a heavy black shawl over her shoulder. In one hand she was carrying a big black bag.

"Greetings, Sister Lucretia," stated Father Salesius.

"Hello Father."

"I need $800.00, Sister. I am a little short of funds. I found a beautiful farm down in Mercer County."

"Sure, Father. Father Joseph has already told me," stated Sister Lucretia, as she began counting the money out.

"I need another favor of you. Would you come back with me and go to each of the convents and assemble enough members for the new place? I will make you the Superior."

"Of course," answered Sister Lucretia, in a very surprised tone.
"When?"

"As soon as possible. I am going back there tomorrow. I would like for you to come along. I will talk to Father John and Mother Johanna and see if it is alright with them. If it is, I should be ready by seven."

"Joseph," continued Father Salesius, as he turned to him, "Let us go see Father John."

All three left — Sister Lucretia back to here convent, Father Joseph, and Father Salesius to find Father John.

"Father John!" shouted Father Salesius, as the two men approached Father Wittmer, who was standing near the barn door entrance, supervising the barn cleaning, being done by several brothers.

"Vas?"

"Are you busy?"

"Not really."

"Good. Come with us, we are going back down to St. Joseph, tomorrow. I've found a farm and want to set a new convent up."

"Very well," replied Father John, as the three men headed back to the seminary building.

The following day, Father Salesius, Father Joseph, Father Wittmer, and Sister Lucretia arrived at the Hemmelgarn farm. As they approached the two blockhouses, Father Joseph noted: "This is it?

This is our new convent?"

"It will take some work, but I'm sure, with a little work and ingenuity, we can develop this farm into a very prosperous community," suggested Father Salesius. "John, don't you think it would be possible to connect these two buildings?"

Father John thought for several seconds, as he looked over the two buildings, and then said: "Yes, I think that could be done."

"Good! Go over to Minster, tomorrow, and get a couple of the brothers. Bring them back here and start right away. I'll stop over at Grunenwald and talk Sister Martha into sending a couple of nuns here to start on the garden. There is an awful lot of work to be done, but I'm sure we can do it."

"It is definitely going to be a challenge," noted Father Joseph.

"Until we get the construction project completed," continued Father Salesius, "you can stay at the parish of St. Joseph. You not only will be in charge of this convent, but also, you will be responsible for the parish of St. Joe, as well as several other small communities in the area."

"I see," happily replied Father Joseph.

"Next week, a couple of nuns should be coming over," added Father Salesius.

"Sister Lucretia will start making her rounds, so in a month or so, that group should be arriving. I have great plans for this place, Joseph. Someday I hope to have a seminary, a convent, a school, everything. This could turn out to be one of our biggest communities, and I want you in charge."

"I am flattered. I will try to build this place up to your expectations."

"I'm sure you will, Joseph. I'm sure you will."

In the early daylight hours of April 29, 1852, Sisters Brigitta Meyer and Fridolina Hess arrived at Himmelgarten, to take charge. Several brothers, under the direction of Father John, were busily putting the final touches on their work.

"Ah, good morning, sisters," exclaimed Father John. "Welcome to your new home. We should have the chapel done in an hour or so. Father Joseph should be here any minute now, with the host for the tabernacle. Feel free to make yourselves at home."

The two sisters walked into the structure and were somewhat surprised at what they saw. There was no furniture, nothing on the walls. Cobwebs were everywhere. Large cracks could be seen in the roof and in the walls.

"Well," remarked Sister Fridolina, "this experience could be quite interesting."

"Father Joseph will see to it that everything is taken care of," assured Sister Brigitta.

Just then, the beautiful sound of church bells was heard. The two nuns ran outside to see where the sound was coming from. Up on the roof, two brothers were putting the finishing touches on the small belfry. Inside were placed three small bells.

"What a beautiful sight!" exclaimed Sister Fridolina.
Just then, Father Joseph approached on foot.

"Hello Father Joseph," greeted Sister Brigitta, as she and Sister Fridolina walked over to meet him.

"Hello Sister Brigitta," replied Father Joseph. "Have you been here long?"

"No, we just arrived."

"I have just come from St. Joseph and have brought the Blessed Sacrament with me. Father Salesius should be here shortly. He plans on having Holy Mass here in our chapel. Let me place the host in the tabernacle, and I'll return to show you where we plan on putting the garden."

Joseph quickly walked into the chapel, placed the host in the tabernacle, and returned to the sisters.

"Come with me," he requested. "There are 520 acres here. The men will begin clearing more land soon. Sister Lucretia will be arriving in a few weeks, with more sisters."

The three of them walked to the rear of the convent building where there was a small open piece of ground. "This will be the garden," stated Father Joseph, as he pointed to the area. "I have seed back at St. Joseph, which I'll bring back with me, tomorrow. If you
get a chance today, why don't you start digging up the soil. There are a couple of spades setting over by that tree. But for now, I think we should go back to the chapel and wait for our guests."

The three returned to the front of the convent, where Father Salesius was just arriving. Father John and several of the brothers were already standing beside the wagon.

"Ah, Joseph," exclaimed Father Salesius, as he got down to the ground. "Do you have everything ready?"

"Yes Father. I believe so."
" I see the sisters are already here. That means nocturnal adoration can start tonight."

"But there are only two of them."

"That's alright. 'm sure they won't mind."

"Of course not," noted Sister Brigitta.

"Come," continued Father Salesius, "let us all go in and celebrate Holy Mass in our newest chapel."

Everyone followed Father Salesius into the chapel.

For the next several months, there was continuous activity at Himmelgarten. Daily, Father Joseph would come over from St. Joseph, and see how everything was progressing. He would check with Father John, concerning the construction projects, and with Sister Lucretia, to see how they were doing.

Sister Lucretia had arrived by the end of May, with her group of recruits: Sisters Sabina Volk, Devota Festi, Thecla Helzinger, Gertrude Aut, Virginia Kenk, Attala Schemmel, Hildetrud Dilger, and Agnes Stuke.

The sight of the sisters' arrival was enjoyed by Father Joseph. His farm was now developing into a full-fledged convent. Soon, the brothers' house would be completed and then he could move over from St. Joe. The daily trip on foot of six miles, back and forth, was beginning to affect his health. Now, he would be able to spend more time being the Superior that Father Salesius had wanted him to be.

Shortly after the arrival of the sisters, a wagon carrying six brothers arrived at Himmelgarten. Father Joseph hastily walked over and greeted them.

"Hello, Father," stated the driver, a short heavy-set young man. "Where would you like us to go."

"Come, I'll show you your new home. It probably isn't done yet, but you should be able to sleep in it tonight."

Father Joseph led the six men into the two-story building, which had been hastily constructed by Father John and his construction crew.

"In about an hour, I would like all of you to come down to the convent chapel, for a short talk. Find a place to put your things, become familiar with your new home, and then come over," continued Father Joseph.

He then proceeded directly to the convent chapel. After saying a short prayer, he got up off his knees and sat down in the front pew. He pulled out a packet of sheets from his pocket, unfolded them, and silently began reading them to himself.

Soon the brothers and sisters began arriving, with the brothers taking a seat to the left, and sisters to the right. Father Joseph then got up and walked to the altar.

"Welcome," he began. "For those who don't know me, I'm Father Joseph Maria Albrecht. I will be your superior. You may call me Father Joseph. I have received a letter from Father Salesius, and he asked me to read it to you, upon your arrival. It goes as follows: 'I have entrusted your souls in the hands of Father Joseph. I'm sure you all will obediently follow his commands. He will direct you in regard to spiritual things. He will assign the daily work. He will be your confessor. Each evening he will conduct an examination of conscience for the brothers, and lead in the meditation after Benediction in the chapel. He will hear confessions for the sisters every Saturday. Besides being appointed your superior, I have also given him the added responsibility of being one of my three consultors for the diocese of Cincinnati. I know you will treat him with the utmost respect. Sincerely, Father Francis deSales Brunner.'"

Father Joseph abruptly stopped. "I have a few more sheets that he wrote but I don't think I need to read them to you. I will be moving into the brothers' house tomorrow. I will try and take care of your needs. Due to circumstances beyond my control, I will be spending much time away from the convent, as will the brothers, for a while. Sister Lucretia, here, is the Sister Superior. She will have complete control of the convent. She and I will discuss the needs of the community and decide on how best 'to attain those objectives. It is her duty to be watchful, at all times, that the rule or mode of life be accurately observed by all. That is all I have to say for now. You may leave."

Folding his papers up, Father Joseph departed the chapel. As he was walking out the door, one of the brothers approached him. "Father," he shouted.

"Yes, Brother Innocent, what is it?"

"I understand Father Salesius has bought some land in Indiana.
Who is taking care of it?" queried Brother Innocent Moorman, the 26-year-old man.

"We will," replied Father Joseph. "As soon as everything gets normalized around here, I will be taking several men over there."

"J would be honored if you would take me along."

"I'll remember that when the time comes. It will probably be sometime next week, or as soon as we get the crops in."

That summer, everything began to take on a semblance of normalcy around Himmelgarten. The brothers and sisters ardently worked on the crops. When time permitted, Father Joseph took several of the brothers over to the new lands in Indiana. This new site, known as Mary's Home, was located about 15 miles west of Himmelparten.

Not much was accomplished that first summer at Mary's Home. It took a lot of hard work on the part of the brothers just to get some of the land cleared. Trees had to be felled. Underbrush had to be pulled away. It got to the point that there was so much more to be
done there, then at Himmelgarten, that Father Joseph decided to give up on the new area for the time being, even though he had already become convinced that one day Mary's Home could be a very important mission for them.

In the fall of 1853, Father Willibald Willi was transferred from Glandorf to Mariastein. His health had improved somewhat, since now he could at least walk with the help of a cane. This proved to be good news for Father Joseph, as now he was sure he would be able to see more of his close friend.

One evening, during a cold heavy rainstorm, Father Joseph had gone out to the newly constructed barn, to check on the animals. Soon, Sister Lucretia came running in.

"Father Joseph. You must do something. Every time the wind blows, or it rains, we have to move our cots around. The living conditions in our house are very bad."

"My dear sister. Are we complaining about personal hardships?"

"No, I'm not complaining," replied Sister Lucretia, as she began to cough. After she cleared her throat, she continued: "All I'm saying is that we should get something done to those cracks and leaks. It would not take much to fix them. Why should the poor sisters suffer unnecessarily?" .

"You are right. I'll] have some of the brothers check it out in the morning."

Sister Lucretia again began to cough.

"It sounds like you are catching a very bad cold. Why don't you find yourself a nice warm bed and stay in it for a few days. Tell Sister Brigitta to come see me, in the chapel. I'll put her in charge until you get better."

"Yes Father," replied Sister Lucretia, as she turned and departed, coughing all the way out.

Sister Lucretia's health continued to worsen. But that wasn't the only problem facing Father Joseph. Sister Brigitta, who had taken over for Sister Lucretia, soon became sick, herself, and on December 8, 1852, died at the convent, and was buried at the cemetery
in St. Joseph.

Since Sister Lucretia was still very sick, the duties of Sister Superior were taken over by Sister Mary Scholastica Dufner.

Life continued on at Himmelgarten. Father Joseph, besides being in charge of the convent, was also responsible for the parishes of St. Joseph, St. Henry, and St. Anthony of Padua. He also helped supervise the construction projects at Mary's Home.

One fall day in 1853, while at Mary's Home, Father Joseph was seen directing the affairs. Several brothers were harvesting the grain, while several others were completing the construction of a storage shed.

Although the health of Father Willibald was still not completely corrected, he did find time to come over from Mariastein, to see how Father Joseph was doing.

"Hello, dear Willibald," shouted Father Joseph, as the wagon, being driven by Father Willi, approached.

"Hello Joseph."

"What brings you over here?"
"Oh, Father, there isn't much for me to do over at Mariastein. I just thought I'd go for a ride and see how you were doing. I stopped at Himmelgarten, and they told me you were over here, so, here I am."

"You look very tired. That ten-hour trip must have been rough on you."

"Oh, it isn't too bad. Although, I do think they should do some work on that road. It is very rough, in some areas."

"Come, sit down here. I have little to offer you, besides this jerky," continued Father Joseph, as he handed him a piece of dried beef.

"Thank-you, but I really don't need anything."

As the two men sat down near a tree, Father Willibald asked:
"How is everything?"

"There is a lot to be done. I just don't have enough time to do everything. This place is too far from any of our mission houses. My new parish, St. Anthony of Padua, is only about three miles from here, but there aren't enough people around here to warrant building a church yet."

"Perhaps one could remedy this situation, at least for a time. I am not of much worth anymore. It matters very little where I live or die, as long as I fulfill the most holy Will of God. Then all things will be right. If only the superiors give me some little indication. If they would only tip the wink, I would gladly and happily come here with full confidence. What I do at Mariastein, offer Holy Mass for our brothers and sisters, that I can do here, as long as God wills it. If the superiors send me, then I am sure that I am fulfilling the Will of God, as if God, himself, spoke to me."

"I will be talking with Father Salesius, tomorrow. I'll see what he thinks of the idea."

"Yes, Joseph. I think I would love to finish out my years in this beautiful place."

"Tt would be good for your health, also. Someday, I believe this mission will be very prosperous. The soil is very rich and fertile. In no time at all, it will be settled, hopefully, by good solid German Catholics."

"Ah, yes. All I need is a few brothers and sisters. Nothing more."

"I'll come over to Mariastein when I find out what Father Salesius decides."

Changing the subject, Father Joseph continued: "Listen, are you planning on going all the way back to Mariastein today?"

"J was thinking about it, but it might be too far."

"Fine. I'm about ready to go back to Himmelgarten. I could ride back with you and then you could stay overnight and continue on your trip tomorrow. Just let me talk to the boys, first. Then we can leave."

"As you wish," stated Father Willibald, as he watched Father Joseph walk over to the brothers and talk to Brother Innocent. While awaiting for his return, Father Willibald made the necessary preparations for departure. After checking the harnesses, he
climbed back onto the wagon seat.

Soon, Father Joseph returned, got aboard, and sat down next to Father Willibald, "I'm ready," he said. "Let's go."

Slowly, the wagon departed Mary's Home, heading eastward toward Himmelgarten. As they were riding along the trail, Father Willibald turned to Father Joseph, and asked: "How were you able to get so much accomplished at Mary's Home and Himmelgarten, in so little time?"

Father Joseph looked back at his friend, and replied:

"It is easy when you have the resources available."

"From Father Salesius?"

"Partly. But I have other ways also."

"What do you mean by that?"

"God works in mysterious ways."

"Ah, yes," laughingly noted Father Willibald. "I see. Well, have him send some my way next time."

Father Joseph shrugged with laughter, as the wagon pulled up in front of the Himmeligarten convent.

"You are welcome to sleep in my bed, tonight," offered Father Joseph, as the two men walked toward his room. "I will take a blanket and sleep on the floor."

"Very kind of you," replied Father Willibald, as he followed Father Joseph into the room.

Both men sat down by the small table, situated in one corner of the room. Father Joseph lit a candle on the table and picked up his small black book. Father Willibald reached into his cassock and pulled out his prayer book. Both men silently sat and prayed for several minutes. Stopping momentarily, Father Joseph put his book down and looked at Father Willibald.

"You know, I have had something bothering me for the past several weeks. Maybe you could help me."

"Me? Help you?"

"Yes. You know that I was picked by Father Salesius to be one of his consultors for the diocese of Cincinnati, along with Kunkler and Van den Broeck. Well, I thought that would mean that I would have some say in what goes on and what rules should be used in the Society. Well, I have been observing some of the younger priests and brothers, and I don't like what I see. I mentioned this fact to Father Salesius, but he seems to ignore me. Sister Mary, the sweet Savior of my soul, always told me to have patience and to trust in

providence and resign myself to the holy will of God. Well, I just don't know. I have some doubts as to what is happening. I just don't know if I have the patience. Tell me, Willibald, could not a person easily be too forbearing and too indulgent?"

"I don't know," replied Father Willibald, as he rubbed his chin, with his right hand. "I, myself, am just a beginner. First, I wish to begin with this test. In this matter, it seems to me, one has to learn wisdom from the hunter. There are hunters who, thinking that real game is moving about, fire upon every little bird. This they do often, or else they fire when they are too far distant. In this manner they expend a great deal of powder to no avail and drive away the better game. Other hunters go about this task more wisely. They follow the trail until surely and unquestionably they come upon the scent of a worthwhile beast. They then lie in wait for the game until it is very close and standing quiet. At that very moment they sight it accurately and penetrate its heart with a bullet. To him it seemed that exhortations and reprimands could easily be such unavailing and harming shots into the air if one did not aim accurately and utilize them opportunely — at the right time and in a suitable manner. One should bide his time, first: investigate all circumstances carefully, consider them maturely, and in the meantime, beseech God for the grace to discover the right word. Then one will not miss the mark so widely."

"What an answer!" exclaimed Father Joseph. "What a beautiful answer! I will always try to remember that. Thank-you."

The next morning, Father Willibald returned to Mariastein, and life went on at Himmelgarten.

The convent was still not completed during the winter of °53, so the poor sisters again had to spend much of their time moving their cots away from the leaks in the roof, that always seemed to reap pear, after the brothers had supposedly patched them up.

MARCH 29, 1854 — On this cool sunny spring morning, activity alt Himmelgarten was beginning. Mass had just been completed, and the brothers and sisters were just leaving to begin their assigned tasks. Father Joseph was walking towards the barn, with several of
the brothers. They were discussing what new items were necessary for the farm work.

"I'm going to be going over to Minster, tomorrow," stated Father Joseph, as he entered the barn. "Brother Innocent, I would like for you to come along. I'll see what they have in the line of new plows. I also want to see if I can find some good oxen. We could use
several pair."

While this discussion continued, the church bells began to ring. Soon, Sister Lucretia came running into the barn, shouting: "Father, Father, the convent is on fire!"

"What!" shouted Father Joseph. "Get the pails!" he demanded, as he ran from the barn, followed immediately by the others.

Soon, everyone was racing toward the convent. Many of them didn't know what to do, so Father Joseph attempted to organize a fire-fighting group, but it was to no avail.

Flames were now pouring forth from the recently completed convent. Soon, the grainery and the storage sheds were also on fire.

They attempted to put as much water on the flame as possible, but it was a losing battle. It was impossible to get enough on the flames, which now were engulfing the entire set of buildings.

"Move back," finally shouted Father Joseph. "We'll just have to let it burn itself out. There is nothing else we can do."

There were tears in everyone's eyes, as they backed up to a safe distance, and stood and watched their home go up in flame. All of the hard work they had done was disappearing right in front of their eyes. Many of them knelt down and began praying, quietly wondering why God would allow such a thing to happen.

Father Joseph was standing beside several of the brothers, watching the fire. "Everything," he remarked, "is gone. Everything that we have accomplished. Now we must start over."

"How?" queried one of the brothers.

"My friend, if we have the determination, we can do anything. With God on our side, and with our faith in his good judgement, we shall succeed."

"Sister Lucretia," continued Father Joseph, as he turned and looked directly at her, "get all the sisters together and take them to Cassella and Mariastein. Find a place for them to stay until we can get this place built back up."

"Yes Father," obediently replied Sister Lucretia, as she turned and began her new task.

"Brother Innocent," continued Father Joseph, "take a few men and go over to St. Joe. See if you can find the necessary building tools, hammers, saws, etc. Anything that you think we could use. I'm going to take a trip over to see Father John. I'll be back in a day or so. Then we can start."

Several days later, the process of rebuilding began. All of the remaining debris, from the fire, was cleaned up and new buildings were started. Within two months, the new convent was built to the point where the 14 sisters were able to move back in.

Everyone worked hard to accomplish the tasks at hand. Besides the building project, the fieldwork needed to be completed, as well as the yardwork and the garden. It was not long, and everything was back to normal. Father Joseph soon was back in his routine of visiting the various convents and tending to the priestly functions of the neighboring parishes.

AUGUST 22, 1854 — Mass was just completed at the sisters' chapel in Mariastein, and Father Willibald was leaving the chapel. He had been very sick during the first part of the year, but, as time went by, he progressively got better. There still was a slight shake in his walk, but he had no need for a cane.

There were two horse-drawn wagons setting in front of the chapel, in which Father Willibald was loading some of his personal belongings. He had his clothes, books, and some church vestments. One of the brothers was putting a newly built tabernacle onto the back of one of the wagons. Several sisters were loading the wagon with the basic necessities of foodstuffs, beds, bedding, cooking utensils, and table equipment.

As Father Willibald placed his books in the wagon, he remarked: "It is as though I am able to withdraw from Nazareth into the poor dwelling of the Mother of God, the place called Mary's Home."

"I think we are ready, Father," shouted Brother Martin, who at the age of 25, was one of the youngest in the group.

"Fine. Do you have my horse ready?"

"Yes. Brother Herman is bringing it over."

"Good. You drive one wagon and have Brother Herman drive the other."

"Sisters," noted Father Willibald, as he looked at the four nuns, standing beside the wagon, "two of you ride in one wagon, two in the other."

Everyone did as they were told, as Father Willibald mounted his horse.

"Let's go," commanded Father Willibald, as the group quietly departed the convent grounds.

The journey was interrupted only twice, with stopovers at Grunenwald and Himmelgarten, where Father Willibald was able to obtain several household items and church articles, for his new home.

At Himmelgarten, Father Joseph handed him a nicely wrapped package. Father Willi carefully unwrapped the box and found a beautiful handearved statue of the Sorrowful Mother, which Father Joseph had brought over from Baden.

"It's beautiful," exclaimed Father Willi, as he held it up. "Thank-you Joseph. I will always treasure it."

"Find a nice home for her."

"I will," replied Father Willi, as he placed it back in its wrapping and set the box in one of the wagons.

"Be sure to come over and visit me, when you get a chance," continued Father Willi.

"I'm sure I will. I've been going up to St. Anthony's about once every month. Maybe you can say Mass for them when I'm not there."

"Fine. I'll stop over and talk to them. But now I must get going. I want to get there before nightfall."

"God be with you, Willibald," exclaimed Father Joseph, as Father Willi mounted his horse and began to depart.

"Good-bye."

Father Joseph stood and watched as the wagons and Father Willi disappeared down the trail.

Mary's Home

CHAPTER XIII

The group arrived at their new destination about seven o'clock, that evening. It was cold and rainy, but that did not dampen their spirits. As the wagon approached the convent, the three brothers, who were already stationed there, came running out to greet them.

Immediately, before all else, Father Willi dismounted, walked over to the wagon, picked out the box, which had been given to him earlier, and went directly to the small chapel. Slowly walking up to the altar, he took the statue out of the box, and placed it on the altar. After looking at it for several seconds, he smiled and stated: "There," and then departed.

It was still light enough outside so that Father Willi was able to take a quick look at his new home. Father Joseph and the brothers had accomplished much in a short time. The small chapel, dedicated to the Sorrowful Mother, had a small lean-to on the back.

There was a small room in this lean-to that was to be used as an eating place for Father Willi and the brothers. The remainder of the building was used as a kitchen and bedroom for the sisters.

A short distance away from the chapel was a small building which was to be used as the dwelling for the brothers. It, like the rest, was made of rough logs. It was a humble setting, but quite sufficient for the men who knew how to be without temporal luxuries. Next to the brothers' dwelling were several storage sheds, as well as an outhouse.

In front of the chapel was a small log cabin, no more than 10 x 10. This was to serve as the home for Father Willi. It was built by Father Joseph and the brothers for the sole purpose of the residing priest.

Father Willi looked inside this empty room. Immediately, he returned to his wagon. After fumbling around for several seconds, he picked out a small wooden table and chair, and took them back into his new home, setting them near the window. Several of the brothers helped bring in the rest of his belongings, a small iron stove, and his personal items. Father Willi picked out several holy pictures from his bag and hung them on the wall. He then took a heavy blanket and placed it on his bed, which was nothing more than several boards, jutting out from the wall. These boards supported a badly-worn straw mattress. This bed was the perfect one for such a humble man.

As he sat down on his new bed, he noticed Brother Innocent carrying in the last of the boxes. "Thank-you, dear Brother Innocent. Just set it beside the table. That will do just fine."

"Is there anything else I can do for you?" queried Brother Innocent, as he walked over to Father Willi.

"Yes, there is one more thing. Could you tell everyone that there will be rosary, at the chapel, in an hour."

"Yes Father," replied Brother Innocent, as he turned and de- parted.

Father Willi remained seated on his bed. As he stared up at the picture of the Blessed Virgin Mary, he said aloud: "Beloved Mary, I want to thank-you and Father Joseph for all you have done for me." The next several months went along very smoothly at Mary's Home. The field work had been completed, twenty more acres of land had been cleared, and a new barn, with an attached shed, to be used as quarters for the brothers, was completed.

On the evening of October 19th, Father Willi, along with Brother Innocent, arrived at the Himmelgarten convent.

"Willibald, hello," stated Father Joseph, as he walked up to the wagon, to greet them.

"Hello, dear Joseph, my friend." "What brings you here?"

"We went to Grunenwald and Mariastein. Our supplies were running desperately low, so I thought I'd go on a little beggar tour and see what I could find. As you see, they have been most generous. Up until now, we only had one chair at the convent. Each day the brothers would carry it from my room to the church, and then back. The little item became known as the house and chapel equipment. Sister Clara was most kind and gave me another, as well as many other useful things."

"Is there anything I can provide you with?"

"Yes. A night's rest, and possibly, any blankets or winter coats that you can spare."

"You are more than welcome to spend the night."

"Brother Joseph," continued Father Joseph, as he turned his attention to one of the brothers, who was standing beside him, "go ring the bell for Sister Lucretia. I need to talk to her right away."

"Yes Father."

"Willibald, you stay with me tonight, and have Brother Innocent stay with the brothers. They'll take care of your horses," suggested Father Joseph, as the two men entered Father Joseph's small room.

Soon, Sister Lucretia arrived, and knocked on the door. Both priests came outside.

"Sister," stated Father Joseph, "could you please get Father any extra blankets and winter coats that you can find? He needs them by tomorrow morning."

"Do you have anything else that my sisters could use?" asked Father Willi, as he looked at Sister Lucretia.

"I have some Indiana paper money, that I can't use here with- out them deducting the value."

"Bring it all to me. I'll make good use of it."

Sister Lucretia departed, heading in the direction of the convent.
"Wasn't that your housekeeper?"

"Yes, it was. She is a kind sweet lady — a perfect example of what a nun should be. She was having some problems with her health, but now she seems to be doing quite well."

As Father Joseph finished speaking, Sister Lucretia returned with a handful of money. "Here it is, Father," she stated, as she handed it to Father Willi.

"Very good. God will reward you."

Sister Lucretia looked quite surprised. "Yes, but I thought you wanted to exchange it for me?"

"You knew from the outset that I am a beggar and never in my life have I been a moneychanger. This I can very well use for our poor brothers and sisters. At instructions, in your childhood, have you never heard that that which one gives as alms to the poor is employed far better and remains more secure than that which one ex- changes or places on interest. God will reward you."

Sister Lucretia looked at Father Willi, in amazement, and then smiled as she left.

"That was quite shrewd," noted Father Joseph. "Huh," shrugged Father Willi, "she doesn't mind."

"I have a little extra," continued Father Joseph, as he handed him a small bag of coins. "Don't tell anyone about this. Do as you wish with it."

"Thank-you Joseph. I will put it to good use."

The two men now walked back into Joseph's room, with Father Willi laying down on the bed and Father Joseph picking a spot out on the floor.

The next morning Father Willi and Brother Innocent returned to Mary's Home. From that time on, Father's health began to worsen. The coughing and hemorrhaging increased as the days went by, until it got to the point where he could not say Mass. This occurred on Saturday, November 11th.

The next day, Father Joseph was preparing to say the late Mass at the small church of St. Henry. He was standing in front of the church, greeting the parishioners, as they entered. As he was about to enter, he noticed Brother Joseph approaching on horseback.

"Father Joseph! Father Joseph!" he shouted. "You must come quick. Brother Innocent came over to the convent and told us that Father \Vi1Ii is very sick and near death. He would like for you to come, as soon as it's convenient."

Without saying a word, Father Joseph hurried into the church, walked to the front, turned around, and said: "I have just been in- formed that Father Willi is quite sick. I would like to go see him. In- stead of Vespers today, I want you to pray a rosary for him. I am going now to Mary's Home."

With that, he hurriedly departed the church, mounted his horse, and rode off to Himmelgarten, where he met Brother Innocent.

By evening, Father Joseph and Brother Innocent had arrived at Mary's Home.

Father Joseph entered Father Willi's room. Inside, lay Father Willi. Sitting beside him, in a chair, was Brother Peter Steiert. Be- side the bed stood a small table, on which was a small bell, crucifix, two candles and a tiny bottle of holy water.

Between coughs, Father Willi shouted with joy, as he seen Father Joseph enter. A smile appeared on his face, as he welcomed his friend.

"Don't say too much," cautioned Father Joseph. "It is time for you to rest."

"I have done plenty of resting. My time is near, Joseph. This cough is getting worse. I would like for you to hear my confession."

"Of course."

"Would you please stay tonight? Maybe then, you could say Mass in the morning."

"Alright," replied Father Joseph, as he patted Father Willi's hand.

"Then you can distribute communion to myself and the brothers and sisters."

"Have you had a visit from the doctor, lately?"

"I have no time or need for him. You would show me great favor in doing this. He would do more harm than good. God will do what is best for me. If you want to do a favor for me, please notify our spiritual father, that he should have everyone in the Precious Blood convents pray for me. That will be my medicine."

"Certainly, the doctor in Minster could help you."

"No, Joseph. I don't want to hear any more about that. I am ready. I only wish that you would hear my confession."

"Of course," replied Father Joseph, as he sat down beside him, in the chair that Brother Peter had just vacated.

As Father Joseph was hearing confession. Brother Peter walked outside, where Brother Innocent was standing.

"I'm afraid Father doesn't have much time left," sighed Brother Peter.

"I know," replied Brother Innocent. "All of our prayers don't seem to be helping."

"Maybe we're not saying the right prayers. Maybe we're asking for the impossible."

Just then, Father Joseph opened the door. As he was coming out, he turned back to Father Willi, and said: "I'll tell Father Salesius right away. He can then pass the word to all of the con- vents. I will also write a letter to Father Oschwald, in Wisconsin, and ask him and his people to pray for you."

Father Joseph closed the door and walked over to where the two brothers were standing.

"I'm going back to Himmelgarten now, he stated to the brothers. "I think Father will be alright for a while. I have to help Father Van den Broeck on some problems with the construction of the new church at St. Henry, and I also have to talk to Father Brunner. You men take care of Father Willi, and if anything should come up where you think I might be able to help, just come over and get me."

With those words, Father Joseph departed Mary's Home.

Father Willi's health did not change much over the next two months. He spent all of his time in bed, patiently awaiting his final departure. The terrible spells of coughing continued. Three brothers—Innocent, Peter, and Herman took turns caring for him, with Father Joseph visiting several times during this period.

On the evening of Thursday, December 14th, Father Joseph once again arrived at Mary's Home.

"Good evening," exclaimed Father Joseph, as he entered Father Willi's cell.
"Hello, Joseph."

"Is there anything I can do for you?"

"Certainly. Could I receive the Last Sacraments again?" "Why, yes."

"We'll have to postpone this task a little while, since you will remain with us tonight. At present, it is practically impossible since I am nearly choking. God is so good that he will give us time."

He again began to violently cough. Brother Peter and Brother Herman helped remove the excess from his mouth, while Father Joseph stood beside and watched.

Once the coughing subsided, father Willi again looked at Father Joseph, and asked: "Did you hear the bells this evening?"

"Yes, I did. They were very beautiful."
"Father Salesius sent them. We ring them morning, noon, and night, just like at Loewenberg."

"When I was coming up, I noticed that you had some construction projects that weren't finished."

"Yes, next spring, would you see to it that they get completed?" Father Joseph nodded his head in approval.

"Joseph when I die will you see to it that I'm buried up on that hill over there," continued Father Willi, as he pointed in that general direction. "I think it would be a beautiful spot for a cemetery."

"If that is what you wish."

"Brother Innocent knows where it is. I showed him the exact spot. Now, I would like to go to confession and to receive Holy Communion. I think the brothers should leave for a while. After my confession, prepare the necessary things, Joseph, and have the sisters pray for me in the chapel."

The brothers quietly left the room, while Father Joseph prepared to give the Last Sacraments.

After a short period of time, the brothers returned and they, with rather Joseph, remained at the side of Father Willi throughout the night, frequently having to raise him up from the bed, to help clear his throat.

At seven o'clock in the morning, of Friday, December 15th, Father Joseph got up from his chair and prepared to go offer Holy Mass at the sisters' chapel.

"Yes, do go," weakly suggested father Willi, "I have nothing more to say to you, but this: It is my wish that whatever I may yet receive from Germany, from home, as well as all other temporal goods, from whatever source they may be, all should revert to the Society of the Precious Blood."

"Are you sure you want to do something like that?" "Yes, that is the way Father Salesius wants it."

"Very well," noted Father Joseph, as he put on his ragged winter coat. "I'm going to hear confessions before Mass, so I better leave now. I'll be back as soon as possible."

Father Joseph departed with Brother Peter, leaving Brother Herman, alone, with Father Willi.

After Brother Herman lifted Father Willi's head up, to help ease the coughing, he again sat down, and asked: "Father, do you think I could go to confession and receive Holy Communion with the others?"

"Just now you cannot leave me. Have a bit of patience. The loving God will direct matters so that all will turn out for the best," replied Father Willi, as he again began to cough.

As soon as the coughing subsided, Father Willi was much more comfortable. He then looked at Brother Herman, and quietly said: "Now you may go, but, immediately after confession, you must return."

"I will, father, I will," he replied, as he got up and began to leave.

After Brother Herman left, Father Willi looked upward and spoke aloud: "Oh Lord, I am ready. Grant me the strength to make the journey. I am very much looking forward to it and hoping you will accept me with open arms. I have tried to lead a simple life, just like my dear and closest friend, Joseph. Ah, yes, Joseph. He has been such an inspiration to me, as well as to the others. He has all ways been there when needed. I have used him as an example to follow. Hopefully, when you decide to take me, he will be nearby, to bury me. That is all I ask, Lord. Amen."

He now closed his eyes and peacefully rested for several minutes, soon to be awakened by the return of Brother Herman, who, immediately upon entering, came over and sat down beside him.

"Ah, Brother Herman! Would you please raise me up so that I may communicate spiritually with Father Joseph, when he returns?"

"Yes, Father," replied Brother Herman, as he obediently held him in his arms. Both of them began to pray the 'Our Father' aloud. During the middle of the prayer, Father Willi abruptly stopped, smiled, and closed his eyes.

With tears flowing down his cheeks, Brother Herman rang the tiny bell, setting on the table. He then proceeded to hurriedly get up and run to the chapel, where Father Joseph had just completed the distribution of Holy Communion.

"Father Joseph," he shouted. "Come quick! Father Willi has died."
Father Joseph stopped the Mass, and gasped: "Oh Lord!" "Brother Herman," he continued, "ring the bells and let the people know." He then turned to the people in the church and said: "Everyone offer your prayers for the repose of his soul. Brother Peter, go to his room and prepare the body for burial. We will have the funeral tomorrow morning at ten. Brother Innocent, take another brother, and dig the grave, exactly where he told you to."

SATURDAY, DECEMBER 16, 1854 — The funeral procession was moving along, slowly, from the chapel to the final resting place. Many lay people from the surrounding area had arrived and were paying their final respects to the young priest whom they had come to love. Sorrow and pain shoz'ed deeply on their faces. As they gathered around the gravesite on this cold wintery day, Father Joseph stated: "My dear people, never forget the instructions and fine admonitions which, in so brief a time, you have received from him, in such an abundance. These were sufficient for entire life, to enable you to become holy. Always hold the priest in the highest es- teem. You have a pressing duty to respect priests highly because of their exalted position. Beseech God for good priests and send up ardent prayers to heaven for priests, whether they be living or dead. Always use to advantage the efforts and labors of priests who have left their fatherland, and all earthly gain, in order to search out the wandering sheep in this wilderness of America. Every sinner, even the greatest, could yet be saved through the priest. In this life, the priest could open heaven to everyone. In heaven, however, the priest can no longer be of assistance. With death, the keys to heaven fall from the hands of the priest so that he can no longer open paradise to others."

As Father Joseph continued to speak, the beautiful sound of the church bells could be heard, in the background. He now took the holy water sprinkler, from Brother Innocent, and blessed the wooden casket, while saying several prayers, in Latin. As the grave was being filled, the church bells ceased.

Father Joseph placed a wooden cross upon the burial mound, and continued: "In the Book of Wisdom, chapter five, the Holy Spirit has revealed and handed down through Holy Mother, the Church, an epitaph regarding the death of this just man. 'But the just man, though he dies early, shall be at rest. For the age that is honorable comes not with the passing of time, nor can it be measured in terms of years. Rather, understanding is the hoary crown for men, and an unsullied life, the attainment of old age. He who pleased God was loved; he who lived among sinners was transported — snatched away, lest wickedness pervert his mind or deceit beguile his soul. For the witchery of paltry things obscures what is right and the whirl of desire transforms the innocent mind. Having become perfect in a short while, he reached the fullness of a long career; for his soul was pleasing to the Lord, therefore he sped him out of the midst of wickedness."

Father Joseph paused for several seconds and looked down at the grave. Folding his hands, he made the sign of the cross, and quietly departed, being followed by the others.

As he was returning to Father Willi's room, he was talking with Brother Innocent.

"You know, I'm going to have to take temporary charge of this place. I believe three simple and holy priests could fittingly care for the two convents, St. Henry's, St. Joseph's, St. Mary's at Philothea, and St. Anthony. This would net a salary of $900.00 of which $300.00 should be allotted to Mary's Home. I am going to ask Father Salesius to appoint Schueli, as a replacement for Father Willi. With Van den Broeck and myself, I think we three could very well take care of everything in this area."

On January 1, 1855, while Father Joseph was again at Mary's Home, the new replacement arrived. Much to the chagrin of Father Joseph, it was not father Rochus Schueli, but rather the young Father Patrick Henneberry.

"What are you doing here?" asked Father Joseph, as Father Henneberry was dismounting from his horse.

"I've come to take over." "What happened to Rochus?" "He could not come."

"This is no place for you. You are too young and weak, and inexperienced, to handle this place and St. Anthony's."

"I'm sorry you feel that way."

"I'm going to have to write a letter to Father Salesius. I purposely requested for Father Schueli. He can at least understand these people. You hardly know any German."

"You must remember, Joseph, that we are in America. English will be the language of everyone, very soon. German is spoken in Europe. It will not last here."

"Foolishness! You young priests think such silly things sometimes. I think Father Salesius always favors you guys and by-passes us older priests. Someday, he'll regret it. I think he is too easily influenced by you, and I'm not afraid to tell him."

Father Joseph immediately went to the stable and got his horse ready. Father Henneberry stood there, in utter amazement, as his colleague got on the horse and departed, without saying another word.

From Mary's Home, Father Joseph headed straight for Grunenwald. As he approached the church grounds, he was met by several brothers, Michael Homburger, Joseph Hog, John Wiederle, John Seifert, Peter Bender, and Blaise Zimmerman, all heading in the opposite direction.

"Where are you men headed for₇ " l f lqLt1I"e d Father Joseph.

"Hello, Father Joseph," stated 23-year-old John Seifert. "We're on our way to help one of the neighbors, up the road. He had a fire and lost everything."

"Have any of you heard anything about being transferred?" "Not yet," replied 30-year-old Blaise Zimmerman.

Looking over at 33-year-old John Wiederle, Father Joseph continued: "And how is my cousin?"

"Fine, Joseph."

"I'm hoping that, someday, I'll be able to have all of you working for me," Joseph continued.

"Father Joseph," interrupted the tall lanky 23-year-old Brother Peter Bender, "have you seen my brother, Anton, lately?"

"Yes, I see him every Sunday. His family is doing fine." "I do miss them all."

"Well, it won't be long, and you all will be back together," consoled Father Joseph, as he patted young Peter on the back.

A Visit With Father Brunner

CHAPTER XIV

March 17, 1855- Himmelgarten Convent-Father Joseph was sitting by his table, in deep thought. He was not feeling very well, so he decided to stay in his room, rather than go over to the retreat that Father Salesius was giving at the chapel. After staring at the crucifix on the wall, for several minutes, he opened his small black book, which had been lying the table, and, silently, began to read.

Just then, there was a knock on the door. Father Joseph looked up and said: "Come in!" In walked Father Salesius. "I missed you at the meeting, Joseph."

"Here, please sit down," offered Father Joseph.

"Thank you" Noted Father Salesius, as he sat down in Joseph's chair, while Joseph sat down on his bed.

"Lately, I have been worried about you," continued Father Salesius. "I have had several reports nothing that you are disagreement with some of our priests. What is the matter?"

"I don't know. It just seems to me that the values of these young guys are really deteriorating. I can't believe some of their ideas. They don't realize how stupid they are."

"Is it really that bad?"

"Yes. It is really bothering me. Several of them even had the gall to try drinking and smoking. Why, that is outrageous! They just don't realize how little time is left. They don't have time to be messing with such foolishness."

"Don't let these little things bother you."

"They do, " shot back Father Joseph, as he slapped his hands on the bed, while jumping up. "They do."

"One thing you must learn, is to have patience. There will always be minor problems, but you must deal with them patiently. Some of them will pass over by themselves, others you will have to use patience. There are malcontents in many places. The convents and seminaries are not immune. For example, take

133

Maria Camp. I was forced to remove several troublemakers and replace them with more docile brothers. I told Father Ganther to rule them with kindness and they would obey him. I tell you the same thing. Be kind and you will be rewarded."

"Sometimes that doesn't work."

"Have you been up to see Father Rochus?" asked Father Salesius, in an attempt to change the subject.

"Yes. I was there last week. He is doing a fine job. Much better than Henneberry every could."

"Why don't you think much of Father Patrick?"

"I have nothing against him. He is a very pious man, but he is too weak for this type of work. He can't speak German, and he doesn't really understand the people around here."

"He has been trying to learn. It just takes time."

"We don't have that much time."

"Did Father Rochus finish those construction projects?"

"No, not yet. I don't think that it might be good idea if you would send Father John over there to complete the work. It would probably only take about one month."

"He's up at Thompson, now. I agree. He should be sent. I'll write to him and get his opinion."

"What do you mean, get his opinion. What is wrong with my opinion?"

"Nothing. I just think he would know more of what is going on."

"Have you no faith in me? Why was I ever chosen as one of your consultors? I never seem to have any influence over what you decide."

"That is not true, Joseph. I always value your judgement."

"Only when it comes to matters of money. Then I'm good enough."

"Joseph, Joseph. Do I sense jealousy?"

"No, not at all. I just feel that I should have more say in what goes on in the Society."
"But you've only been a priest for five years."

"That should make no difference. We've known each other for a lot longer than that. That should be worth something."

"It is, Joseph. It is."

"I don't believe you," shot back Father Joseph, as he stood up and looked straight at Father Salesius.

Father Salesius stared back at Father Joseph, and then said: "I plan on returning to Europe this summer, and don't know when I'll be back. I have decided to send Father Ringele to Defiance and replace him with

Father Kramer. Father Herbstritt is going to Grunenwald and Father Ruf to St. Johns. Father Kunkler will take charge of Maria Stein, while you will be going to Liverpool." "Liverpool? Why there?"

"I need a strong-minded priest there, to care for the needs of those people. They are having some problems and I believe you can take care of them."
"But that is so far away."

"You will be in full control. You won't have to deal with any of the problems of the brothers or sisters, or other priests. It will give you time to think things over."

"When is this supposed to take place?"

"Next June."

"Are you trying to get me out of your hair?"

"No. Absolutely not."

"Well, I want you to know, I don't like it."

"You have no choice in the matter. The change will do you some good."

"Do you remember that sermon about the Swabians, who came into the valley? There was a large pond there and a walnut tree stood at the edge of the water. The nuts were just ripe, and the outer shell had split open. These Swabians had never seen such a thing before and thought that the nuts, holding their mouth ajar, were suffering from thirst. How could they help them? One of them had an idea. Why not pull the top of the tree into the water? And so, the heaviest one climbed the tree first, almost to the top, another followed, hanging to the feet or the first, and so on, until the living chain almost reached the water. The tree did not bend much, and the hands of the top man were slowly slipping. He called to those below him: Hold tight, while I spit into my hands. You can imagine what happened. Now, are you that top man? Do you need to spit on your hands? Are they slipping?"

"Joseph, you are talking nonsense. There are problems out there that I feel only you can correct. There are two factions arguing amongst themselves. I just think that you can mend things up."

"But, what about everything here? Father Van den Broeck and I are in the middle of supervising the construction of the new church at St. Henry's. I have several unfinished projects here at Himmelgarten, plus there is work to be done at St. Joseph's and St. Mary's. Who will do that?"
"You will get it done before you leave."
"Huh, I suppose."
"I also wanted you to know that I had to dismiss Brother Joseph Riesterer, up at Maria Camp. He was not getting along with the others. We are also having difficulties with Marder and Haener."
"I find that hard to believe. I know them all, and they have always been perfect, God-fearing Catholics."
"Ah, but people change. The environment in which they live have changed tremendously since they arrived in America." "I'll have to talk to Mr. Riesterer."
"That will do no good."
"I think it will."
"Tell me, Joseph," continued Father Salesius, in another attempt to change the subject, "how has Father Stephen been doing since he came here?"
"Father Falk is a very good priest. He does have some dumb ideas, like the other young priests, but, with my guidance, he'll be alright."

"Father John is going to be in charge, while I'm gone."

"Why him? Why not me? Why not let me run things while you're gone?"

"Father John has much more experience. Besides, he knows how to handle the younger priests and brothers."

"And I don't?"

"No Joseph. You are very set in your ways, and no matter what someone will tell you, you still hold onto your own opinion. You aren't as open-minded as Father John."

"Sometimes you can make me so disgusted," noted Father Joseph, as he paced back and forth.

"Are you having any problems here that you have not told me?"

"No, not really. Some of the brothers think that I'm too strict, but they still do whatever I tell them. I never have any problem with the sisters."

"You have nine brothers here, right?"

"Yes. I have Karl Schuler, John Brans, Aloysius Kiefer, Joseph Renz, Max Hummel, Frederick Wiersch, John Wiesler, Francis Helg, and Jacob Zissener."

"Which ones give you the most problems?"

"The two youngest ones."

Just then, 34-year-old Brother Aloysius, a short, stocky man with a full beard, came running into the room. "Father Joseph," he exclaimed, "Brother Maximillian is hurt."

"Father Joseph jumped up and followed Brother Aloysius out the door, toward the small meadow, between the stable and one of the storage sheds, where 28-year-old Maximillian Hummel was lying, in the lap of 33-year-old Brother Jacob.

"What happened?" asked Father Joseph, as he knelt down beside Brother Max.

"We were cutting a tree down, " exclaimed the tall lanky Brother Jacob. "When it came down, Brother Max slipped, and a large branch hit him."

"Where does it hurt?"

"Mt ribs, Father," weakly replied Brother Max, who was showing signs of grave and excruciating pain.

"Let me see," continued Father Joseph, as he felt Brother Max's ribs.

"I don't think you broke anything. Probably just bruised them. Is this where they hurt?"

"Ah, ouch. Yes. Yes."

Father Joseph kept his hand on the sore ribs and quietly said a short prayer.

Looking at Brother Jacob, he continued: "Take him to his room. He'll be alright."

While Brother Jacob helped Brother Max back to his room, Father Joseph got up and began walking back to where Father Salesius was. Along the way, he was met by Father Salesius, who asked: "Is everything alright?"

"Yes. Brother Max had an accident, but I think I took care of it."

"What did you do?"

"You'll see, replied Father Joseph, as the two men went back into Father Joseph's room.

"Say Father," continued Father Joseph, "I've had several men ask me when you were going to write down the rules for the Society, so that they would know what to do."

"I'm working on it. But we really don't need one. For myself, if I have no printed or written paper at hand, I note what is best that I, as a priest of the Society, should do or should not do. If I were to console or pacify myself that I can get by before the judgement seat of God with 'I didn't know,' I would someday discover that this was unavailing self-deception."

"You mean, we should do what we think best?"

"Yes, Joseph, you are wise enough to decide what is correct."

"But what am I supposed to tell the younger priests when they ask why we do certain things in such a way, when it is not written down?"

"Before I leave, I'll write a letter to everyone. I'll try and explain it to them. Our Society has come a long way since its beginning. We have accomplished much with little resources. With the help of the Blessed Virgin Mary, we have prospered. We now have ten convents and farms, with over 300 people. Surely, with that many people under our supervision, we are bound to have a few malcontents. It will all work out. I assure you. Always remember to place a big emphasis on silence. Avoid all novelties. Tolerate no abuses or malpractices. See that everyone does their daily spiritual exercises of 1) morning examin, 2) evening examin, 3) a visit to the Blessed Sacrament, 4) have a definite time set aside for study. If you follow these basic rules, you should have no problems. Always strive for uniformity. When you are saying Mass, after reading the gospel, you should have a 5 to 10 minutes talk on clarifying what the gospel means. Keep your sermon between ½ and ¾ hour. No more, no less. Your Sunday vespers should not exceed an hour. Always remember that the more time people spend with religion, the less time they have to spend on other things that might be dangerous to their spiritual well-being. When they are occupied with religious matters, the devil cannot influence them."

"I have always tried to do as you wished. But it is the other priests that I have the problems with. They are not like you and me. They are too open to new ideas. They are too readily influenced by outside interference."

"Then, it's up to you, to try and straighten them out, before it is too late."

"Then I should be put in charge when you leave for Europe."

"It is the responsibility of each member to see to it that no other member falls along the wayside, whether it be a priest, sister, or brother. You don't have to be the Superior in order to be the watchdog over everyone."

"I sometimes wonder if I shouldn't leave here and go see Father Ambrose. He brought his group over here last August. I received a letter from him last week. They are having a pretty rough time up there in the wilderness of Wisconsin."

"How many people are up there?"

"He came over with a group of over 100, but he only has about 70, or so, that are still with him."

"What does he plan on doing?"

"He set up a colony that will be able to support itself, without outside help. According to him, he has a paradise on Earth, where his followers can practice their Catholic faith, without being interfered with by anyone. It really sounds like a good idea. I would like very much to go up and see how he is doing.

"Perhaps someday you will get the chance," suggested Father Salesius, "but you have so much to do down here for now."

"Just then, Brother Max came walking into the room, accompanied by Brother Jacob.

"Look Father!" exclaimed Father Jacob, as he pointed at Brother Max.

Father Salesius was quite surprised to see that Brother Max was walking, without assistance.

"I feel much better," remarked Brother Max, as he looked first, at Father Joseph, and then at Father Salesius. "I laid down for several minutes, and then felt the pain go away. Surely, it must have been your prayers, Joseph."

"Father Joseph just looked at Father Salesius and smiled.

Liverpool

CHAPTER XV

Father Joseph remained in charge of the Himmelgarten Convent until June of 1856, continuing to make his rounds with visits on foot, to the neighboring parishes, where he would fervently spread the holy gospel and follow the strict guidelines of Father Salesius. He continued to place a heavy emphasis on contemplation and would always stress that point to whomever he came in contact with. He was a fine example of a gentle, pious, strong-minded priest, a priest that everyone came to honor and respect. During his tenure at Himmelgarten Convent, he grew to become very close with the parishioners of the small community of St. Joseph's, where on the morning of June 6, 1856, he had said, what he thought was to be his final Mass at the Church. Outside the small log church, the entire congregation was awaiting the appearance of Father Joseph. Everyone had a sad look on their face, as they knew that they probably would not see their beloved priest for some time to come, if ever.

They were all mingling on this warm sunny Sunday morning — the men with the men and the women with the women, while the children played. As Father Joseph came out of the church, he was approached by Mr. Riesterer, Mr. Scheidecker, Mr. Grismer, and Mr. Anton Doll. "We are all going to miss you, Father," noted Mr. Scheidecker, in a shaky voice.

"Yes, Victor, and I shall miss all of you. But I shall return. I had a dream, and in it, I came back. So, wait three years. My dreams always seem to come true. Always remember me in your prayers, as I will you, and don't forget the time is short on this Earth. Our reward is waiting. Always remember what was said in the Book of Zephaniah: T will completely sweep away all things from the face of the Earth, says the Lord. I will sweep away man
and beast, I will sweep away the birds of the sky, and the fishes of the sea. I will overthrow the wicked, I will destroy mankind from the face of the Earth. Remember, silence in the presence of the Lord God. For near is the day of the Lord."

By now, all of the people had gathered around him. His eloquent speaking always seemed to arouse their interest, and today was no exception.

"Fear not, my people," he continued, "the time is at hand, but I will be with you. Be patient and prepare yourselves."

Everyone tried to personally say good-bye with a handshake, hug, or kiss. Father Joseph stood near the church entrance and repeatedly thanked them as they walked by, in single file.

"You have been an inspiration to all of us," exclaimed the widow, Sophia Doll. "We all feel a sense of numbness at your leaving."

"Don't worry, Mrs. Doll, I will soon be back. My job is not yet done."
"Good-bye, Father," noted Sophia as she shook hands.

The next person to talk to Father Joseph, was Michael Doll, the 14-year-old son of Sophia. "Good-bye," he exclaimed.

"Ah, Michael, my young man. When I return, I hope to see you at Himmelgarten. You have been a good child and we could always use men like you in the priesthood."

Michael politely smiled and left.

"Well, Father," stated 32-year-old Joseph Weis, who had been standing beside him, "If you would like, I could drive you back to Himmelgarten."

"No, Mr. Weis. Today, I would like to walk. It gives me a good chance to contemplate, and I have a lot to think about."

"Very well," replied Mr. Weis, as he shook hands, and added:
"Good-bye then."
"Good-bye."

The people slowly departed the church grounds, while Father Joseph began heading down the trail which he had so often traveled over the past four years. It was a beautiful day for a walk. The abundant wildlife was seen everywhere. The trees and shrubbery were at their greenest. Wildflowers were in full bloom. The sky was clear, and the wind was calm. It was a perfect setting for Father Joseph to think about what lie ahead, to think about his future, to reflect on his past, to think about his shortcomings, as well as on his
accomplishments.

As Father was in the midst of humming a tune, he arrived back at Himmelgarten. He immediately went to his room, where all of his personal belongings were packed and waiting to be carried away. He picked everything up and carried them out to the awaiting
wagon, which one of the brothers had just brought over from the stable. Setting them on the back of the wagon, he noticed Sister Lucretia approaching. He walked to the side of the wagon and awaited her arrival.

"Oh Father," she lamented, "please don't go."

"Now Lucretia, you know that I must. From what Capeder told me, I'm going to have my hands full out there, but Father Salesius has faith in me, so I can't let him down."

"But, what about us? What are we to do?"
"Do as Father Van den Broeck tells you."

"No one can replace you."

"That's not true. I, like everyone else, have weaknesses. One of them is that I have become too attached to the people of St. Joe, as well as to some of the brothers and sisters here, at Himmelgarten. It hurts me very much to be leaving them now, but I feel relieved
when I know I shall one day return. Take good care of everything here. I am leaving the relics here and entrust you with their safekeeping. I will keep you in my prayers, and I hope you remember me in yours. If you should happen to see Mary, please give her my regards. Good-bye now, my dear sister."

"Good-bye Father Joseph," she replied, as she gave him a hug. Father Joseph got aboard the wagon and began to leave. Farewells were given by the brothers and sisters, as he rode down the trail.

Once away from the convent grounds, he stopped and looked back. After several moments of quiet thought, he proceeded on his journey.

The trip to his new destination was long and arduous for the 55-year-old priest. His goal, Liverpool, was a small village located about 40 miles east of St. Alphonse. Three miles from town, he found the small German settlement, which surrounded the small brick church of St. Martin, a beautiful structure of 40' x 60', which had been built under the supervision of Father Capeder, back in 1849. Father Capeder had also been responsible for the construction of a small rectory, next to the church.

A few miles away, was located the Abbeyville mission of St. Mary, built in 1842. It was a small brick church of 24' x 40'. Most of the families soon became affiliated with St. Martins, simply because Mass was held there more often.

In 1849, when the question of building a new church arose, certain members disagreed as to the location. Therefore, they returned to their former mission church. This was the situation that Father Joseph entered. It was going to be up to him to take care of both missions.

"Why have I been honored with such a task?" asked Father Joseph to himself, as he thought about his predicament. "How could Father Salesius do this to me? Am I to be eternally damned?"

When he rode up to the front of the rectory, he was greeted by three middle-aged men: Mr. Kramer, Mr. Huttinger, and a Mr. Weigel.

"Hello," greeted Mr. Kramer. "You must be Father Albrecht?"

"Yes, that is correct."

"My name is Mr. Kramer, and this here is Mr. Huttinger and Mr. Weigel. Welcome to St. Martins."

Father Joseph got down from the wagon and looked around, and then asked: "Are you the trustees?"

"Yes," replied the heavy-set Mr. Weigel. "We are a small parish at present but are hoping that the people at St. Mary's decide to come back to us."

"Where is St. Mary's?"

"Across the creek, a few miles down the road," pointed out Mr. Weigel.

"I've been told the problems, but I must check them out for myself."

As the three men escorted Father Joseph into the rectory, Mr. Kramer continued: "This will be your new home."

The rectory was a small log building, simple, yet nice. It was sparsely furnished with a short wooden bed in one corner, near a window. Beside the bed was a small kneeling bench. Directly in front of that, was a beautiful hand-carved crucifix. Next to the kneeler, was the fireplace, with all the necessary cooking utensils hanging on a nearby wall. In the middle of the room was a large wooden table, with four poorly built chairs around it. In the opposite corner was a small table and chair. Beside the table was wooden box, filled with an assortment of papers.

"You'll find all of the church records in this box," noted Mr. Kramer, as he pointed at the box. "All the baptisms, marriages, deaths, financial reports, and the like."

"Alright," replied Father Joseph. "If you would excuse me, gentlemen, the trip has been very hard on me, and I am very tired. I would like to rest now. Please pass the word that we'll have Mass on Sunday at 8 o'clock."

"We will," replied Mr. Huttinger, as the three men departed. Father Joseph now sat down by the small table and quietly thought. "Oh, Father Ambrose, what would you do if you were in this situation? How did I ever let myself get in such a fix? I feel like
I'm out in the middle of nowhere. Oh God, why do you torture me so? Is it because of my sins? How can I make it up to you? Are you testing me? If you are, surely, I will fail. Please, make this easier for me."

The next morning, after checking out the church, Father Joseph decided to make a trip over to St. Mary's. The two-mile trip didn't take very long, but it was treacherous. The trail ran through a densely wooded area. Approximately half-way there, he had to cross a fast-moving, five-foot-deep creek. He carefully made it across and continued on his way, soon arriving at the small brick church.

He entered the building and knelt down by the altar, which had a statue of Jesus, Joseph, and the Blessed Virgin Mary on it. After a short prayer, he got up and walked back out. He placed a small note on the church door, and then returned to St. Martins.

The situation of Father Joseph did not change much during his tenure at St. Martins. His lifestyle soon fell into a pattern. On one Sunday he would say Mass at St. Martins, the next at St. Mary's.

On the evening of December 1, 1856, he sat down by his small table, and began to write a letter to his close friend, Mr. Adam Edelmann, of St. Rosa. As he was writing he read aloud: "My friends Adam and Mary Ann, if I otherwise had no responsibilities and were only to give missions, I would like this place. I had intended to ask the Bishop, when he was here, to absolve me from my priestly vows.

He ordained me, as you know, and at that time already I felt the burden. I feel somewhat easier now, but if I would be free, I think I could find a place where I could work out my salvation."

He stopped writing and paused for several minutes. He thought to himself, how much nicer it was here, not having to put up with the young upstart priests, who, at every opportunity, would try to introduce new ideas. I am gratified, he thought, for the chance given me to be able to think about what I have done, what I am doing now, and what I should be doing in the future. The more I think of it, the more I believe that I should follow the ways of Father Oschwald.

Surely, Father Salesius wants to put me aside. I just know it. If I would start my own congregation, I would have the power and the control. I have given much to the Society, and what have I received in return? A chance to live the lonely life of a parish priest, out in the country, away from all of my close friends. I should be in charge of the entire Society, while Father Salesius is gone. Surely, Wittmer had something to do with that. I'll show him. Someday I'll be back.

Father Joseph now returned to writing the letter. Shortly thereafter, he put his pen down on the table, set the paper aside, and laid down on his bed. He continued his priestly functions at Liverpool, until May of 1859. During this time, he was successful in several undertakings. In 1858, he supervised the construction of a new parochial school near St. Martins, but he never did accomplish his goal of combining the two parishes.

Return To Himmelgarten

CHAPTER XVI

What a joyful moment when Father Joseph read the letter, informing him that he was being transferred back to Himmelgarten, in May 1859! It seems that Father Van den Broeck had been too strict with the sisters, and this led to his transfer. Father Joseph was to immediately return to Himmelgarten, while Father Van den Broeck was to replace him at St. Martins. Father Joseph quickly prepared to leave, being anxious to return to his favorite parish of St. Joseph. He was also anxious to see how much things had changed at Himmelgarten, since his departure of three years ago. He was overjoyed at the thought of returning to the 'Black Swamp Area', where stagnant pools in the summertime, aided in the appearance of millions of mosquitoes. He was overjoyed at returning to the place where he had developed such a wonderful rapport with the parishioners. He could hardly wait to get back to the job of influencing the brothers and sisters under his wings. He could hardly wait to get back to recruiting new men and women for vocations.

Upon his arrival, he was met by several brothers, who happily aided their leader back into his house.

"From the looks of things, there have been some changes around here," he noted, as he looked around.

"Yes Father," replied Brother Innocent. "Father Van den Broeck and Father Ruf kept us very busy."

"Is Father Engelbert around?"

"Yes," answered Brother Peter Steiert. "He is saying Mass at the chapel. He should be back soon."

"I see my house has changed quite a bit," continued Father Joseph, as he looked around the room. Just then, Father Engelbert Ruf entered.

"Welcome back, Joseph," he exclaimed, as he walked up to the tall Father Joseph and shook his hand.

"Hello, Engelbert."

"I am glad to see you back here. Things have become quite hectic. Maybe now, they will return to normal."

"It seems that things have been that way all over. I have heard many reports these past few years about our Society. It seems that Father Salesius should get back here as soon as he can. I don't think Father John can handle all of the problems."

"I agree with you," noted Father Engelbert.

"Say, could you tell me what happened to Father Meyer?"

"Anton left the Society and is now a priest in Wisconsin."

"That's too bad. He is a fine man and priest. He sent me a letter while I was out at Liverpool. He told me of his disgust with the idea that priests have to render account to the sisters, and that the main purpose of the Precious Blood priests was to look out after the sisters. He also could not see why all the goods of the priests and brothers, their inheritances, and stipends, and the like, should be shared with the sisters. I tell you, Engelbert, he had some good arguments. I agree with him completely. I'm sure there are others who feel the same way."

"We've lost Meyer, Obermueller, Falk, and Dambach," continued Father Engelbert.

"Doesn't Father Salesius know what is happening?"
"I'm sure he does. But he probably can't do anything about it."
"If there aren't some changes made soon, he'll probably be losing more priests. Mark my words."

Soon, everything was back to normal at Himmelgarten. Father Joseph was in full command of the situation, and everyone was satisfied and content. The surrounding parishes of St. Henry, and St. Joseph, were also pleased at the return of their saintly Father
Joseph.

Much to the chagrin of Father Joseph, Father Francis deSales Brunner was never to return to America. On December 29, 1859, he died at the Precious Blood convent, at Schellenberg.

The news of his death was a deep blow to Father Joseph. He had tried to model his life after that of Father Salesius, for he greatly admired the man. Now his closest friend had departed this world.

What was he to do?

On the 23rd of August 1860, the entire Precious Blood congregation of priests assembled at the Mariastein Convent, with the sole purpose of electing a successor to Father Salesius.

The group was slowly walking from the church, where Father John had just performed Mass, heading towards the brothers' quarters.

Father Joseph was walking amongst this group, talking with Father Schueli and Father Capeder.

"Well, my friends," stated Father Joseph, "today is the day we decide who is going to become our leader. Have you given it much thought?"

"Not really," replied Father Rochus.

"I would imagine that Father Wittmer would be the most likely candidate," added Father Capeder.

"Yes, I suppose you are correct," replied Father Joseph, "but Father John would not be the ideal Superior. We need someone who is strong-minded, someone who has respect from everyone, someone who knows how to handle money wisely, someone who has the desire to carry out all the wishes of Father Salesius. We need someone who is the perfect example for the others to follow."

"Are you suggesting Joseph Albrecht?" queried Father Rochus, as he smiled.

"Yes," bluntly replied Father Joseph. "Father John may have been the vice-Superior, but I have been a very close friend and confidant of Father Salesius. Not only that, but I have given large donations to the Society, and this would be a way that the Society could
repay me."

"I wouldn't get my hopes up too high," cautioned Father Capeder. "There are a lot of young priests here who probably think you are too old for the job."

"One is never too old for a job. With age, comes experience. With age, comes wisdom."

"Yes, but is that what these younger priests think?" asked Father Capeder.

The group now arrived at the meeting place, outside of the brothers' house. They congregated in a circle, around Father Wittmer. After sitting down on the ground, they listened to Father John, who had remained standing.

"Gentlemen," he began, "we have an important task at hand.

Hopefully, you have all had a chance to think about whom you would like to succeed Father Salesius. It was his wish that we would all have a say in this matter."

As Father John began handing out small pieces of paper to everyone, he continued: "Take this paper and write down the person, whom you think would best be able to conduct the duties of Superior. When you have this done, place the paper in this box, and I will check the ballots."

Each of the men busily wrote down a name and then placed the paper in a box.
Father Joseph had high hopes and aspirations of becoming the Superior, but the outcome did not turn out in his favor. Father Andrew Kunkier was elected. When the results were given, Father Joseph got up from his place and stormed away from the meeting, not even remaining for the High Mass, which Father Kunkier was to offer, nor staying around to listen to the administering of the oath of allegiance, nor offering his pledge of obedience, respect, and loyalty, to the new Superior. He hurriedly walked to his horse, mounted it and left for Himmelgarten, saying not a word to anyone. The outrage and bitterness of this defeat were always to linger in his mind.

He was now sure that it would only be a matter of time before he would have to leave. Father Joseph returned to Himmelgarten, a changed man. He continued to supervise the work of the brothers and sisters, and to offer Holy Mass at the convent, and the surrounding parishes, but everyone could see that, inside, he was showing signs of a struggle.

As time went by, he became more and more embittered with the conditions of the Society. He would spend much time with the brothers and sisters of Himmelgarten, and the parishioners of St. Joseph, but tried to avoid, as much as possible, anything that had to do with the Society.

He was still in charge of the Himmelgarten convent, but he allowed the 24-year-old Father Joseph Dwenger, to take care of the seminarians, who resided at Himmelgarten. This young priest was responsible for teaching nine students in becoming priests. In 1860, these students were: Henry Best, age 27; Barney Dickman, age 20; Bernard Rumalseling, age 20; Christian Fine, age 32; Peter Sont, age 24; Gregory Moore, age 22; Henry Drees, age 30; and William Strulcer, age 19.

Father Dwenger took care of their needs, while Father Joseph took care of the spiritual and temporal needs of the brothers, which included: Peter Steiert, age 48; Joseph Riley, age 49; Philip Rist, age 15; Edward Klarer, age 30; Innocent Moorman, age 34; and
John Frey, age 28. He also continued to be the confessor of the sisters, who now numbered 31 at Himmelgarten, as well as to the sisters of the surrounding convents.

The sisters, in their habit, which consisted of a black dress, black sunbonnet, an elbow-length cape, and a crucifix around the neck, were easily influenced by the powerful oratory of Father Joseph.

The brothers, in their simple garb of a black suit jacket, black pants, and black shoes, or boots, also continued to admire and respect Father Joseph.

Early in the spring of 1861, as the American Civil War was breaking out, Father Dwenger realized that Himmelgarten was not the ideal location for a seminary, and went out, along with a certain Christopher Schunk, in search of a more suitable place. They succeeded in their task.

One day, while Father Joseph was standing along the fenceline, watching the brothers diligently planting the crops, Father Dwenger approached. "Father Joseph," he shouted, "we have permission to buy the old Emlin Institute. It will be an excellent location for a seminary."

"Good," dejectedly replied Father Joseph. "The sooner, the better."

Father Dwenger looked surprised. "I thought you'd be happy for us."

"I am. I am."

Father Dwenger knew better. He could sense that something was bothering Father Joseph, but he did not know exactly what.

"Could I have the use of some of the brothers, to help fix up the place?"

"No," Father Joseph bluntly replied. "I need them all for the crops."

"Then, we'll do it ourselves," shot back Father Dwenger, as he turned and departed.

Father Joseph stood and watched Father Dwenger for several seconds, and then turned to mount his horse, which had been tied up alongside the fence. He got on and headed off in the direction of St. Joseph's.

Upon arrival at the church grounds, Father Joseph notices several men laying the groundwork for a new church. He had discussed this topic with the parishioners, and now they had finally decided to go ahead with the venture. It was to be a brick church and was to be located right in front of the old log church.

"Well, Mr. Weis," noted Father Joseph, as he dismounted, "do you think we can have it done before winter sets in?"

"I'm not sure," replied John, "it will all depend on how much free help we can get from the other parishioners."

"Well, I said last Sunday that there is no hurry. We can still use the log church. Tell me, is there anything I can do?"

"No Father. You have already done more than your share. It is our responsibility now to accomplish the task. Mr. Bender and Mr. Boedigheimer are good masons. I'm sure we can manage. If a problem should arise, we'll ask for your help."

"Very well," replied Father Joseph, as he looked around at the completed work, and then continued: "Have you men seen the town site plots that the Bishop had drawn up?"

"Yes, I have," replied Mr. Weis. "Several people have already bought lots and have given the money to Father Dwenger."

"I don't know why Dwenger should have anything to do with this parish," objected Father Joseph. "The proceeds from the sale of those lands are supposed to help pay for this new church.

The Bishop knew that this is my church, and not Dwengers. He continually tries to slap me in the face and make it look like I'm not needed."

"I'm sure he figures you are overworked as it is, Father," replied Mr. Weis.
"Huh. I don't think so."

As Father Joseph walked around, inspecting the work, he continued: "Are you getting the clay from the schoolyard, for the bricks?"

"Yes Father, we are doing just as you suggested."

"Good. That should save us some money."

"Say Father," interrupted the 30-year-old Anton Bender, "did you hear what happened to Mr. Johe, yesterday?"

"No, I didn't."

"There was a group of soldiers around looking for young men, who haven't volunteered to go fight for Lincoln," continued Anton, as he wiped the sweat off his forehead. "They went to Joseph's house and searched it. He almost suffocated in a wooden trunk, because his wife was sitting on the keyhole, while the soldiers were there."

"Is he alright?"

"Yes, he's fine now. Luckily, the soldiers didn't stay very long. After they left, Mrs. Johe got up and Joseph was able to get out of the trunk."

"Good. I'm glad to hear that. I'm also glad for what he did. There is no reason why our boys have to go fight a stupid war that really has no purpose. It makes no sense. It makes no difference to us if those Southern states secede from the Union, or not. As a matter of fact, it would probably be better for all concerned. Why, we have Negroes right in this area, and there is nothing wrong with them. Yes, John, wars are a bad thing. It seems that all my life has revolved around one kind of battle or another. It is surely a sign of God's displeasure. Whenever I talk to parents, who have boys, I stress the point that, if at all possible, keep them from having to fight. If they can pay the $300.00 to keep them at home, fine. If they can't they should come and see me."

"But that isn't very patriotic," remarked Mr. Weis.

"Call it what you like, but, under the circumstances, we are doing the right thing. There is no need for unnecessary bloodshed.

The end is approaching fast enough for all of us. There are more important things to be doing than to kill each other off."

Father Joseph now stopped, put his hand in his pocket, and pulled out a handkerchief. After blowing his nose, he continued:

"Well men, I best be getting back home. I have to pay a visit to the sick yet."

He mounted his horse, and as he was leaving, he said: "Goodbye. I shall see you all in church on Sunday."

The men bid farewell to their religious leader, as he departed. Upon his arrival back at Himmelgarten,

Father Joseph immediately went to the nuns' convent. He entered a small room where four nuns were lying, each in separate beds. They were being cared for by Sister Margaret Fisher, a short solidly built lady of 33.

"Sister Margaret, how is everyone?"

"Much better. I was afraid that Sister Franceska wasn't going to make it, but now she is much better."

The two walked over to the bed where the heavy-set 35-year-old Sister Franceska Strecker was lying.

"How do you feel?" queried Father Joseph, as he gently took a hold of the nun's hand.

"Ah, Father Joseph," she weakly noted. "I feel much better. You are a most welcome sight. Now, I know that I will return to full health."

"Don't speak too much, Sister. I shall pray that you will soon be back in the fields."

"Thank-you, Father."

Father Joseph now turned to the next sister. "Hello, dear Sister. What are you doing here?"

"Hello, Father Joseph," replied the 51-year-old Sister Cecelia Spitts, a short, slender lady, with glasses and a small scar on her forehead. "I have not been able to eat for the past several days. I have trouble keeping my food down."

"I shall pray for you, Sister," noted Father Joseph, as he put his hand on her forehead, and silently said a short prayer.

"I feel much better, already," smilingly replied Sister Cecelia, as he took his hand off her forehead.

Next, he walked over to the bed where Sister Mary Ann Ruh, age 51, was sleeping.

"What is the matter with her?" he asked," as he looked at Sister Margaret.

She replied: "She is very weak. All she does is sleep. I'm not sure what to do about it."

Father Joseph stood by her bedside and said a short, silent prayer, after which he added: "There. Now, she will be better."

He then proceeded to the fourth bed, where Maria Fritz, a young 17-year-old postulant, was lying.

"Maria. How are you?"

"Hello Father Joseph," she replied, as she sat up in bed. "I broke my leg this morning while doing my chores. Sister Margaret has fixed me up, but it will be a while before I can get around again."

"My! My! Such an unfortunate accident! Have no fear, Maria, you will be back to full health in no time."

He now turned to Sister Margaret, as both of them headed in the direction of the door. "I shall return in the morning, after Mass, and hear confessions and distribute communion. Have them prepared for me when I arrive."

"Yes, Father," replied Sister Margaret, as she walked outside with him.

"I have to talk to Sister Lucretia," continued Father Joseph, as he turned and departed.

He immediately walked over to the room of Sister Lucretia. He never entered, because Sister Lucretia had seen him approaching, and came out to greet him.

"Sister Lucretia, how did everything go today?"

"Fine. We accomplished everything that you wanted done."

"Good. I was just over to the infirmary and have seen the girls."

"Yes". Maria had a most unfortunate accident."

"Don't be surprised if she is up and about very soon."

"But she has a broken leg."
"God works in mysterious ways."

"Ah, yes, that he does."

"I shall be in my room, if you need me," stated Father Joseph, as he turned and began to leave.

"Alright."

Father Joseph walked back to his room. Upon entering, he sat down by his table, took out a piece of paper, dipped his quill pen in the ink bottle, and began to write some notes. After a minute, he put the pen down, folded up the paper, and placed it under his mattress.

He then got up from his chair and laid down on his bed, quickly falling to sleep.

The next morning, after having said Mass at the convent chapel, he returned to the infirmary. As he entered, Sister Margaret came running over to him. "Father Joseph," she exclaimed, "what kind of prayers did you say for these people, yesterday?"

"Why do you ask?"

"See for yourself," replied Sister Margaret, in an excited tone, as she motioned with her arm for him to make the rounds.

They first stopped at the bed of Sister Franceska.

"Father Joseph," remarked Sister Franceska, "thank-you for your prayers. This morning, when I awoke, I felt like a new person. I am ready to go back to work, all because of you."

"Don't thank me. Thank the Lord. It is his work." Next, they went to Sister Cecelia.

"Hello Father Joseph," she noted. "I was able to eat this morning. My stomach feels much better."

"Fine," he replied, as he took her hand. "That is very good news."

"Thank-you. I will never forget this."

Father Joseph smiled, and moved on to the next bed, where Sister Mary Ann Ruh was sitting up, wide awake, and in very good spirits.

"Good morning."

"Good morning, Father."

"I see you are doing much better today."

"Yes Father. I had been so tired the past few days, but today I awoke and feel much better."

"Good to hear that," he added, as he now turned to young Maria. "And, how about you?"

"I am doing fine."

"I have come to hear your confessions and to distribute Holy Communion. Does everyone want to partake?"

All five of the women nodded their heads in the affirmative, so Father Joseph proceeded with the task at hand.

Upon completion of his duties, Father Joseph departed the infirmary, being escorted by Sister Margaret.

"I will never forget what you did here," she exclaimed.

"It is nothing."

"Don't be so modest. Surely, it was a miracle."

"Think what you may," continued Father Joseph, "but, it is merely a coincidence. God has a way of getting things done."

As this conversation was being held, Brother Innocent came running up to him.

"Father Joseph! Father Joseph!" he exclaimed, half out of breath, "Come quick!"

Brother Innocent led Father Joseph out into one of the nearby grain fields. When they reached the fenceline, they stopped, and Brother Innocent pointed to the ground, and said: "Look!"

Father Joseph looked down at the ground and was quite surprised at what he saw. "Oh my God! he exclaimed, "Worms.

Thousands of them."

"What are we to do?" asked Brother Innocent.

"I don't know, but we surely don't need this."

The two men slowly walked back to the convent grounds. "Keep a close eye on this matter," ordered Father Joseph. "I'll see what I can do."

A week later, not a worm could be found. No one was ever able to figure out why.

Progress on the new church at St. Josephs continued at a snail's pace. Father Joseph continued to keep a close watch on the construction. With the departure of Father Dwenger, and the seminarians, from Himmelgarten, to the new St. Charles Seminary, near Carthagena, Father Joseph now took financial control of the building project at St. Joseph. With the coming of winter, work on the building had to cease, but Father Joseph was determined that by the end of the next year, the job would be completed. Sure enough! On the 22nd of August 1862, Archbishop Purcell came to St. Joseph, to dedicate the new church. Father Joseph, not desiring to have anything to do with the Bishop, sent Father Ruf in his stead.

The next year, or so, went by without any major incidents. All was going well for Father Joseph, and his convent. He was spending more and more time in reading and contemplation, and at the same time, becoming more and more attached to the people at St. Joseph.

On January 21, 1864, while holding a discussion with a group of the brothers, in the church at Himmelgarten, a stranger entered and walked up to Father Joseph.

"Can I help you?" asked Father Joseph.

"I have a message for you," replied the young man, as he handed a note to Father Joseph.

He took the note, opened it, and silently read it. "Oh Lord!" he exclaimed. "Mary Ann died yesterday." He put down the note and sat down in a chair. The lady whom he had married years ago, back at Kirchzarten, the lady that had so much influence over him, the lady who gave him a daughter, the lady who had been responsible for his success, was gone.

"She died, peacefully, at Marywood. Oh, how I would like to go to her funeral!" he exclaimed. "I must leave now my brothers. I would like to be by myself."

He slowly walked to his room. With a distraught look on his face, he went directly to his kneeler, knelt down, took out his rosary, and began to pray. Several minutes later, he stopped. "Surely," he thought, "God is trying to tell me something." He got up from the kneeler and walked over to the bed and pulled out a small wooden box. After lifting the lid, he picked out a small book, and set it on the table. He opened up the book and began to read.

"Where did I read that," he said to himself, as he continued to peruse the book. "Ah,
here it is. Grace is poured out upon your lips; thus, God has blessed you forever. In your splendor and your beauty ride on triumphant, and reign."

As he closed the book, he remarked: "Mary, someday I shall join you."

Several weeks later, while Father Joseph was at the parish of St. Henry, the following occurred: Mass had just been completed. It was very cold and snowy outside, so some of the parishioners remained in the church, to talk to each other. Father Joseph came out of the sacristy and went down to talk with them. Among the people were: Barney Drahmann, age 50, his wife Mary, age 35, and their children: Henry, Daniel, Anna, Theresa, Elizabeth, John, Mary, and Joseph; Henry Kemper, age 59, and his wife Clara, age 54, with their children: Henry, Philomena, and Ben; Ignatz Schoeneberger, age 52, with his children: Casper, Martin, Mary Ann, Michael, and Andrew.

The children were busily playing, while the men sat together and talked in one area, and the women, in another.

As Father Joseph approached the men, Ignatz remarked: "Ex-cellent sermon today, Father."

"Thank-you," replied Father Joseph. "I only hope that I was able to reach the minds of some of the younger ones. We really do need more candidates for the priesthood and sisterhood."

"Casper has already been talking about that. And so have Martin and Michael."

"Well, perhaps someday," continued Father Joseph. "They will know when and if they are being called. Have another talk with him and send him over to Himmelgarten if he wants to come. I'll gladly welcome him."

On the Feast of Corpus Christi, 1866, at St. Josephs parish, the procession of the Blessed Sacrament was beginning. It was a beautiful day for the annual three-mile trip from St. Joseph to Himmelgarten.

The first people to come out of the church were three brothers, one in the middle with the long cross, the other two flanking him on each side, with candles. Next, came the women, two by two, then the men, and the children. They were followed by the mens' choir, which was joyfully singing hymns. Finally, Father Joseph came out, holding the monstrance high in the air. He was walking under a canopy being held by four men. Beside Father Joseph was Father Engelbert, who had recently returned to the Himmelgarten convent, after the death of Father John Butz, who died at Himmelgarten, on 26 May 1865.

The procession slowly moved down the trail which, earlier that morning, had been strewn with wildflowers.

These flowers were found in the surrounding woods and added an extra touch of beauty to the procession.

Father Joseph carried the monstrance in an elevated position for the entire length of the trip. This small feat did not go unnoticed by the people. Once arriving at Himmelgarten, the Blessed Sacrament was placed in the tabernacle of the convent church.

The procession had been completed and now the very tired Father Joseph was taking off his vestments and was to return to his room.

"I'm going to take a short rest, and then go over to the Boedigheimer farm," he stated, as he looked at Father Engelbert.

"That dreadful cholera has struck there, and I need to help them."

Upon entering his room with Father Engelbert, he sat down by the table and grabbed a chunk of cornbread and began eating. "I guess I can eat this on the way," he noted, as he got back up and left.

The trip to the Boedigheimer farm did not take him very long. He entered the small log house and walked directly over to the bed of Mr. Boedigheimer. The sickly man was very dehydrated, and his skin was very dry.

"Water/" begged Mr. Boedigheimer. "I need water."

"Yes, my friend," replied Father Joseph, as he fed him a cup of water, which was conveniently setting on the table, beside the bed.

"Here you are."

Mr. Boedigheimer quickly grabbed the tin cup and drank the water, after which he said: "Ah, thank-you, Father," and handed the cup back to him.

"I have fervently been praying for you and your wife," noted Father Joseph. "But sometimes they seem to go unheard. Tell me, where are the children?"

"In the barn."

"They are of no use to you in there."

"We didn't want them to get sick, too."

"I will continue to pray for you," comforted Father Joseph, as he held Mr. Boedigheimer's hand. Looking at Mrs. Boedigheimer, who was lying in another bed across the room, Father Joseph continued: "Now, how is the Mrs. doing?"

"Hello Father," she replied, as she raised her hand. "I feel that the time is near. I am too weak to carry on. Bruno and Mary are coming over to take the children. Father, please forgive me of my sins."

She looked upward, smiled, and breathed her last. Father Joseph closed her eyes and said several prayers. He then gave her the final rites and then covered her body with a sheet. As this was occurring, Bruno and Mary Boedigheimer entered. 29-year-old Bruno was quite short, while his 29-year-old wife was short and stocky. As soon as they entered, they knew that something was wrong.

"Bruno, could you go to the church and ring the bell, announcing that your sister-in-law has passed away? Then, go see if you can find Mr. Bender. Have him go to the cemetery and dig a grave.

Spread the word that we will have the funeral tomorrow. I will prepare the coffin you made. Mary, you stay with your brother-in-law. I have to go to the barn and talk to the children."

Father Joseph departed the house and walked directly to the barn, which was only a short distance away. Inside, he found five children, lying in a loose pile of hay.

"Listen, my children," he quietly exclaimed. "I have something to tell you. Your mother has been very sick. Just now, the Lord decided that it was time for her to go to heaven. She is in peace now. It is the most precious thing that can happen to a person."

All five of the children began to sob.

"Now, now," consoled Father Joseph. "You should be happy for her. You should be shedding tears of happiness and joy, not of sor-row and pain. Come with me now. Your Uncle Bruno will take care of you."

Father Joseph helped the children up and guided them out into the yard, where several people had already gathered.

"Ah, Mr. Doll," exclaimed Father Joseph, as he looked directly at the 27-year-old John Doll. "Could you help me? Bruno had Mr. Schoeneberger make a coffin for Mrs. Boedigheimer. He put it in the storage shed over there. Could you help me get it and prepare it?"

"Of course," replied Mr. Doll. "What about her husband?"

"He doesn't look very good, either. I'm sure it will just be a matter of time."

"That's too bad."

"Could you have your wife take the children over to your place for a few days? Tell her that the funeral will be tomorrow morning at ten."

"Yes Father," replied Mr. Doll, as he went toward his wife, Catharine, who was standing in the distance, talking with several other women.

Father Joseph walked directly over to the storage shed, opened the large doors, and entered. Inside, lying in a wagon box, was a small wodden coffin. He picked it up and carried it into the house.

He set it down on the floor, next to the bed of Mrs. Boedigheimer. John Doll then entered and helped Father Joseph put the body into the casket. They then proceeded to set the coffin on three chairs, which were placed side by side along the wall.

"Would you take all of her clothes, soak them, and have them burned?" asked Father Joseph, to Mr. Doll.

"Yes Father."

While all of this was going on, Mr. Boedigheimer was lying in his bed, watching.

There wasn't a thing he could do, except cry and scream, and that is exactly what he did.

"Mary," noted Father Joseph, as he was about to depart, "I'm going back to Himmelgarten. I will return later this afternoon, for the rosary. If his condition should worsen, send someone to get me right away."

Mary nodded her head in approval as Father Joseph left the house and returned to Himmelgarten.

As Father Joseph approached the convent lands, he noticed something — grasshoppers. He could see them everywhere. They were devouring everything in their path.

"Grasshoppers," he thought. "It's too early for grasshoppers." Quickly, he reached into his pocket and pulled out a small bottle of Holy Water. He sprinkled it along the fenceline as far as he could until the bottle was empty. As he was doing this, he proclaimed:

"Oh Lord, with this Holy Water, make these small monsters turn and retreat. Do not allow them to devour our crops. Do not allow them to cross this line. Oh Lord, I know you will help us in this time of need. Amen."

As Father Joseph placed the empty bottle back into his pocket, he watched for several seconds, and then proceeded to the convent grounds. The next morning, at ten, the funeral Mass was held for Mrs. Boedigheimer. As always, the funeral turned out to be a parish event. All of the people left their work behind in order to attend.

Sadness was evident everywhere, as all of the relatives present, both men and women, wore mourning clothes. The men were dressed in black ties and a black veil folded around their black hat band. The women wore complete black — black hat, black veil, black shoes. The children too, were distinctively marked with various garments of black.

The procession from the church to the cemetery was led by Father Joseph and followed by the casket-bearers and then the relatives and friends.

Upon arriving at the gravesite, Father Joseph said the final prayers. With his loud voice, he stated the words used in the burial ceremony. As he grabbed a shovel and, symbolically threw three shovels of dirt over the coffin; while it was slowly lowered, the choir sang: 'I'm Grabe ist Ruh.'

Upon completion of the ceremony, almost everyone gloomily left the cemetery. Father Joseph and Brother Innocent, momentarily, remained behind.

"Father," noted Brother Innocent, "while you were saying Mass, Mr. Boedigheimer passed away. Father Ruf was able to give him the Last Rites before he died."

"Those poor children!" exclaimed Father Joseph. "I should go over there right away."

"Also, Father," continued Brother Innocent. "Brother Peter was out in the fields this morning and he noticed something very strange."

"Oh! What was that?"

"He saw locusts in the neighbors' fields, but there wasn't any in ours."

"I know," bluntly replied Father Joseph, "I know."

Father Joseph now walked over to Mr. Bender, who was busily filling in the gravesite.

"Well Anton, you might as well dig another grave right beside this one. Mr. Boedigheimer died this morning."

"Oh my!" exclaimed Mr. Bender.

"I have to go to Mariastein, so I'll have Father Ruf come over
for the funeral tomorrow."

The next morning, at Mariastein, Father Joseph was holding a retreat meeting for Mother Kunigunda and a group of the sisters.

"Father Joseph," noted Mother Kunigunda, "the Reverend Bishop Purcell has proclaimed that it is not necessary for you to hold these retreats any longer."

"What does he know?" asked Father Joseph, in an irritated tone. "He sits on his chair in Cincinnati. He doesn't know what is really going on. He is too busy in his own little world."

"Why," exclaimed Sister Kunigunda, "surely, the hand of God is not here. The Bishop is the legitimate authority. Why, I'm surprised to hear you talk like that. I am recommending to all that you should not return to Mariastein, without our invitation."

"Very well," replied Father Joseph, "but, it will be your loss." Father Joseph quickly left the room. It was very evident that he was utterly upset, to say the least. As he was heading for his horse, he blared out aloud: "Surely, Kunkier had something to do with this.

The spirit of Father Salesius is departing the congregation. My followers and I should break with the Kunkleranerians and call ourselves, the Salesianerians."

Father Joseph mounted his horse and departed the grounds of Mariastein, never again to return.

Crinolines

CHAPTER XVII

Father Joseph arrived at St. Josephs about 15 minutes before Mass was to begin. The weather was excellent this particular June morning so, as customary, he had walked the three miles from Himmelgarten. He was greeted at the church by several men and women.

"Good morning, Father Joseph," they stated.
"Good morning, my dear people."

With that, he entered the church and proceeded to the sacristy. Upon arrival, he opened his little knapsack and pulled out his chalice, ciborium, and vestments. He hurriedly began preparations for Holy Mass. First, he put on his amice, then the alb, cincture, stole, chasuble and finally the maniple. Placing his biretta upon his head, he was almost ready to say Mass. The only thing left was to make sure he had wine and water and that his Mass vessels were ready.

9-year-old Leander Boedigheimer and 8-year-old John Eifert entered the sacristy and prepared to assist him in the Mass. As Father Joseph began to place the paten and purificator on the chalice, a large increase in noise began in the church. He went over to the sacristy door to find out what was causing the commotion. He could not believe his eyes. He watched in utter amazement as two daughters of Andrew Siegrist came waltzing into church, all decked out in the latest French fashion — crinolines.

The men on one side, the women on the other, were all stunned. How could anyone dare go against the demands of Father Joseph? The girls walked up to the front of the church, and took a seat, as if nothing was happening. Father Joseph was boiling. What was he to do? The past several Sundays he had been warning his people that crinolines were forbidden, as long as he had anything to say about it. The nerve of those girls to disregard his command. He stood and thought for a minute.

He remained calm. "Ring the bell, John. It is time to start."

Holy Mass was begun. As he approached the altar, the people could see that he was irritated. He genuflected, made the sign of the cross and began saying Mass, in Latin. As usual, he was having trouble with the Latin. He knew the Mass by heart, yet he always seemed to have difficulty saying them.

After he finished singing the 'Gloria', he approached the pulpit. Rather than read the Epistle for the days Mass, he thumbed through his book for several seconds, stopped, quietly read for a few seconds, and began to smile.

"My dear friends in Christ. Today, I will read the First Epistle of Paul to Timothy." He then began to read: "It is my wish, then, that in every place the men shall offer prayers with blameless hands held aloft and be free from anger and dissention. Similarly, the women, must deport themselves properly. They should dress modestly and quietly, and not be decked out in fancy hairstyles, gold ornaments, pearls, or costly clothing; rather, as becomes women who profess to be religious, their adornment should be good deeds."

With that, he set the book down, looked around the church for a few seconds, and then zeroed in on the two Siegrist girls, sitting in the front.

"The message of today's epistle is very appropriate. Many times, I have mentioned to you how much I despise the latest invention of Empress Eugenie of France. Many times, I have warned you that as long as I have anything to do, or say, concerning the parish, I will not allow hoopskirts in the house of the Lord. If anyone should wear them one more time, I will refuse to say Mass. This is my final warning," he continued, as he slammed his fist down on the pulpit.

"Enough said," he added. "Let us continue on with the gospel."

The remainder of the Mass went by without incident. After Mass, outside the church, much discussion was held among the parishioners. Sides were being taken. Most of them seemed to favor the view of Father Joseph, but there were a few who fervently disagreed.

Father Joseph, himself, stayed in the sacristy. He was still fuming. He took off his vestments, while in deep thought. He then went out to his kneeler, knelt down, and began to pray. With hands folded, he looked upwards. "Oh Lord, help me in this time of trial. Give a sign to these people, to show them how wrong they are. Let them see their erring ways. Give me the courage to deal with this problem. Give the willpower and patience. Oh Lord. Hear my prayer."

That afternoon, vespers were held. Among the people who entered the church, were the two Siegrist girls, again wearing their crinolines.

Immediately, Father Joseph noticed them. This was the last straw. He quickly walked over to the pulpit, opened his book, and began to read: "The Gospel according to Luke, chapter 19, verses 41 through 47. At that time, when Jesus drew near to Jerusalem and saw the city, he wept over it, saying, 'If you had known, in this your day, even you, the things that are for your peace. But now they are hidden from your eyes. For days will come upon you when your enemies will throw up a rampart about you and surround you and shut you in on every side and will dash you to the ground and your children within you, and will not leave you one stone upon another, because you have not known the time of your visitation.' And he entered the temple and began to cast out those who were selling and buying in it, saying to them, 'It is written, that my house is a house of prayer, but you have made it a den of thieves.' And he was teaching daily in the temple. Amen."

Father Joseph calmly closed the book. He proceeded to take off his vestments. He grabbed a hickory stick, which had been setting near the sacristy entrance, and drove the two girls from the church, shouting: "You have defied the word of God. You have chosen to go against my will. For this, you must pay. I will not allow you in my church. You are to get out and stay out until you decide not to wear those silly garments."

The girls ran, screaming, out the door, shouting for help. A couple of teenage boys made an attempt to stop Father Joseph, but they stopped as soon as Father Joseph gave them one look, straight in the eye.

Once the girls were outside, Father Joseph locked the door, and went back to the front of the church and continued with vespers. Several of the families, showing their disgust, got up and proceeded to leave the church. The remaining people expressed their approval of the way that Father Joseph handled the situation.

After vespers, Father Joseph walked back to Himmelgarten. Upon his arrival, he met Godfrey Schlachter, a young candidate who had recently arrived at Himmelgarten, to begin studies for the priesthood. "Godfrey, my dear friend, I have problems," stated Father Joseph. "My health has been good for 65 years now, but mental problems are arising. The devil is at work at St. Joe. Many people nowadays are falling into the grasp of his arms. They know not what they are doing. I have lost my patience, and now, I suppose, will have to pay the consequences. I really don't know what to do. My mind seems to be getting boggled up. I don't know which way to turn. Today at St. Joe, I chased two young ladies out of church because they were wearing crinolines. Now, I have several parishioners mad at me. Pray for me, Godfrey, and for those who err in their ways."

Young Godfrey just sat there quietly and listened to what Father Joseph had to say. The episode at St. Joseph was, immediately, reported to Archbishop Purcell of Cincinnati, who, upon hearing the story, wrote a letter of reprimand to Father Joseph.

The following Sunday, Father Joseph read the letter at Holy Mass, at St. Joseph. "I received a letter from Archbishop Purcell, yesterday, and I would like to read it to you." He opened the envelope, took out the letter and began to read: "Dear Father Joseph, I have just received word from some of your parishioners at St. Joseph, informing me of the situation that occurred at Sunday vespers. I must emphasize that you are wrong. You may preach against the fashion, but you must tolerate it. You have no right to keep people from attending church, just because of what they wear. I repeat, do not refuse the Sacraments to those who wear the hoop. You made a serious mistake. Fancy clothing is not pride, but only a current fashion and, a modest dance, or an occasional game of cards on Sunday afternoons and Holy Days, for the purpose of recreation, does not constitute sin. I am hoping you will clear this matter up soon. Sincerely yours in Christ, Bishop John B. Purcell, Bishop of Cincinnati."

Father Joseph placed the letter on the pulpit. He took his right hand and rubbed his chin. "My dear people, the Archbishop is wrong. If bishops make laws, which are contrary to God, and therefore, also contrary to the true religion, then no priest, nor anyone else, need obey them. I cannot agree with him. I will not, I repeat, will not obey the work of the devil. Many bishops have fallen off and were like Luther. This letter is simply imprudent."

"According to the Gospel of Mark, Jesus said: 'Be on guard against the scribes, who like to parade around in robes and accept marks of respect in public, front seats in the synagogues, and places of honor at banquets. These men devour the savings of widows, and recite long prayers for appearance's sake, it is they who will receive the severest sentence.'"

"My dear people, I still believe in the Holy Scripture, and I condemn those people who do not consider fancy clothes, greed, lust, and games, to be sinful, as heretics. The vices of pride, vanity, and lust are abundant, and we must not allow such problems to continue. I have come to the conclusion that I will never celebrate Mass again in this sacred place, after this abomination of desolation. My days here are numbered."

Father Joseph returned to Himmelgarten, never to say Mass again at St. Josephs. Several days later, Father Andrew Kunkier, the Superior, came to visit Father Joseph.

"Welcome," stated Father Joseph, as he got up from his chair and greeted Father Kunkier at the door.

As Father Kunkier sat down by the table, he asked "Joseph, Joseph. Why have you despised the orders of Bishop Purcell?"

"I cannot agree with him. If I did so, I could not face my people."
"Then, maybe it would be a good idea if I transferred you to Glandorf."
"No. I will not do that either. I cannot."
"Then, you leave me no choice, but to forbid you from saying Mass and preaching."

"Alright. If that is what you wish. I am glad. You have taken a heavy burden off my shoulders. When I came to America in '48, I had an agreement with Father Salesius. I could leave the Society, whenever I wanted to, and that, when I did, I was to receive back all of my money, which I had given."

Father Kunkier got up from his chair and stormed out of the room in complete disgust. Father Joseph remained sitting and began to laugh.

As soon as Father Kunkier had departed, Brother Joseph Boedigheimer, a tall solidly built man of 25, entered the room.

"Ah, Brother Joseph. What can I do for you?"
"Father Joseph, you have been in my prayers. I only wish there was something I could do for you."

"Oh, but there is. It will not be long, and I will have to leave this place. I need you to go and talk to the other brothers and those that you think feel the same way I do and tell them to come to the meeting room tonight at 8, as I need to talk to them. I am going to talk to Sister Lucretia. I have a plan and would like to inform all of you about it, this evening."

"Yes Father, that I can do," remarked Brother Joseph, as he turned and departed.

Father Joseph left with Brother Joseph, proceeding over to the nunnery. Upon entering, he was met at the door, by Sister Lucretia.

"Dear Sister, I need your help. Be at the meeting room tonight at 8. I am going to hold a meeting. I would like you to talk to each of the sisters and novices and find out their feelings concerning me. If you think they are favorable towards me, please invite them to the meeting. I have a plan that I would like to share with them."

"Of course. Anything you say, Father."

That night, at the appointed time, the meeting was held. Among those in attendance were the following: Brothers Joseph Boedigheimer, John Wiederle, Joseph A. Doll, John Frey, and Godfrey Schlachter. Sister Lucretia, Sister Lydia Mahl, age 26, Sister Seraphim Hummel, age 40; Sister Barbara Flaif, age 44; Sister Cherubim Schummher, age 57; Sister Afra Mary Ann Ruh, age 56; Sister Theresa Arnold, age 19; Sister Agamonti Engelberta Dietsche, age 22; Sister Rustika Bishof, age 21; Josephine Thoening, Rosa Wahl, Mary Graf, and Caroline Schuh.

"I suppose you are wondering why I have gathered you here. As you know by now, I am having some difficulties with that Irishman in Cincinnati. I'm afraid that his commands are becoming intolerable. It is one thing to obey your superiors when you know they are right, and it is another thing to obey them when you know they are wrong. My conscience tells me that I should listen to what the Bible says, in this instance, rather than what the Bishop says. Keeping this in mind, I'm sure that I will be receiving a letter, shortly, from the Bishop, concerning a suspension."

"Over the years, I have spent a considerable amount of my own personal wealth in building up the Society. I have not only helped build this beautiful convent but have freely given to Father Salesius, when he needed it. Bishop Purcell believes that priests should not have money, that they should give all their personal wealth to their Superiors, for the betterment of the Church. I do not agree with him, and that, my dear friends, is really the main reason why we do not get along. I feel that I can better use my money by seeing first-hand who needs it, rather than giving it to some Irishman in Cincinnati."

"Anyway, it will not be long, and I will have to leave here. As of yet, I know not where I'm going to go. Perhaps, I will go visit Father Ambrose, up at St. Nazianz, or perhaps, I will go to California. I have been reading some of the articles in the newspaper, concerning the need for good Catholic settlers in Minnesota. A certain Father Pierz makes it sound very interesting. I am going to be checking that out in more detail. Perhaps, some day we could set up a Precious Blood Society there and run it the way Father Salesius wanted it to be run."

"Everything that has been built or bought around here, has been put in my name, and not in the name of the diocese, or the Society. So, when Father Kunkier comes to remove me, he will have problems. I have set it up with Mr. Beckman, a lawyer, so that the civil law would protect me, if it comes to that."

"For the next few days, I beg that you remember me in your prayers, asking God to give me strength in these trying times. Thank-you."

As Father Joseph pulled a rosary out of his pocket, he continued: "And now, I think it would be a good time for us to pray a rosary. Let us begin."

Preparations for Departure

CHAPTER XVIII

Life at the convent continued on, with the sisters and brothers doing their normal duties. However, Father Joseph's routine changed drastically. He did not say Mass at any of the area churches, nor at the convent, spending most of his time in solitude. The next Sunday, he again went over to St. Joseph's church. Only this time, he was not offering Mass, but was just a spectator.

Father Bernard Austermann, another Precious Blood priest, from Himmelgarten, said the Mass. He was 42 years old and was one of the main enemies of Father Joseph.

When it was time for the sermon, this is part of what Father Austermann had to say: "I have been asked by Father Kunkier to take care of this parish, for the time being. I am hoping that you will cooperate fully with me. Father Joseph has finally had his downfall. He is a disobedient, contumacious, vile person, who has fallen prey to lack of humility, and an outpouring of vanity. The Bible tells us that we are to always obey our superiors. Father Joseph believes that he should only obey his superiors, when it is in his own best interest. That is not the way it is supposed to be. You must be careful not to be led astray by a wolf in sheep's clothing. I would rather have my right hand cut off than to give Holy Communion to such a person."

Father Joseph was sitting in the front pew, taking the sermon in stride. All he could do was shake his head in disgust. "The nerve of that man to cut me down like that in front of all my friends," he thought.

The Mass continued on. By looking throughout, the church, one could see that many of the parishioners were also quite riled. Many of them had known Father Joseph for over ten years. They knew what he was really like. They knew that there was more to the story than just the fact that he did not like hoopskirts. During Holy Communion, Father Joseph went up to the communion railing, to receive the Sacrament. When it came to his turn, Father Austermann passed him by. This was the most degrading thing that could have happened to him. He got up and stormed out of the church, followed closely behind by many of the parishioners. Bruno Boedigheimer, Anton Bender, and Joseph A. Doll stopped him outside of the church.

"Father Joseph," shouted Bruno. "Wait up! We would like to talk to you."

Father Joseph stopped and turned around. His usually kind gentle-looking face was now stern. You could see that he was very mad and upset.

"Father, we do not agree with Father Austermann," continued Bruno.

"We believe you are right. There are many others in this parish that also believe in you. If there is anything we can do for you, don't hesitate to ask. When we needed help, you were there.

Maybe, now we can pay back our debt."

"Yes Bruno," stated Father Joseph, "there is something you could do for me. There is no way that I am going to be able to stay at the convent now, after what Father Austermann just did. I am going to pack up my things and leave. If you know of some place where I could stay for a while, I would surely appreciate it."

"You can stay at my place," interrupted Anton Bender. "You are always welcome at my house."

"My house also," added Mr. Doll.

"Thank-you."

"Father," continued Bruno, "I have a good-sized barn which you would be free to use for as long as you needed it. There is plenty of room for you to store your things, live in, and say Mass."

"Bless you, Bruno. That is probably exactly what I need. There is a good chance that I will not be the only one coming. Some of the brothers and sisters have expressed a desire to come with me. Give me a couple of days to get everything in order, and then I'll be seeing you."

As Father Joseph began heading towards Himmelgarten, he turned around to the three men, and said: "Thank-you for your support."

The next morning, Father Joseph awoke early and went over to see Sister Lucretia.

"Sister," he said, "you have known me almost your entire life. You have been by my side in times of agony and despair. You have witnessed good times and bad times. I need to know if you will come with me. I must leave Himmelgarten. I feel it is my duty, as a true member of the Precious Blood Society, to start a community of priests, brothers, and sisters, who will follow the ideals of our dearly beloved founder Blessed Gaspar, and our former Superior, Father Salesius. I'm sure the Archbishop will be coming soon, and I am going to refuse to see him. All he really wants is my money."

"Yes Father Joseph, whatever you say."

"Bruno has kindly offered me the use of his barn. Please get all of your belongings together and be ready to leave in a few days. Pass the word to the others, to do likewise, if they so wish. Emphasize to them that it must be done as secretly as possible. When you get a chance, go over to St. Joe, and pick up some of the vestments. Since you and the other sisters here, made most of them, they are rightly ours, anyway. I will pass the word on to the brothers. Remember, we must be ready to leave in two days."

Sister Lucretia busily scurried about doing her assigned tasks. Within a short time, she had passed the word to the other sisters. All of them were excited, believing that Father Joseph was their true leader and that he could do no wrong. Just as Sister Lucretia was getting ready to take off for St. Joe, a visitor arrived. It was Sister Milburgis Fischer, the Mother Superior from Minster.

"Greetings, Sister Milburgis," shouted Sister Lucretia.

"Hello, Sister Lucretia."

"What brings you to our home?"

"I figured it was about time I came to see how everyone was doing here."
"Everything is just fine. As you can see, we are all busy as ever."

Sister Milburgis could tell that something was wrong. She could tell by the way the other sisters were acting in the background, that her presence was really not needed.

"How was your trip?" queried Sister Lucretia, as she helped Sister Milburgis down from the wagon.

"The usual. Long, grueling, boring. I cannot stay long as I still must get to Mariastein yet, today."

"Oh yes, I'm sure Mother Kunigunda will be happy to see you. We have much work to do yet, so we must hurry with our conversation. You know how Father Joseph is, when he wants something done on time, he expects it to be done on time."

"Ah yes, I do. I certainly do. How is Father Joseph? I hear he has been having some difficulty over at St. Joe."
"Nothing serious. It will all blow over in due time. Just a slight misunderstanding."

"Well, I suppose I better get going then, so I don't keep you from your work. When you get a chance, maybe you could come visit me in Minster."

"Yes, I will do that. Maybe in a month or so, after harvest."

"Good-bye then," stated Sister Milburgis, as she got back into her carriage.

"May God grant you a safe journey."

And so, Sister Milburgis was on her way. She knew something was wrong at Himmelgarten, but she lacked the finesse to find out what it was. Maybe Sister Kunigunda would know something.

As soon as Sister Milburgis was out of sight, the sisters dropped what they were doing and proceeded to begin the arduous duty of
packing.

Sister Lucretia headed for St. Joe. The others packed everything that they figured they could use in their new endeavor. They packed away all of the eating utensils, cooking utensils, and all the provisions from the pantry. The only thing left of the beds were the
wooden frames, themselves. The feather-bed mattresses, blankets, and sheets were all placed on the wagons.

The chapel too, was cleaned out. Even the life-size wax figure, containing the holy relics of St. Candidus, was taken from under the high altar. The beautiful replica had been clothed in velvet, sprinkled with an abundance of precious gems. This prized treasure, which Father Joseph had purchased years ago, in Europe, had been donated to the convent for safe keeping. Father Joseph now believed that it would be better to take it with him, rather than leave it for someone else to plunder.

Within a day, everyone was ready to depart. Several of the sisters and novices had arrived from Mary's Home and were willing to move on to wherever their leader would take them. Among these were Mary Ann Graf and Caroline Schuh.

"Well, Sister Lucretia, everything looks about ready," stated Father Joseph, quite pleased with what was occurring.

"Yes Father, there will be 23 members going with you. Eight brothers and fifteen sisters.
Father Andrew is very upset. He has taken off to spread the word about what we are doing. I tried to reason with him, but he was as stubborn as ever."

"We should be gone by the time he gets back," suggested Father Joseph.

The next morning, there was much activity at Himmelgarten. Little Emma Bliley, an 8-year-old girl, who had been sent to Himmelgarten, for a religious education, by her grandfather, knew that something important was happening, but she did not know what. She noticed Sister Rosa Wahl, a novice, dressed in her Sunday best. Seeing this, Emma ran back to her room and donned her Sunday dress. She then came back outside and ran towards Sister Rosa.

"Why Emma!" exclaimed Sister Rosa. "Why have you put on your Sunday dress? Today is not Sunday."

"You have yours on, and if you go away, I am going with you. I have already noticed that several sisters have departed."

"But you cannot go with me, for your mother will not know where to find you."

Hearing these words, Emma began to cry. Tears came rolling down her cheeks. "I will not stay, if you don't. I will not. I will not," continued Emma, as she began to cry louder and louder.

"Alright then, my dear child, if you insist. Get your things and we will be on our way. We are leaving with Father Joseph, very soon."

Later that same day, Sister Milburgis reappeared at Himmelgarten. She was aghast at what she saw. It was a complete mess. There were only a few members who remained, and Sister found them in the chapel.

"What has happened here?" she asked.

"Father Joseph has gone. And with him, went many of the brothers and sisters. They have taken all of our food supplies and left us with nothing," stated one of the poor sisters, who was almost in tears.

"Where did they go?"

"We don't know. All they said was that Father Joseph was taking them to a nearby farm. I'm sure that is where all the provisions are."

"Please get in the wagon," insisted Sister Milburgis. "I'll take you over to Mariastein, until we find out what is going on. "Meanwhile at Bruno Boedigheimer's farm, the group was arriving. Father Joseph, driving the first horse and carriage, followed by several more wagons, loaded down with trunks and various household goods, pulled up near the house. The other wagons were being driven by the brothers, while the sisters were walking alongside.

"Welcome," shouted Bruno, as he and his wife, Mary, came running out of the house. Behind them came the kids — Julia (13), Frank (15), Joseph (8), William (6), Aurilia (3), Ignatius (11), Ferdinand (9), LeAnder (7), Frank (5), and Emma (16). All of them were overjoyed at the sight of having so many brothers and sisters at their home.

"Thank-you Bruno," replied Father Joseph, as he got down from his carriage. "It is a joy to know that I still have some friends left in this day and age."

"Oh Father, you have many friends in this area. I only wish that you had better accommodations than what I have to offer." I'm sure they'll be fine. We've never needed much. All that we ask for is a roof over our head."

"There are two small block houses over there," pointed out Bruno. "You can store your wagons in the barn. One of the block houses can be used by the sisters, the other, the brothers."

"Very well," remarked Father Joseph. "Brother Joseph, please supervise the unloading. I must have a private conversation with Bruno.

"Yes Father," stated Big Joe, as he turned, and began giving orders to others.

Father Joseph and Bruno walked into the house. Once inside, they sat down by the kitchen table, situated in the middle of the room. The house was modestly furnished with several pieces of large, beautiful furniture. Bruno was not considered to be a well-off farmer, but was not poor, by any means.

"I don't know what is going to happen in the near future, Bruno," stated Father Joseph.

"It seems that every day brings more and more obstacles. I have had little sleep the past few days. The uncertainties have been plaguing my mind. If only I could go and live in the wilderness of Michigan, or Wisconsin, or even Minnesota, as a hermit. I could then fulfill my life in complete dedication to God. This was my main goal when I came to America, but Father Salesius was able to persuade me to join the Sanguinists. Ever since, my heart has been burdened by one problem after another."

"I realize now that I must not only think of my own salvation, but I also must look out for the safekeeping of all my children. These poor souls need to be led on the right path. It is so easy to be led astray," continued Father Joseph.

"Father," interrupted Bruno, "last night I had some visitors. Several men from the parish came over and we had a very interesting conversation. Anton Bender, Frank Staab, Charles Foltz, Joseph Riesterer, Anton Doll, Victor Eifert, Luis Sarbacher, Joseph Doll.
They were all here. We all agreed that, if at all possible, we would like to move to wherever you go. You have been our spiritual leader and our guiding light for quite some time now, and we would consider it an honor if you would allow us to join you."

"Well, thank-you Bruno. I am flattered. The Bishop has suspended me, but I do not believe I have been suspended by God. Life must go on. My duties to my children continue. Go and tell these men to bring their families here this Sunday and we shall partake of the Lord's Supper, in your barn."

Now Bruno, I must go out and see how my children are doing. Thank-you again. We will try and stay out of your way." After departing the house, Father Joseph walked over to one of the block houses, where Sister Lucretia was busily unloading the bedding and foodstuffs.

"Sister Lucretia," he stated. "Have everyone come over by the barn as soon as they finish their duties. I think it would be appropriate if we held a small prayer service this evening. I also have some things to say."

Father Joseph then walked over to the barn and entered the main door. One of the wagons had already been placed there. He glanced through the remainder of the freight, which had been left on the wagon, and stopped when he came to the large bell. He silently read the inscription: "The Blessed Virgin Mary — Her sorrows penetrate the Hearts of all men." He thought to himself:

"How true! Oh Mary, my pains and sorrows have been small compared to what you have gone through. I must stop feeling sorry for myself. Help me rid myself of vanity and have me make the proper decisions in the future."

He knelt down beside the wagon. Folding his hands, he began to pray: "Oh Lord, I am unworthy of your goodness. Make me strong and able to provide the necessary leadership in the future. Make Father Kunkier and Bishop Purcell realize their mistakes. Grant my wishes, not only for my sake, but also, for the sake of your children that have followed me. Amen."

He then abruptly arose, turned around, and noticed that the sisters and brothers were already beginning to come towards the barn. Within several minutes, the entire group was situated around Father Joseph.

"My children. This will be our temporary home. I am sure it will suffice until we have made our final preparations for departure. I have here a copy of the Community Constitution."

As he lifted up a small booklet and showed it to the brothers and sisters, he opened it up, and said: "It says here that any member of the Community has no ties or obligations to each other and can leave whenever they wish. Each and every member can demand a return of his property from the Community, whenever he, or she, feels it necessary. We, therefore, have the right to what is actually ours. Be not bothered by misconception. It is we who have toiled in the fields and in the gardens. It is we who have earned that right.

That right is to have what is truly ours. Do not think for a moment that we are doing something wrong. We are only doing what the Bible says, and we know that the Bible is the truth. We must now try harder to act as the good Lord would want us to act. We must try harder to serve for the betterment of our community—a community which will be based on what Father Salesius wanted, not on what Father Kunkier wants. Our obligation to Father Salesius did not die when he died. It continues on. Our obligation to Father Kunkier and to the Archbishop must end. They have fallen astray. It is they who have been influenced by the evils of today's society. It is they whom we must pray for. It is our duty and our obligation to see that we receive salvation by means of leading a truly Christian life and setting a good example for others to follow, just like Father Salesius would have wanted it."

"I also have here a newspaper," he continued. "In it, is an article by Father Francis Xavier Pierz, of Minnesota. He describes a virtual paradise on Earth. Virgin soil, never before touched by the plow. Cheap land. Rich soil. An abundance of trees and water and healthy air. This land could be ours if we so desire. This Sunday, I will be holding Mass here. After Mass, we are to have a meeting.
Many of our friends from St. Joe will also be in attendance. We will then talk more about this land called Minnesota. But for now, it is time to say our evening prayers."

The next morning, a visitor arrived at the Boedigheimer farm. It was Father Andrew, who had come to take his niece, Emma Bliley, back to Himmelgarten. Father Joseph, seeing him approach, mentioned to Brother Joseph: "Joseph, go get Julia and Frank and LeAnder, and William, and tell them to take Emma, quickly, to the wheatfield. Have them play hide and seek. Make sure Emma is hidden."

"Yes Father," replied Big Joe, as he hurried into Bruno's house. Soon he reappeared and walked over to Father Joseph. "It is done. They went out the back door. Father Andrew will not find them." Father Andrew approached the barn. He stopped his horse,
jumped off and tied it to a nearby post.

"What have you done with little Emma?" he shouted towards Father Joseph. "Where is she? I have come to save her from your evil clutches."

"Why Father Andrew, I don't know what you are talking about."

"Don't lie to me, Albrecht. I know you have her here. I have been told that she left Himmelgarten with Sister Rosa."

"Look for yourself. She is not here."

Meanwhile, Emma and Julia were hiding under a shock of wheat. Little William Boedigheimer was having a difficult time searching for them. He would go from shock to shock, but with no success.

Back at the farmstead, Father Andrew was going from building to building, trying to find some clue of Emma's presence. He too, was having no luck.

Bruno and Mary were standing by their door to the house, watching very closely to what was happening. Father Andrew called out to them: "Have you seen my sweet innocent niece, Emma?"

Bruno replied: "Can't say that I have, Father."

Finally, Father Andrew gave up. He stomped over to his horse, untied the bridle, mounted, and took off, heading back towards the convent of Himmelgarten. As soon as he was out of sight, Father Joseph looked over to- wards a couple of the older Boedigheimer boys, and said:

"You can run out and get the children. It is safe for Emma to come back."
The boys did as they were told. Soon, Sunday arrived. Father Joseph, the brothers, and the sisters, were all up very early.

"Good morning," offered Father Joseph, as he met Sister Lucretia, near the entrance to the barn.

"Good morning."

"I need you to get all the women together. I want to talk to them, in the barn, before Mass."

"Yes Father."

As Sister Lucretia went off on her task, Father Joseph went inside and began preparing for the Holy Mass he was to offer that morning.

Within 15 minutes, all the women were gathered around the makeshift altar, built out of wooden crates, in the barn.

"My dear sisters, I have called you together to make sure that there are no doubts in your minds concerning the move we are making, and to let you know about the possible repercussions that Father Kunkier will probably throw upon us. According to the Precious Blood rules, you only take the vow of fidelity. It says nothing about poverty, chastity, or obedience. Six of you have taken this vow, but it does not mean you have committed a grave sin for leaving. Your vows of fidelity still hold true. We are still members of the Precious Blood Community. Actually, we are better members than those who remain here, because our Society will reflect the true Society. As long as we continue to observe my rules, based on Father Brunner's rules, we will do alright. Continue to pray for our success."

As Father Joseph was finishing his meeting, several wagons were approaching the yard. They included families from St. Joe, consisting of the Bender, Weis, Dolls, Staabs, Foltzs, Riesterers, Eiferts, as well as several single men. Father Joseph came to the entrance of the barn and invited them in to partake of the Holy Mass.

It made Father Joseph very happy to see so many people who shared the same views as himself.

After all the people had entered the barn, Father Joseph proceeded to prepare for Mass. He put on his vestments and began the ceremony.

After completion of the Holy Mass, he took off his vestments and began talking to the crowd, which remained: "For the past several days I have had many doubts as to what we should do. The ideas that Father Ambrose had put to use at St. Nazianz, continue to come into my mind. The idea of a community farm sounds very interesting. This farm would consist solely of Catholic families, making up a parish, being aided by religious brothers and sisters. All temporal things would be held in common. We would live as the apostles did.

In the Book of Acts, chapter 4, verses 32 through 35, it says: 'The community of believers were of one heart and one mind. None of them ever claimed anything as his own; rather, everything was held in common. With power, the apostles bore witness to the resurrection of the Lord Jesus, and great respect was paid to them all; nor was there anyone needy among them, for all who owned property or houses sold them and donated the proceeds. They used to lay them at the feet of the apostles to be distributed to everyone according to his need.' Father Ambrose has put these words to practice in Wisconsin, and from what I have heard from his letters, it is working out well. It may be a good idea to write to him again and ask for suggestions. Do any of you have anything to say?"
Anton Bender raised his arm.

"Yes Anton?"

"Your ideas of communal life sound very interesting and I am all for it. I have done some reading on a place called Minnesota. It seems that that would be a great place to move to. Maybe we should look into moving there."

"Yes Anton, I too have read much about that state. It sounds good. I will look into it, in more detail. I will write some letters and see what I can find out. For now, I think that we should hold Mass every day, right here."

The next month seemed to go by very fast. The brothers and the sisters helped with the harvest on the farms around the area, while Father Joseph was busy planning the future.
One day he held a meeting with several men of the area. They were Anton Bender, Bruno Boedigheimer, and Victor Eifert.
"Gentlemen," he stated, "I have received several letters this past week. I believe we should move to Minnesota. I would like to send five or six brothers to go ahead and check out the area and buy some land for us, if they feel that it is a good bargain. It will have to be quickly. I am still being haunted by the Bishop and the other Precious Blood priests, so the sooner the better. We do not have much time left here."

That afternoon, Father Joseph talked to some of the brothers. They were John Wiederle (29), Joseph Boedigheimer (25), John Frey (34), Joseph A. Doll (24), Michael Doll (25), and Casper Schoeneberger (22).

"Men," stated Father Joseph, "I have decided to send you on a trip. You are going to Minnesota. The trip is all planned. I am sending you by train to St. Paul. From there, you are to proceed to St. Cloud. There you will be fitted out and will go by horseback, along
the Crow Wing Trail, until you find suitable land. You are then to buy about 700 acres, or so. As soon as you find the land, send word back to us, so we can prepare to leave. I have some money here that should take care of the expenses. Brother Joseph, I am putting you in charge. Take this bag and protect it. Use what you must, but be frugile, wherever possible."

As Father Joseph handed him the bag, he continued: "Take care and God be with you."

The brothers continued to look at the map that Father Joseph had placed in front of them. Meanwhile, Father Joseph departed. AUGUST 17, 1866 — The six men were riding along the Leaf River It was a cool dry day with clear skies.

"Ah, just breath that wonderful fresh air," sighed Big Joe.

"Ah yes, brother, it sure is no comparison to back home, is it?" queried John Wiederle.

"According to our map, we should be coming up to Leaf Lake soon," stated Big Joe.

"Ottertail City is our goal, before noon. When we get there, we can query more about available land. From what I've seen so far, no matter where we choose to settle, we are going to have a lot of work to do. There are trees everywhere."

"Yes, and I've noticed quite a few Indians along the trail," added Mike Doll.

"Johnnie how are we doing with our supplies?" asked Big Joe.

"About two days' worth," replied Mr. Frey.

"Good. We'll be in Ottertail City soon. Then, we can stock up again."

The group was now approaching Leaf Lakes. The lakes were a beautiful sight. The water was crystal clear and as blue as the sky. There was an abundance of shrubbery and trees hugging the shoreline, which seemed miles long.

The caravan continued onward, arriving at Ottertail City around noon. The town was a bustling community, located on the shores of Ottertail Lake. One could see people, many people, moving here and there, all seeming to know what they were doing and where they were going. There were French fur traders, Indians, and speculators.

The six men stopped at one of the many hotels. Big Joe was the first to dismount. He tied his horse up and walked into the hotel. The rest of the men got off their horses and just stood nearby.

"Greetings sir," proclaimed the innkeeper, as he looked at Big Joe. "What can I do for you?"

"Hello, I'm looking for some information. I am representing a group of farmers and religious people from Ohio. I have been sent here in search of some fertile land, where we can take up homesteads. Whom do you suppose I should talk to?"

"Well sir, I know quite a bit about this area. From here, the Red River Ox Trail goes northward, towards Winnipeg. I have been over to Rush Lake and up the Red River, about 20 miles or so, and have seen plenty of choice land. There are hardly any white settlers up in that area, but I'm sure that'll soon change. There are Indians everywhere, but they are very friendly. I think if you just follow the cart trail, you will be able to find what you're looking for."

"Thank-you," stated Big Joe, as he turned and went back outside, returning to the other men. "Johnnie," he continued, "take this money and go get some grub at that supply house down the street."

He handed John Frey a small bag and watched him depart.

"I've been told that if we head north on that trail over there, we should be able to find some nice lands. As soon as Johnnie returns, we'll take off."

Soon, Johnnie returned with the necessary supplies, and the men mounted and began the next stage of their journey. The trail they were traveling on was very rough. In some areas, it was just wide enough for one two-wheeled cart. It seemed that there were Indians on all sides of them. Many of them were just standing alongside the trail, gazing at the new strangers who were entering their territory. It gave an eery feeling to the six men, but they continued onward, without incident.

Several hours later, they were following the shoreline of Rush Lake. They approached the mouth of the Red River, on the northern side of the lake. It was a beautiful location, and that is exactly what the men thought. Just by looking at the banks of the river, they could tell that it had been a dry summer in the area. It looked as if the river should be 10-15 feet across, but, in some areas, it was only a step wide.

"I think we'll spend the night here," noted Big Joe. "Tomorrow, we can go out and scout the area. This might just be the spot we've been looking for."

The men hastily built a campfire, for the night. The sun was just beginning to set, and it was already cooling down. Johnnie busily prepared a meal of beans, while the others gathered around him.

Over the next few days, the men split up in pairs and scouted the area. All reports were the same when they came back. Excellent soil, but plenty of trees. It would mean a lot of hard work, but they all agreed that a settlement could be built here. It was far enough away that Father Joseph could run his society, without much interference, and it would be far enough away so that the parents could raise their children under ideal Christian practices.

Big Joe immediately sent word back to Ohio, informing Father Joseph that land had been found, and they should prepare immediately for the trip to Minnesota. After delivering the letter for the stage line at Ottertail City, Big Joe went over to the land office, to stake a claim for all the land located on both sides of the Red River, on the northern side of Rush
Lake. Enough land was claimed to provide subsistence for the religious community, as well as for 15-20 families. The title to the land was put in the name of Father Joseph, as he was the one who was financing the entire deal.

As Big Joe returned to the campsite, he noticed several Indians, dressed in their native garb, at the campsite. They all had long black hair and paint on their faces. It looked as if they were trying to show the men something. Although the men couldn't understand
the language of the Indians, and the Indians were unable to comprehend what the white men were saying, they each seemed to be getting their point across.

The Indians were showing the white men, rutabagas. These hardy vegetables were easy to plant and grew quickly. There would still be enough time for the men to plant and harvest them before the cold winter set in.

"Joseph," stated John Wiederle, as he noticed Big Joe approaching, "look what these Indians brought us. Rutabagas. They have enough here for us to plant. I think they are trying to tell us to plant them now, and that we would be able to harvest them before winter."

Big Joe looked down at the huge pile of seeds and rutabagas that the Indians had placed on a blanket, near the campfire. As he looked them over, a smile came to his face, and he said:

"How kind they are! Pick out a spot and plant them right away. See what we have in our supplies that they might like, in exchange."

Mr. Wiederle walked over to the knapsack and began rummaging through it, being watched very closely by the five Indians. Soon, he came up with some bread. He took several loaves and gave them to the Indians. They looked at it very strangely. John tore a piece off and began to eat it, as the Indians watched. Then one of them decided to try it. After chewing on it for several seconds, he expressed his appreciation and told the others how good it was. Soon, all of them were eating it. They took the remaining loaves, smiled, and left the campsite.

These native Americans proved to be of much help to the newcomers. Over the next few days, they showed the men how to find, and shoot, the abundant wild game that seemed to be everywhere in the area.

One morning, the cook, Johnnie Frey, decided to take his shotgun and venture into the woods, in search of more food for the camp. He walked along the river for quite some distance. Then, he went into the thick forest. He was aghast at the beautiful sights his eyes were beholding. Not paying any attention to where he was heading, he soon realized that he was lost. He sat down by a big rock and wondered which way to go. It was getting late, and the sun was already beginning to set. What was he to do? He became frightened. He thought he heard strange noises, but he could see nothing. There was plenty of wild game in the area, but there was also something else that he did not realize. There were Indians everywhere, and they were not friendly.

The longer Johnnie sat there, the more frightened he became. He kept looking around. Hearing a snap of a twig, he would jump up and turn around. Seeing nothing, he would sit back down. Then something happened. Instantaneously, an arrow pierced his forehead. It was a mortal blow. He fell to the ground, in excruciating pain. He was quickly losing blood. Lying on the ground, he gasped: "Oh my God! What have they done?"

Once word was received in Ohio, plans were hastily made for the upcoming trip. The men proceeded in selling their lands and much of their personal property. Since most of the crops had already been harvested for the season, they also sold them. Those who were not able to sell, appointed someone to sell for them. Each farmer saved some of his income for his own personal use, but each gave a sizable share to Father

Joseph, for safekeeping. This money was to be used by him for the betterment of the community — partly for the trip, and partly for the new settlement. On the 26th of September, Father Joseph sat down by a makeshift table and chair and wrote a letter to Archbishop Purcell.

He was there for several minutes, before he began to write the following:

Dear Most Reverend Archbishop, Experience teaches. I am sorry for having transgressed, the cause I could not agree, as you are aware, with some of the Congregation of Sanguinists in Ohio. And, for peace's sake, I would prefer living in the wilderness. My wish is to be submissive to your commands and all Catholic bishops. My desire is to go to Minnesota and establish a convent there. At present, there are some of the brothers, as

you are aware, who bought some land. As to the remarks I have made at St. Josephs, I recall all I have said or done that displeased you. I humbly ask my restoration and the necessary papers for leaving the group.

Respectfully yours,
Your humble servant,

P. Joseph M. Albrecht.

Father Joseph laid down the pen and sat back. He knew that he would have to have episcopal permission to leave Ohio and transfer into the jurisdiction of another Bishop. He figured that this letter may be the key to weaken the Archbishop. He felt it was worth a try.

Father Joseph sent the letter off, but he did not remain in Ohio long enough, to get a reply. Several days later, on October 4, 1866, the entire group departed.

Altogether, there were 60 people making the trip. They were to be transported to the railroad station, by friends and relatives, who chose to remain in Ohio, for the time being. The list included: Godfrey Schlachter, Father Joseph, Sister Lucretia, Sister Lydia, Sister

Agamonti, Sister Afra, Sister Rustika, Sister Cherubim, Sister Barbara Flaif, Sister Seraphim, Teresa Arnold, Mary Ann Graf, Rosa Wahl, Josephine Thienig, Caroline Schuh, Emma Bliley, and Martha Eifert; Bruno and Mary Boedigheimer, and family, Frank, Joseph A., William, Aurelia, Ignatius, Ferdinand, LeAnder, Frank, Emma, Julia, and Cornelius; Anton and Matilda Bender, his father, Joseph, and their children: Frank, Joseph, George, John, Mary, and Anna.

Joseph Weis and his wife, Magdalen, and their newborn son, Charles; Frank and Susan Staab, and their children: John, Maria, Joseph, Anton, Adeline, Theresa, and Charles; Victor Eifert, and his wife, Matilda, and their children: John, Catharine, Frank, and Martha, as well as several single men: John Weis, Joachim Weis, and Clemence Cole.

This group of ardent followers had all originated from the same area of Baden. Some of them had even known Father Joseph, when they were still back in the old country. They all had the same type of upbringing — the same as Father Joseph's. Consequently, it was,

therefore, very easy for them to pull up stakes once more and move with him.

Religion was not the only reason why they were so willing to leave. Most of these settlers had been in Ohio long enough to see their children born, grow up, and get married. With usually large families, the farmland began to get divided up. Soon, there were too many people for the amount of land available. This trip to Minnesota would help alleviate that problem.

Another problem that the settlers were hoping to overcome, was that of health. Cholera was still a commonly feared household word in Ohio. By moving to Minnesota, they were hoping to leave that part of their vocabulary behind.

Mr. & Mrs. Anton Bender

Trip To Minnesota

CHAPTER XIX

The group slowly departed the Boedigheimer farm. Father Joseph was in the lead wagon, along with Sister Lucretia, and several other nuns. They were followed, one after another, by each of the families.

Tears came to the eyes of many as they were leaving what had been their home for the past 20 years or more. Many happy moments, as well as some sad ones, were spent there. Now, it was time for them to move on again. It was time to move to a new land, a new
land that held many question marks. They were placing their futures in the hands of God, for only he knew what was in store for them.

It was not long, and the group arrived at the train station. They had very little time to transfer their belongings from the wagons to the awaiting cars — one for their belongings, and two for themselves.

Father Joseph took care of all the financial affairs, with each of the adult males being responsible for their own individual families. Considering the circumstances, everything went very smoothly. Anton Doll, Joseph Riesterer, Charley Foltz, Wendolin Doll, and Ignatz Schoeneberger came along with the sole purpose of returning the wagons.

"Well, my dear friends," stated Father Joseph, as he was about to board the train, "I shall miss all of you. We'll make sure to let you know how everything goes once we get to Minnesota. Hopefully, by next summer all of you will be able to come also."

"Good-bye Father Joseph," exclaimed Ignatz, as he gave him a big hug. Take good care and say hello to my son for me."

"Ah, that I will, Ignatz."

"Be sure to save us some good farmland," added Wendolin. "I just know that we will be seeing you again."

"Good-bye Wendolin."
"I don't know what we will do here in your absence," noted Charley Foltz, as he took his turn at hugging Father Joseph.
"You all will be in my prayers,"

continued Father Joseph, as he waved his arm to them. Hugs and kisses were noticed coming from other friends who were at the station, to see the departing members off. Finally, as the train whistle blew, Father Joseph looked at the small crowd and gave them a blessing. The people responded by genuflecting and making the sign of the cross. With that, Father Joseph turned and boarded the train, as it slowly began to leave the station, gradually picking up steam, and heading for the next destination — Chicago.

It was an exciting trip for everyone, especially the children. They enjoyed sitting by the windows and watching the beautiful countryside scenery go by them. Father Joseph was sitting near the front of the car, with Bruno and Anton. Several of the women were by the cookstove, making supper for their families. Several of the nuns were sitting in the back, busily praying the rosary.

"We will soon be in Chicago," stated Father Joseph. "We are to transfer to the Milwaukee line, which will take us up to Wisconsin. This will give us a first-hand chance to see the community that Father Ambrose has built."

"Are we going to have much time in Chicago?" asked Anton.
"No Anton. According to my tickets, we will only have about an hour to get to the next train. So, when we do get there, we will have to make sure we all stay close together and transfer our belongings as quickly as possible."

When the train approached Chicago, the children really became excited. Never before did they see such a sight. So many buildings! It seemed as if there were miles and miles of the same thing. The closer the train came to the station, the slower it went. Finally, it came to a halt.

"Make sure we all stay together," shouted Father Joseph, as he got up from his seat, and looked at the followers. Everyone quickly got their belongings together and got off the train. The older boys helped the single men transfer the baggage, using four-wheel carts to move them to their next train.

The men, women, and children all stayed close together, as they followed Father Joseph into the depot. "Watch out for pick-pockets," shouted Bruno, as he turned around and looked at some of the other men. "I've heard that kind of thing happens quite often around here."

As he finished saying this, he checked his own money belt, which was wrapped around his left shoulder. It was hidden under his shirt, so no one could really notice it. The transfer almost went without incident. It so happened that young Godfrey Schlachter had second thoughts. During the trip from Ohio to Chicago, he had spent his time contemplating the move. When he left Himmelgarten, he was sure that Father Joseph was right. Now, he was beginning to wonder. While they were at the depot, he approached Father Joseph.

"Father Joseph. I need to talk to you," he shouted, over the noise of the crowd. "I have been thinking it over and have decided that I want to return to Ohio. I think my heart remains with our Sanguinist brothers and sisters, in Ohio."

"What! Now is a fine time to say that. What do you propose me to do?"
"Nothing. All I ask, is that you give me permission to return."

"Sure, but you won't get a cent from me. If you want to return, fine. You will have to find your own way back."

"I'll walk, if I have to," blurted Godfrey, as he turned away from Father Joseph, and left.

"Godfrey," shouted Father Joseph, "I hope you know what you are doing."

"I do Father Joseph, I do."

This first defection bothered Father Joseph, immensely. Ever since Godfrey had first arrived at Himmelgarten, he was a favorite of Father's. Now, he turned his back on him. Father Joseph had no time for that. He thought maybe he had been too hard on him. Maybe he should have given him some aid to get back. Maybe if he would have tried to convince him to continue on, he could have succeeded. No, he finally thought, if he would give in to one, he would probably soon be giving in to others. He now was convinced that he made the right decision.

The group now boarded their next train and were soon on their way out of Chicago. It was not long, and they had entered the state of Wisconsin. Everyone on board was enjoying the trip. It was to be an experience they would never forget. The landscape was beautiful. Trees were everywhere. Tall jack pines spread out as far as the eye could see. Lake Michigan, on the right, was an awe-inspiring scene. To some, it brought back memories of their trek from LeHavre to New York. To others, it just looked like an awful lot of water. The journey continued onward. Finally, the train pulled into the small town of Manitowac. As they approached the station, Father Joseph immediately picked out Father Ambrose, who was standing on the platform, in front of the depot.

The group again proceeded to transfer their belongings. Father Joseph was the first to get off, and he was welcomed by Father Ambrose. Father Ambrose Oschwald, born one day before Father Joseph, on March 14, 1801, in Mundelfingen, Baden, still looked quite young for his 65 years. He had a receding hairline, was quite thin, and somewhat shorter than Father Joseph.

"Welcome Joseph," stated Father Ambrose, as he hugged his old friend.

"Welcome to Wisconsin. It is good to see you again."

"Yes Ambrose, it is good to see you also. It has been quite some time. I have often thought of you, since our days together, back in the homeland. How is everything?"

"Fine. Just fine. I have had several of my men bring their farm wagons along, to get your belongings over to St. Nazianz."

"Anton," shouted Father Joseph, "make sure everything gets unloaded."

"Yes, Father."

"Ambrose," Father Joseph continued, "Here is Sister Lucretia. You probably remember her as my maid, Barbara."

"Ah, yes. Hello dear Sister," stated Father Ambrose, as he shook hands.

"Hello, Father Ambrose," quietly replied Sister Lucretia.

"Come ride in my wagon, Joseph," continued Father Ambrose.

Father Ambrose Oschwald

"This is our community," stated Father Ambrose to Father Joseph, as he pointed to both sides of the road. "We live a very simple life here. When we arrived in '54, all the property was held in common.

Whenever anyone needed help, the community provided it. No one needed to worry about starving or doing without the necessities of life. As time went by, we made several minor changes. Now, each family personally owns some land."

"Has this way of life been satisfying to the people?"
"Overall, I would say yes. We have had a few who were influenced by the devil and thought of nothing but themselves. We have no place for those types. They are free to leave whenever they want."

The group was now approaching the village of St. Nazianz, from the east. The town was platted out in 90-degree angles. Very clean looking. At the end of the main street was the convent. In the middle of town, to the left, was located St. Gregory's Catholic Church. This was one of the first buildings erected by the early settlers. The two-story wooden-framed building pointed to the north. It was 32'x24'.

There were four windows on the west and east sides of each floor. Entrance to the church was from the west side. There were two doors there, one for the parishioners, and one for Father Ambrose. There were three windows on the first floor of the front, and three on the second. Two windows were located higher, and still one more up near the top of the roof. The church tower was quite small, with air vents located on all four sides. There was a chimney protruding about ten feet behind the steeple. The group momentarily, stopped at this building, where Father Ambrose stated:

"This is my church, and my home. Joseph, please come in with me."
While Father Joseph and Father Ambrose got off the wagon and walked toward the church, the others remained in their wagons. As the two men entered the rear door, Father Ambrose continued:

"The other door leads upstairs. That is where the church is located. The first floor is where I live."

As they entered the room, Father Joseph noticed how neat it was. There was a small cookstove immediately to the left, with several pots and pans on top. A desk was located to the right. Next to that was a small table and chair. On the table was a large crucifix, Bible, and several papers. Beside the table, was located Father's bed, with a rocking chair next to that. There was a large, framed picture of Father Ambrose on the wall, above the bed. Near this picture was also a framed picture of Jesus on the Cross. On the wall, to the left of the doorway, was a picture of the Blessed Virgin Mary. The floor was made of planks, and it squeaked in several places, as the men entered.

"Welcome to my home."
"Very nice, Ambrose. An ideal atmosphere."
"Please, have a seat, and rest your bones," continued Father Ambrose, as he pushed a chair in the direction of Father Joseph.
"Thank-you."

As the two men sat down, there was a knock at the door. Father Ambrose got up and walked over to see who it was. "Ah, Anton," he exclaimed. "Come in."

"Joseph. You remember Anton Stoll, don't you? He is my assistant. Without him, I would have failed years ago."

"Why, yes. Hello, Anton," stated Father Joseph, as he shook hands.

"Hello Joseph."

"Father Ambrose has told me a lot about you," continued Mr. Stoll. He then turned to Father Ambrose, and continued:

"Where should we house these people?"

"Put the sisters and girls in the convent and find room in the monastery for the families. I'm sure you will have plenty of room."

"We won't be able to stay very long, Ambrose," interrupted Father Joseph. "We have to get to Minnesota before winter sets in. I have several brothers already there, and I'm sure, they could use our help in building the houses."

"I understand. Tomorrow, I'll show you around. Hopefully, you will find everything to your liking. Much of the community was set according to our ideals, set up back in Baden."

"Yes. I'm very interested in finding out how you set this up.

Please tell me about it."

"I've told you quite a bit in my letters, but this is basically what has happened. Before we left, I drew up a set of rules. This is it,"
stated Father Ambrose, as he gave several sheets of paper to Father Joseph. Father Joseph took the papers and began to read.

"Pay particular attention to numbers 4, 5, 9, 15, 24, and 29. The money at hand shall be put together for the purchase of lands in common. #9 is the public morality shall be guarded by the Ephorate, which shall consist of 12 elders and the priest of the place. #15 is the mode of living will be in common as much as possible. And here is #29, which reads: those who will not obey the rules and regulations of the Senate, and of the undersigned, cannot be admitted in the parish, nor remain there. There must be charity, harmony, true Christian fraternal love, and real Christianity in the parish, as well as in the convents."

After several minutes, Father Joseph set the sheets down on the desk, and looked at Father Ambrose. "Very interesting. When I get my group set up in Minnesota, that is exactly the way I want it. Has it worked out for you, so far?"

"We have had to make several changes, but only minor ones. Problems sometime arise, usually when newcomers arrive. Then, on several occasions, we had people become too selfish and worldly. The only way we could correct it was by having them leave. Tomorrow, when I show you around, I'll let you talk to some of the people who live here, then you'll see how much of a success we have had."

"Very well," replied Father Joseph. "Now, I think I should like to lie down for a while. I have not been feeling very well these past few days."

"Hope it isn't serious."

"No. Just a minor headache, once in a while."

"Here, lie down on my bed. You are more than welcomed to use it."

"Thank-you," noted Father Joseph, as he laid down. The next morning, Father Ambrose was busy writing a letter by his desk, while Father Joseph was just awakening.

"Good morning," exclaimed Father Ambrose. "You must have been tired. You slept straight through."

"Please forgive me. I didn't mean to take your bed."

"That is quite alright. You apparently needed it more than I." Father Joseph slowly got out of bed. As he scratched his head, and yawned, he asked: "What time is it?"

"Nearly ten o'clock," replied Father Ambrose, as he looked at his pocket watch.

"Dear God, forgive me. I must go to the chapel."

"Fine. Just go in the front entrance, and up the steps."

Father Joseph did just that. As he entered the chapel, he was awed. The small hand-carved altar was decorated with flowers of every color. Small statues of the Blessed Virgin Mary, Joseph, and Jesus adorned it. Three candle holders were on each side. The altar cloth was a hand-made linen of the most superb white quality. A small communion railing was situated to the left and in front of the altar. The wooden pews were all hand-carved and very ornate. He knew that many hours had been spent in creating such a splendid home for the Holy Eucharist.

"This is the way I want my church to be built," he said to himself, as he stopped by the communion railing, knelt down, and began to silently pray.

Meanwhile, Father Oschwald and Mr. Stoll were having a discussion in Father's room.
"That is an excellent group of sisters that Father Albrecht brought along," stated Mr. Stoll, as he poured himself a cup of coffee.

"I know many of them and would consider it an honor if they would stay here and help us out. Maybe we can convince Father Joseph, to leave them here for the winter."
"That is exactly what I was going to suggest."

"I'm sure he won't mind. If I can convince him that it would be better if he went ahead without the sisters, he would have less difficulty preparing for the winter."

Just then, Father Joseph reappeared. "Well Ambrose, are you ready to show me around?"
"Of course," replied Father Ambrose, as he arose from his chair.
"We can't take much time though. I'd like to be leaving by at least tomorrow."

The two men left the house and began walking down the street.
"The first building that I'll show you is the Holy Ghost Convent. We finished it in 1860. It is that building over there,"

Father Ambrose stated, as he pointed to a large quadrangular structure. The three-story building was 84'x84'. The first two floors, each had 8 windows on each side. Each window had 12 small panes of glass. The third floor had small 4-pane windows jutting out from the roof. The stucco walls were painted pink, and that is what made the building stick out so much more than any other building in the area.
"This is where the sisters stay," continued Father Ambrose.
"As you can see, there is plenty of room."
"Yes Ambrose, maybe you would have enough room to keep some of my sisters over the winter."
"Of course, we would be glad to have them. That would be an excellent idea."

"I've been thinking about when we get to Minnesota. I'm not so sure what kind of conditions we are going to have there. It might be too hard on the women, until we get some housing built. It might be better if I only took a couple of the older ones, and left the rest with you, until next spring."

"You can be assured that I will take good care of them," noted Father Ambrose.
"I'm sure you would."
"The next building over there," continued Father Ambrose, as he pointed, "is the Loretto Monastery. This is where our brothers stay."
This was a 5-story, stucco building. The sides, each had 4 rows of windows, each containing nine. The front and the rear sides had six, in each row. Again, like the convent, there were windows protruding from the roof, on each side.

"We built the basement and the first floor out of stone, and for the remainder, we used brick."
"We have everything here that anyone needs," noted Father Ambrose, as the two continued to walk. "We have a community kitchen, blacksmith shop, barn, flour mill, smokehouse, and tannery. We have shoemakers, tailors, ropemakers, bakers, coopers, turners, carpenters, masons, brewers, brickmakers, and weavers. Just about every trade is represented."

"That is an excellent idea. The more self-sufficient you can be, the better. That way there is no need for outside help and that lessens the chance for corruption. An excellent idea."

"We are in the process of building a new church. It is to be larger than the present one. It is located on the west end of the settlement. Hopefully, it will be completed in a year or so.

It is to be 120'x55', with the spire rising to 148 feet. Last year we completed an orphanage. I still would like to have a hospital, but that might have to wait."

"I am very impressed. Someday, I hope my community will be just like this. Tell me, Ambrose, do you still practice medicine?"

"Yes, more than ever. I have learned a lot of new remedies that I would gladly show you. That might help you when you get to Minnesota."

"I would like that very much "

As this conversation was being carried out, several men approached.

"Well, well," exclaimed Father Joseph. "Wanibald, George, Joseph, what a surprise! You're all looking good."

"Hello Father," replied young Wanibald Neumaier, as he shook hands.

"Are you going to be staying long?" queried Joseph Schwab, as he took his turn at shaking Joseph's hand.

"No, I'm afraid we must leave by tomorrow."

"Good to see you again," stated George Wolfle, as he hugged Father Joseph.

"Hello Joseph."

"We understand you are taking a group to Minnesota," noted Wanibald.

"Yes, we are going to a place called Rush Lake. We are anxiously hoping that we can set up a settlement, just like yours. We too, stress the fact that it is better to live the old ways, like in the Bible. We are emphasizing community togetherness. We want to lead our own lives, and be able to practice our own religion, without any outside interference. We want to be able to speak our native language. We want to teach our children what we think is right."

"We wish you success," offered Mr. Wolfle.

"That is exactly what we are trying to do here," continued Joseph Schwab.

"Yes, and from the looks of things, everything is working out fine."

"Father, when do you want us to have the wagons ready to transfer the visitors?" queried George, as he looked at Father Ambrose.

"When will you be ready?" asked Father Ambrose, as he looked at Father Joseph.

"What time do you have Mass, in the morning?"

"Seven thirty."

"Then, have the wagons in front of St. Gregory's at nine."

"There is one more place that I'd like to show you yet, Joseph," continued Father Ambrose, as the two men began walking, away from the others.

"Come with me." Father Ambrose and Father Joseph walked up a small hill and stopped at a little stand.

"This is our shrine to the Lady of Loretto," exclaimed Father Ambrose, as he pointed at a small pedestal. Upon this stand was a statue of the Lady of Loretto, encased in glass. "We already have many pilgrims come to this shrine, each year. It is becoming a very popular place."

Father Joseph knelt down in front of the shrine, made the sign of the cross, and silently said a short prayer. After which he again made the sign of the cross and got up.

"It is beautiful. Thank-you for bringing me up here."

"It is always nice and quiet here. Very conducive for contemplation and prayer. Whenever I feel a need to be alone, here is where I come."

Just then, a young sister came running up. "Father Ambrose!

Father Ambrose!" she shouted.

"I have just come from the convent. One of the sisters from Ohio is very sick. Please come!"

"Yes, yes, sister, we will come," assured Father Ambrose, as the three began to head in the direction of the nunnery.

Upon arrival at the convent, they entered one of the side doors and walked into one of the nearby rooms. It was Sister Lucretia. She was lying in bed, all covered with several blankets. Only her head was protruding from under the covers.

"Sister Lucretia," exclaimed Father Joseph, "What is wrong?"

"Oh Father, I don't know. I haven't felt good all day. I can't eat a thing. My head is continuously spinning." As she took Father Joseph's hand, she continued: "Please forgive me."

"I'll pray for you. You just stay in here and have the good sisters take care of you."

With those words, the two priests left.

Once outside the room, Father Joseph looked at Father Ambrose, and said: "I would like to go back in and talk to Sister Lucretia, alone. Would you mind?"

"Why no. I'll go back to the church and see that the preparations are going along smoothly."

Father Joseph re-entered the room.

"Sister," he said, as he looked at the nun that was tending to Sister Lucretia, "would you please leave the room for a minute?"

The young sister nodded her head and departed, without a word.

"Sister Lucretia, I have decided to take Sister Seraphim, Sister Cherubim, and Sister Afra with me. You are to remain here, with the other girls, until I come back for you in the spring."

As he reached under his cassock, and pulled out a large black bag, and handed it to her, he continued: "Keep this bag. Do not use any of it. It will be your responsibility to take care of this and of the others, and be sure that nothing happens to them."

"I'll be better in a day or so," begged Sister Lucretia. "Can't you wait till I can come along?"

"No. It will be better this way. We don't really know what it's going to be like in Minnesota. I have no idea if the men have houses built already, or if we'll have to build them when we get there. I don't want to put too much hardship on the women. If I wait, and come back next spring, it will be much better for all of you."

"Whatever you say, Father."

"I will keep you in my prayers. Do as Father Oschwald tells you, while I'm gone. Make sure the others do likewise. It will just be a matter of months before I come back for you. Good-bye now."

"Good-bye Father," replied Sister Lucretia, as tears began forming in her eyes.

The next morning, after Mass had been completed, the travelers were making final preparations. As Father Joseph approached the lead wagon, he could see that the group was about ready to depart.

When he got up to his wagon, one of the St. Nazianz settlers came up to him, and said: "Father, there are three of us that would like to go with you. My name is Engelbert Tresch. Joseph Schwab and Carl Ottleberg would also like to go."

"Of course. You are most welcomed."

Father Ambrose, who was standing next to the wagon, overheard this request and was not the least happy at what he heard. He said nothing, but the look he gave was one of resentment. Mr. Tresch smiled and ran back to tell the others. Another young man, who had been helping get the wagons ready, now approached Father Joseph. "My name is Sebastian Hertel," said the short, 21-year-old man. "I have been talking with several of your people and am very interested in what you are doing. I would like to hear from you, once you get to Minnesota. Let me know what it's like. I plan on getting married and am really not happy here."

"Of course, Sebastian. You could come now if you wished."

"No. I better stay here for now."

"Very well," continued Father Joseph, as he turned towards Father Ambrose.

"I didn't mean to invade your domain," apologized Father Joseph, as he pulled a handkerchief from his pocket, and blew his nose.

"I realize that."

"It's just that I know so many of your people from back home. It has been a long time since I've seen them, — the Zaehringers, the Reicherts, the Goetzs, the Freys, the Clarers, the Mayers, the Kaltenbruns, the Kunzweilers, the Fehrenbachers, the Metzgers, the Mohrs, the Stahls, the Riesterers, all of them. It is such a joy to see old faces."

"I know what you mean." Father Joseph now walked around the wagon and talked to several other old friends that he had not seen for over 20 years. As he was doing this, Father Ambrose walked over to Anton Stoll, and said:

"Get everyone ready. If he stays here much longer, we won't have anyone left."

"Yes Father."

Finally, everything was ready. As Father Joseph climbed aboard the lead wagon, he turned to Father Ambrose, and said:

"Thank-you for your hospitality. Take good care of the women. I shall return for them, as soon as possible. Perhaps in March, or April. I will write to you and let you know how everything is going."

"You do that, my friend," replied Father Ambrose, as he waved good-bye.

As the wagons began departing St. Nazianz, final farewells were given. The farm wagons trudged through the heavy forests, along a narrow trail, towards their next destination of Calumetville.

As the small caravan entered the village, the local populace came out to see what these strangers were up to. The wagons went down the main street and headed directly to the waterfront. There, everything was transferred to two small awaiting boats.

"We are making good time," remarked Father Joseph, as he stood along the dock, and watched the other men and women loading the boats. Bruno and Anton, who were standing beside him, agreed.

"We should be in Minnesota, in no time," replied Mr. Bender.

"Are you ready?" asked a heavy-set, bearded man, dressed in a heavy blue coat, as he looked at Father Joseph. "I am the boat captain, and we'll be taking off across the lake, as soon as you get aboard."

The three men hurriedly climbed aboard one of the small boats. They sat down next to Father Joseph's belongings. As the boats began to leave the shoreline, on their journey across Lake Winnebago, Anton looked at Father Joseph, and asked:

"Aren't you afraid of leaving the other women back at St. Nazianz?"
"Why should I be afraid?"
"I got the impression from the look on Father Oschwald's face, that he had plans for them."
"That is nonsense. My girls are too faithful to me, to ever think of doing anything else other than what I ask of them."

Well, I don't think he was too happy when you let those three guys come along with us," interrupted Bruno.

"Father Ambrose is not that kind of person. When I come back for them next spring, I'm sure they all will be anxiously waiting to return with me."

"Oh, my side," stated Bruno, as he grabbed his left side. "I think I'm getting sea-sick."

"Grab one of those buckets," shouted Father Joseph.

The wind was blowing quite fiercely, causing huge waves to form, which in turn, caused the boats to bob up and down at a very rapid pace. Bruno was not the only one to feel the effects of the undulating movement. Several of the others made their way over to the pails, and immediately used them. Father Joseph could do nothing to help them. He sat and watched for a short time, and then took out his rosary, and began to pray. The boat trip took the following course: across Lake Winnebago, to Oshkosh, on the Fox River, down the river to Prairie du Chien, where the Fox River flowed into the Mississippi. From there, they proceeded northward on the Mississippi, to the bustling city of St. Paul, Minnesota.

As the group of travelers disembarked from their boats, they were greeted by several of Bruno's relatives, who had already moved to St. Paul. St. Paul was a prospering city. It seemed that there were people everywhere. Several steamboats were tied up along the docks, either loading or unloading freight and passengers.

"Anton! Keep everyone together," ordered Father Joseph.

"We won't have much time here. We have to find the train station."

"We can take you over there," offered Bruno's cousin. "But, if I were you, I'd think twice about going up into that wilderness. There are all kinds of Indians there and I don't think it is safe for anyone."

"Impossible! We already have some people up there."

"Well, we've heard a lot of bad reports come from people who've been up there."

"Please, take us to the station," continued Father Joseph, as he picked up his black bag.

With that, the group was led over to the railroad station. It so happened that there were many other travelers heading northward, also. All seemed to have the same goal in mind. Cheap and abundant land. Many of them were just like Father Joseph's group. They were of German descent and from Ohio, all heading for the area around St. Cloud, and points further west. Once the group arrived at the station, Father Joseph walked inside, to get information on where he was to find the two passenger cars, which he had previously requested. Within several minutes, he returned.

"My people, come follow me. I'll show you where to go."

With that, he turned and led the group to the correct location, where a five-car train was waiting.

"Anton," continued Father Joseph, "make sure all of our belongings get on the train. The first two cars are ours."

The tired travelers once again boarded a train. Just by looking at the group, one could tell that the long journey was already taking its toll, especially among the women and the children. Soon, the train was heading northward, with its destination being St. Cloud, a small city about 85 miles away.

Father Joseph was sitting in the front seat of the first car. Beside him was Anton Bender, and across the aisle was Bruno and Mary Boedigheimer.

"Well, gentlemen," stated Father Joseph, "we don't have too much more left of this journey. I have asked God to speed things up, but I suppose he will let us get there when he thinks it is time."

"Have you noticed the beautiful scenery?" queried Bruno, as he looked out the window.

"Yes, isn't it marvelous?" replied Father Joseph. "Just like Father Pierz described it. Beautiful fall colors, rich black soil, clear blue water. Everything looks so perfect."

Upon arrival in St. Cloud, much work remained, as Father Joseph led the entire group to a nearby hotel.

"Anton, I'm going to need your help. Bring along Bruno, Frank, and Victor. We need to go down to a supply house and get everything set for our final journey."

When all five men were together, they departed. They walked along the busy street until they spotted a supply store, into which they entered.

"Gentlemen, can I help you?" queried the elderly bearded storekeeper.

"Yes," answered Father Joseph. "We need to be outfitted for a wagon trip. How much are your oxen?"
"$160.00 to $200.00 a pair, depending on which ones you buy."
"We need eight pair. How much would that be?"
"Eight pair? Let's see," replied the storekeeper, as he paused for several seconds and thought, "$1350.00."

"Fine. I'll take them. I also need six wagons, six stoves, this pile of cooking utensils here and enough salt, sugar, flour, and coffee, to last 60 people for the winter."

"Let's see, 60 people, ah, flour ... 12 barrels at $18.00 a barrel. Salt, sugar, coffee. We have plenty of sugar and coffee, but I'm a little short on salt. I'll give you as much as I can spare. These pots and pans. Let's see O.K. Here is the total bill."

"He handed the list to Father Joseph, who took and read it over, and then said: "Fine. Here is the money." He reached into his pocket and pulled out a small black bag, and quietly began to count.

"There, that should be more than enough."

The storekeeper silently counted the money. Finally, he said:

"Thank-you very much. Now, let's go get your oxen."

The five men and the storekeeper proceeded to the back of the store, where a livery stable was located.

"Pick out the eight best teams that you want," ordered the storekeeper, as he pointed at the oxen, which were in a pen, right outside of the livery.

"My wagons are located over there, next to the fence. The necessary gear is on them. Just hitch the teams up and bring them around to the front. Then, we can load up the other supplies."

As the men began looking through the herd, and picking out the good ones, Father Joseph stayed with the storekeeper.

"I would also like to buy some cows, pigs and chickens," he noted.

"Come with me," requested the storekeeper.

"I know a man down the street who just might have what you are looking for."

After leading Father Joseph back through the store, out the front door, and down the street for about a half a block, the storekeeper stopped at another small store. "Ben!" he shouted,

"I have a gentleman here, who's in need of some farm animals. Can you help him?"

"Why yes. What do you need?"

"I need about 10 milk cows, 1 bull, 10 pigs, and 30 to 40 chickens," replied Father Joseph.

"I can take care of that. You come back in about a half an hour, and I'll have everything ready."

"Good," replied Father Joseph, as he turned and followed the other storekeeper out the door. When the two men arrived back at the supply house, they found out that the men had already picked out the oxen and had them hitched to the covered wagons. They were now loading them with the supplies that Father Joseph had just purchased.

"Bruno," shouted Father Joseph, "when you get the wagons loaded, I need you and a couple of the others to come with me and get some animals. Anton, maybe you should go back to the hotel and get some of the other men. Have them take the loaded wagons back and wait for us."

"It has been a pleasure doing business with you," noted the storekeeper, as he shook Father's hand.

"Likewise. If we should run low on supplies, and need to come to St. Cloud, I'll make sure my men stop here."

Soon, Anton returned, with several other men. Father Joseph, Bruno, and a couple of others went down the street, to get the animals, while Anton, and the others, drove the loaded wagons back to the hotel. It was not long, and the last segment of their long journey began. Slowly, the wagons made their way along the Mississippi River. Father Joseph was riding in the lead wagon, which was being driven by Bruno. Each wagon that followed, was driven by one of the older men, as some of the women and children walked alongside. It was the responsibility of several of the older boys to watch over the pigs. Each of the wagons had a couple of cows tied to them, as well as several crates, which contained the newly purchased chickens. As they moved northward, they noticed fewer and fewer population centers. There were small villages springing up along the river, and farmsteads here and there, but the number of people were few. The small wagon train followed the Mississippi River, until they arrived at the small village of Pillager, which was a tiny Indian center located where the Crow Wing River flows into the Mississippi. Its location was only a few miles from the sight where Father Francis Pierz had his home. As the caravan entered the village, Father Joseph had Bruno drive the wagon up to a point where several white men were sitting, carrying on a conversation. "Can you tell me where I can find Father Pierz?" he asked, looking directly at the men.

"He lives up by Crow Wing. Just follow the Mississippi. You can't miss it. There's a small log church near the river. He spends a lot of his time taking care of the Indians, and the Catholics in the area, so you might have a problem finding him at home."

"Thank-you."

"Bruno, keep everyone here, for the night. I'm going up-river for a while. I should be back by morning."

Father Joseph turned around, looked under the seat of the wagon, picked out several of his small books, and quietly departed. Following the trail along the Mississippi, he arrived at the little village of Crow Wing, in less than an hour. As he entered, he noticed that this village was no more than several log houses and teepees. He saw several Indian children playing along the path, as well as some Indian women, working near their teepees. He then spotted an old gentleman, dressed in priest's garb, sitting near a small log building, which resembled a church.

Father Francis X. Pierz

"Hello," he exclaimed, as he walked up beside the man.

"Greetings," returned the old man, as he got up off the ground. "I am Father Joseph Maria Albrecht. I'm looking for Father Pierz."

"I am he."

"I have read many of your letters, Father, and have heeded your call. I have a group of about 60 people with me. We're headed for a place called Rush Lake. I felt that I just had to meet you before we continued our journey."

"Welcome, welcome," excitedly exclaimed Father Pierz. "It is a pleasure to my eyes to see another priest, in my midst. Please sit down here," he continued, as he pointed to a spot on the ground. Father Pierz was a short well-rounded man. He was already 81 years old, and the years of missionary work could be seen taking their toll on his body. He was slow in his walk, yet very fast in his mind.

"Please tell me more about your plans," he continued.

"I have with me several good Catholic families, sisters, and brothers. I want to set up a convent at Rush Lake, for the Precious Blood Society. We want a place where we can live alone in peace, with no outside interference."

"An excellent idea. You say this is going to be by Rush Lake?"

"Yes."

"That will be an excellent spot. The land over there is beautiful. I go up to that area once in a while. There are Chippewa Indians living around there. They are a good people who need much help. You will see."

"Precious Blood, huh?" he continued. "Are you from Ohio?"

"Why yes. Have you heard of our Society?"

"Yes. I once met Father Brunner. A very nice humble man. I don't know much about your group, but from what I've heard, it sounds very good. Tell me, have you received permission from Bishop Grace?"

"No, not yet. I plan on doing that at the earliest convenience. My main goal now is to get my people to the settlement."

"Yes, you won't have much time before winter sets in, and these Minnesota winters can be very rough. I tell you what, next month, when I'm making my rounds through that area, I'll stop and see how you are doing."

"Fine. I'll be looking forward to it."

"Where is the rest of your group?"

"I left them down at Pillager. I had sent several brothers out earlier, and they are the ones that found the spot at Rush Lake. They should be building houses there right now. I do have many more German settlers, back in Ohio, and some in Wisconsin, who have expressed an interest in our settlement, but they want to wait and find out from us what it's really like up here."

"Sounds good. We are getting quite a large number of German settlers in this area, especially around St. Cloud, and west from there. It is a pleasure to hear that now I will have some German friends up by Rush Lake."

"Tell me Father," noted Father Joseph. "What can you tell me about Bishop Grace?"

"Ah, Bishop Grace. He is a very good man; quite elderly, but very smart. He is an Irishman, but he can speak and understand German. He has his office in St. Paul, so he doesn't get up this way very often. It's too bad you didn't stop and see him when you were down there."

"He's an Irishman, huh?"

"Yes, but like I said, he does speak some German."

"But does he understand the German mind? I have yet to see an Irishman who could fully understand the mind of a German."

"You will see. I'm sure it won't be long, and you'll meet him."

"Are you the only priest around the area?"

"No, but sometimes it seems like it. There are several others, but we are so spread out, that we hardly ever see each other."

Looking at his pocket-watch, Father Joseph got back up, and said: "I should be getting back to my people. I just remembered that there were a few things I wanted to get done before nightfall. If I leave now, it still should be light when I get back."

"Must you leave so soon? You just got here."

"Yes Father, I must. I shall see you next month."

"Very well, then. God be with you."

Father Joseph shook Father Pierz's hand and departed back down the trail, towards Pillager. The thick forest hugged the shores of the Mississippi. The leaves of the birch trees were falling, but the pine trees continued to hinder his way. At several points along the river, it was very difficult for him to follow the trail. It was very quiet at this time of the evening, yet he thought he heard several strange noises, never heard before, by his ears. Upon hearing it, he would stop in his tracks, and listen, to see if he could find out where they were coming from. But he had no success. As soon as he began walking again, he would hear the same noise. Little did he know that they were the sounds of Indians, hiding in the underbrush, keeping an eye on the new stranger.

Finally, Father Joseph arrived back at Pillager. What a relief!

He was so overjoyed that when he reached the campfire, he gave a big hug to Bruno, who had just finished putting more firewood on the fire.

"Ah Bruno. It is good to be back with my people."

"What happened?"

"Oh nothing. I met Father Pierz, and had an interesting discussion with him, but the trip back here was very lonely, and the one feeling I despise is the feeling of being lonely."

"I had Mary set out your blankets over here," continued Bruno, as he pointed next to his bedroll. "I hope you don't mind."

"Not at all," remarked Father Joseph, as he hurriedly crawled under them, and quickly fell asleep.
The next morning, the group was up, bright and early. The sun had barely risen above the horizon, and Father Joseph was already preparing to leave.

"Today might be the day, my people," stated Father Joseph, as he looked at Bruno, Victor, and Anton, who were busily eating their breakfast.

"If we get going soon, we could be able to make it to our new home by sundown."

Father Joseph was excited. He had been looking forward to this day for quite some time. Many a night he had spent dreaming about what it was going to be like in his new surroundings. Finally, he was going to find out.

The travelers were still very weary, even though they did get a good night's sleep. Even though they were tired, they still found enough ambition to continue on. Soon, the eight wagons were moving. They followed the Crow Wing River, until it split into the Wing River.

"Where do we go from here?" asked Bruno, as he looked over at Father Joseph. Father Joseph took out his large map and looked it over for several seconds. "It looks like we follow the river to the left. According to this map, this is supposed to be the Wing River."

Just then, one of the men from the rear began to holler: "Stop! Stop!"

Father Joseph set his map down and looked around to see what the problem was. The last wagon had just lost one of its wheels. The caravan stopped, and several of the men walked back to the rear wagon, which had been driven by Victor Eifert, and helped him put the wheel back on. Once completed, Father Joseph looked around and noticed that the sun was already getting quite low in the sky.

"We might as well set up camp here for the night," he suggested, in somewhat of a disgusted tone. "It looks like our trip is going to take longer than I thought."

The men went back to their wagons and moved them into a circle. Preparations were made for camp. Father Joseph had hoped to be at Rush Lake, already, but several other difficulties had also arisen that day. The trail, that they were following, was of very poor quality. Due to the heavy rains of the previous few days, there were deep ruts in many areas of the road. Several times, some of the wagons got stuck. Precious time was spent getting them back onto the trail.

"Well Bruno, maybe tomorrow," he exclaimed, as he sat down near the campfire.
"Yes Father. We will just have to be patient. God will get us there when he wants us there."

"Father! Father! Can you come with me?" shouted Joe Weis, as he came running up to Father Joseph. "There's something wrong with my baby."

The two men hurried off to the Weis wagon. As Mr. Weis opened the back of the covered wagon, Father Joseph noticed Magdalene busily taking care of little Charles. He was crying. No matter what Maggie did, he continued to cry.

"What can I do?" asked Maggie. "He has been like this for the past 30 minutes."

"Give him to me."

Maggie picked up the baby and handed him to Father Joseph, who gently held the baby and rocked him in his arms.

"Oh Lord, bless this child. Make him well. Give him the health that he needs."

Within seconds, the baby stopped crying. No one ever found out what the problem was, but Charles now seemed to be fine. Father Joseph handed the infant back to his mother.

"There Maggie, I think he is alright, now."

"Thank-you, Father Joseph."

"There is no need to mention this to anyone, Joseph," noted Father Joseph. "The baby was probably just overtired from the long trip."

The next morning, the group was once more on the move. With each passing hour, the suspense mounted. They knew that soon they would be at their destination. They were all anxious to see what was in store for them. Around noon, the wagon train stopped. Father Joseph got off and walked over to Anton, who was standing beside his wagon.

"From here, we go across country. We're not far from Clitherall, and, I would venture to say, we are no more than 25-30 miles away from Rush Lake."

"Do you think we can still make it there, before nightfall?"

"I don't know. I'm beginning to wonder," replied Father Joseph, as he walked back to his wagon.

Once he sat down and grabbed the reins, he turned around and shouted to the others:

"Follow me!" The wagons continued onward, along the rough trail, which was becoming more and more difficult to travel. The hills were becoming more numerous. In some places, it seemed that there was no trail at all, and Father Joseph had to decide which way to go. After handing the reins back to Bruno, Father Joseph looked at his map. He knew that if they would head to the left, they would arrive at Clitherall, but he felt there was no need to go there, now. So, he decided to turn to the right. As the caravan slowly made its way along the eastern shore of the beautiful Battle Lake, another problem arose. Once again Victor Eifert's wagon broke down. The same wheel had fallen off again, only this time, the axle broke. As Father Joseph, Bruno, Anton, and Victor looked over the situation, Anton stated: "It seems to me that we are going to have to cut a whole new axle. There is no way we will be able to use this."

"I'm afraid you're right," replied Father Joseph. "It looks like we'll have to camp here for the night." Once again, the group prepared for the night. Several of the men and some of the boys went down by the lake, cut off some branches, whittled them down, attached a long piece of string to it, put a hook on the end, and went fishing. All they needed was some bait. One of the men grabbed a shovel, from one of the wagons, and began digging. In no time at all, he had enough worms for everyone. With that distributed, the men and boys spread out along the shore, and began searching for supper. Father Joseph took one of the makeshift poles and tried his luck. He stood along the shoreline, next to 15-year-old Frank Boedigheimer. As soon as Frank put his pole in the water, he had a bite.

"Nothing to it!" he shouted, as he pulled it onto shore.

"Some people have no trouble fishing for fish," noted Father Joseph. "And some people have no trouble fishing for men, but it looks like I'm having trouble fishing for both."

Young Frank just laughed and put his line back into the water. He really didn't understand what Father Joseph had just said, but it didn't matter anyway, because he was having fun. While some of the men were fishing, Anton, Victor, and Clemence Cole went into the nearby woods to find a log, for the broken wagon. They soon arrived back at camp with a small pole, which they believed would suffice until they got to Rush Lake. As the three men finished their task, the fisherman came back. They had been very lucky, as they had caught an abundant supply, surely more than needed. The group gathered around the campfires, and prepared for a fish fry, a meal that the new settlers would soon become accustomed to. Father Joseph got himself several pieces, and sat down next to Frank and Susan Staab, who already were eating.

"How do they taste?"

"Fine," replied Frank, as he wiped his face. "They are very fresh. This is a meal fit for a king."

Once Father Joseph was seated, he began to eat, only to be interrupted by several of the younger boys, who came running up to him. They were 6-year-old Anton Staab, 7-year-old LeAnder Boedigheimer, and 8-year-old John Eifert.

"Father Joseph," shouted LeAnder. "Will you tell us a story?"

"Of course, my children," he answered, as he continued to eat.

"What would you like to hear?"

"Anything," replied John, as the three boys hurriedly sat down around the priest.

"Well, let me see," continued Father Joseph, as he thought for several seconds. "Once upon a time there was an old man who lived in a cave. Every day he would go out and look for food. He would hunt for the wild deer, and turkeys, and ducks, anything that was edible. He would take it back to his cave and store it for the winter. Since he was a very good hunter, he soon had his entire storage area full of meat. Nevertheless, he continued to go out each day and search for more. One day, while he was getting ready to go out, a young boy, who was also out hunting, stopped at the cave.

'What are you doing young fella?' he asked. 'I am trying to find some food for my parents, who are very sick,' replied the young boy. 'Aren't you having any success?' asked the man.

'No, I've been out all day and have seen nothing. I don't know what I'm going to do.' The old man invited the boy in. Once inside, he showed him all of the food that he had stored up for the winter. 'Can I have some of that to take back to my parents?' asked the boy. 'Of course not,' replied the old man. 'I spent a lot of time getting this.' The boy, dejectedly turned, and left.''

"The next day, the old man was again out hunting. While he was gone, the young boy went into the cave and took some of the meat and hurried back home. When the old man came back, he noticed that someone had stolen some of his supplies. Thinking about it for several seconds, he decided that it must have been the boy, since he was the only one that knew about it. He became very angry, yet there wasn't a thing he could do, because he did not know where to find the boy."

"About a week later, the old man was again in the forest, hunting. Again, he met the young boy. 'Were you at my cave last week?' asked the old man, in a very gruff voice. The little boy, knowing that it was a sin to lie, replied:

'Yes sir.' 'Did you take some of my meat?' 'Yes sir.' 'Don't you know that it is a sin to steal?' 'Yes, I do.' 'What should I do to you?' 'I did not steal it,' objected the boy. 'I only borrowed it so that my parents would not starve to death. As soon as I get some more, I'll repay you."

"The angry man raised his right arm, as if to strike at the young boy, and just then, he had a heart attack and died. Now, can any of you tell me the moral of the story?"

The three little boys looked at each other and shook their heads in the negative.

"Well, my boys," continued Father Joseph, "it is always better to give than to receive, and there is a difference between stealing and borrowing."

"Now," added Father Joseph, "I think it is time for children to be sleeping. Find your blankets, and don't forget to say your prayers."

"Good night, Father Joseph," stated each of the children, as they scurried off.

"Good night."

The next day, the caravan was again on the move. As each hour passed, the more anxious everyone was becoming. As they slowly made their way around Ottertail City, large mounds could be seen to their right. "What a peculiar place for hills!" stated 12-year-old John Staab, who was riding in the lead wagon, with Father Joseph.

"Those aren't hills. They are Indian mounds. That is an Indian cemetery."

As they continued on, the people noticed more and more Indians standing alongside the trail. They were quite shy, yet very curious. They were wondering what all these people were doing on their land. The wagons continued onward. A little futher down the trail, Father Joseph and John Staab noticed a big black bear, tied to a chain. He was growling at them as they went by.

"I never saw a real live bear before," stated John, as he moved closer to Father Joseph.

"It looks like that one is a pet. It's tied up, so there's nothing to be afraid of."

Soon, they arrived at Rush Lake. Father Joseph stopped the wagon near the creek, that flowed out of the lake. He got down and walked to the shore.

"Bruno," he shouted, "it looks pretty deep here. I don't think we can cross here."

"I think you're right," replied Bruno, as he walked up beside Father Joseph, and looked at the river. "But look over there," he continued, as he pointed toward the mouth of the river.

"See that sand ridge out there? Maybe we can drive the wagons on that. It doesn't look like more than a foot deep."

Bruno walked into the water and followed the sandbar around to the other shore. "It looks good," he shouted, as he began returning to the wagons.

"Anton, you go first. I'll follow," stated Father Joseph, as he looked at Mr. Bender, who had just walked up beside Father Joseph.

"If we follow the shoreline, I think we should run into the settlement," stated Father Joseph, as he looked at his map. "Once everyone is across, I'll take over the lead again."

Anton returned to his wagon and began the trek across. One by one, they began to cross over, following the trail that Bruno had discovered. When they were all safely across, they continued onward. The area along Rush Lake was densely wooded. There was a cart trail to follow, but sometimes it was very difficult. As they began to 'follow the north side of the lake, they had to cross another river. This creek was about four feet wide, and very shallow. The wagons were able to cross without incident. However, two of the boys, 8-year-old Joseph Staab, and 7-year-old John Bender, had been following the last wagon. They realized, too late, that they had been stranded. They hollered for help, but no one heard them. They decided to run and jump across. They didn't make it. They landed in the icy, cold water. They both got up and ran after the wagons. As soon as they caught up with them, they jumped into their wagons in search of blankets, and the security of their mothers.

Finally, the wagons approached the mouth of the Red River. Their long journey was coming to an end. At last, the people could see where they were going to be making their new home. A large smile was on Father Joseph's face, for he was very pleased at what he saw. Near the river were several brothers, busily building small log houses. Two of the houses had already been completed and they were working on two more.

These houses were being built in a circle, on about an acre of cleared land. Each house had only one door, at the front, and one window in the gables. Father Joseph jumped off his wagon and ran up to the brothers, giving Big Joe, a hug.

"We made it!" he shouted. "We finally made it!"

"Good to see you again, Father," remarked Big Joe. "Welcome to your new home."

The entire group of newcomers were now off the wagons and looking around at the settlement. They all seemed very relieved and pleased at what they saw. The children were running here and there, having a good time, not really knowing what was happening.

"We have some bad news for you, Father," stated Big Joe.

"Johnnie Frey is no longer with us. He went hunting one day, by himself, and never returned. We don't know what happened to him."

"Oh my!" exclaimed Father Joseph.

"The houses that we are building are not the best, but they should suffice for the winter," noted Big Joe. "We had hoped to have eight of them built, by the time you got here, but we have been having problems. Now that we have more help, we should be able to get a lot more done."

"Have you started on the church, yet?"

"No. We thought we'd have you pick out the sight. Then, you could also tell us how you wanted it built."

That evening, everyone gathered around the campfires. Father Joseph held a prayer service, which included the rosary. All seemed to be content at the settlement.

Early Life at the Rush Lake

CHAPTER XX

When morning arrived; the people were startled. They were surrounded by Indians; at least 200 of them. They entered the camp in large groups, curious to see what the white men had brought with them. All of them were wearing blue paint stripes on their faces.

They looked fierce but were actually quite gentle. They had brought with them several piles of calico corn. They began trading this corn for some of the wares and clothes of the settlers. They also had fish and deer meat. They offered this in exchange for flour and baked bread. Within an hour, their trading was completed, and they departed, much to the relief of many of the women.

Work continued fiercely on the houses. It was just a matter of days and eight of the shelters were completed. All of them were built exactly alike. Wild reeds, from near the river, were used for each of the roofs. The floors were strewn with these reeds, also, three to four inches deep, to protect the inhabitants from the cold ground. There were no nails in the settlement, so all of the logs were fastened together by small wooden pegs.

As the men put the finishing touches on the houses, Father Joseph walked up to Brother John Wiederle. "Brother John," he said, "come with me."

As they entered one of the houses, Father Joseph continued:

"Since we have no beds, we'll have to improvise. If we bore holes into the wall, here, put a pole into it, take a large pole, stand it up, and attach them, we will have the framing for a bed. Then, we can put flat boards and grass on top of them and we'll have a bed."

"Take several men," he added, "and do this in all the houses."

Since the settlers were unable to bring much of their furniture with them, they also had to improvise there. Wooden crates were used as tables. Stumps were used as chairs. Along with the pole beds, this is what the houses contained, as far as furniture was concerned.

Father Joseph had picked out the sight for his new church and was in charge of its construction. It was located near the houses, and several hundred feet from the river. It was to be a log building, facing westward. Within several weeks, after their arrival, the exterior had been completed. It would not be long, and Father Joseph would be able to celebrate his first Holy Mass in Minnesota.

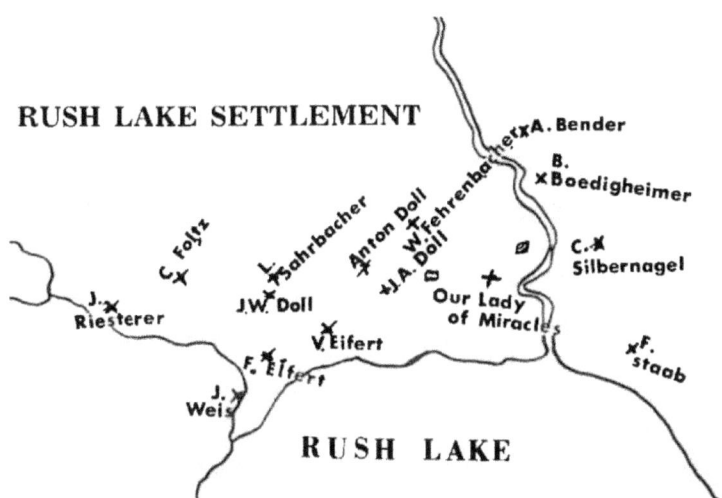

During these first few weeks at Rush Lake, another tragedy occurred. The 27-year-old Brother Clemence Cole had become ill, almost immediately upon arrival. He was kept in one of the covered wagons. Sister Theresa Arnold, the regular nurse, had remained in St. Nazianz, so Father Joseph and Sister Cherubim attended to his needs.

As each day passed, his condition worsened. "Brother Clemence, there is no more we can do for you," noted Father Joseph, one morning. "I have been praying for you, day and night. Your pneumonia attack just doesn't seem to be getting any better."

"Father, I realize that my days are numbered. All I ask is that you give me a proper burial and pray that I have the good fortune of entering heaven."

"That I promise."

With those words, Brother Clemence died. A tear came to Father Joseph's eyes. His group was slowly becoming smaller and smaller. First it was Godfrey Schlachter, then Johnnie Frey, and now, Clemence Cole.

"Oh Lord, Jesus Christ, King of Glory, deliver the soul of Brother Clemence from the pains of Hell and from the bottomless pit; deliver him from the lion's mouth, that he'll not swallow him up, that he falls not into darkness, but let St. Michael bring him into that holy light, which you promised of old to Abraham and to his seed. May light eternal shine upon him, Oh Lord, with your saints, forever. Amen," stated Father Joseph, as he knelt beside the lifeless body of one of his ardent followers.

Father Joseph then wiped his eyes, got up, and left the wagon.

"Anton, we need a coffin built. Brother Clemence has just died," noted Father Joseph, as he got out of the wagon, and looked at Mr.

Bender, who had been patiently awaiting Father Joseph. "Yesterday, I was up on that hill over there," he pointed out. "I think it would be a beautiful spot for a cemetery. It's right next to the river, and you can see for a long distance from there. I think we'll bury Clemence up there."

Anton proceeded to knock apart several crates, from which he was able to build a makeshift coffin.

The next day, Clemence was buried. It was a sad occasion for everyone at the settlement, especially for Father Joseph, for it had been Father Joseph who had convinced Clemence to lead a life as a brother, in the Precious Blood Society. He had come from the parish of St. Henry, and had become the pride of Father Joseph, at Himmelgarten. He had plans for him, to study for the priesthood, but those plans now had been cancelled.

As the people were returning from the cemetery, they noticed a visitor approaching from the west. It was the 81-year-old Father Pierz.

"Greetings Father," exclaimed Father Joseph, as he walked over and met Father Pierz.

"Hello my dear friend."

"Welcome to our community."

"How is everything coming along?"

"Good. We are prepared for the winter. We all have shelter, and our church is almost complete. Would you like to see it?"

"Yes, I would."

The two men walked toward the new church. It was a small structure, yet beautiful in its own way. Upon entering, one could see the altar. It was a simple wooden structure. There were three pictures on the wall, directly behind. On one side was the Blessed Virgin Mary. In the middle, the Sacred Heart of Jesus, and on the other, the Holy Family. To the rear of the structure was joined a large square convent, for the sisters. Toward the Blessed Virgin

Mary side of the sanctuary was attached a small chapel. It was separated by a long sliding window of three glass pains, which faced directly upon the altar. The tabernacle, a simple wooden box, could be pivoted upon its base to face the chapel. It was in this chapel, that the sisters would assist in the Mass. It was here that they were to make their nocturnal hours of adoration of the Blessed Sacrament. It was here that they would perform their daily spiritual exercises, according to the Precious Blood rule.

"Very nice," exclaimed Father Pierz.

"We are going to dedicate it to 'Our Lady of Miracles.'"

"Is the Bishop coming to consecrate it?"

"I haven't had time to talk to him, yet. Maybe, I could get your help. Could you write a letter to Father Kunkier, in Ohio, asking for my pardon, and for a legal dismissorial, sanctioned by Archbishop Purcell? I need that, in order to get legal admission from Bishop

Grace, in St. Paul. Maybe you could also mention to him that I would like for him to come and see our new convent and church, and that we could use more new members."

"Yes, I can surely do that much. In the meantime, I think you should still try and talk to Bishop Grace. I'm sure he would be very

interested in what you are doing here. Under the circumstances, he would be very sympathetic to your cause."

"Yes, I plan on doing that at my earliest convenience."

"Would you like for me to say Mass here tomorrow?"

"That would be a very good idea," answered Father Joseph, with a smile.

Word quickly spread throughout the community, that Mass would be held the next day. How overjoyed everyone was! They would finally have the chance to receive Holy Communion again. Up to this time, on Sundays, they had prayed the rosary and Father Joseph had read from the book. Their first Mass in Minnesota was finally to be held.

The three sisters were especially excited. They hurried about the small church, getting everything prepared. It was already the middle of November, so they made sure there was enough wood by the new stove, so that no one would get too cold the next day.

The next morning, everything seemed perfect. The skies were clear and the air, refreshing. It had rained the night before, but now the sun was brightly shining. It was a cool day, but that was typical for this time of the year.

Everyone in the community, even the youngest of children, came to church. All were anxious to partake in the Holy Mass. After Mass was completed, Father Pierz and Father Joseph met outside of the church.

"Thank-you for coming," noted Father Joseph.

"Thank-you for having me. I must be on my way, though. I will give you the authority to carry on your church work here, under the condition that you go see the Bishop and obtain the proper credentials, at your earliest convenience."

As he handed Father Joseph a piece of paper, he continued:

"Show this to the Bishop, when you get there."

"Yes Father, I will leave for St. Paul, tomorrow," replied Father Joseph, as he took the paper.

"Then, I will be on my way. Take care, and God be with you. I'll try and stop by again in about a month."

"Good-bye Father," stated Father Joseph, as he stood and watched Father Pierz head northward, along the river. After he was out of sight, Father Joseph went over to several men, who were talking in front of their house. "Anton, Bruno, Victor, greetings," he stated. "Tomorrow, I must make a journey to St. Paul. I must talk with Bishop Grace and get his permission to say Mass here. While I'm gone, I want you three to make sure everything goes alright. The rutabagas should be about ready to harvest. Get them picked and put in the cellar. Give out to the people only what they need. These vegetables will have to last us all winter. I don't know how long I'll be gone, but it shouldn't be more than two weeks."

Father Joseph then turned, and walked over to his house, which was a simple little building, just like the others. He sat down on a block of wood and picked up his breviary and began to pray. All at once, he stopped, put down the book, and began to daydream. Would it be worthwhile even to go to St. Paul?" What if Bishop Purcell or Father Kunkier had already written to him and told him their side of the story? Who would Bishop Grace believe? Surely, he would take the side of Bishop Purcell. Surely, he would hold the same view. Why not? They were both Irishmen. They wouldn't understand his predicament. Surely, one Irishmen would be as stubborn as the next. Oh well, he had better try anyway."

The next day, Father Joseph was off on his journey. Dressed in his usual garb of worn-out clothes and shoes, he carried only a small knapsack in one hand, and a rosary in the other. Rather than ride a horse, he walked. He walked the entire distance to St. Paul, a distance of over 200 miles.

The journey was uneventful. He would walk at a modest pace, usually praying the rosary, and just admiring the surroundings. It was starting to get quite cold at nights, with the day temperature getting into the low 50's, and into the 20's during the night. The leaves were falling from the trees, a sure sign that winter was near. He realized this and knew that he could not waste any time along the way. He had to get to St. Paul and back before the snows came. On the seventh day of his trip, he arrived in St. Paul. He had been told that he could possibly find the Bishop at the St. Paul Cathedral, which was located on St. Peter Street. All Father Joseph had to do was ask someone where St. Peter Street was. This he did, and in about one hour's time, he had found the cathedral. It was a large building, with a basement, two stories, and an attic. It was a rectangular building with a long stairway, leading to the front entrance. There were three rows of windows on each side. Each row had six windows. The front of the building had a door to the left of the steps, leading into the basement. A window was located on each side of the entranceway. There was a row of three windows on the third floor, spread apart at an equal distance. There was one window in the attic. There were three chimneys protruding from the roof, with a small wooden cross attached at the rear.

Father Joseph walked into the front entryway and was greeted by another priest.
"May I help you?"
"Yes, I'm looking for Bishop Grace?"

I'm sorry, but he left yesterday and won't be back for at least two weeks," replied the priest. "Who may I say called?"

"Never mind," replied Father Joseph. "I don't have time to wait for him, anyway."

He now turned around and walked back out the entrance, and down the steps. He was very upset. "Surely," he thought, "the Bishop must have known I was coming. If he doesn't have time for me, then I don't have time for him."

Father Joseph returned to Rush Lake, without the necessary permission from the Bishop.

"Oh well," he thought. "I have God's permission. I don't need the Bishop."

Upon his arrival, the Rush Lake settlers were pleased to see him. He was greeted several miles from the settlement, by several of the men, and was given a much-welcomed wagon ride back to the settlement.

"How has everything been here, while I was gone?"

"The weather has been very cold," replied Mr. Bender. "We got the rutabagas picked and put in storage. It looks like a good crop. It should help us make it through the winter. The kids have been spending a lot of time down by the river, fishing. The river is full of them."

"Good. I was beginning to wonder how we were going to survive the winter."

Several days after Father Josephs' return, Father Pierz, again, arrived on the scene. This time, he had a companion with him. It was a young priest by the name of John Ireland. Father Joseph greeted them, and they entered Father's house.

"Did you see His Excellency?" asked Father Pierz.

"I went to see him, but he wasn't there."

"My! My! That means you still can't properly administer to the people. We can't have that. I'll have to try and get special permission for you. If it's alright, I'll offer Mass tomorrow. Father Ireland would like to talk to the children. Would you mind?"

"Not at all."

The next morning, while Father Pierz was saying Mass, Father Ireland had gathered all of the children in one of the neighboring houses and held catechism with them. After telling some stories and asking a few questions, concerning religion, he began to ask personal questions.

"How many of you have had your First Holy Communion?"

Most of them raised their hands.

"Those who haven't, should start preparing for it. If you study your catechism well, I will give you Communion the next time I'm here."

The children were overjoyed, although, they really didn't understand why Father Joseph couldn't do that. After Father Pierz said Mass, and heard confessions, he talked a short while with Father Joseph. One could tell that each admired the other. A true friendship was developing.

"I received a letter from Father Kunkier, the other day," stated Father Pierz. "He says that if you fulfill the following steps, he will grant you legal dismission: 1) If you make good the scandal given by you by sending a letter in which you retract everything said against the Catholic Church, the Most Reverend Bishop, and the Precious Blood Society, which letter they will read at St. Joseph's, and the surrounding congregations; 2) If you do not make any claim against the Precious Blood Congregation, but stay content with the gift which shall be given to you willfully; 3) If you send back the sisters, whom you have taken with you; and they have the intention to reassume them to the novitiate; 4) That you never pretend to have permission from our part to form a convent in our name, which permission we never intend to give you."

"How can that man be so stubborn? I have already told them that I was sorry. What more do they want? They have been a constant thorn in my side. Why? Why?" he shouted over and over, while pounding his fist on the table.

"There, there, Joseph," stated Father Pierz. "Don't let this upset you too much. I'll try and straighten everything out. Have patience, my friend. Everything will be alright. It sounds to me that they are quite mad that you took the sisters with you."

"I didn't steal them," replied Father Joseph. "They all wanted to come on their own."

"Don't get too excited. I'll try and take care of it."

Just then, Father Ireland came into the room.

"Well John," stated Father Pierz, "we best be leaving. We have very little time to get to our destination."

"Joseph," he continued, "feel free to go out amongst the Indians, and try to learn their ways. They have been living around here much longer than any white man, and they know how to survive the Minnesota winters. You will soon find out that the winters can be very dangerous. Learn as much as you can from them. I'm not sure when I'll be back. Perhaps next spring. These bones of mine are beginning to tire, so I don't know how much more I will be able to do. God be with you, and I'll remember you in my prayers. I will try and talk to the Bishop, the next time I'm down in St. Paul, and I also will write another letter to Father Kunkier."

"Thank-you."

"Good-bye now, my friend," continued Father Pierz, as he gave him a big hug.

"Good-bye," replied Father Joseph, as he followed Father Pierz and Father Ireland out to the front. "John, it's been a pleasure meeting you," he continued. "I hope to see you again."

"Good-bye Joseph," replied Father Ireland, as the two men began walking down the trail. Once Father Pierz and Father Ireland had departed, Father Joseph entered the church. Walking in front of the altar, he noticed that the old missionary had left the Blessed Sacrament in the tabernacle. "Surely," he thought, "this must be a sign from God. Surely, he wants me to carry on my priestly functions."

He quickly ran over to the sisters and told them of the discovery.

"Now we can start our adoration," exclaimed Sister Cherubim.

"Yes sister, that you can. I must write to him and tell him, but as long as it's here, we will protect and adore it."

Thereafter, the three sisters spent much time in the chapel. They would take turns, during the night hours, in the adoration of the Blessed Sacrament.

Several days later, Father Joseph took a short walk up the river, to where there was a large Indian camp. He bravely walked right into camp, with the eyes of everyone watching his every move. He was carrying a small knapsack filled with dried meat and fish. He stopped in front of the makeshift hut that he thought was the chief's. The elderly chief came out and walked straight up to Father Joseph. He stared at him, for several seconds, saying not a word. Father Joseph took the knapsack and handed it to him. The chief carefully opened up the sack and looked inside. Upon realizing what Father Joseph was trying to do, he looked up at him and smiled. He proceeded to take each piece out and distribute them to several men, who had approached. The men took the meat and happily ran back to their teepees. The chief then took a beautiful stone necklace from around his neck and handed it to Father Joseph. Father Joseph graciously accepted it, with a smile. The two men shook hands and Father Joseph returned to his home. This marked the beginning of a friendship which was to develop over the next several years. When Father Joseph arrived back at the settlement, he was met by Frank Staab, who had just returned from Ottertail City.

"Father Joseph," he stated. "When I was in Ottertail City, I picked up a letter, addressed to you. It's from Father Pierz," he continued, as he handed the small envelope to Father Joseph.

"Thank-you," replied Father Joseph, as he took the envelope, and opened it. As he was reading it to himself, he became elated.

"Listen to this," continued Father Joseph, as he now began reading aloud. "I realized only too late that I had left the Blessed Sacrament there. Please take good care of it. I am sure that it would be alright if, on Sundays, you would give Benediction to your people.

I will soon be talking to the Bishop, but, in the meantime, feel free to say Benediction."
"I knew he could help me out," exclaimed Father Joseph. "I'm sure he will be getting the permission I need. I will be saying Mass in no time."

Frank Staab stood there and smiled, as Father Joseph continued: "I must go tell the brothers and the sisters."

As he was saying these words, he began to head in the direction of the convent. Father Joseph's belief was right, for within a week, Father Pierz again returned to the Rush Lake settlement.

This particular morning, in the early part of December 1866, was very cold. It had snowed during the night, but with sunrise, came clear skies and a chilling wind out of the north.

"Greetings," stated Father Pierz, as he approached Father's house.

"Hello Father," replied Father Joseph. "Please come in out of the cold."

As Father Pierz entered and began to take off his heavy black winter coat, he stated:

"I have good news for you. Pope Gregory has granted a period of grace. We shall celebrate todays Mass, together. If you would like, I will hear your confession, and then we will have Mass."

As Father Joseph smiled, he looked at Brother Joseph, who was also in the room, and said,

"Did you hear that?"

"Yes Father."

"Prepare your music, for a grand entry," ordered Father Joseph.

"I am going to say Mass."

Immediately, the three men headed for the small church of 'Our Lady of Miracles.'

While Father Pierz was hearing the confession of Father Joseph, in the sacristy, Brother Joseph was preparing his music, for the first Mass of Father Joseph, since his arrival in Minnesota. With the bells ringing loudly, and the church filling to capacity, Father Joseph and Father Pierz walked outside and around to the front entry of the church. With Brother Joseph playing the organ, and the choir joyfully singing, the two men made their entry in. When they reached the altar, and after the music stopped, Father Pierz genuflected, turned around to the parishioners, and said:

"Father Joseph may now say Mass." He then turned and walked to the side, as Father Joseph began Mass.

The people were overjoyed. What a day to remember! Their prayers had been answered. Their spiritual leader was once again saying Mass.

After Mass was completed, and Father Pierz had left, Father Joseph walked over to talk with Anton and Bruno.

"It sure was good to have you up at the altar again," stated Anton, as he looked toward Father Joseph.

"It was a good feeling. It was a relief to find out that I could celebrate again. Finally, after all those problems, I have partaken of Holy Communion. I want you two to pass the word that I will have three Masses on Christmas. Have the people prepare for a joyful holiday. We shall celebrate one Mass to symbolize Christ's human birth from a Virgin, one for his spiritual birth in our souls, and one for his eternal birth from the Father. I will have the sisters decorate the church and set up a Nativity scene. I want you men to make
sure, that everyone comes."

"That won't be a problem," answered Bruno. "Everyone will be happy to."

Soon, Christmas arrived. Father Joseph was in the sacristy, busily preparing for the Midnight Mass. The church, that night, was beautifully decorated. It was well-lit, with candles appropriately positioned throughout the church. There was a simple Nativity set placed on the Blessed Virgin Mary side of the altar, surrounded by several small pine trees, which Father Joseph had, earlier, cut down. The colony gathered early that night to join with Brother Joseph, the organist, in singing Christmas carols. While the singing was taking place, Father Joseph stood at the side of the main altar, and showed the people that he was pleased with what was going on.

Soon, Mass began. Father Joseph approached the altar, with two servers, one on each side. After genuflecting and making the sign of the cross, he began: "In Nomine Patris, et Filii, et Spiritus Sancti. Amen. Introibo ad alt are Dei."

The servers replied: "Ad Deum qui laetificat juventutem meam."

With difficulty, Father Joseph continued on. After the Kyrie, he stood at the center of the altar and chanted: "Gloria in excelsis Deo." The choir joined in singing the 'Gloria.'

After several more Latin prayers, Father Joseph walked over to the right side, by the newly built communion railing, and read the gospel. After kissing the book, he put it down on the podium, paused for several seconds, and then began: "My people in Christ. I am pleased to be able to partake of the Holy Mass with you. It gives me great pleasure to honor and serve the Lord, in this beautiful house, with my close friends."

"This time of the year is one of the most joyous periods for the Holy Mother Church. It is a time when we can reflect on the beautiful story of the birth of Jesus, in a small manger, in Bethlehem. How Joseph took care of Mary, the Blessed Virgin, and the newborn child."

"We can reflect on how it was then and how it is now. How simple, life was then. How the poor carpenter couldn't understand that Mary was conceived by the Holy Spirit. And an angel had to appear and reassure him that everything was alright. How from the simple
life evolved the Son of God, Jesus Christ."

"We must reflect on our lives today, on how the birth of Jesus affects us. He was born into this world to save us. We can make this job easier, just by leading a good life, setting a good example, and staying free from sin. Follow the Ten Commandments and when your day at the judgement seat arrives, you will have no problem entering the gates of heaven."

"For the day will come, and will come soon, when the Lord will end this life. The day of the Final Judgement will be upon us. Are you prepared? Are you ready to face the Master? Will you be able to satisfy his desire? Will you be ready to defend yourselves? I hope so. If you follow me, and do as I say, I will guarantee you peace, ever after."

"The life you lead here on Earth is just a small period, compared to the hereafter. We have no time in this life for temporal things. We have no time for vanity. We have no time for pride. We have no time for fancy dress. We have no time for drinking. We have no time for card playing. We have no time for people who lack humility. We only have enough time to save ourselves and our brethren."

"The Holy Bible tells us: 'Pride goes before disaster, and a haughty spirit before a fall. When pride comes, disgrace comes; but with the humble is wisdom. For it is better to be humble with the meek than to share plunder with the proud. Arrogant is the name for
the man of overbearing pride.'"

Father Joseph was becoming very excited now. His voice was unwavering and strong. He was working the people into a frenzy, as he continued: "In the Book of Sirach it is said:
'No matter the wrong, do no violence to your neighbor, and do not walk the path of arrogance. Odious to the LORD and to men is arrogance, and the sin of oppression they both hate. Dominion is transferred from one people to another because of the violence of the arrogant. The beginning of pride is man's stubbornness in withdrawing his heart from his Maker; For pride is the reservoir of sin, a source which runs over with vice; Because of its God sends unheard-of afflictions and brings men to utter ruin. The root of the proud God plucks up, to plant the humble in their place. He breaks down their stem to the level of the ground, then digs their roots from the earth. The trace of the proud God sweeps away and effaces the memory of them from the earth.'

"My people do not be misled by the unbelievers, or by those who will tell you that I am wrong in my beliefs. Do not fall for their lies. Do not adhere to their requests to fall in a state of sin and moral degradation."

"The Lord chose Peter to run his Church, and down through the ages, the Holy Father has led the Catholic Church along the road to salvation. I follow him. I believe in him, in what he stands for, and in what he says, not in what some Irish bishop has to say. I am his representative here. If you abide by my rules, as I abide by his, you will be saved."

"The Bible also says: 'As for the exact day or hour, no one knows it, neither the angels in Heaven, nor the Son, but the Father only.' The coming of the Son of Man will repeat what happened in Noah's time. In the days before the flood, people were eating and drinking, marrying and being married, right up to the day Noah entered the Ark. They were totally unconcerned until the flood came and destroyed them. So will it be at the coming of the Son of Man."

"Be prepared, my people. Do not indulge in over-eating and drinking. There is no time for that. Be not concerned with marriage. There is not enough time left. Spend your time in prayer. Pray to the Lord for your salvation. Be prepared to be gathered to the right of the Lord, in the next world."

"Now, my dear people, I realize it is difficult in this day to live a pure life without sin. That is why our dear Jesus Christ came into this world. He came to save us and forgive us of our sins. He came to show us how we can prepare for the kingdom of God. He came to set an example for us to follow. We must follow that way. For if we don't, we shall spend the hereafter in the flames."

"Be compassionate, as your Father is compassionate. Do not judge, and you will not be judged. Do not condemn, and you will not be condemned. Pardon, and you shall be pardoned. Give, and it shall be given to you."

"If we follow the word of the Bible, rather than man, we cannot go wrong. For the Bible is the truth and man can be misled. The word of the Bible does not change, while the word of man does. The word of the Bible was influenced by God, while the word of man can be influenced by the devil."

"Yes, today we celebrate the birth of Jesus Christ. The Birth of the Lamb of God who came to take away the sins of the world. He prepared the way. He gave us an example to follow. Follow this example in your everyday lives, and you will be saved. Follow me, and you will be saved. Amen."

Father Joseph was smiling now, as he turned and walked back to the altar, to continue the Mass. Sweat was still rolling down his forehead, but he did not mind. He was content. He was able to succeed in getting his point across to his people, who seemed to have become hypnotized by what he had to say.

Outside, the snow was gently falling against the small log church and the eight temporary homes of the Rush Lake colony. Peaceful and serene was the countryside, except for the joyful singing coming from the choir at 'Our Lady of Miracles' church on this particular Christmas Eve in 1866.

The first winter in Minnesota was setting in. It seemed that an endless string of cold snowy days prevailed for the next several months. As time went by, the role of the rutabaga came to the forefront. Sure, there was plenty of deer and other wild animals, and the settlers did have pistols and old guns, but not a single deer was shot that first winter, simply because the men did not really know how to go about it. Therefore, more and more meals were being served with rutabagas, as the main course. Flour and smoked meat were almost gone, by the end of January. With ice covering the lake and river, the people did not know that they could cut through the ice and fish. This was not realized until the following winter.

By March, the colony ran out of another important staple—salt.

One morning Father Joseph had Brother Joseph in his house. "Brother Joseph," he declared, "take Joe Weis with you, and go, immediately, to St. Cloud. We only have a few days' supply of salt left. Take the two sleighs, that the boys just built. Bring back this list of items," he continued, as he handed him a slip of paper, and a small bag. "There should be enough money in this bag to pay for it." Brother Joseph quickly got up and walked outside, into a windy snowstorm. He made his way down to Joe Weis's house and knocked on the door.

"Come in," stated Joe Weis, as he opened the door.

"Father Joseph wants us to go to St. Cloud for supplies."

"In this storm?"

"Yes. We are just about out of salt, and he thinks we can make it with those two sleighs."

"Go start hitching up the oxen then. I'll be over as soon as I get

dressed."

After Big Joe departed, Joe walked over to his wife, who was holding their son, Charles, in her lap.

"How can he expect you two to find your way back to St. Cloud in this kind of weather?" she asked.

"He must figure we can do it," replied Joe, as he began to dress for the cold winter, outside. "We shouldn't be gone too long. Besides, if we run out of salt, how are we to survive around here?"

After getting his long winter coat and cap on, Joe departed, walking over to the barn, where Brother Joseph was busily hitching up the oxen. Soon, the two men had everything ready. Before they left, Father Joseph, Bruno, and Anton entered the barn.

"Rather than follow the river," stated Father Joseph, "take the trail south, past Clitherall. It should save you some time. My prayers will be with you and I have faith that you will return safely."

After the good-byes were said, Brother Joseph and Joe Weis were off on their trek, with Joe driving the first sleigh and Brother

Joseph right behind.

They slowly made their way around Rush Lake and in the direction of Ottertail City, through the vicious snowstorm. By the time they reached Ottertail City, the snow had let up considerably, and they had no problem the rest of the way to St. Cloud.

Two weeks later, on their return trip, the two men again ran into difficulty with the weather. While traveling on the prairie, south of Clitherall, they were caught in a blizzard. It was a blinding storm, and seemed to be getting worse, with each passing minute.

Joe was driving the first sleigh, being pulled by three pair of oxen, while, right behind him came Brother Joseph, who had two pair attached to his sleigh.

They trudged along as best they could. It was getting harder and harder for the cattle to move. Finally, it got to the point where they had to stop, simply because the snowdrifts were getting too deep and they also could not see where they were going.

"I think we better unhitch the teams and see if we can make it to Clitherall. It can't be more than a couple of miles from here," shouted Mr. Weis, as he looked toward Big Joe.

"And leave the supplies here?"

"Yes. We have no choice. Once this storm is over, we can return for the goods."

It was beginning to get dark, and the temperature was dropping, as the two men quickly unhitched their teams, and proceeded to the small Mormon village of Clitherall. They were anxious to find a warm fire. Although they had heavy clothing on, it seemed that the cold wind was blowing right through them. "Oh, the warmth of a fire," they thought, as they slowly made their way along.

It was now completely dark when the two men, practically frozen, reached Clitherall. They walked up to the nearest log cabin and knocked on the door. There was no answer. They continued to knock. Finally, an old man, holding a lit candle, opened the door.

"What are you two doing out in weather like this?" he asked.

"Come in."

As the two entered, Mr. Weis stated: "We are from the Rush Lake colony. We desperately needed supplies, so we went to St. Cloud. Unfortunately, the weather did not want us back just yet. We got about a mile or so from here. We had to leave the supplies there. It was either that or freeze to death."

"Hopefully, tomorrow we will be able to continue on," added Big Joe.

"Is it possible for us to stay here, tonight?" asked Mr. Weis, a he walked over to the fireplace, in an attempt to warm his body up.

"Of course. You are welcomed in my home, anytime."

"Is there a place where we can keep the oxen?" asked Big Joe.

"Why yes. I have a small barn on the other side of the house.

You can put them in there."

"We have them right outside," noted Joe, as he walked toward the door. "Perhaps, we should get them under cover before it's too late."

"Yes," added Big Joe, as he too headed for the door.

"Father Joseph would never forgive us if we lost all those animals. Can you show us the way?"

The old man hurriedly put on a heavy black coat, his cap, and a pair of gloves, and led them outside. They took the animals and put them in the barn. Once inside the building, Big Joe stated: "There. This should protect them from the cold."

The three men returned to the house and sat down by the fireplace.

As the old man was taking off his cap and coat, he asked: "So, you're from Rush Lake, huh? We've heard a lot about your little settlement. It sure was good news when we heard about your arrival.

That Father Joseph must be quite a man?"

"Without him," replied Joe, "we would never be able to make it.

He has been our leader. He is a very wise man, who always seems to make the right decision."

"Whatever made you people decide on settling up here?"

"There were several reasons. The population in Ohio was getting to be too much. Land was becoming scarce for us farmers. We heard so many good reports about Minnesota — cheap, fertile land, no cholera, beautiful scenery, a place where we can practice our Catholic faith without any interference, and a challenge."

"Those are all very good reasons," replied the old man. "They are the exact reasons why we came here."

"Well," he continued, as he got up from his chair, and walked to the storage box, located near the door. "I have several blankets in here that you are welcomed to use. I wish I had a bed for you, but the floor will have to do."

"That will be fine," replied Big Joe, as he took one of the blankets from the man.

The old man handed a blanket to Joe, and the two travelers placed them on the wooden floor, next to the fireplace. As they proceeded to crawl under the blanket, the old man threw two more logs on the fire. "There," he said, "that should keep you warm enough till morning."

"Good night," noted the old man, as he went over to his cot, and blew out the candle.

The snowstorm continued on into the next day. Although, by noon, it was letting up.

"Do you think we should try and make it back?" queried Big Joe.

"Yes, I do," replied Joe. "Hopefully, we will be able to find our supplies."

"I'll get some of the men from the village to help you," offered the old man, as he began to put on his coat.

Around one o'clock, in the afternoon, a group of six men left Clitherall, with the oxen, in search of the supplies.

After much difficulty, the wagons were finally spotted. The snowdrifts had practically covered them up, completely.

The men began shoveling the snow away, and soon, they had the sleighs uncovered. As Mr. Weis thanked the men, Big Joe hitched up the teams. Once again, they were ready to continue on their trip. However, due to the heavy snows, the oxen were having much difficulty.

After a short distance, Joe stopped his sleigh, and walked back to Big Joe. "I think we're going to have to stop," he suggested. "It's already getting late, and we won't be able to find our way in the dark."

The two men proceeded to unhitch the oxen, once again. They then unloaded one of the wagons, and turned it over, and crawled underneath. It was not the best place to spend a night, but it was better than outside. The cold winds were very active, so at least, the sleigh provided somewhat of a protective shield for them.

"Maybe we should have gone back to Clitherall," suggested Big Joe.

"It's too late now. We'll have to pray that it will be much nicer in the morning."

The two men huddled together, as they became colder and colder. They could hear the fierce wind blowing down upon them.

"If only spring would get here," they thought. The next morning, they arose to somewhat of a surprise.

"Oh Lord," exclaimed Big Joe, as he crawled out from under the wagon, "I can't feel anything in my toes, nor on my face."

Joe took a look at his face. "It looks very red. It's possible that you froze it. I'll see if I can find some wood and start a fire."

The sun was rising in the east. During the night, the skies had cleared, and the wind died down. Truly, this was a welcomed sight for the weary travelers. Joe looked around at the surroundings and noticing that there were no trees for some distance, decided to tear parts of the wagon apart, for firewood. As he was doing this, Big Joe, who was in great
pain, went over to check on the oxen. Realizing that they were alright, he began to hitch them up.

After he had the first teams hitched up, he walked over to the fire that Joe had started.

"Here," remarked Joe, "you sit here and try and warm up. I'll load the other wagon and take care of the oxen."

Big Joe gratefully huddled up to the fire and attempted to thaw himself out. He was suffering, but not once did he complain. Soon, the men were, again, on their way. However, they were still having problems with the tall snowdrifts. Upon arrival at Clitherall, they decided to unload half of their supplies, and return for them at a later date. Once this was completed, they continued on.

Meanwhile, back at the colony, the people were anxiously awaiting to see some sight of the two men. Several of the children were standing near the upstairs window in one of the houses, looking across the frozen lake, for some sign. Father Joseph and Bruno were standing outside Bruno's house.

"Do you think we should send some of the men out to look for them?" asked Bruno, with a worried look on his face.

"No. I think they are alright. We just have to have patience and put our trust in God. He'll make sure that they get back here safely."

"You realize, of course, that we used the last of the salt yesterday."

"Yes, I know. We will just have to learn to live without it."

Just then, seven-year-old LeAnder Boedigheimer, one of the boys standing by the window, shouted: "Father Joseph! Father Joseph! I see two sleighs coming."
"See, I told you they'd be alright."

As word passed that the men were returning, a large crowd gathered in front of the church, patiently awaiting the arrival of the men and the much-needed salt. When the men did finally arrive, they were warmly greeted.
"Bruno," shouted Father Joseph, "have the men unload the wagons, and put the supplies in the storage shed. Let me know when you are done. Then, we can distribute it."

As Bruno obediently left to do his task, Father Joseph walked up to Mr. Weis and Big Joe.

"Welcome back," he stated, as he gave them each a hug. "You are a most welcomed sight."

"You don't know how good it feels to be back," exclaimed Big Joe.
As Maggie gave a big hug and kiss to her husband, Father Joseph continued: "Please come into my house and tell me about your trip."

"First, I'd like to see my son," stated Joe.
"Fine. You do that, and then come over to the house."

As Joe and his wife headed for their house, Father Joseph and Big Joe entered Father's house. On the way in, Father Joseph asked:

"What took you so long?"
"We had some difficulty down by Clitherall. That storm almost did us in."
"Yes, I'm beginning to believe that Father Pierz was right, when he warned us about these Minnesota winters. I had no idea they were going to be so bad."

As Father Joseph placed several logs into the fire, he continued:
"Did you get everything on that list?"

"Yes. But we left some of it down at Clitherall. The loads were too heavy for the oxen. We figured that we could go back down for it when it got nicer."

There was a knock at the door. "Come in," shouted Father Joseph, as he looked toward the door.

The door opened, and in walked Bruno.
"Father Joseph, we got the supplies unloaded, and we noticed that there was no salt."

"No salt!" exclaimed Father Joseph, as he looked at Big Joe.

"Oh no!" stated Big Joe. "We must've unloaded it all at Clitherall."

After thinking for several seconds, Father Joseph stated:

"I'll have to send someone down, as soon as possible."
After the second day without salt, nothing tasted right to the settlers. Soon, people were having trouble eating at all, and they began to get sick. Father Joseph walked over to the house of the brothers. Upon entering, he asked young Michael Doll, who was sitting next to the fireplace, smoking his pipe: "How would you like to go to Clitherall, and get the rest of the supplies?"

"In this weather?"

"Yes. Just bring the salt back. It would probably be easier to walk."

"If you insist, Father," replied Michael, as he began getting dressed for the cold winter weather outside. Father Joseph stood by and watched as Michael put on a pair of home-made snowshoes and departed.

The trip to Clitherall took Michael two days and one night. Even though it was snowing the entire trip, he had no difficulty with the weather. On the late afternoon of his second day, he arrived back at the colony, with the salt, much to the pleasure of the other colonists. Now, they would at least be able to eat salt on their rutabagas. It was not long, and the cold Minnesota winter began to give way to the long-awaited spring. The snows began to disappear, and the ice started to melt. As each day passed, the weather became nicer and nicer.

One day, Father Joseph held a meeting with the entire colony, in the church. As he stood in front of his congregation, he stated:

"Soon, spring will be upon us. We must think and decide what we are going to do. I have drawn up some construction plans for the convent, that I want built, as well as several other buildings. We should get started on them as soon as possible. We also must decide
on setting up permanent homesteads. I think most of you men have had ample time to look over the countryside and choose a place to live."

"Yes Father," interrupted Joe Weis. "I have a place picked out. It's back down the trail a mile, or so, where the creek flows into the lake."

"I found a spot just north of the cemetery, across the river," noted Bruno.

"And I, next to Bruno, just a little further north," added Anton.

"I want to be near the lake," stated Frank Staab. "I saw an area across the river that would be ideal for a house."

"And Victor, where would you like to go?"

"About a mile back down the trail. Near Joe."

"Alright," continued Father Joseph, "tomorrow, we'll go over to Ottertail City, and find out what is necessary to stake claims. It is quite possible that all we have to do is pay for the survey fee, and from what I've been able to gather, that will only cost about $14.00."

For the next couple of months, there was much activity going on around the settlement. During the past winter, the men had cut down some timber, but now, with spring here, a sawmill was set up, just north of the church, on the river, and many trees were felled.

The various farmhouses were built as a community project. All the men worked on one house together, and then moved to the next, and continued until each family had a home of their own. Much time was also spent on building up the convent grounds. There was a huge barn, grainery, pig sty, and chicken house built. The barn was located north of the church. The ground was dug out first, then the wooden building was put on it. This not only saved in the amount of lumber needed, but it also would keep the building warmer in the winter.

A large blacksmith shop was built near the barn. This would give old Joe Bender a place to work when it rained or snowed. On the top floor of the shop was a classroom which was to be used as a German school for the young children.

An addition was put on to the rear of the church. It was a refectory for the sisters. There was also an addition to the chapel, for the nuns, added to the right side of the church.

Much time was also spent by several of the men in making better kneeling benches and a nicer altar for the church. Once these additions were completed, Father Joseph set a pattern of living, which soon, became routine. Every morning at 5, the settlers would assemble for meditation, at the church. After a brief period of silent prayer, they would have Mass, after which there would be a communal breakfast. Then, everyone would do their assigned tasks for the day, returning to the settlement, at noon, for lunch. They then would work till 5, and then gather for a spiritual reading. Every once in a while, Father Joseph would include Benediction. After this, the women would rush back home, to prepare supper.

Dress was modest throughout the colony. All of the women would wear black aprons, around the waist, over their black dresses, and they would wear black veils on their heads. The men wore simple black or brown pants and jackets, and brimmed hats. Each of the farmers tried to get enough land cleared on their plots, in order to plant a small crop. This job was very difficult. No more than 5 or 6 acres per farmer were cleared that first year. Once the trees had been felled by ax, the logs had to be hauled away. The women and the children came along and cleared the underbrush. The men then would return, with the oxen, to pull the stumps. Quite often, that job was too difficult, so they would just dig the land around the stump.

One bright sunny day, Bruno was out clearing some of his land. Several of his boys were with him. They had been working hard all day. Getting close to evening, something happened to one of the oxen. As Bruno was hauling a log down to the river, one of the oxen fell over and died. It had been overworked. 15-year-old Frank Boedigheimer and LeAnder were nearby, burning some brush. When they saw what happened, to the ox, they ran over to see if there was anything they could do.

"LeAnder," shouted Bruno, as he looked over the dead animal.

"Let me see your knife."

As LeAnder took his knife from the sheath, he asked: "What are you going to do, Father?"

"I can save the hide," replied Bruno, as he began to cut into the animal.

Several Indians, who had been standing close by, came rushing up. They patiently waited and watched as Bruno took the hide off. When this was completed, one of the Indians came over to Bruno, and motioned to him that he wanted the rest of the animal. Bruno, thinking about it for a second, agreed. After giving them permission, the Indians took out their knives and began cutting up the animal.

Bruno, realizing that they wanted the meat, took LeAnder's knife and helped them cut the meat off. Once this was done, the Indians carried the pieces off into the woods.

"Are they actually going to eat that meat?" asked Frank.

"Yes, I believe so."

After several seconds, Bruno continued: "Well, I'm going back to the house. You two, stay here until this fire goes out, and then head straight home. I'll have to go see if I can borrow an ox from Father Joseph."

As Bruno began heading in the direction of his house, Frank and LeAnder returned to their small fire. The next morning, the three Indians reappeared at the Boedigheimer farmstead. They had brought several items with them. Bruno, who was walking from his barn to the house, greeted them, near the entrance. The long-haired Indians were smoking pipes. They handed him a basket of tobacco, and then proceeded to show him how it was made. They used the inner bark of the kinkinik tree, discarding the red bark and scraping the white inner bark into a fine shred and then letting it dry.

Bruno took some of the tobacco and put it in his pipe. After lighting it, and taking a puff, he began to cough. It was too strong for him. What was he to do? He had to continue smoking it, to show the Indians his appreciation. But, after each puff, he would begin to
cough. The Indians just stood there and laughed. After several minutes, the Indians decided to leave. When they were out of sight, Bruno put out the pipe and walked into the house.

"I'm going down to the church to talk with Father Joseph," he stated, as he walked over to his wife, who was busy preparing some bread. Little 3-year-old Aurelia, was standing nearby, watching very closely. "Bring the rest of the children down at noon," continued
Bruno. "I'm going to take Frank and Cornelius with me."

Bruno grabbed the basket of tobacco, walked outside, and got Frank and Cornelius, who had been in the barn taking care of the animals. The three of them headed for the church grounds.

When they arrived, they were first met by Joe Weis and Anton Bender, who were standing in the front of the church.

"Look what I got from several Indians this morning," exclaimed Bruno, as he showed them the basket of tobacco.

Joe picked some of the tobacco out and put it in his pipe. After lighting it and taking a puff, he too began to cough. "This stuff is terrible!" he exclaimed, as he knocked it out of his pipe.

"It's Indian tobacco. They showed me how they make it. It comes from the kinkinik tree."

"Tobacco from a tree?" queried Anton, in a tone of disbelief.

"That's exactly what I thought. But they seem to enjoy it."

"Wait till we get some good tobacco up here," interrupted Joe.

"Then, we'll show them what real tobacco is supposed to taste like."

As this conversation was being held, Father Joseph came out of the church, and approached the group.

"Ah Bruno! How are you?"

"Hello Father Joseph. As you've probably heard by now, I lost one of my oxen, yesterday. I was wondering if I could borrow one of yours until I get another?"

"Why, of course. What's mine is yours. Have one of the boys go behind the barn and pick one out and use it for as long as you have to."

"Thank-you Father."

"I was going to come over this afternoon and see how you are coming along on the land clearing. How many acres do you think you are going to be able to plant this year?"

"Well," answered Bruno, "I was hoping to have about 15 to 20 acres opened, but it probably will be closer to 10."

"It looks like we are going to have a shortage of seed, anyway. We have some oats and wheat seed, and the Indians did give us some calico corn and rutabaga seed, but that is all we have. I'll have to portion it out so each of the men get at least a little of each."

"Is it too late to send someone down to get more seed?" asked Anton.

"I'm afraid so. We should already have the crops sewn. It's going to be a late harvest the way it is now."

"Cornelius," continued Father Joseph, as he turned to the young Boedigheimer boy, "have you decided to move into the brother's quarters, yet?"

"In a couple of weeks, Father, if it's alright with you. I would like to help my father out with the crops."

"You could still help him, even if you lived here. I will be more than glad to have you. I could use a strong man like you around here, and then we can get your training started, for the religious life."

"I promise in two weeks."

"Very well," noted Father Joseph, as he turned his attention to a wagon approaching from the west. The wagon pulled up in front of the church. Victor Eifert was driving.

As he pulled on the reins, to stop the horses, he exclaimed: "Father Joseph, I have good news. I just received a letter from my brother, Ferdinand, and he tells me the group is ready to leave Ohio."

As Victor got down from the wagon, and walked up to Father Joseph, he continued: "He wrote down the names of the people that were coming, and it is quite a large list."

"May I read the letter?"

"Why yes," replied Victor, as he pulled the letter out of his side pocket and handed it to him.

Father Joseph took the letter, unfolded it, and began to read aloud: "Dear Victor, Hope this letter finds everything fine with you and the rest at Rush Lake. I would like to inform you that we are planning on leaving here around the 7th or 8th of May, and arriving there, no later than the end of May, or the first part of June. We have all the necessary travel arrangements made. Here is a list of the people to expect: My family, and the families of Joseph W. Doll, Wendolin Doll, Anton Doll, Charles Foltz, Joseph Riesterer, Louis Sarbacher, Ignatz Schoeneberger, John Foltz, and perhaps, several others. We will try to inform Father Joseph when we are to leave, exactly. Please let him know, that we all sorely miss him, and that we are looking forward to the day when we can once again be under his wing. Sincerely, Ferdinand."

While folding the letter back up, he smiled and handed it to Victor.

"This is the best news I've heard in a long time." Meanwhile, in a nearby woods, Ferdinand, young Frank, and LeAnder Boedigheimer, and George and John Bender, were out herding the cattle. While doing this, they also found time to chop rails, and even play.

"Look it here!" shouted young Frank, to the other boys, as he pointed towards a skull, lying beside a tree.

Ferdinand dropped his ax and ran over to see what his brother had found. LeAnder and John, who were climbing trees some distance away, quickly jumped down and headed over to Frank.

George, who had been piling up several poles, dropped what he was doing, and like the others, ran over to Frank. As the five boys surrounded the tree, Frank picked up the skull.

"Who do you suppose this was?"

George took the skull from Frank and examined it. "It has a knife cut on top and there is a small hole in the scalp."

"Let's take it to Father Joseph and see what he says," suggested Ferdinand.

The five boys hurried off for the church grounds. As they approached, they were noticed by Father Joseph, and the others, who were still standing in front of the church. "I wonder what they are up to?"

"Look Father Joseph!" shouted Ferdinand, as he showed him the skull. "Look what we found in the woods."

Father Joseph grabbed the skull and looked at it for several seconds. He could plainly see the marks on the head.

"Put this back where you found it, and leave it there," he demanded, as he handed it back to Ferdinand. He then looked at the others, and after the boys left, he stated: "Do you suppose that was Johnnie Frey, who disappeared last fall?"

The other men just stood there, for none of them really knew if that was the case, or not. Needless to say, the subject was never again brought up.

The Summer Of '67

CHAPTER XXI

"Are we about ready?" shouted the 52-year-old Wendolin Doll, as he looked at 43-year-old Joseph Riesterer. "I think so," replied Joseph, as he looked around at the group of people who had just boarded several horse-drawn wagons. "As soon as the Schoenebergers get here, we can leave."

"Well, we can't wait much longer. We got a boat to catch in Cincinnati."

Today was May 21, 1867. The sun was shining brightly down upon the group, who had met at the Wendolin Doll farm, near St. Joseph, in Mercer County, Ohio, on this particular morning. They had arrived, fully prepared for the long journey they were about to take. Once again, they were pulling up stakes and moving onward. They were headed for Rush Lake, to be with their old leader, Father Joseph.

The group included: Joseph W. Doll, age 29, his wife Barbara, age 21, and their son August, age 3; Wendolin Doll, age 52, and his wife, Mary Ann, age 50, and their children: Leopold, Theresa, and John; Anton Doll, age 57, and his wife Mary Ann, age 48, and their
20-year-old son, Anton; Charles Foltz, age 36, and his wife Mary Ann, age 33, and their children: John, Theresa, Magdalene, Elizabeth, Rose, and Katharine; Joseph Riesterer, age 43, and his wife Esther, age 39, and their children: Joseph, Maria, and Agnes; Louis Sarbacher, age 39, and his children: Magdalen, Joseph, and Anton; Ferdinand Eifert, age 23, and his wife Antoinetta, age 21, and their new-born son, Julius; Ignatz Schoeneberger, age 55, and his children: Martin, Mary Ann, Michael, and Andrew; Victor Scheidecker, age 57, and his children: Joseph, Sophia, John, Christopher, and Henry; as well as several others.

Wendolin walked from wagon to wagon, to see that everything was alright. When he reached the last wagon, he stopped to talk to Charley Foltz. "Well Charley," he said, "we're finally going to get the chance to see Father Joseph again. Do you have everything in order?"

"Yes sir," replied the short stocky Mr. Foltz, with a smile. "I've had my family prepared for weeks now."
"I sent a letter to Rush Lake," continued Wendolin. "Father Joseph and the rest should be expecting us."

Another wagon was now approaching the group. It was Ignatz Schoeneberger and his family. Ignatz was riding in the front, with the 22-year-old Henry Drahmann driving the team. The children were riding in the back, amongst their belongings.

"Well, Ignatz," exclaimed Wendolin, as the wagon pulled up beside Wendolin and Charley, "good to see you. Now we can depart. Just pull in behind Charley and follow us." Wendolin hurriedly went up to the front wagon and climbed aboard, and sat down next to 22-year-old Henry Kemper, who was to drive the wagon. "Let's go Henry!" exclaimed Wendolin, as he first looked at Henry, and then turned, and motioned for the others to follow.

The small wagon train slowly took off, with Cincinnati as their first destination. Meanwhile, back at Rush Lake, preparations were being made by Father Joseph, and the others, for the arrival of their friends. The crops for the year were planted. Work was continuing on at the church grounds, where several new buildings were being constructed.

One morning, Father Joseph was standing alongside the river, with several young boys, who were busily working with a large homemade fish trap. The net was about six-foot square, with light wooden poles along the sides and a strong pole in the middle. Father Joseph was attaching this pole to a 15-foot sapling, which was overhanging the river.

9-year-old John Eifert stood on the other side and looked down river as Father Joseph and the other boys put pressure on the sapling and lowered the net into the river.

"They're coming in," shouted John.
"We'll wait a minute," quietly suggested Father Joseph. "Let the net fill up first."
"Now," shouted John.

With that command, Father Joseph, Ferdinand, LeAnder, and John Bender let go of the sapling and swung the pole over towards the bank. George Bender stood along the river and grabbed the net, as it reached the shore. He dumped the catch onto the ground. Once
this was done, he straightened it back out, and the others swung it back into the river.
"Now that you know how to do it," stated Father Joseph, as he looked at George, "I'll leave. I'm going to go up to the sawmill."
After he departed, and the boys were waiting for the net to fill again, several canoes, each carrying three Indians, passed by.

As they were going by, LeAnder and Ferdinand picked up several wood chips and threw them into the river, aiming for the passengers. In the last canoe there was a short heavy-set squaw, who happened to be the main target of the mischievous boys. As she went by, she raised a finger of warning at them. Just then, she was hit. After grabbing her face, she had the two men turn the canoe towards shore.

Seeing that she was about to land, the boys backed away from the river and began to run into the woods, being closely followed by an irate woman, with a canoe paddle. After chasing the boys for a short distance, she stopped, in disgust, and returned to the canoe.

As this was happening, Father Joseph arrived at the community sawmill. When he got there, he went over to talk to Bruno, who was standing on top of a 7-foot scaffold. The sawmill was set up on the side of a hill, so that logs could be rolled onto a platform. One man would stand on top of the scaffold, while another stood below, and together, they operated a long ripsaw.

"Hello Father Joseph," greeted Bruno, as he saw the elderly priest approach.

"Good morning, Bruno," returned Father Joseph. As he walked onto the scaffold, he looked between the floor logs, and continued:

"Hello Joseph."

Joe Weis looked up and replied: "Hello Father Joseph."

"Don't let me stop your work. I just came up to see how you were doing."

As the men began to saw another log, Bruno stated:

"We're coming along just fine. With Anton and Victor hauling, we should have enough logs cut for Frank's house, by this afternoon."

"Where is Frank?"

"At his house," replied Bruno.

"I should go over there and see how they are doing, but I have to go over to Ottertail City this afternoon on some business. I'm going to put in a claim for some more land, so when our friends from Ohio get here, they'll have some land to choose. I won't be at the church
for lunch today, but I should be back in time for prayer meditation tonight."

Father Joseph turned and began to depart. "Good-bye my friends."

"Good-bye Father," replied Bruno, as he continued to saw. When Father Joseph got back to the church, he noticed a wagon parked in front, with four men standing beside it.

"Hello," he greeted, as he walked up beside them. "Can I help you?"

"Hello Father," stated a 30-year-old man, with a beard. He was a short, stock, well-built man, who had on a heavy buckskin coat and a broad brimmed hat. "My name is Gustav Morgenroth, and these are my friends. We have just arrived from Ohio and are looking for some good fertile land, where we can set up homesteads.

When we were in Ottertail City, a man told us to come and see you/'
"Are you married?"

"Yes, we are. We left our families back home, but plan on going back after them as soon as we find a place for them."

"Are you all Catholic?"

"Yes."

"Well, I'm sure I can find some place for you. I'm supposed to go to Ottertail City, but I can put that off for a little while."

"It would be most appreciated."

"Are you hungry? The sisters could fix you something."

"No. We just ate."

"Well, this is 'Our Lady of Miracles'," continued Father Joseph.

"We have a small church here, along with a convent for the sisters and a place for the brothers. We plan on opening up an orphanage very soon. We like to think of our little settlement as the perfect place to live, and I hope that you will find it to your liking. We haven't been here very long ourselves, but we have big plans. If it's alright with you, I'll ride with you up north, along the river, and I'll show you some choice land?"

"Fine," replied Gustav, as the five men boarded the wagon.

"Just follow this trail," continued Father Joseph, as he pointed to the path which headed northward.

As they were going along, Father Joseph continued to tell the men about his colony. It was not long, and they were at a site that Father Joseph thought would be ideal for them.

"How about this area?"

Gustav and the other three looked around for several seconds, and then Gustav said: "It looks perfect. What do we have to do to claim it?"

"Well, I own all this land along here, so I'll just sell it to you. I'm sure each of you could get 160 acres a piece if you want. All I will charge you is the $14.00 filing fee."

The four men looked at each other in amazement. "We'll take it," replied Gustav.

"Fine. We'll take care of the necessary paperwork later. Now, I'm sure that you would like to set up camp. Although, if you would like, you could stay at the church grounds, until you have your houses built."

"No, that is alright."

"Well, if there is anything you need, just come down and ask." As Gustav got down from the wagon, followed by Father Joseph, he said: "Thank-you very much Father. You have been a great help."

"That's the least I can do."

"How often do you have Mass?"

"Every day. In the morning. I hope to see you all there as soon as you possibly can make it. I must get back there now, but remember that if you should need any help, please don't hesitate to ask."

"Would you like a ride back?"

"No. The walk will do me good. When I get to Ottertail City, I'll draw up the boundary lines for your homesteads, and I'll bring them back out to you. Perhaps, by tomorrow."

On June 8th, the next large group of settlers arrived from Mercer County. What a welcomed sight for Father Joseph! These people all believed in the actions of Father Joseph, but, due to their financial situations, were unable to move with him, the previous fall. Father Joseph and the others stood near the church and welcomed the newcomers, as they arrived.

"Greetings, my people. What a joy to see all of you!" exclaimed Father Joseph. "I hope your trip went well."

"Fine Father," replied Mr. Riesterer, who was driving the first wagon. "The information you sent us was a great help. We traveled by boat from Cincinnati to St. Paul. Then, we took the train to St. Cloud. It was nice of you to have the wagons and oxen awaiting for us there."

"I was hoping that that would make it much easier."

As the newcomers entered the settlement, much joy was seen. Friends and relatives were greeting each other. Father Joseph ran from wagon to wagon, greeting each of them, and offering assistance to anyone who needed it.

"Hello, my dear Anton," he exclaimed, as he greeted Mr. Doll.
"Welcome to your new home."

"Hello Father. We have been looking forward to this day ever since you left Ohio. We all have missed you. It hasn't been the same there. The Sanguinists have said much about you, most of which we found hard to believe."

"Surely, they are mistaken. They do not know what is going on here. Here we are leading a life of true Christian communal living, away from the sickly world, and away from the devil. We lead a simple life, in common, where we look out for each other. This is a place where one can live with himself in peace, and prepare himself, and his family, for the life afterwards. There are no loose morals here. I will not permit it. We practice no new religion. It is the true Catholic religion. It is the way Father Salesius wanted it to be."

"Excellent. We knew what to expect. We knew what you were doing. It's just that the priests back there were putting doubts in our minds."

"You will see how our community is functioning," continued Father Joseph, as he helped Anton and his wife down from the wagon.
"We don't have too many crops planted this year," he added.

"We were short on seed, but we did get some oats and wheat planted, along with some rutabagas, potatoes, and corn. The married folk have taken up homesteads, and have cleared some land, but there still is much more to be done."

"Anton," he continued, as he looked at the young Mr. Doll, who had just gotten out of the back of his father's wagon. "Good to see you."

"Hello Father Joseph."

"Would you please pass the word to everyone, that I would like for them to go into the church? I'll be there shortly and offer a prayer of thanksgiving."

"Of course," replied young Anton. Shortly, everyone was in the church. Father Joseph walked out from the sacristy, with a big smile, for it gave him great pleasure, to see his small church filled to capacity.

"Welcome to 'Our Lady of Miracles', he began. "I am so happy to see so many faces that, a short time ago I thought I probably would never see again. I would like to take this time for each of us to say a silent prayer of thanksgiving to our dear Lord, for the safe deliverance of all of you."

He folded his hands and bowed his head, and the entire congregation did likewise. After the short prayer, he continued: "There is much work to be done. I'm sure you all realized this before you left. If we help each other, it will all work out smoothly. I have here, in my pocket, a piece of paper."

As he pulled out the paper and unfolded it, he continued: "It is a map of the area. After this meeting, I would like to talk to the married men, and see if we can't get homesteads set up for you. We won't have time to plant any new crops this year, but we can get some of the land cleared, and make preparations for next year. We do have several temporary houses available here on the church grounds that you are welcome to use, until you have your homes

built. Once again, I welcome you all here."

As the women and children got up and went back out of the church, the married men walked to the front.

"I would like to take all of you out tomorrow morning to look at the available land around here," continued Father Joseph. "With the help of this map, we can probably get everything set up."

"How much is this land going to cost us?" asked Charley Foltz.

"Very little. I have already bought it from the government, so you just have to go through me."

"We have 4 vacant houses here at the settlement," he continued.

"The 4 oldest members and their families can use them. The rest of you will have to camp out, until the houses are built. We have church services in the morning at five, and I want all of you to be there, so now I'll let you get back to your families and friends."

As the men departed the church, Father Joseph went back into the sacristy, where Brother Joseph and Brother Engelbert were standing.

"Get the brothers, and meet me at my house," requested Father Joseph. "I need to talk to all of you."
"Yes Father," replied Big Joe, as the two men left.

Father Joseph went over to his small table and pulled out a box from underneath. He opened it up and looked through some papers. Finding what he wanted, he took the sheets, folded them up, put them in his pocket, and left the sacristy. He walked over to his house, where the brothers were already waiting. There was John Wiederle, Joe Boedigheimer, Cornelius Boedigheimer, Michael Doll, Joseph Schwab, Engelbert Tresch, Joseph A. Doll, Casper Schoeneberger, and Joachim Weis.

"Gentlemen, please come in," offered Father Joseph, as he led them into his house.

Once everyone was inside, and seated, he continued: "We have a lot of work to do. With all of the newcomers arriving, we are going to have to help them. I must go back to St. Nazianz and get the rest of the sisters up here."

"Who's going to be in charge, while you're gone?" queried Brother Joseph.

"I'm going to leave you in charge. I shouldn't be gone for more than two or three weeks."

"Are you taking anyone with you?" asked Brother Engelbert.
"No. There is no need."
"When are you leaving?" queried Brother John.
"I was hoping to be gone already, but it looks like I'll have to wait for a while, yet. At least, until the people get settled in."

"Almost every day," he continued, "we see more and more visitors coming along the trail. Many are continuing through, but I noticed that several families have settled to the west of here. I must go out and see to their religious needs. It is getting to be too much
for Father Pierz, and I'm sure he would be glad to hear that I'm helping him out. Tomorrow, I'm going to take a walk over that way, and introduce myself."

"Father, you must remember that you are 66 years old, and you shouldn't work as hard as when you were younger," objected Brother Cornelius.

"Oh, this is not work. This is pleasure. It does my heart good to see these strong German souls coming here, and it's my duty to see to their needs."

"Yes Father, but I still think you should have some help," continued Brother Cornelius.

"I have great plans, Cornelius. Someday I will have a seminary and I will have priests to help me carry on the work of the Lord, but for now, I must do it. The Lord put me in this wilderness for a reason. I must comply with his demands. As long as I have brothers,
like you men, I shall have no problems."

"I thought you were taking the married men out tomorrow morning," interrupted Brother Michael.

"I am, but I should be done with that by noon. Then I'm going over to the other area. Now, getting back to what I was talking about earlier, as soon as we decide where everyone is going to set up a homestead, we are going to have to help them clear their land. I want each of you to pick out a person and offer to them your assistance. We could clear more of our land, but right now, these people are more important."

The next morning, Father Joseph walked around the campfires of the newcomers, as well as the temporary houses, and gathered all of the married men, and led them westward away from the church-grounds.

"As you can see, there are many trees here, but you must also notice the rich virgin soil. Once the land is cleared, I envision abundant crops, within a year," noted Father Joseph, as they walked along the trail.

"I have the land all plotted here on this map," he continued, as he picked out two sheets from his pocket, and unfolded them. The men gathered around him, to take a closer look.

"As you can see here, Victor has the land to our left, but all of this land to the right is available."

"How about this area?" asked Joseph W. Doll, as he pointed to an area to their left.
"That's open."
"I'll take it."
"Alright," replied Father Joseph, as he wrote down Joseph's name on the sheet. "Let's see, that's 160 acres."

"What about the land across from his?" asked Mr. Sarbacher.

"Can I get that?"

"Of course."

As the group continued onward, Charley Foltz picked out an area, and then Joseph Riesterer. Ferdinand Eifert picked out 160 acres between Joe Weis and Victor.

"Joseph," continued Father Joseph, as he looked at Mr. Riesterer, "the lake that lies beside your land is called 'Boedigheimer Lake.' Bruno and I checked this land out last winter, and he named it after his descendants."

"I do have more land available on the other side of the river," he added, as he looked at the others, "around by Bruno and Anton."

It was now getting close to noon, when the men arrived back at church, just in time for the noon meal. Father Joseph walked over to Bruno and Mary Boedigheimer. "Bruno," he stated, "could you take Victor and Ignatz up past your place this afternoon, and show them some of the available lands? I have to get over and see someone, so I can't."
"Sure. Is there any particular spot?"

"Take them along the river, north of Anton's."

"Very well," replied Bruno, as he watched Father Joseph turn and depart.

Father Joseph went to his house, grabbed his knapsack, and left, heading in a westerly direction toward Boedigheimer Lake. From there, he headed to Marion Lake, going along the river route. He followed the shoreline to the north until he reached a small log hut.

This hut was the new home of Michael Schmitz. Michael, and his wife Anna Maria, had recently arrived in the area, and were in the process of building their shelter. He was a
short man of 37, while his wife, sometimes called Mary Ann, was 38. They had three children: Nicholas, age 11, Peter, age 9 and a new-born daughter, Margaret. The two boys were playing in front of the cabin as Father Joseph approached.

"Hello my friend. My name is Father Joseph Albrecht. I am wondering if there is anything I can do for you. I am in charge of a Catholic settlement not too far from here, at a place called Rush Lake."

"Hello Father," replied Michael, as he stopped what he was doing, and shook hands. "Mike Schmitz here."
"Yes, I've heard quite a bit about you," continued Michael.
"Father Pierz has mentioned your name on several occasions."
"You are more than welcome to come and have Mass with us. We have built a small church, and it is getting quite crowded, but we can always find room."

"Why, thank-you. We would like that very much."
"Where are you from?"
"We originally came from Ohio. Then, we moved to Wisconsin for a couple of years, and then on to Clinton, Minnesota. There is a strong Catholic community down there, in Stearns County, but already, land is getting hard to find. Florian Fehr came up here with
me awhile back, and we checked this land out. We had heard that you were living over by Rush Lake, but we just didn't have the time to visit you. We just got back a few days ago, with our families."

"Florian Fehr? Where does he live?"

"Not too far from here," answered Michael, as he pointed eastward. "Just go east, you can't miss it, if you follow the old Indian trail."

"Are you having any problems?"

"No, not really. We get along real good with the Indians, and that was my main worry."

"Well, if you should ever need any help, feel free to come see me. My door is always open. And, when you get the chance bring the family over to church."

"I will Father, I will."
Father Joseph now headed for the house of Florian Fehr. It was in a very short time that he arrived at another small, crude, log cabin. A tall man of 21, was working outside the cabin.

"Greetings. My name is Father Joseph Albrecht. I live several miles from here, at Rush Lake."

"Florian Fehr is my name. What can I do for you?"
"Oh nothing. I just came to visit and meet you, and to welcome you to my church on Sundays."

"Well, thank-you Father. I will be there. I thought about coming earlier, but it just seemed that there was so much to do."

"I understand. Is there anything I can get for you?"

"No, not that I can think of. Mike and I planned this move out pretty well. If all goes as expected, there'll be more people coming up here."

"Splendid. There is plenty of room up here for good Catholic families."

"Yes, there are quite a few young men from St. Joseph parish, who are anxious to come up here."

"Good. Just let me know when they come, and I'll see if I can help them. Remember, feel free to come to my church, when you get a chance."

"Thank-you Father."

Return to St. Nazianz

CHAPTER XXII

ister Lucretia was lying in bed, still in a very sickly state. Father Ambrose had spent many hours administering to her, yet she did not seem to be getting any better. On this one particular day, she seemed to be taking a turn for the worse. "Father Ambrose," she noted in a very weak voice, "could you please send Sister Mary Ann to me? I would like to talk to her." "Why yes. I will get her right away."

Within several minutes, Sister Mary Ann arrived in the room.

"Dear sister, what would you like?"

Sister Lucretia reached under her blanket and pulled out a satchel. Handing it to Sister Mary Ann, she stated:

"I believe that the good Lord will be taking me away soon. Take this bag and protect it. Hide it and give it to no one except Father Joseph."

She took the bag and looked inside. She pulled out a smaller bag and opened it. As she did so, she gasped. She was amazed at what she saw. "So much money! What would a sister be doing with so much money?" she thought.

She quickly put the bag back inside the satchel, and after stammering for a second, she finally said:

"Yes, I will keep it for you."

"Thank-you. Remember, don't give it to anyone except Father Joseph."

"Yes Sister Lucretia."

"Now, I must go to sleep."

"Good-bye," noted Sister May Ann, as she departed the room, with the satchel under her right arm.

Sister Lucretia nodded her head in approval and closed her eyes.

Sister Mary Ann returned to the convent. Upon arriving, she took the satchel and placed it under her bed. She then went to talk to Sister Rosa Wahl, who was working in the garden.

"Sister Rosa!" she shouted. "I need your help."

"Hush Sister," stated Sister Rosa, as she put down the hoe, and walked over to Sister Mary Ann. "You must be quiet. What is the matter?"

"I have just come from seeing Sister Lucretia," continued Sister Mary Ann, in a very quiet tone.

"She gave me a bag, which contains over $2000.00. I am supposed to take care of it. It bothers me that she should be in possession of such a large amount of money."

"I'm sure it must belong to Father Joseph. Sister Lucretia is probably just keeping it until we get to Minnesota."

"It still bothers me."

"Maybe, it would be a good idea for you to go see Sister Theresa Gramlich, at Clark's Mill. She might be able to ease your mind. I would like to go with you, but I must stay here and teach."

"Yes, I think I will."

The next day, Sister Mary Ann left for Clark's Mill. This small hamlet was located nearby on the Manitowac River, and Sister Mary Ann enjoyed the beautiful scenery on this peaceful walk. Upon arrival at the small church of the Immaculate Conception, she was greeted by young Sister Theresa, who had been from the colony, and had been asked by Father Joseph Fessler to come to Clark's Mill and teach the children.

"What a welcomed sight, you are! Why have you come?"

"I needed to get away from the rest for a while. My mind is confused, and I needed to go somewhere to try and unsettle things."

"You are welcome to stay here for as long as you wish. I have been very busy here, and I could use some extra help."

Sister Mary Ann remained for several days, spending much of her time in prayer, searching for the answers she most definitely was looking for. While there, she also helped Sister Theresa,- and it was then that she realized she could use more help. Deep down inside, Sister Mary Ann was already deciding that she wanted to stay here and live with Sister Theresa. She still had much faith in Father Joseph, but with each passing day, the faith diminished.

Several days later, she returned to St. Nazianz, a completely changed woman. Her heart had been lifted. She now was smiling and content. She knew that when Father Joseph returned from Minnesota, she would not go with him. She could hardly wait to tell Sister Rosa of her experiences at Clark's Mill.

"You must go and visit Sister Theresa," suggested Sister Mary Ann, to Sister Rosa, who was standing near the convent, with Josepha Thoenig.

"I'm sure you will get the same feeling that I did. There is a need for our assistance."

"But, what about Father Joseph?" queried Sister Rosa.

"I have decided that I'm more needed here."
"I still feel that my allegiance should go to Father Joseph," argued Sister Rosa. "It is he who has helped us the most. We should not give up on him."

Just then, Father Ambrose approached the threesome. "Excuse me, but I just read something in the newspaper, here, that I must show you, especially you Rosa," he noted, as he opened the newspaper and prepared to read: "To Rosa Wahl — wherever she may be. Your mother, near Minster, is very sick. She is at the door of death and would like to see you, if at all possible. Please come home at your earliest convenience."

Sister Rosa sat down on the doorstep and gasped. What was she to do? Oh, how she longed to see her mother again.

"Take Caroline with you and return home," suggested Father Ambrose.

"I will get you train tickets back to Ohio."

Caroline Schuh had previously expressed a desire to return home to see her parents. She had just celebrated her 17th birthday and had hinted that she was homesick. She had left without the consent of her parents, so she thought it would be a good idea to straighten matters out, before she headed for Minnesota. The next day, the two women departed for Ohio. After a brief stay, Rosa Wahl returned to St. Nazianz. Caroline Schuh was never allowed to return. She gave in to her fathers' demands and remained in Ohio.

SEPTEMBER 1867 — Father Ambrose was standing in front of the church, with Anton Stoll, one particular sunny morning, when they noticed a wagon approach. This wagon was being driven by Father Joseph.

After the wagon pulled up in front of the church, Father Ambrose shouted: "What a surprise! Why didn't you write and let me know when you were coming?"

As Father Joseph was getting down, he noted: "I had been hoping to return much sooner, but I have been so busy in Minnesota. Finally, I decided I had to get back here and get my girls to their new home."

"They have been a great help to me. Several of them have been helping Father Fessler, over at Clark's Mill."

"I have missed them dearly," added Father Joseph. "I sure could have used them this past summer."

"I have some sad news for you, Joseph," stated Father Ambrose, as he led Father Joseph toward his room," Caroline Schuh is no longer with us."

"Why?"

"She returned to Ohio, and her parents did not allow her to come back."

"She reminded me so much of my daughter. She looked and acted just like Rosalie. I was looking forward to having her in Minnesota. She always seemed to brighten up my day."

As the three men continued toward Father Ambrose's room, they were met by Sister Lucretia.

"Hello dear sister," shouted Father Joseph.

"Father Joseph! What a relief to see you again! We were starting to wonder when you were going to come back. We had been praying diligently for your return. Our prayers have been answered."

"How has everything been here, since I left?"

"Not so good. While I was sick, I confided in Sister Mary Ann. I gave her my satchel for safekeeping. She snooped in it and found the money. She hasn't been the same since."

"I'll have a talk with her. Why not get all the girls together, so I can see them again?"

Sister Lucretia obediently went on her errand.

"There is something else I should tell you, Joseph," interrupted Father Ambrose, after Sister Lucretia was gone.

"Several of your sisters told me that they wished to stay at Clark's Mill, rather than move on to Minnesota."

"I don't believe you," shouted Father Joseph. "Why would they want to leave me? I have been their guardian. I have taken care of them. If it weren't for me, they would be in a bad state, right now."

"They have been helping Father Fessler and have decided that he needs them."

"Who are they?"

"Rosa Wahl, Mary Ann Graf and Josepha Thoenig."

As the two men continued to talk, the women arrived. "That is four of them, that you snatched away from me," continued Father Joseph, as he looked coldly into the eyes of Father Ambrose.

"Believe me, Joseph, I didn't have a thing to do with it." After the women arrived, Father Joseph turned to Sister Lucretia, and said:

"Sister, get everything ready. We are leaving immediately. There is no need to stay here any longer."

"But Joseph," interrupted Father Ambrose, "surely, you can't be mad or angry over what the girls really want?"

Father Joseph thought for several seconds, and then seemed to settle down.

"Yes, I suppose you are right. It will be better this way.
But I still would like to leave right away. Could you have your men take us over to Manitowac in a couple of your wagons?"

"Certainly."

"Anton, could you take care of that?"

Anton nodded his head and left.

"What about the wagon you came in?"

"I borrowed it from a gentleman, back at Calumetville. He will be coming over to pick it up," replied Father Joseph.

Among the sisters was little Emma Bliley. She now began to wonder what she was to do. She had left Ohio to be with Sister Rosa. She now knew that Rosa was not going to Minnesota. Her close friend, Julia Boedigheimer, too, had been with her at St. Nazianz, but she was preparing to leave. What was she to do?

Two sturdy wagons arrived in front of the convent. The sisters began putting what little belongings they had, into the wagons. In no time, they were climbing aboard. They were ready to go with Father Joseph.

Little Emma Bliley was sitting in the back of the second wagon. She glanced back and saw Rosa. Rosa saw her. Both had tears in their eyes. In a flash, Emma jumped off the wagon and ran towards Rosa. They hugged each other.

"I want to stay with you," she pleaded.

"You can't," replied Rosa. "You must go with Father Joseph.

He can take better care of you than I can."

"Emma! Get back here!" shouted Father Joseph. "We are leaving."

Emma looked at Father Joseph, and then at Sister Rosa. Then she began running toward the convent. Father Joseph jumped down from the wagon and ran after her. Finally catching her, he forcibly carried her back to the wagon.

"Sister Theresa, you take care of her," he shouted to Sister Theresa Arnold, who was sitting in the back of the second wagon, next to little Julia Boedigheimer.

"Now you stay there," continued Father Joseph, as he scolded Emma.

As Father Joseph returned to the first wagon, Emma was glancing toward the sun. In an instant, she acted entirely different.

Through the rays of the golden sun, she had a vision. She saw the Holy Mother, dressed in white, with a flowing blue mantle over her shoulders. The Holy Mother stretched out her hands to Emma.

Right then, Emma knew that Mary desired for her to go forward with the journey. Emma became overjoyed. She smiled at Sister Theresa and Julia. The others could not figure out what happened, but they could see a marked difference in her. It was a difference that no one but Emma could explain.

The trip to Minnesota began. Father Joseph and his small band of 8 women and girls departed St. Nazianz, taking the same route that Father Joseph had traveled a year earlier.

While going down the Fox River, heading for Prairie du Chien, Father Joseph held religious instructions and Mass for the women.

When Mass was completed, he sat down between Emma Bliley and

Julia Boedigheimer. "Well, my children," he stated, "it won't be long now, and we'll be in Minnesota."

"I do long to see my parents again," stated Julia.

"Ah, that you will."

"Father, are we going to live at the convent?" asked Emma.

"Yes. I have plenty of room. Not only for you girls, but for many of the others in the settlement. I have big plans for my group."

Finally arriving in St. Paul, by riverboat, the group headed for St. Cloud, by train. Once arriving there, they transferred to two ox driven wagons, which were awaiting them.

The journey from St. Cloud to Rush Lake lasted eight days. They had difficulties with the chuck holes, which seemed to be everywhere along the trail. Sometimes, it was so bad that it was easier for the women to walk beside the wagon, rather than ride.

On Saturday, the seventh day of their wagon journey, they approached a cabin which was situated right along the trail. A man and his wife were standing outside. He walked toward the wagon of Father Joseph.

"Hello sir," stated Father Joseph.

"Hello. Where are you headed for?"

"We are returning to Rush Lake."

"Ah, you must be Father Albrecht. I have heard about you."

"Why, yes I am."

"You are welcomed to stay here tonight. It is still quite a way from here to Rush Lake."

"It is getting late," thought Father Joseph. "I think I'll take you up on that."

That night, Father Joseph slept in the wagon, while the others slept in the log cabin. The next morning, Father Joseph arose very early, and was standing near a campfire, with several of the sisters. Just then, the woman came running over to them.

"If you value your lives, you better hurry up and get out of here. My husband has taken some of your things already. Please, leave before he tries something else."

"Very well," replied Father Joseph. "Sister Lucretia, get everyone together, and we'll be on our way."

In a matter of minutes, the group was again on the move. It did not take them long and they arrived at Ottertail City.

"Sister Lucretia," stated Father Joseph, as he stopped the wagon and got down. "Bruno is supposed to meet us here. We will stop and have a break. If he does not come in fifteen minutes, we will take off again."

Everyone got off the wagons and sat down under some nearby oak trees. Sister Lucretia took out her guitar and began to sing a song. When she was done, Bruno came riding up on horseback, with another horse behind him.

"Welcome back Father," stated Bruno, as he came up alongside

Father Joseph. "Here is the horse, just like you asked for."

"Hello Bruno," replied Father Joseph, as he walked over and took the reins of the other horse. "Thank-you."

"Sister Lucretia," he continued, "take the wagons and follow the trail north, out of town. I'm going to ride ahead with Bruno. When you get to the river, wait there. I will come back and meet you."

As Father Joseph mounted and left, Sister Lucretia got all of the women together, and likewise departed, with her driving the lead wagon, and Sister Lydia driving the second. When the group of women approached Rush Lake, they were met by Father Joseph and Bruno, in a canoe. Several of the older Boedigheimer boys were closely behind, in another canoe. Father Joseph and Bruno led the women back to the settlement.

Immediately, upon their arrival, the cloistered life of the sisters began. They took possession of their convent and assumed their roles in the religious life.

The next day, Father Joseph walked over to Sister Lucretia, who was standing beside the small convent building, looking over the surrounding area.

"It is rather small," he stated, as he pointed to the convent, "but that will change. Some day we shall have a large 3-story building that can house from 50 to 60 sisters."

"It is fine. Simplicity is beauty. We don't need an extravagant building to carry out our work."

"There is still plenty of daylight hours left," continued Father Joseph. "Send four of the sisters to that wooded area on the other side of the cemetery. Have them help the brothers clear the land.

Have one sister wash the clothes by the river, one to clean the church, and one to mend some of my vestments, that I have laying out in the sacristy. Plus, make sure they continue the nightly adoration."

"Yes Father."

"Also, send Sister Theresa over to Frank and Anna Staab's house. She had a baby boy this morning, and I would like to find out how she is doing. Just tell her to follow the path along the lake, and she will find the house. This evening, after our prayer meeting, I would like the sisters to gather in the church. I want to make clear the rules and regulations of our society."

"Yes Father," answered Sister Lucretia, as she turned and departed.

That evening, after services, all of the sisters and novices gathered in the small log church.

Upon entering, Father Joseph walked to the front, and said:

"Thank-you for coming. I would like to set down some rules for our society, here at Rush Lake. As you may have already assumed, we have a lot of work to be done. In order to best get this accomplished, we must have some rules to live by. First of all, we must always remember that our work is mainly for God. He is our Master. It is for him that we suffer. It is for him that we do without many temporal things. But, for our society to function correctly, they must have a human leader. Sister Lucretia is your Mother Superior, but I am your leader. I am your guardian. What I say, goes. Do not question my ability, as I have had much experience."

"Many of our rules will be based on the ideals of Father Brunner. The main ones are: 1) The only time you can talk to each other is when you are in the garden, wash house, barn, or field. Otherwise, there is no need, except for when you feel it is necessary to talk to Sister Lucretia. 2) No time will be wasted in gossip. 3) There must be a complete detachment from friend and family. 4) Parlor visitation will be allowed only on very rare occasion. 5) Nightly adoration of the Blessed Sacrament will continue. Each vigil will last two hours. Sister Lucretia will be responsible to tell each of you when you are to be there. 6) Each morning, I will tell Sister Lucretia what needs to be done for the day. She will then pass it on to you. 7) We will have no oaths to take. You are free to leave whenever you want. 8) You are expected to be up at 5, for morning prayers. Sister Lucretia will talk to you at 7."

Father Joseph paused for several seconds and looked around at the poorly dressed women. He smiled, as he continued: "I will have simple outfits made for you. They will be black robes. The brothers will wear the same type, as you, but you will wear the hood over your head, at all times. That is all I have to say to you for now. Good night."

As he began to depart the church, he turned around, and said:

"Oh, by the way, confessions will be heard every Saturday." Outside of the church, he met Anton.

"Anton, I think we better send some men back to St. Cloud, tomorrow, for more supplies."

"Yes Father. I'll talk to some of the brothers."

"Also, tomorrow I am going over to Millerville. I'll be gone for a couple of days. I'll ride along with the brothers. Before I leave, I would like to talk to you, Bruno, and Victor. Please pass on to them that I want to speak to you three in the morning, after prayers."

The next morning, Mike Doll, Joe Boedigheimer, Joseph Schwab, and Casper Schoeneberger, were prepared to leave, as they waited in the freight wagons, in front of the church. Soon, Father Joseph, followed closely by Anton, Bruno, and Victor, came out of the church.

"Remember Anton," stated Father Joseph, as he climbed aboard the lead wagon, "I shall be back in two or three days."

"God be with you," exclaimed Anton.

"Good-bye," stated Father Joseph, as the wagons began to pull out. Brother Joseph and Brother Mike Doll were sitting in the first wagon, with Brother Joseph Schwab and Brother Casper in the second.

The sun was shining brightly as there was hardly a cloud in the sky. The leaves were already turning to their fall colors, and this added to the beauty of the surroundings that the travelers enjoyed.

As the wagons meandered down the trail, to Ottertail City, and southward to Clitherall, the men chatted, while Father Joseph sat and read his breviary. Along the trail, they met several caravans heading northward. Some of them were immigrants, coming in hopes of finding a new beginning. One of these wagons contained the Gustav Morgenroth family. He was returning to his homestead with his family, which included: his wife, Katharine, age 21, and their new-born son, Gustav.

"As soon as I get back, I shall come up to see you/' promised Father Joseph, as he talked to the Morgenroth family.

"That would be fine," replied Katharine.

"I must tend to some business down at Millerville, but I should be back in a few days."

As the men approached Millerville, a heavy thunderstorm occurred. Dark clouds, loud thunder, fiece continuous lightning, and strong winds, were prevalent.

The men stopped the wagons and crawled underneath, for cover. It was a downpour that lasted for over an hour.

"We are only a little ways from Millerville," stated Father Joseph. "I think I'll walk over there as soon as it lets up some. This will save you men some time."

The men continued to watch the heavy rains come down. When the rains finally did let up, Father Joseph decided to leave.

"I shall see you when you return to Rush Lake."

"Good-bye Father," replied the brothers. Meanwhile, back at the Rush Lake settlement, Gustav Morgenroth had just arrived. Upon reaching the small farmstead, he got off the wagon, and helped his wife and son down. She looked at the house, as her husband said: "This is your new home, my dear. I realize that it isn't a mansion, but it will have to do for now."

He opened the door and Katharine, with baby in arms, walked in. It was a small one-room log cabin, with a fireplace on one end and two beds on the other, with a small table and two stumps, for chairs, in the middle of the floor.

"This is only temporary," continued Gustav. "As soon as I'm able, I'll build a bigger and better place."

"This will do just fine."

"I'll bring in some of the belongings," added Gustav. "It's getting close to dusk, so we better prepare for the night."

He went to the wagon, and soon, was back in the house, with several household items. Just then, they heard a loud whooping sound, coming from the direction of the river.

Katharine was frightened. "What was that?"

"Oh, don't worry dear. It's probably just some of the Indians having a little fun. They are very friendly people. You have no need to be afraid of them. While we were building our houses, they would come around and snoop, but they did us no harm."

The yelling was getting louder. Gustav ran over to the window and looked out. He was quite surprised to see about 50 Indians, all wearing warpaint, approaching the house.

He ran over to the door and bolted it. Then he proceeded to open a trap door, which was conveniently located right inside the doorway. He grabbed his gun and stood in front of his wife and child. There, he patiently waited.

The Indians came right up to the house. They danced around and made a lot of noise, for quite some time. Then, suddenly, it became quiet. Gustav walked over to the window and looked out. "What a relief!" he stated. "They're gone."

"I wonder why they left?"

"Maybe they just wanted to check us out. Needless to say, I don't think we'll have to worry about them anymore, tonight. When Father Joseph comes back, I'll have him go see their chief, and find out what happened. Now, I think it's time for bed."

"Yes, I think you are right," added Katharine. After Mass, the next Sunday, Gustav approached Father Joseph. "Father Joseph," he exclaimed, "we had a frightful experience out by our place, the first night we were here."

"Oh! What happened?"

"A large group of Indians came up from down by the river and gave us a good scare. I wish you would find out why they did such a thing."

"They probably got a hold of some more of that whiskey. They can't seem to handle that devil's tea. Those fur traders keep on giving it to them though."

"That may well be, Father, but I still wish you would go talk to them. I've been told that you are very influential with them."

"Alright Gustav. I'll go see them as soon as I can," replied Father Joseph. "Say Gustav, we could use a teacher for our school. I heard that you had done some teaching before you came up here. Could you possibly help out?"

"Why, I would be more than glad to. When would you want me to begin?"

"Right away. You can use the room over the livery stable. That should be big enough. Let me know what supplies you need, and I'll see to it that you get them. I'll pass the word to all the parents to bring their children here, let's say next Monday."

"Very well Father," replied Gustav. "I'll come back tomorrow and get everything ready."

As the Morgenroths departed, the freight wagons arrived in front of the storage shed. Brother Joseph and Brother Michael Doll began to unload the goods, as Father Joseph walked over to greet them.

"Father," exclaimed Big Joe, "Casper didn't come back with us. He said he wanted to return to Ohio."

Father Joseph stood speechless, for several seconds. "Why would he want to do something like that? His family just got here.

Why would he want to leave now? He seemed to be enjoying himself here."

"He told me to tell you that it was nothing personal against you, Father. He just wanted to return to his home."

"My! My! What will his father say?" thought Father Joseph. "I guess I'll have to go tell Ignatz."

"Here are the receipts," continued Big Joe, as he handed several pieces of paper to Father Joseph.

After looking at them for several seconds, he put them in his pocket, and stated: "I have to go over and see how Margaret Doll is doing. She is supposed to have a baby any time now."

Father Joseph turned and headed for the new homestead of Joseph A. and Margaret Doll, which was located just a short distance from the church.

Mr. Doll was standing outside the entry way as Father Joseph approached.

"How is she doing?"

"I haven't heard a thing. Sister Theresa and Maggie are in there with her."

Just then, the sound of a crying baby was heard. Mr. Doll and Father Joseph looked at each other and smiled. Shortly thereafter, Sister Theresa appeared in the doorway. She looked at Mr. Doll, and said:

"Congratulations Joseph, you have a son."

Mr. Doll jumped up and down, as he shouted: "A son! I have a son! "

As he calmed down, he continued: "How is Margaret?" She is fine. Maggie is beside her. She is resting comfortably."

"Father," continued Mr. Doll, as he turned toward Father Joseph, "can I bring him down to church, tomorrow, and get him baptized?"

"Of course. Do you have a name?"

"Yes. We talked about it last week and decided that if it was a boy, we would name him Leopold?'

"Ah. Leopold Doll. The first child born at Rush Lake. Come to church at ten. I'll have everything ready."

"Fine," replied Mr. Doll, as he shook hands, and watched Father Joseph and Sister Theresa depart.

On their return trip to the church grounds, they walked through the golden wheat field, that was ripening along the trail. There wasn't much there but it was ready for harvesting.
When they got back to the convent, they were met by Sister Lucretia and Sister Seraphim.

"It is getting late, Sister Lucretia," he stated. "Tomorrow, we're going to have to get that wheat harvested. After Mass, I want all the sisters out in the field. I'll have Brother Joseph and Brother John take care of the hauling and Brother Michael and Brother Engelbert can do the stacking."

The next morning, all of the women were seen, with flails in hand, cutting the small wheatfield. Brother Joseph and Brother John were loading the cut grain on oxen-driven carts to take back to the church grounds.

After the baptism of Leo Doll was completed, Father Joseph walked out to see how everything was progressing. He met Brother Joseph coming back, with a load of grain.

"How is everything?"

"There isn't much wheat in this straw."

"Yes, I know. The grasshoppers did quite a lot of damage. Just shock the wheat up near the grainery. We'll thresh it later this fall."

"Say Father," continued Brother Joseph, "last night Brother Engelbert was acting very strangely. I think you should have a talk with him. I got the impression he is not happy here."

"Yes, I've noticed that too. It does worry me, but you know as well as I, that I can't force him to stay. Anyone is free to do as they want. If he wants to leave, then I'll have to let him."

"But Father, you should have some kind of binding rule, or oath, that we should have to take."

"This is not a slave camp, Joseph. I will never hold anyone here, against their will. If they do not find true happiness here, then it is my fault. I am failing somewhere."

"You can only do so much. You always stress that we must suffer on this Earth, in order to celebrate in the next. Some of the brothers don't want to share in that suffering."

"Who may that be?"

"Michael Schoeneberger, Engelbert Tresch, Michael Doll, Mr. Ottleberg, and even your cousin, John Wiederle."

"In other words," continued Father Joseph, "you are saying that most of the brothers aren't happy here?"

"In a way. They may be good Catholic men, but I believe, they will all be married someday."

"If that is the way they want it, then I'll let them. That will not change my way of thinking, concerning marriage. I cannot stress enough the fact that we have only a short time left."

"I still think you should have a talk with Brother Engelbert."

"I will. I will."

He then waved to Brother Joseph, and proceeded to the wheatfield, where he watched the women, busily cut the grain.

"Sister Lucretia," he stated, as he walked up to her, "it looks like you'll be able to get the whole field done today."

"Yes Father," answered Sister Lucretia, as she wiped the sweat from her forehead. "The girls have really been working hard."

"I noticed that. Surely, you will all be rewarded."

"We should have had this crop done a couple of weeks ago, already," continued Father Joseph, "but those unnecessary rains changed that. We're going to be lucky to get enough seed for next year."

"We know everything will work out," noted Sister Lucretia.

"The potato crop looks excellent. If nothing else, we will have plenty of potatoes this winter."

"Yes, and some of the men are getting to be excellent hunters," added Father Joseph. "We should have plenty of meat."

"Well, anyway," continued Father Joseph, "I must get back to the church. I'll talk to you all this evening, at meditation."

When he returned to the church grounds, he walked over to the grainery, where Brother Michael Doll was shocking the wheat.

"Have you seen Brother Engelbert?"

"Yes, I did," bluntly replied Michael. "I saw him head west just a short time ago. He was carrying a small bag."

"Oh my!" exclaimed Father Joseph. "I may be too late."

He quickly turned and walked away, heading for the brothers' quarters. Upon entering, he walked over to Engelbert's bunk. All of his personal belongings were gone. Father Joseph was too late. Engelbert Tresch had departed, never to be heard from again.

Father Joseph sat down on a nearby chair, looked upward, and exclaimed: "Oh Lord, what is happening?"

Lightning Strikes

CHAPTER XXIII

On a bright sunny spring morning in 1868, Michael Schmitz and Florian Fehr approached the home of Father Joseph. They walked up to the entrance and knocked on the door.

"Good morning. Please come in."

"Good morning," answered the two men, as they entered.

"We were wondering if you could help us," stated Michael.

"Several families from St. Joseph's are on their way up here. We are expecting them any day now. All of them are good Catholic families and are going to be needing some good Christian leadership. Can you help?"

"Sure. How many are there?"

"Five families," noted Florian. "Balts Fuchs, George Seifert, Martin Fiedler, Joe Zimmerman, and George Rieder."

"Do they all have homesteads picked out?"

"Yes," replied Michael. "We've had several visits by the men, and they all picked out some property."

"When they arrive, let me know. I'll gladly help in any way that I can. After they get settled in, I will start saying Mass in that area, every once in a while. That would be easier for you people, rather than having you all come over here."

"That would be wonderful," replied Florian.

"My church is really not big enough to hold them all anyway."

"I'll let you know Father," stated Michael, as he and Florian began to head for the door.
"Yes. You do that."

Several weeks later, Father Joseph made another journey over to the Michael Schmitz homestead.

"Good morning," stated Michael, as he came out of the house.

"Are you ready?"

"Yes Mike. Who are we going to see first?"

"All of the families are going to be over at Joe Zimmerman's."

"Good. That'll give me a chance to meet everyone, in the least amount of time."

The two men walked over to the Zimmerman homestead, which was located next to Florian Fehr's place. As they approached the shanty, they noticed a small group of people gathered out front.

"Joe," stated Michael, as he walked up to a short young man of 32, who was standing near the doorway, "I would like you to meet Father Joseph Albrecht. Father, this is Joe Zimmerman."

"Hello," stated Joe, as he shook hands. "Mike has told me a lot about you. Welcome to my home."

"Hello," replied Father Joseph. "I am looking forward to saying Mass for you people, as well as anything else I can do."

"Could you say Mass this Sunday?" asked Joe.

After pausing for several seconds, Father Joseph stated: "Why yes. I'll say Mass in the morning, at Rush Lake, and then come over here. Let's say, ah, at two o'clock."

"Good. I'll make sure everyone knows about it."

"Father," continued Joe, as he took the hand of his wife, who had been standing beside him, "this is my wife, Mary. Mary, Father Joseph."

"Please to meet you," stated the thin 25-year-old lady, as she looked at Father Joseph.

"Hello Mary. My, what a beautiful name!"

"Come Father," interrupted Michael, "I want you to meet the others."

Michael led Father Joseph over to several men, who were busy talking under the shade of a large oak tree.

"Men," stated Michael, "I want you to meet Father Joseph. Father, this is George Seifert, George Rieder, Balts Fuchs, and Martin Fiedler."

"Hello men. I am overjoyed at the sight of more new settlers. I will be honored to take care of your spiritual needs. If there is anything you need, just ask, perhaps I can help. If you need help clearing your lands, maybe I can get some of the men from Rush Lake to
come over and help. I, also might have some extra seed for those who may not have enough."

"Thank-you, Father," stated the strong muscular 38-year-old Martin Fiedler, "but,*I think we have everything necessary to get started."

"I have Mass over at my church in Rush Lake, every day of the week. You are all more than welcome to come."

"Father has offered to say Mass here next Sunday afternoon," interrupted Michael.

"What about Father Pierz?" queried the 36-year-old George
Seifert. "He said he was going to come over here when he got the chance."

"Ah, you met Father Pierz?" asked Father Joseph.

"Yes," continued George, "he stopped by at our church before we left."

"He is an excellent man, but, he has too much territory to cover, so I will help out when he is not around."

"That would be nice," noted George.

"Are all of you married?"

"Yes Father," replied Martin.

"Would you get your families together, so I can meet them?"

The men quickly rounded up their families, in a row.

The first family he was introduced to was the George Seifert family. "Father," stated George, "this is my wife, Elizabeth, and

my children Martin, age 9, George, age 11, Margaret, age 7, Mary, age 3, and my baby, Barbara."

"Father," interrupted Martin Fiedler, "this is my family, Margaret, my wife, she is a sister to George. My children Balthasar, age

14, and Martin, age 10."

Father Joseph continued on down the line, until he was introduced to everyone present.

"There are more people coming up," stated Michael, as he

walked with Father Jospeh, back to the start of the line.

"Well, I'm not sure how many of you I remember right now, but, give me a little time and I'll get to know you. I should be getting back to Rush Lake now."

After all of the farewells were given, he departed, heading in an easterly direction, back to his home. "Surely," he thought to himself, "God has sent these people to me, for me to take care of."

TWO WEEKS LATER.

Father Joseph had just walked out of the stable, when Ignatz Schoeneberger came driving up in an ox-driven cart, followed by another cart, driven by his 22-year-old son, Martin.

"Well, I see you are ready to leave."

"Yes, we are on our way. I just stopped by to see if there was anything else we could get you, in St. Cloud."

"No. I'm sure your wagons are going to be overloaded the way it is. Have a safe trip. I hope to see you in a couple of weeks."

"Thank-you Father," continued Ignatz, "and thank-you for letting my son, Michael, come along with us. He'll be a great help.

Would you please check on Mary Ann and Andrew, once in a while, to make sure they are alright?"

"Sure."

"Good-bye Father."

"Good-bye Ignatz."

The trip to St. Cloud happened without incident, but problems arose on the return trip. Approximately 7 miles north of Alexandria, a small town about 50 miles from Rush Lake, the men noticed a storm approaching from the west.

"I think we better stop," stated Ignatz, as he looked at his son, Michael, who was driving the first wagon and sitting next to him.

"We should put another cover over the wagon, so the flour don't get wet."

Michael obediently stopped the wagon. Martin, who was driving the second wagon, did likewise.

"What are we doing?" asked Martin, as he walked up to his father.

"We're going to put another cover on the wagon," replied Ignatz, as he got down from the wagon.

Michael went to the back of the wagon and brought out a large tarp, as the thunder became louder and the lightning sharper.

As it began to rain heavily, he handed Ignatz one end of the covering. Ignatz took it and threw it over the wagon. He then got aboard the wagon tongue, between the two oxen, and attempted to get the covering completely over.

At that instant, disaster struck. A sharp bolt of lightning struck Ignatz. He gave a loud yell and fell to the ground.

Michael and Martin, wondering what happened, came running up from behind the wagon. They noticed the lifeless body of their father, lying on the ground, next to one of the oxen, which had also been stricken.

"Oh my God!" shouted Michael, as he knelt down beside his father. "Help me Martin," he continued, as he began to pull his father away from the oxen.

When the two men had the body safely away from the animals, Michael continued: "Now what are we going to do?"

Martin wiped the tears from his eyes and replied: "I'll get the shovels from my wagon."

As Martin went over to his wagon, Michael got down on his knees and made the sign of the cross. "Why Lord?" he asked. "My father never did a bad thing all of his life. Why couldn't it have been me instead?" He reached down and touched the body, and immediately, burst into tears.

Music To Their Ears

CHAPTER XXIV

Life continued on at the Rush Lake settlement. On the morning of March 18, 1869, Father Joseph held a baptismal ceremony at the home of Joseph W. and Barbara Doll, for their new son, Joseph Leopold. Besides the godparents, John and Theresa Doll, those present included Charley Foltz, and his wife; Wendel Doll, young John A. Doll, Wendolin Doll Sr., Catharine Doll, Jacob, and Mary Doll, and Joseph and Barbara's other children: August and Sophrona.

When the ceremony was completed, Father Joseph walked over to Charley Foltz, who was talking with Joseph Wendolin Doll. "Thank-you for coming, Father," stated Joseph.

"It was my pleasure."

"Say Father," interrupted Charley, "did you know that Joseph's sisters, and their families, will soon be coming out here to live?"

"No, I didn't. When?"

"We're not quite sure," replied Joseph. "We have a place picked out for both John and Maggie, and Adam and Veronica."

"You finally convinced your brother to come out, huh?" stated Father Joseph, as he looked at Charley.

"Yes. They have three young girls now. Bridget, Magdaline, and Sophrona. Adam and Veronica have two, John and Annie, but are expecting a third."

"Well," continued Father Joseph, "I received a letter from a certain Christof Silbernagel, from Wisconsin, and he is bringing a group out here also."

"It won't be long, and this entire area will be settled," stated Joseph, as he puffed on his pipe.

It was not long, and the new arrivals came. Christof Silbernagel, age 35, with his wife Mary, age 29, and their 3-year-old son, Christopher, picked out a homestead across the river, a short distance from the church. Sebastian Hertel, age 24, and his wife, Margaret, age 24, also arrived from Wisconsin, along with Wanibald Neumaier, and wife Caroline; Wendolin Fehrenbacher, and his wife Caroline; Anton Friedsam, age 40, and his wife, Elizabeth, age 44, and their children: Barney, Catharine, Mary, and Alois.

Even though the Adam Kerber's and John Foltz's did not arrive until 1870, other settlers did arrive from Ohio, in 1869. Among these were John and Sophia Grismer, and John Reinhart, and his two boys, John, and Lawrence. The scene now turns to August of 1869. Father Joseph, having just completed Holy Mass, was mingling with his parishioners.

"Have you met any of those surveyors?" asked Bruno.

"No," replied Father Joseph,

"but I have seen them working. I sure hope they don't decide to put a railroad through where they have been surveying."

"That would be rather bad, wouldn't it?" stated Christof.

"Perhaps, we should send our band out to visit them, some evening," suggested Bruno. "Maybe we can show them good hospitality, as well as convince them to choose a different route."

"That is an excellent idea," replied Father Joseph. "Have the men gather this evening here, and we'll pay them a visit."

As this conversation was being held, a group of strangers came riding up to the church.

"Who are those men?" asked Anton, as he watched them approach.

"I don't know," answered Father Joseph. "I never saw them before."

Several of them were on horseback, while a group of four were riding in a carriage. After the carriage came to a stop, right in front of Father Joseph, one of the men from inside the carriage yelled: "Who do we have here?"

"I was wondering the same thing," stated Father Joseph.

"The gentlemen riding with me here," continued the heavy-set man, as he got out of the carriage, "is none other than Mr. Schuyler Colfax, Vice-President of these United States."

"Vice-President!" exclaimed Father Joseph. "What are you doing out here?"

Mr. Colfax got out of the carriage and shook Father Joseph's hand.

"My name is Father Joseph Albrecht. Welcome to Rush Lake."

"Please to meet you, Father. What are you people doing out here?"

"We live here. We have for the past three years."

"I didn't think there were any permanent settlements in this area," stated Mr. Colfax.

"Bruno, go get the men together," requested Father Joseph.

"I'm sure these people wouldn't mind hearing some music."

"Yes Father."

"We are on a tour of this area," continued Mr. Colfax. "We left Minneapolis and went to Breckenridge. From there, we went to Fort Abercrombie, and over to Georgetown, and then over to Detroit. Now we are heading back to Minneapolis. It won't be long, and the railroad will be coming through this area. Major George Brackett, here, and Bill King, have come along to check out the best route, westward. I understand the Northern Pacific has survey crews out just a little north of here, and the St. Paul and Canada have survey crew around here, also."

"Yes," noted Father Joseph, "I've seen them working."

Just then Bruno came back with a group of men and boys. They were playing music on their brass instruments. They slowly marched around the carriage, and into a circle. There were twelve men, altogether, in this little brass band. The visitors were quite surprised at what they heard. They all sat down under the shade trees and listened to the beautiful sound of music, coming from the coronets, tubas, trombones, and a drum. Father Joseph sat down next to Mr. Colfax and seemed to enjoy the music. After they played several songs, Mr. Colfax looked at Father Joseph, and said: "Father, that is excellent music! It gives me a good feeling. You should be proud of your musicians."

"Oh I am."

"We should be on our way," interrupted the heavy-set middle-aged man, who went by the name of Bill King.

"Yes Bill, I suppose you are right," replied Mr. Colfax.

"Thank-you for stopping by," noted Father Joseph.

"Thank-you for the entertainment," replied Mr. Colfax.

After the group departed, Father Joseph continued: "Bruno, have the men here at about five, and we'll take them over to the survey crew."

"Very well, Father," replied Bruno, as he put his instrument back into the case.

That evening, more music was heard in the area around the

Rush Lake church. The men had gathered at the church and Father Joseph led them, in a march, out to the survey crew that was encamped about 2 miles away. Brother Joseph Boedigheimer was walking alongside Father Joseph. He was carrying a torch, as was Brother Cornelius and Brother John. They were followed by the band, which was playing tunes, all the way. When they arrived at the camp, they got in a circle, and continued to play. Upon completion of the song, Father Joseph walked up to one of the men, standing near the fire, and said: "Hello, my name is Father Joseph Albrecht. We have a settlement not too far from here. We just received these instruments a few weeks ago from Cincinnati, and the boys have really been enjoying themselves. We thought maybe we could entertain you for a little while, since we know how lonely it can be out here in the night."

"Thank-you," replied a tall slender man of about 30. "My name is Carlson, and Pm a reporter for the Boston Journal. I have been with this crew for about two weeks now, and I agree with you. It does get very lonely out here."

"We can't play much yet," interrupted Bruno, "but we do the best we can. We have sent to Toledo, for an instructor, who will spend the winter with us. You will pardon our poor playing, but we felt so good when we heard you were here looking for a route for a railroad, that we felt like doing something to show our appreciation and good will. You see, we are just getting started and have to work hard, but we wanted some recreation and we concluded to get up a band. We thought it would be better than hanging around a grocery. We haven't any grocery yet, and if we keep sober, and give our attention to other things, perhaps, we shan't have one, which I reckon will be all the better for us."

"Your men sound wonderful," noted Mr. Carlson, "please, play some more."

The group played one more song, after which Father Joseph stated: "Well, we should be getting back home. I'm sure everyone is very tired. How long do you plan on being around here?"

"We should be gone in a day or so."

"What do you think of all this railroad business?"

"I think it's great. Someday a person will be able to travel from the East Coast to the West Coast, and never touch the ground. There will be railroads. That is the thing of the future."

"What are the chances of one coming through this area?"

"I'd say that within two to three years, there will be one here.

Maybe not right here, but somewhere in the area."

"That is what I'm afraid of."

"I take it, you are against them?"

"Yes, I am. We left Ohio, not too many years ago, because it was getting crowded, and we wanted to find a place where we could live out our lives, in quiet. With the railroad coming, that means there will be many people coming. I don't want to think about what

will happen then."

Turning to Bruno, Father Joseph continued: "Come Bruno. It is time to leave."

Father Joseph, dressed in his long black robe, and black broad rimmed hat, led his group back to Rush Lake.

More Settlers Arrive

CHAPTER XXV

"Do you have everything ready for the Kempers when they arrive?" asked Father Joseph, as he looked at young John Doll, whom he was visiting on this particularly cold March day in 1870.

"I think so," replied the 31-year-old. "We just finished the log cabin over there on that hill. We're expecting him and his wife any day now, although Mr. Steinbach has been awaiting a letter from him, and up to now, hasn't received one."

"You know how the mail is."

As this conversation was being held, 22-year-old Ignatz Steinbach walked into the room.

"Have you heard anything from your brother-in-law, yet?" asked Father Joseph.

"No, I haven't, Father, but surely, they must be on their way by now."

"Tell me John," continued Father Joseph, "do you really think that Henry can make a go of a store out in this area?"

"Yes, I believe he can. That way, we won't have to depend on you for everything. And it will also make it easier for you. You won't have to worry about making sure that there are always enough supplies on hand."

"I suppose you are right, but for some reason, I have my doubts about it."

"Why do you say that?" asked Ignatz.

"It just seems that there are bigger and better things in store for that man."

"That may well be," noted John, "but, from what I gathered from the letter I received, he is really excited about moving up here."

Just then, there was a knock on the door. John walked over and opened it. Outside, were standing the young couple of Henry and Regina Kemper. Henry, who was 25, and his wife of 2 years, Regina, who was 24, were standing in the cold air, heavily dressed in winter apparel.

"Henry! Regina!" shouted John. "Come in!"

"Hello John," stated Henry, as he took off his cap.

"How did you get here?" asked Catharine, John's wife, who was standing beside John.

"We walked from Ottertail City," replied Regina.

"Oh my!" exclaimed John. "I wish I would have known you were there. I would have come and got you. It's awful cold to be walking."

As Henry rubbed his hands and walked toward the fireplace, he continued: "I agree John. I didn't think it would be that bad, until

we got close to Rush Lake. That last mile was very long."

"Henry," stated Ignatz, "good to see you again."

"Hello Ignatz," replied Henry, as they shook hands. "I wrote you a letter about a week ago, or so, but when we stopped at the hotel in Ottertail City, I asked Mr. McArthur, if there was any mail for Rush Lake, and he handed me a letter, and sure enough, it was

the letter I wrote to you."

"Please sit down," offered John, as he pointed to a nearby chair. You remember Father Joseph, don't you?"

"Ah yes," replied Henry, as he walked over and shook Father

Joseph's hand. "Hello Father."

"Hello Henry. Welcome to Rush Lake."

"Thank-you Father," replied Henry, as he sat down.

"Tell us about your trip," suggested Ignatz, as he sat down next

to Henry.

"Well, we left Ohio by train, as far as St. Cloud. Then we switched trains to Sauk Centre. From there, we traveled by stage up to Chippewa. From there, we left by sleigh, to Ottertail City, and we walked the rest of the way."

"Did you have any problems?" asked Father Joseph.

"A few," continued Henry. "When we were riding the stage to Chippewa, there were four young soldiers riding with us. They were going to Fort Abercrombie. They had so much baggage that the stage kept tipping, whenever they hit a rough spot in the trail."

"Did anyone else come with you up to Ottertail?" inquired John.

"Yes. There was a Mr. Lent. He is going to be running a sawmill in Ottertail City, for a certain Mr. R.L. Frazee."

"Well, I'm sure you must be very tired," noted John. "We have your house built for you, but it probably would be a good idea, if you stayed here for a couple of days, to rest up."

"Well," stated Father Joseph, as he got up from his chair, "I must be leaving now. It sure is good to see you again, Henry. I hope to see you in church this Sunday."

"We'll be there, Father," replied Henry, as he got up and walked with Father Joseph to the door.

"Good-bye Father," stated John, as he opened the door.

As Father Joseph put on his heavy black coat and walked through the doorway, he turned and said:

"Good-bye my children."

"Good-bye Father," replied Henry. "Be sure to stop over at my house, in a few days, and bless it."

"I will," answered Father Joseph, as he began to walk back to the church grounds.

When he arrived back at the church grounds, young Anton Doll was patiently standing in front of his house.

"Anton," stated Father Joseph. "What are you doing here?"

"I've come to live here," replied the 25-year-old man. "I've decided to become a brother."

"Well, that is very good news. Please come inside."

"You know very well what it's like living here. I shouldn't have to explain any of my rules to you. You can go over to the brothers' quarters and pick out an empty bunk. I shall expect you to lead a quiet, simple, holy life, while here, and to obey what I say and what

Brother Joseph says."

Yes Father, I am fully aware of what is expected of me."

"You don't know how good it makes me feel to see you join my society. It seems that I have been losing more than gaining. I was beginning to wonder what I was doing wrong."

"There are no papers to sign" he continued, "nor oaths to read. You will find plenty of room in the brothers' quarters, since Mike Doll has left, as you probably already know. Brother Michael, Brother Joseph, and Brother Cornelius are the only ones left. Joseph Bender is still living here, but I'm going to have to ask Anton to take him back. He is already 75 years old and is getting too old to do blacksmith work. This afternoon, I'm going over to see John and Sophie Grismer. She is expecting a child soon, and I've been told that she is having some difficulties, so I will see you this evening for meditation."

Without saying another word, Anton turned and departed, heading for the brothers' quarters.

As soon as Anton had left, Father Joseph went over to the church. He went up to the front pew, knelt down, made the sign of the cross, and silently, said a short prayer. While he was praying, Sister Lucretia entered from the side entrance, and walked over to Father Joseph. Noticing her, Father Joseph made the sign of the cross, and got up.

"What is it, Sister Lucretia?"

"Father. While you were gone this morning, we had some visitors. The Mohr family brought their daughter here."

"Anna?"

"Yes Father. I found a place for her and told her that I would let you know of her arrival as soon as you got back."

"Excellent. That is very good news. She will fit right in with Magdalene Bender and Maria Doll. They are all about the same age?'

"Yes, that should help out."

"Tell her that I will talk to her this evening," added Father Joseph, "but, that now I must go see the Grismer's."

"Very well," replied Sister Lucretia, as she genuflected and de-

parted. The long journey to the John Grismer farm was very excruciating on Father Joseph, but he tried not to show it. His 69-year-old body was beginning to show signs of getting worn out. Ever since his arrival in Minnesota, the winters were causing his arthritis to flare up. It was becoming a constant reminder for him that he was get-

ting old.

Upon his arrival, he was met at the door by the 49-year-old John Grismer. "Father Joseph," he stated, "please come in. I really didn't expect you to come in this kind of weather."

"Hello John. How is your wife doing?"

"Not so good. She is really having difficulty."

"Do you have anyone tending to her needs?"

"No. I'm trying to do the best I can."

"I'll send Sister Theresa over. Can I see her?"

"She has been sleeping for the past several hours."

"I'll let her sleep then. I'll just go in and say a few prayers for her."

John led him over to where Sophie was peacefully resting. Father Joseph took out his prayer book, opened it, made the sign of the cross and said a few short prayers. Upon completion of the prayers, he again made the sign of the cross, and walked back over to John, who was now sitting by the table with his children, Henry, Joseph, Martin, John, and Katharine.

"I'll make sure that Sister Theresa comes tomorrow. I'm sure she will be able to help you."

"Thank-you for everything, Father," stated John, as he got up and showed Father Joseph to the door.

One morning, in early April, as Father Joseph was standing in the garden, watching the sisters planting seed, he noticed several visitors approaching. There were two ox-driven carts coming from the west.

"Hello," he shouted from a distance.

"Hello Father," replied a 35-year-old man, who was driving the first wagon. "My name is Adam Gerber. We are from Pennsylvania and have come here to find a new homestead. When we were in St. Cloud, a man told us about you. He said that you could possibly help us."

"Perhaps I can," replied Father Joseph. "Who else do we have here?"

"This is my wife, Crescentia," continued Adam.

"My name is George Altstadt," answered the 40-year-old man, in the second wagon. "And, this is my wife, Genovieve. The children are ours. They are Charles, John, August, Louis, Maria, William, Edward, and the baby, Crescentia."

"Please to meet all of you," noted Father Joseph, as he turned back to Mr. Gerber, and asked: "What do you need?"

"Do you know of any land around here that is still open for homesteading?"

"Yes, I do," answered Father Joseph. "There is some land, not too far from here. Come! I'll take you over there. Leave the families here, and I'll show you."

"Would you do that for us?" asked Mr. Altstadt.

"Of course. That is the least I can do. I always make it a point to help those out, who need it."

Sister Lucretia and Sister Seraphim came over from the garden, and gave comfort to the children, and talked with Mrs. Gerber and Mrs. Altstadt, while Father Joseph departed with the two men.

As they were riding along, Father Joseph stated: "The entire populace around here is Catholic. There are a few Polish and Irish, north, and west of here, but right in this area, it is all German. You should find the area ideal for raising a good Christian family."

They continued along until they came upon a hill. Pointing in an easterly direction, he said: "This land, following this line and northward, is still vacant. There is 120 acres here, but as you see, there are a lot of trees."

"This is a beautiful spot," stated Mr. Altstadt.

"Let us continue on," requested Father Joseph. "Further north, there is another piece of land."

They rode on for a short distance, and there, Mr. Gerber picked out a choice site for a homestead.

"There will be a meeting on the 16th of this month, at the home of Balts Fuchs," continued Father Joseph. "We are going to discuss the formation of a new Catholic church. You are more than welcome to come."

As the three began their return trip to Rush Lake, he continued:

"I'll show you where he lives, on our way back."

Several days later, Father Joseph made the short walk over to the new home of Henry Kemper. When he arrived, he noticed several men standing in front of the house. They were Henry, Bruno, Ignatz Steinbach, Clemens Steinbach and a young stranger.

"Hello men," stated Father Joseph, as he walked up to them.

"Ah, hello Father, " replied Henry. "Bruno and I are just getting ready to take off for St. Cloud. If I'm to have a store here, I need to have supplies to sell. Bruno was kind enough to offer his assistance."

"I noticed another building beside here. What is that going to be?"

"A blacksmith shop."

"A blacksmith shop?"

"Yes. Andy Mutschler, here, is going to run it."

"But we already have a blacksmith shop here, down by the church."

"Well, I guess he feels that there is enough business for two."

Changing the subject, Father Joseph looked around and said:

"This looks like a very nice little place you have here, Henry. Are you going to live upstairs?"

"Yes. I'm going to try and get a post office here too, to go with the store. There should be enough room. Regina and I don't need much."

"Well, if there is anything you need, feel free to ask."

"Thank-you Father, but I would like to try and make it on my own."

As Father Joseph took out his small prayer book, he looked at Henry, and asked: "Is it alright if I bless the building?"

"Fine. Please do. I must go out now and make sure that everything is ready with the team."

"Have a good journey."

Tragedy among Father Joseph's flock struck again, on May 2, 1870. While giving birth to a son, who was named Anton, Sophia Grismer died. The young child was baptized the next day, and on the 6th of May, the funeral was held, with burial in the Rush Lake cemetery.

As the bereaved friends and relatives were coming back to the church, from the cemetery, Father Joseph was walking beside Mr. Grismer.

"Thank-you for everything," stated John, as he wiped his eyes.

"You have been a great help to me. But I was wondering if there was one more thing you could do for me?"

"What's that?"

"Would you take Yny son, Joseph, in?"

"Of course. He can move in anytime."

"He had mentioned it to me several times that he would like to become a brother. He has nothing but adoration for you, and for what you stand for."

"Good. He is most welcome."

The group was now arriving back at the church. As they were dispersing, Father Joseph walked over to Joseph A. Doll.

"Mr. Doll, I understand that the new schoolhouse is going to be starting on the tenth of this month. Is that correct?"

"Yes Father."

"Is it alright if I come over and have a talk with the children, on that day?"

"I don't see why not."

"On May 10th, 1870, the settlement organized their first public school. It was to be called District 13. Joseph A. Doll was elected chairman, Louis Sarbacher, treasurer, and H.R. Moeller, clerk. Mr. Anton Button was the first teacher. Wendolin Fehrenbacher had built the small one-room building on his property. Up to this time, the children of the area had been attending the church school at 'Our Lady of Miracles.' This new school bothered Father Joseph, so on the day of its opening he came for a visit.

As he entered, he noticed all of the familiar faces of the children that belonged to his church. He walked straight up to the front of the room, where Mr. Button, was sitting behind his desk.

"Mr. Button," he stated, "I would like to speak to the children this morning before you start classes."

"Fine, go-ahead Father."

Father Joseph turned to the children and began: "Good morning my children."

"Good morning, Father Joseph," they replied.

"I hope you enjoy your new school. I am sure that Mr. Button will teach you well. But you must remember, your religion is still more important than reading, writing, and arithmetic. Never forsake your religion. Always find the time to say your prayers, in the

morning, in the evening, before and after meals, always. Sure, it's fine to learn the three R's, but it is much more important to learn your religion. Thank-you."

With those words said, Father Joseph left the schoolhouse. He knew that it would now be more difficult to control these children. When they were at his school, he had much more influence on them. Now, only time would tell. On May 31st, Father Joseph was sitting by his table, busily writing. The burning candle was now beginning to hurt his eyes, so he

stopped, once in a while, and wiped them. Over on the other side of the room were seated two men, Bruno Boedigheimer and John Mower, a lawyer from Alexandria.

As Father Joseph finished writing his note, he said: "There. It's ready for you to sign."

He turned back to the first page and began to read aloud: "I, Joseph M. Albrecht, of the county of Ottertail and State of Minnesota, do make, publish, and declare this my last will and testament as follows — All my debts, dues, and charges, after my death to be paid promptly and without any unnecessary delay, out of my property. After the payment of my debts, I give, devise, and bequeath forever, all my property of whatever kind, real, personal, or mixed, to those members, both brothers and sisters, of the Society of the Most Precious Blood, who are under my control, and subject to my authority, at the time of my death. The aforesaid brothers and sisters of said Society shall, at my death, appoint from among their members (in case I do not make such appointment previous to my

death), three persons, who shall be Trustees, to take and receive said property so devised to said Society. I further direct that all of my property, herein devised, or which shall in any manner be received by said Society from me, shall be held in common by all the

members of said Society, as above described, and by their successors, and by all others who may join said Society, subject to my control as aforesaid hereafter, forever, but in no case is to descend to any of the natural heirs of any of the members of said Society, and I

further direct that all of my said property, and the proceeds thereof, is to be used by said Society in a humble and meek way. Not in any luxury, pride, or self-esteem, but to be used by the brothers and sisters, members of said Society, to live according to the rules as first laid down and practiced in the beginning and founding of said Society, the benefits of all my property herein devised and bequeathed, shall endure as well as to all who may, at any time hereafter, join the said Society as to those who may be members thereof at my

death.

All my property, herein devised and bequeathed, shall be used for the support and benefit of said order or Society of the Most Precious Blood, for the support of the members thereof, when necessary. For the founding of more permanent homes or houses for said

Society, and for the support of the poor and needy, whom said Society can relieve in a benevolent manner. I hereby nominate and appoint the three trustees who may be selected, as I have already directed at my death, Executors of this my last will and testament, and hereby authorize and empower them to settle compound or compromise any claim or demand in favor of, or against, my estate, as they may deem best and most practicable. And I further authorize and empower the said Trustees, acting as my executors, to collect, by law, or compromise, from any person and especially from the Society of the Most Precious Blood, to institute suits, and prosecute all suits already began, and as such execution to receipt for all debts due me, and release the same as I might do in my own name. I further direct that the three trustees selected, in accordance with this my last will and testament, and their successors who shall be selected by said Society, in case of death of any of them, shall have full power at all times, hereafter, to sell and convey any real estate which may descend to said Society, by virtue of this my last will and testament, and to make deeds for any lands sold, and give as full and perfect title and conveyance of any land, so sold as I could do, if alive. In witness whereof I have here unto set my hand and seal this 31st day of May A.D. 1870."

"Signed and published and declared by the said Testator to be his last will and testament, in the presence of us, who have signed our names at his request, and in his presence, and the presence of each other."

Father Joseph set the papers down on the table and continued: "I am getting near 70 years. It is about time that I have a will, so that our Society can continue on, after I'm gone. I would appreciate you gentlemen signing your name to these documents." Bruno walked over, grabbed the quill pen, looked at the document for several seconds, and then signed it. He then handed the pen to Mr. Mower, who, likewise, signed it.

"Thank-you gentlemen," stated Father Joseph, as he took the papers and neatly folded them up and placed them in a small box. The three men walked outside, where Father Joseph headed in a westerly direction, while Bruno and Mr. Mower went northward.

A short time later, Father Joseph arrived at Kemper's store.

"Good evening, Henry," he stated as he entered.

"Hello Father Joseph," replied Henry, who was standing behind the counter, putting some stock on the shelf.

"How is Regina?"

"Fine. She is getting bigger and bigger, with each passing day."

"When is she expecting?"

"As far as we can figure," replied Henry, as he rubbed his right hand over his chin, "the first part of August."

"That's not too far away."

As Father Joseph browsed around, he continued: "I also came over to see how Mike Doll has been doing."

"Just fine. He still plans on getting married in October, to my sister-in-law, Catharine."

"I was afraid you would say that. I had so many plans for that young man. I noticed him in church last Sunday. He was sitting with Ignatz and Clemens. After church, he was with Catharine, and Ignatz was talking with Anna Schoeneberger. Are they getting serious too?"

"Yes. I don't imagine it will be long before he asks her to marry him."

"For the life of me, I can't figure out why everyone wants to get married," objected Father Joseph, in a disgusted tone.

"It's only natural. Each person has their calling. Some hear it and some don't. Some have a calling to become priests, some to become sisters, and others to become married, and raise a family."

"Natural, you say? That is not what we should be thinking about now. We must worry about the end. What's going to happen then?"

Henry just looked at Father Joseph, in bewilderment, and went about doing his work, while Father Joseph turned and headed toward the door.

"Say hello to Regina, for me," he added, as he left. The year 1870 also saw one final visit to the Rush Lake settlement by Father Pierz. On August 28, he went to the home of George Seifert and performed a marriage ceremony for Elizabeth Seifert and Florian Fehr. Immediately after that, he went to the Hassler homestead and married Joseph Hassler and Elizabeth Roesner.

From there, he went to visit Father Joseph.

"Hello Francis," stated Father Joseph, as he noticed his old friend approaching.

"Hello Joseph," replied the tired old priest.

"Please come in. I haven't seen you for so long, I was beginning to wonder what happened."

"I've been very busy. I just came from the Hasslers."

"Did you marry Joe and Lizzie?"

"Yes."

"Why? I was supposed to."

"Joseph," continued Father Pierz, as he stopped in his tracks, and looked sternly at him, "I have been ordered by His Excellency Bishop Grace, to forbid you from saying Mass, and doing any other priestly functions, anymore."

"What!" exclaimed Father Joseph. "But Francis, the Bishop had not, as yet, accepted me as a priest. I have been referred to the Pope, by Bishop Purcell. I now stand in front of the Pope, and therefore, accountable only to him.

"How can you say that, Joseph?" queried Father Pierz. "You continue to press charges against the Precious Blood Society. You continue to claim that they owe you money. They have offered time and time again to grant you your leave, but, yet you are so stubborn

and refuse to do what they want you to do. You continue to refuse to do anything about your situation. Why?"

"Why?" replied Father Joseph. "Why should I give in to them? I am right and they know it. If I give into them, it will look like I'm admitting to be wrong. That, I cannot do. Father Dwenger wrote me a letter awhile back, and he offered to give me a present of all I had taken from St. Joe. He also offered me $300.00 a year, for the rest of my life, and the proper papers for exeat. How riduculous!

Everything I took from Ohio was mine in the first place, and $300.00 a year? What a joke! Here I am, almost 70 years old. How many years do I have left? Maybe a couple. Those people owe me more than that. How can I accept their conditions? No! No, there is no

way."

"You stubborn old fool," continued Father Pierz. "I can no longer help you. I wash my hands. I will not be coming back here again. Father Ignatius Tomazin will be taking care of the missions from now on. I am getting too old. I am sure he will come and visit

you. Hopefully, by then, you will have thought about your situation and straightened everything out. If you continue your ways, it is possible that not only you, but your entire congregation, could get excommunicated from the Catholic Church. Enough is enough. I must leave. I shall remember you in my prayers." Father Pierz turned and departed, as Father Joseph continued to stand beside a tree, in bewilderment, saying nothing. "Excommunication? How can they?" he thought. The more he thought of the idea, the madder he got. He pounded his hand against the tree, turned towards his house and shouted: "Never!"

These times were very trying for Father Joseph. Everything seemed to be crumbling around him. He was losing his grip on the situation. His influence was beginning to falter. His power to control the people was being questioned more and more. And now, the threat of excommunication.

A Letter To The Pope

CHAPTER XXVI

One morning, while on his visits to the area farmers, Father Joseph stopped to talk to Christof Silbernagel, one of the latest arrivals at the colony. As he crossed the Red River, he watched a log drive coming down the river. There wasn't much water in the river at that time, but it still was enough to float the lumber into Rush Lake. After standing alongside the riverbank for several minutes, he turned and headed for the Silbernagel homestead.

Christof, age 36, was out in his garden, when Father Joseph approached.

"Good morning, Father Joseph," he exclaimed, as he got up off his knees. "What a pleasure to see you!"

"Hello dear Christof."

"What can I do for you?"

"I am having some difficulties," replied Father Joseph. "I need to get all of the men together, for a parish meeting. Is it possible that you could ride and tell everyone to come to the church as soon as possible? I must talk to all of them."

"Why not tell them on Sunday?"

"Sunday is too late. I must talk to them right away."

"I'll saddle my horse immediately."

"Good! Have them be down at the church by six, this evening.

I'll be waiting."

By late that afternoon, all of the men of the parish had arrived at the church. There were 40 people present, besides Father Joseph. They included: Anton Bender, Bruno Boedigheimer, Charley Foltz, Anton Doll, Joseph Riesterer, Joseph A. Doll, Victor Eifert, Sebastian Hertel, Clemens Steinbach, John Reinhart, John Doll, Joseph W. Doll, Frank Staab, Louis Sarbacher, Christof Silbernagel, Ignatz Steinbach, John Widerle, Wendolin Fehrenbacher, Paul Klarer, Joseph Weis, Martin Schoeneberger, Joseph Hassler, George Wolfle, Michael Schmitz, Martin Fiedler, Joseph Zimmerman, Friedrich Mohr, John Rock, Ferdinand Eifert, Joseph Schwab, Victor Scheidecker, Michael Doll, Michael Schoeneberger, Gustav Meyer, Brother Joseph Boedigheimer, Brother Anton Doll, Cornelius Boedigheimer, William Hassler, Joseph Boedigheimer, and young Henry Drahmann, who had just arrived the day before, from St. Henry, Ohio.

"Gentlemen," stated Father Joseph. "I was hoping everyone could make it to this meeting, but I notice a few that are missing. I suppose you are all wondering why I have called you together, in such a short notice. To be honest, I am having some difficulty and

need your help. I had a letter written up to be sent to the Pope, in Rome, asking him for his assistance, on my behalf. I would like to read it to you, and, if you agree with the contents, I would like for you to sign it."

He picked up several sheets of paper and began to read aloud: "Most Esteemed Lord! In the name of Jesus, Mary, and Joseph. We the undersigned petitioners, turn to you with confidence of receiving from you a decision that is just in the sight of God, on an important matter. Necessity compels us to take this step. It is a matter first of all of honoring God and of freeing an old, venerable, pious priest, who has been oppressed and maltreated in every way, one whom even his opponents, themselves, call saintly, namely, Reverend Joseph Maria Albrecht, and of the good of an entire congregation. We above all beg your pardon, should we employ perhaps unsuitable and clumsy expressions. All of us, petitioners, and scribe, are but simple, ordinary country folk, whom Christian duty has compelled to seek redress at your hands from a wrong that cries to heaven.

Here in America, it appears that a divinely just redress in said matter — in so far as it has been attempted — has been frustrated totally by the malice of the old serpent. In order for you to arrive at the necessary understanding in this matter, perhaps it would be necessary for us to place before you a short life sketch of Reverend Albrecht. Reverend Albrecht was the only son of prosperous farmers in the grand duchy of Baden, in Europe. He received a very Christian upbringing from his parents. He showed, already in his early years, a very special zeal for the defense of the true Catholic religion. In compliance with his parents' will, he entered, against his own will, the state of marriage. This, however, did not deter him from continuing to defend his religion, which he did more and more

zealously as time went by. Later, however, under God's special providence and the direction of his chosen spiritual advisor, a pious and indeed saintly missionary and former Probgant, Francis Aloysius Maria Brunner, he and his better marital half, were counselled to bid farewell to the married state and to dedicate themselves without reserve with their goods and property to the religious life. Reverend M. Brunner was the leader and director in spiritual matters, and Reverend Albrecht carried them out by his support with material contributions. The two of them made a pilgrimage to Rome shortly after the death of Gaspar del Bufalo, whose Community they entered in 1838, with the approval of Pope Gregory XVI. Fully authorized by the Pope to spread further the Community of the Precious Blood, their goal was Switzerland and France. God in his love, however, wanted them in America, and this they accepted without hesitation. Here, by means of the material support already mentioned, land was purchased, houses built, young priests, brothers, sisters, admitted and trained for their tasks, and everything during the earliest years proceeded smoothly with God's blessings. Already in the earliest years in America, he was ordained a priest, against his own wishes, but now he could without reserve continue his defense of religion, which God blessed visibly and abundantly, so that all the people who heard him were astonished. Yes, even animosity against him was created among his priestly confreres. And when at times they erred — as sometimes happens — he admonished them quite sharply. This stirred and intensified their envy and animosity against him, but always in secret, waiting for an opportunity when they might pour out their poison against him. It was at this time that God's love called Reverend Brunner into the next world.

Reverend Albrecht continued to preach with great success. In fact, by his prayers and blessings, he even healed various sick persons, to which all of us can testify. He preached very clearly and plainly against vices, especially pride, vanity, and lust, so that people, and even priests from other parishes, marvelled at the discipline and church order that he maintained in his congregations. He inveighed especially against the practice of women wearing hoopskirts, and he had succeeded not only in discouraging their use, but in eliminating them entirely in the parishes under his charge, until, finally, one lone head of a family in his parish on several occasions maliciously sent his daughters wearing hoopskirts into the church, against the will of the entire congregation. Reverend Albrecht preached against it kindly, calmly, prudently, plainly, energetically, at last however seriously and sternly and was often encouraged by his superior to enforce it. Finally, after many admonitions and warnings it got so bad that Reverend Albrecht found himself compelled — in order not to give offense and irritation to the parish — to drive the above-mentioned daughters out of the church with a rod and to excommunicate them until they should desist from their great wickedness. The matter was later reported by us to the Most Reverend Bishop, John Baptiste Purcell, of Cincinnati, Ohio, in whose diocese the event occurred. The latter, however, replied that Reverend Albrecht had made a serious mistake in this, that fancy clothing was not pride, but only a current fashion, and that a modest dance and an occasional game of cards in the afternoon on Sundays and holy days, for the purpose of recreation did not constitute a sin. Yes, he went so far as to put down the venerable old man publicly in the parish church, in front of the entire congregation, as a proud, simple-minded old man. He was still allowed to preach, but he was not to give the people commands anymore. Reverend Albrecht was ordered to continue to conduct services, but he was not to meddle in the people's daily-life affairs, anymore. He replied, however, that he would never celebrate Mass in the sacred place after this abomination of desolation. In his last sermon in June 1866, he once more sharply and publicly condemned the above-mentioned vices and called all those — but nobody by name — who did not consider fancy clothes, greed, lust, and games, to be sinful, as heretics. This was the opportunity for those who nourished envy and animosity against him.

Suspension and excommunication ensued, reserved to the Holy See, so that no one but the Pope alone could absolve him. He was labelled a heretic because he is supposed to have said: "Bishops can make laws, but priests don't have to obey them." He did indeed say something like that, but with a difference, namely: If bishops make laws which are contrary to God and therefore also contrary to religion, then no priest nor anyone else need obey them. It was alleged further that he had called the Most Reverend John B. Purcell, Archbishop of Cincinnati, a heretic in the above-mentioned sermon in June 1866. Even a prominent priest of the Community, publicly in the pulpit, before many people, called him by name, a disobedient, contumacious, vile person, and that he would sooner have his right hand cut off than to give such a person

Holy Communion. It actually occurred there afterwards, before the eyes of all the people present that he passed him up at the distribution of Holy Communion."

Father Joseph now paused and wiped his forehead. After glancing over the group for several seconds, he continued: "Since he was no longer able to endure living in the Community house, because of the overwhelming malice, he retired to a private home, and many brothers and sisters of the Community did likewise. At the beginning of this time, he intended — as he later revealed to trusted friends — to retire from the world and to live alone in the wilderness of America, as a hermit and dedicate his life to God. God, however, did not want it so, but revealed to him in a wondrous fashion, that he was not to be concerned for himself alone, but also for the souls entrusted to him. Since there were now no prospects for effective work in an area in which he was so despised and slandered, it was decided to move into a new, far-distant, quiet area still inhabited by Indians, and there, await what God would further impose upon him. To accomplish this, required great expenditures. These were requested from the Community but were spitefully and obstinately denied. And this, even though nearly all their livelihood and prosperous condition had derived from Reverend Albrecht, as mentioned already.

God, however, so disposed it that that plan has been carried out until now, through the support of right-thinking and through many and great deprivations of all kinds. The Most Reverend Bishop Grace of St. Paul, Minnesota, in whose diocese we are now located, was blinded by his enemies shortly after our arrival. A veritable flood of slanders against Reverend Albrecht, both in person, and in writing, were made. He was called a robber of churches because he had taken along the relics of a saint from the Community church.

He had transported them on his back to Germany from a Roman pilgrimage, and later on, to America. It was said that he had the brothers and sisters who followed him, break their oath of allegiance, whereas, the Constitutions of the Community, which were written down in Rome, and of which he has a copy, clearly state that the members of the Community have no ties of obligation to each other and can leave whenever they wish. They say that he set an entire parish into an uproar. This indeed he has. A part of the parish followed him immediately. In fact, with few exceptions, the entire parish would have done so, if the means and circumstances had not hindered them. And so, there are many more things which would make an honorable man blush with shame. Relief from this injustice was requested from the Most Reverend Bishop Grace, but the latter, as mentioned before, partly from deception, and partly for the sake of the dead letter of the law, demanded first of all his release, otherwise he could not negotiate. And this is still the situation after a three-year stay in his diocese. Reverend Albrecht's release was frequently requested, but always stubbornly refused, because they wanted thereby to gain his relinquishment of the afore-mentioned considerable amount of property. This can be seen crystal clear from all their actions in this matter, in person, and in writing. Thus, they still insist on the return of the stolen property, the recanting of the afore-mentioned sermon, and a formal apology for the wrong done. But it is crystal clear in the above-mentioned Constitutions that each and every member can demand a return of his property from the Community, and, after approval, do with it what he wishes.

If one speaks of getting it back by secular authority, then they threaten with excommunication and every conceivable ecclesiastical penalty. And before the spiritual authority, where they absolutely want to have it, it has already been judged, as one can see in this. And so, it continued under the yoke of ecclesiastical penalties, from June 1866 to June 1869. However, a traveling missionary priest occasionally administered the Sacraments of Penance and Communion, to the people, with the exception of Reverend Albrecht, until, finally, Pope Piux IX, in his proclamation of a great period of grace, obsolved and released him from his excommunication. However, the jurisdiction from the bishop, which was still withheld, was recently offered to him, by a priest delegated for this, publicly in the church, before all the people. If he would not renounce the recovery

of his property and not agree upon the points written or cited above, then his priestly functions would again be removed and the entire parish, without exception, would be excommunicated, which on the part of the bishop, they now actually are. This is now, in brief, a clear, unvarnished presentation of the matters as it stands before God. We, the undersigned petitioners, beseech you, Most Reverend Lord, in the name of Jesus, Mary, and Joseph, for an early response and a decision which is just in the sight of God, for the vindication of the innocense of a pious priest, and for the glorification of the honor

of God, for all eternity. Amen."

After pausing for several seconds, Father Joseph continued:

"I shall pass this letter around for each of you to sign if you wish. I would like to get this sent to Rome, as quickly as possible."

He handed the letter to Anton Bender, who immediately took out a pen, and signed the letter. He passed it on to Bruno, who did the same.

While the signing was taking place, Father Joseph talked with Anton and Bruno.

"Did you really go to Rome and bring back those relics?" asked Bruno.

"Well, I may have stretched the truth a little, in a few areas."

"Do you really think that sending a letter to the Pope will help? queried Anton.

"I have no other place to turn to. Nobody around here seems to want to believe my story."

Just then, young Henry Drahmann carried the letter back up to Father Joseph, and handed it to him. Father Joseph looked at the

signatures, and then said: "Fine." He then folded them up and put them in an envelope.

"Gentlemen," he continued, "I want to thank all of you for coming. Hopefully, this matter will soon be cleared up."

Turning his attention to Martin Fiedler, he stated: "Martin, before you go, I would like to have a word with you. Everyone else may leave."

As the men got up and began departing the church, Martin Fiedler walked up to Father Joseph.

"Martin," stated Father Joseph, "did you notice that some of the men didn't come? Do you know why?"

"No, I don't, but I'm sure they must have had a good reason."

"I was hoping to have everyone in the parish sign this. It would've looked better when the Pope read it."

Taking a handkerchief from his pocket, and blowing his nose, Father Joseph continued: "When is your next county board meeting?"

"I haven't heard yet, but it should be soon."

"Let me know when you find out. There are a few items of business that I need to discuss with you before the meeting."

"I sure will," replied Martin, as he began to leave the church, with Father Joseph.

Once outside, Father Joseph turned to Martin, and continued:

"Say hello to your wife, for me, and have a good evening."

"Thank-you Father," replied Martin, as he walked over to his buggy.

Father Joseph now walked over to his house and entered. He went directly to his table and sat down. After leaning back in the chair and staring at the ceiling, for several seconds, he looked over at a picture of Jesus, which was hanging on one of the walls, and

quietly said: "0 Jesus, what am I to do?"

Construction of St. Joseph's

CHAPTER XXVII

The year of 1871 was to be one of the most important years in the life of Father Joseph. He accomplished much during this time, but all for naught, as we shall see. On January 21st, township elections were held at the home of Henry Kemper. Father Joseph used his influence to get the representatives that he wanted on the board. He was successful in this goal as he was in his attempt to get Martin Fiedler the position of County Commissioner, representing the entire area of Rush Lake and Ottertail City.

On January 22nd, Father Joseph held Mass at the home of Joe Zimmerman. After Mass was completed, he had a visit with several of the neighborhood men. "Father Joseph," began Balts Fuchs, "remember that talk we had a while back? Well, since there still are more Catholics coming into this area, to settle, we have been giving a lot of thought to the idea of building a new church of our own. What do you think?"

"I think it's an excellent idea," replied Father Joseph.

"I have 40 acres that I could donate," continued Mr. Fuchs. "It's just down the road from here. The other men and I think that it would be an ideal location for a church. It's all woods now, but with a little work, we could really make it into a thing of beauty."

"It would be easier for you," added Martin Fiedler. "You wouldn't have to carry everything with you, every time you came to say Mass."

"Yes, that is true. Have you mentioned it to the bishop?"

"No, but we did mention it to Father Tomazin, and he said he would talk to him," answered Mr. Fuchs.

"When will you begin?"

"We can start cutting the logs right away, and then, when spring gets here, we can begin building."

"Very well. Get all the men together and I'll have a talk with them."

"I think just about everyone is here now," stated Martin, as he looked around. "Why not have the talk right now?"

"Alright," agreed Father Joseph, as he looked at his pocket watch. "Have everyone go back into the house."

Mr. Fiedler and Mr. Fuchs went over to the wagons, which were beginning to depart the homestead and told the men to stop and come back into the house.

As Father Joseph entered the house, he was met at the doorway by Mr. Zimmerman. "Did you forget something?"

"I was just talking with Martin and Balts, and they mentioned something about building a church, so I thought I'd talk to all of you about it."

"Good. Please come back in."

When everyone was seated again, Father Joseph walked up to the front of the group. "I understand that you have been discussing the idea of building a church. Well, I am all for it. I give it my blessing."

The small group was pleased at what they were hearing.

"Just where is this site?"

"A quarter of a mile from here," replied Mr. Fuchs, as he pointed in a northerly direction. "At the northwest corner of my property."

"I see," continued Father Joseph. "Well, I would like every available man down at that area tomorrow morning, and we'll get started. Make sure you all bring your teams, as well as axes and saws. I'll meet you there at ten."

The next morning, after completing Mass at Rush Lake, Father Joseph headed straight for the church site, riding a horse-drawn carriage.

Upon arriving, he noticed that the men were already waiting for him.

"How many men are here?"

"12," replied Mike Schmitz.

As Father Joseph looked around at the wooded area, he continued: "This looks like a very good location. It is centrally located. I like that. I think we should plan for the church to be laid out in an east-west direction."

As Father Joseph led the group of men, which included: Mike Schmitz, Balts Fuchs, George Altstadt, Adam Gerber, George Seifert, Florian Fehr, Joe Zimmerman, Martin Fiedler, Joseph Lein Sr., Joseph Lein Jr., Joseph Hassler, and John Grismer, into the woods, he stated: "Mike, have the men start cutting these trees through here. We'll lay the foundation right in here. We should only have to work on it for a couple of weeks for now, and then when springs gets here, we can complete it." Immediately, the men began cutting away at the trees. Father Joseph stood by and watched for several minutes, before he walked over to Mike Schmitz, and said: "I'm going to head back to Rush Lake."

"Thank-you Father," stated Mike, as he helped Father Joseph get back into his wagon.

Soon, spring arrived. The snow was melting, and the trees were beginning to green. Kemper's store was as busy as usual. In order to help out, Henry Drahmann had become a partner. On this particular day, both Mr. Kemper and Mr. Drahmann were in the store.

"I'm going to St. Paul, tomorrow," stated Mr. Kemper. "We have about $3,000.00 that we can use to purchase new goods. You will have to take care of the place, while I'm gone. Is there anything special that you know of that we need?"

"No, not really."

As the two men were talking, four rough-looking men entered the store. One of them was a tall husky young man, who wore a gray broadrimmed hat. The other three were much smaller. They didn't say much but did spend a lot of time looking around. "Say Henry," stated the big man, "we've been waiting for the railroad work to start up again, but it has been pretty slow. I've had to dig into my savings. I have a $1,000.00 bill, and was wondering if you could change it for me?"

"Why, yes I can," replied Mr. Kemper.

"I'll bring it over tomorrow."

"Tomorrow, I'll be gone. I'm heading for St. Paul for supplies."

"Oh! Well, then I'll wait till you get back."

"But Mr. Drahmann will be here."

"That's alright. I'll wait for you."

"Very well."

"Well men, I guess we better be leaving then," noted the man, as he headed for the door, followed closely behind by the other three. As he shook Mr. Kemper's hand, he added: "Good luck on your trip."

After they had departed, Mr. Drahmann looked at Mr. Kemper, and said: "Do you think that was wise to tell them that you could give him change for a $1,000.00 bill?"

"Why not? I can. Father Joseph has always stressed that we should never lie. Besides, I don't really think he had a $1,000.00 bill anyway."

"Yes, but they could be waiting along the trail for you tomorrow, knowing that you are going to be carrying a lot of money."

"I'll just have to take that chance."

At three in the morning, Mr. Kemper started out on his journey, by walking to Ottertail City. As he approached the outlet of the Red River from Rush Lake, he noticed a bright campfire. He didn't think too much of it, since it was not at all unusual for campfires to be there, nightly. As he came closer, he realized, however, that these campers were not people just passing through. They were the four men that had been at his store, earlier. He immediately turned, and walked around them, making sure he was not seen.

After crossing the river, he proceeded to Ottertail City, where he caught the seven o'clock stage. Meanwhile, back at the settlement, Father Joseph was just finishing Mass, and was about to have a talk with the sisters, who were all seated in their pews, in the small chapel. "Sister Lucretia," he stated, "I want all of the sisters to go up by the cemetery and work on that field. I have a meeting this morning with the trustees, so I won't be able to come up there with you. Sister Theodilda should be arriving any day now, so I should be close by to greet her. If any problems arise, send someone back. I should be here all day."

Sister Lucretia nodded her head in approval, and silently led the others out of the chapel, as Father Joseph headed for the sacristy, and over to his house. Upon entering, Father Joseph noticed the three trustees, Bruno, Anton, and Charley, seated by the table.

"Well gentlemen," stated Father Joseph, as he walked over to his bed, reached underneath, pulled out a large brown book, and carried it over to the others, "this should not take very long. All I need for you to do is verify the financial report for the year."

As he opened the book to the front pages, and laid it on the table, he continued: "Just look over the receipts and expenses and then sign it. As you will see, we didn't get much this year, but it was enough so that I didn't have to use much of my own." The three men briefly looked over the statement, and without question, signed it, and handed it back to Father Joseph.

"There is one other thing," continued Father Joseph, "Charley, you will be replaced as a trustee, by Frank Staab, starting next month. If there are no other questions, you may all leave. I will be staying around here today, as I am expecting Sister Theodilda to arrive. Gentlemen, have a good day."

The three men arose and quietly departed, leaving Father Joseph alone. On June 19, 1871, Bishop Thomas L. Grace arrived in the area. He was accompanied by several other priests, among which was Father Ignatius Tomazin. The Bishop was on his Confirmation tour and was planning on paying a visit to Father Joseph. The small entourage was traveling along the shore of Rush Lake. When they approached the eastward turn, Father Tomazin headed in a northwesterly direction, to the home of a certain Mr. Karsnia, where he was to perform a marriage for Julianna Karsnia and John Gerber.

Bishop Thomas Langdon
Grace, O.P.

Bishop Grace, being transported by a team of horses, headed for the Rush Lake settlement.

Anton Bender and Bruno Boedigheimer were standing in front of the church, while Father Joseph was inside, praying.

"Greetings," stated the two men, as the wagons pulled up in front of the church.

"Hello," replied one of the priests, who was driving the lead wagon. "Can we speak to Father Albrecht?"

After Anton and Bruno looked at each other, Anton replied: "I'm sorry, but Father Joseph is not available. He is very busy, taking care of some personal matters. We don't really know when he will be free."

"Oh!" exclaimed the priest. "Well, when he returns, tell him that His Excellency, the Bishop, is in the area, and would like to personally see him."

"We certainly will," replied Anton, as he watched the wagons turn and depart.

Anton and Bruno stood there, watching the wagons disappear into the distant. Just then, Father Joseph came out.

"Who was here?"

"Oh, just a couple of priests," answered Anton. "They wanted to see you, but we told them that you were busy."

"Oh," replied Father Joseph.

The next morning Father Joseph, again, headed for the neighboring area. As he arrived at the site of the new church, he noticed that it was almost completed.

"What a beautiful sight!" he exclaimed, as he approached several of the men. "You have done an excellent job."

"Thank-you Father," replied Balts Fuchs.

The small church, facing westward, had an addition attached to the rear, which was to serve as the quarters for the pastor. As Balts and Father Joseph entered the front, Father Joseph noticed how modest the building was. George Seifert and Joseph Lein were busily building benches on the dirt floor. "Keep up the good work, George," stated Father Joseph, as he looked at the pews. "They look beautiful."

Next, Father Joseph and Balts walked up to the front of the church, where Adam Gerber and Mike Schmitz were working on the altar.

On the small simple altar was a statue of St. Joseph. As Father Joseph stopped and looked at the statue, Balts Fuchs stated: "We are going to call the church, St. Joseph. I am donating this statue. Many of us have come from parishes that were dedicated to him, and since he is also the patron saint of the farmers, we feel it is only right that we honor him. Bishop Grace was here yesterday, and I signed over the deed to this 40 acres to the St. Paul diocese. He said that he would like to come back this fall and officially dedicate the church, if possible."

"Bishop Grace was here?"

"Yes. He said he was over to visit you, but that you weren't there."

"He did?" What a surprise! No one told me."

"Really?"

As this conversation was occurring, Father Tomazin arrived.

"Father Albrecht?" queried Father Tomazin.

"Yes."

"My name is Father Ignatius Tomazin. I have replaced Father Pierz. He will no longer be coming around here. I have talked to Bishop Grace, and I've been wondering how you have been doing?"

"I am doing just fine."

"Have you gotten everything straightened out in Ohio?"

"I have done nothing wrong back there."

"You mean, you never got your permission to leave, nor permission to continue here?"

"No, not yet. The Bishop is too stubborn!"

"You mean that you are still staying Mass and performing the other priestly functions, without permission?"

"I have God's permission. I have the approval of the Pope. That is all I need."

"That's not so. You can't do a thing without the Bishop's permission. He is your superior."

"Nonsense! I have done nothing wrong. Why should I recant for something I never did?"

"Father, this is insane. If you can't see how wrong you are, then I believe you are actually a heretic, or else a little touched in the head. You do what you want, no matter what anyone else says. I feel so sorry for you."

"Don't feel sorry for me. Feel sorry for the bishops. They are the ones who have the problem."

Father Tomazin was now getting very disgusted, as his face began turning red. "I am going to tell everyone in the area, not to have a thing to do with you, or your people. You are insane."

Father Joseph began to laugh. "Don't you see that they are all wrong? It is me and our Holy Father who, alone, are right. I will do as our Holy Father in Rome does. I will keep on and do all I can against those 'hoops'."

Father Joseph continued to laugh, louder and louder, while Father Tomazin turned around and left.

Meanwhile, George, Balts, Adam, and Mike were standing off to the side, listening intently.

After Father Tomazin left, Father Joseph turned and looked at the other men. After a several second pause, he stated: "Father Tomazin is a young man. He doesn't know what is really going on around here. Pay no attention to him. Someday he'll learn the

truth."

The men didn't say a word, as they stood in bewilderment, wondering what was really happening, and wondering what the truth really was.

Dedication and Excommunication

CHAPTER XXVIII

October 1871 — The train had just arrived in the newly-created town of Perham, situated about 7 miles northwest of the Rush Lake settlement. It was one of the first passenger trains to come this far west on the Northern Pacific tracks, which were gradually making their way towards the west coast. When the train came to a complete stop, a short man, with a large black bag, got off. His name was Father Francis Xavier

Weninger, a Jesuit missionary. He was 66 years old and had already been a priest for 43 years. He had spent many years in the missionary field and those years were taking their toll on his body. He had a receding hairline, wrinkles on his forehead, and a very serious

look on his face. There was very little to see in the town of Perham, except for a few small shanties. The sight did not impress Father Weninger in the least. "How do I get to the Rush Lake settlement?" he queried, as he looked at one of the young railroad men, working at the station.

"Just head southeast, along the tracks, until you come to the river. Follow that river south, and you'll come right up to it."

"Thank-you," politely noted Father Weninger, as he began to head in that direction.

Meanwhile, out at Rush Lake, Father Joseph was busy overseeing the potato harvest. Sister Lydia, Sister Cherubim, Sister Theresa, and Sister Lucretia, along with several younger girls, were digging with forks, while several of the men filled the sacks, and hauled them back to the storage sheds. Father Joseph was standing alongside the sisters, talking with Sister Lucretia.

Soon, young Johnnie Bender came running up to Father Joseph. "Father Joseph!" he shouted, as he stopped and attempted to catch his breath.

"What is it?"

"There is a priest coming this way. He's about a quarter of a mile from here."

"Thank-you Johnnie."

Father Francis Xavier Weninger

"Sister Lucretia, continue the supervision," added Father Joseph. "Be sure they get all the potatoes. Even the small ones. This should be one of our best crops ever."

"Yes Father."

Father Joseph began to head towards the church. When he arrived there, Father Weninger was already sitting in front of the church.

"Hello Father," stated Father Weninger.

"Hello. Is there something I can do for you?"

"My name is Father Francis Xavier Weninger."

"And I am Father Joseph Maria Albrecht."

"Bishop Grace has sent me up here to give a mission, dedicate a new church, and talk to you."

"What new church?"

"St. Joseph's."

"When?"

"I am going over there tomorrow."

"Why did he send you? Those are my people. I helped them build the church. Whenever they needed assistance, I was there to provide it. I am their leader. They all look up to me. I should be the one to dedicate the church. I should be the one giving the mission.

Why did he have you do it?"

"The Bishop sent me because of you," replied Father Weninger.

"You are going down the wrong path. You have no right to be doing what you are. You should actually be ashamed of what you are doing."

"Who are you to talk like that?" shouted Father Joseph. "You are just a pawn of the Bishop, jumping at his every whim. You have no right to come around here and tell me that I am doing wrong."

"How stubborn can you be?" shouted back Father Weninger.

"You old fool!"

"I don't have to stand here and take this abuse," yelled Father Joseph. "Get out of here! I never want to see you again," he continued, as he stormed into the church. Father Weninger just stood there and shook his head. "God forgive him," he noted, as he prepared to depart.

The next morning, Father Weninger arrived at the small parish church of St. Joseph. He was being escorted by George Seifert, at whose home he spent the previous night. Everyone in the neighborhood had known for weeks about the mission, so many of them came to the church early that day, to welcome the highly regarded Jesuit priest.

He shook hands with several of the people, as he walked into the small log church. As he put on his surplice and stole, he looked around. There were approximately 15 families present. Not as many as he had expected, but it would be a start. After he picked up his crucifix, he walked to the front of the altar.

"Greetings, my dear people in Christ. I am overjoyed at the chance of dedicating this beautiful little church, and at the chance of giving you a mission. Bishop Thomas L. Grace sends you his regards and wishes to tell you that he is sorry he could not come."

"I will be giving a mission here, daily, for the next two weeks. Hopefully, everyone in the area will be able to attend. Before I can hold a mission, however, we must have a blessed building. Therefore, today, the 17th of October, in the year of our Lord, 1871, we shall dedicate this new temple of God's. We shall dedicate it to St. Joseph. Let us begin."

"As in the Book of Psalms, chapter 95, verses one through seven:
'Come, let us sing joyfully to the Lord; let us acclaim the Rock of our salvation. Let us greet him with thanksgiving. Let us joyfully sing psalms to him. For the Lord is a great God, and a great king above all gods. In his hands are the depths of the earth, and the tops of the mountains are his. His is the sea, for he has made it, and the dry land, which his hands have formed. Come, let us bow down in worship: let us

kneel before the Lord who made us. For he is our God, and we are the people he shepherds, the flock he guides.'"

He stopped momentarily and walked over to the side of the altar and put on his vestments. He then returned to the center of the altar, and began to say Mass. Several minutes later, after the opening prayers and the epistle were said, Father Weninger walked over to the left side of the altar and began reading from the book: "The Gospel, according to Luke, chapter 19, verses 1 through 10. Jesus, upon entering Jericho, passed

through the city. There was a man there named Zacchaeus, the chief tax collector, and a wealthy man. He was trying to see what Jesus was like, but being small of stature, was unable to do so because of the crowd. He first ran on in the front, then climbed a sycamore tree which was along Jesus' route, in order to see him. When Jesus came to the spot he looked up and said,

"Zacchaeus, hurry down. I mean to stay at your house today." He quickly descended

and welcomed him with delight. When this was observed, everyone

began to murmur,

"He has gone to a sinner's house as a guest."

Zacchaeus stood his ground and said to the Lord: "I give half my belongings, Lord, to the poor. If I have defrauded anyone in the least, I pay him back fourfold." Jesus said to him:

"Today salvation has come to this house, for this is what it means to be a son of Abraham.

The Son of Man has come to search out and save what was lost." Praised be to you, oh Christ."

Father Weninger put the book down. Pausing for several seconds, he collected his thoughts, and then began: "In the name of the Father, and of the Son, and of the Holy Ghost. Amen. My people in Christ. The Gospel, today, tells us of Zacchaeus, a rich man whom Jesus favored because of his use of money. We have a man near here who claims to be a modern-day Zacchaeus. But he uses his money for his own end. Yes, he gives to the poor and needy. But what does he expect in return? He claims to be their spiritual leader, but yet has not even talked to the Bishop about getting the proper admission papers. Why? Why does he refuse to see him? The answer, my friends, is that he is afraid. He is afraid that the Bishop is right and that he is wrong. He is afraid that if he does what he is asked, he would look bad in the eyes of his people. He is afraid that he would lose his grip on his people. He would lose his influence. Without this power, he would be unable to function. He preaches against vanity yet does not practice what he preaches. He preaches against pride, yet it is his pride that is his downfall. He is a foolish man who has clearly been influenced by others. He cannot continue the way he has. Surely, you people must see that. He has a clever mouthpiece and knows how to delude the common people. He maintains that the Pope is on his side, but that is pure foolishness. Yes, my people, there is a man nearby who calls himself a priest. Beware! Have nothing more to do with him. Tell your friends and relatives the same. We must stamp this enemy out, for I pursue my enemies, and overtake them. I smote them, and they cannot rise; they fall beneath my feet. Pray to the Lord, that we can succeed in our task. With God's help, we shall overcome. Father Ignatius Tomazin will be coming here to say Mass, after I leave. Have him do all of your works. Have him hear your confessions, marry your sons and daughters, and bury your dead. Always remember, the Bishop is the Pope's representative here. It is the Bishop whom the priests are subject to. Bishop Grace has tried time and time again to talk with this so-called priest and has not succeeded. We must follow the decision of the Bishop. We must do what we have to. Praise the Lord."

"Alleluia," replied the people.

"Praise the name of the Lord," shouted Father Weninger.

"Alleluia."

"Praise, you servants of the Lord, who stand in this house of the Lord."

"Alleluia."

"Praise the Lord, for the Lord is good."

"Alleluia," replied the people, as they became more and more excited, with each passing minute.

"Praise, you servants of the Lord, who stand in this house of the Lord."

"Alleluia."

"Praise the Lord, for the Lord is good."

"Alleluia."

"Sing praise to his name, which we love."

"Alleluia."

"My people," continued Father Weninger, as he walked to the center of the altar, "listen to what St. Paul says to the Romans: 'Let everyone obey the authorities that are over him, for there is no authority except from God, and all authority that exists is established by God! As a consequence, the man who opposes authority, rebels against the ordinance of God; those who resist thus shall draw condemnation down upon themselves.' Oh Lord, we pray that Joseph heeds this authority. Please answer our prayers."

"Amen."

Father Weninger returned to the altar and continued Mass. The following day, before Father Weninger said the morning Mass, and began his mission, a group of men approached him, outside of St. Joseph's church. It was Joseph W. Doll, Wendolin Doll,

Michael Doll, Anton Friedsam, and Ignatz Steinbach.

"Father Weninger," stated Joseph, as he stepped up beside the priest, "my name is Joseph Doll, and these men here are my friends and relatives. We belong to the Rush Lake church of Father Joseph. Last night we had a meeting and heard what you are doing here.

We have decided that Father Joseph has erred, and we want to join this parish."

"Excellent! I am going to be giving missions here, three times a day — morning, noon, and evening, for the next two weeks. You are all welcomed to come and partake. Bring your families with you."

"Well do that," replied Joseph, as the men began to enter the church.

Meanwhile back at Rush Lake, Father Joseph was becoming irate. He could not just sit back and watch his people desert him. What was he to do? He finally decided that on Sunday he would say Mass and fight back.

"My dear people," he stated in his Sunday sermon, "I am saddened to see that some of our brethren have decided to leave our parish. The Irishman from St. Paul has sent a Jesuit up here to confuse everyone. Neither one knows what is really going on. We must

pray that they are not successful. We must ask God to help us out in these hard times. We must ask God to help those people to decide to reject the ideas of this Weninger."

"Over the past few years, we have been through a lot. The Lord has looked out for us. We have suffered hard times and we have witnessed good times. I thought that since we were a good people, we did not need confession. Confessions are good for the sinners, for those who dance and for those who wear obscene hoops, but it was unnecessary for us. I have been wrong. So, from now on, I will gladly hear your confessions, if you so desire."

"If we would have been left alone, we would not need confession. But now we are being invaded on all sides. Our community is being weakened. Our settlement is being gnawed at. Our sense of values is being weakened. We must prepare ourselves for a strong battle,

for it was my calling to lead my people down the right path. It was my calling to be your faithful leader. It was my calling to be your guardian. It was my calling to help you find salvation."

Father Joseph paused and looked around the church. Many of the people had tears in their eyes, some because they were sad, others because they were overjoyed.

With a smile, Father Joseph continued: "My people. We are the chosen ones. We are in the right. We shall overcome."

This strong sermon did not, however, seem to help the cause of Father Joseph, for on the last day of Father Weninger's missions, there were only 15 families who remained loyal to Father Joseph. Everyone else decided to go over to the new parish. The scene was now set for a parting service at the log church of St. Joseph. As Father Weninger walked to the front of the church, he noticed that it was packed.

"Greetings, my people in Christ," he began. "What a beautiful sight! "What a beautiful scene to behold! I am only sorry that I will be leaving today. It has been a pleasure being here and witnessing the spiritual growth in each of you."

"Let us now renew the promises of holy Baptism, by which we formerly renounced Satan and his works, as well as the world, which is at enmity with God; and let us promise to serve God, faithfully, in the Holy Catholic Church. Therefore: Do you renounce Satan?"

"We do renounce him."

"And his works?"

"We do renounce them."

"And all his display."

"We do renounce it."

"Do you believe in God, the Father Almighty, Creator of heaven and Earth?"

"We do believe."

"Do you believe in Jesus Christ, His only Son, our Lord, who was born into this world and suffered for us?"

"We do believe."

"And do you believe in the Holy Spirit, the Holy Catholic Church, the communion of Saints, the forgiveness of sins, the resurrection of the body, and life everlasting?"

"We do believe."

"Now let us pray together, as our Lord Jesus Christ taught us to pray," suggested Father Weninger, as he led the congregation in

saying the 'Our Father.'

"We beseech Thee, oh Lord,"

he continued, in the same strong voice,

"We pray for our souls. We pray for our salvation. Grant unto us, oh Lord, the will to defend our true faith. Defend us against the wicked. Defend us against those who pretend to have powers. Defend us against those who misunderstand. Defend us against those false prophets. Oh Lord, hear our prayer. Oh Lord, rescue us, your lowly sinners, from the arms of the wicked."

The people were now getting very emotional. Some were crying aloud, while others quietly wept. All of them were very touched by what Father Weninger was saying.

"My people, outside the entrance I have a wooden cross. Let us now, in solemn procession, go and plant this cross as a sign for your spiritual renewal."

As Father Weninger began to go to the exit, followed, two by two, by the people, he continued: "Repeat after me. Live Jesus!"

"Live Jesus!" shouted the people.

"Live Jesus and Mary!"

"Live Jesus and Mary!"

"Long live the church!"

"Long live the church!"

When Father Weninger reached the outside of the church, he proceeded to plant the five-foot wooden cross, in front, saying:

"Long live the holy Cross!, with the people repeating the same.

"We ask you, oh Lord, to watch over us and make this parish grow. Make this parish grow in Christ. Help them to become perfect Christians. Amen."

The mission was complete. Father Weninger was ready to return to St. Paul. After taking off his stole and biretta, he climbed aboard an awaiting wagon. A large crowd followed him to the train station, in Perham, where he departed.

Upon arrival in St. Paul, he went to see Bishop Grace, who was in his living quarters, reading.

"Hello Father," greeted the Bishop.

"Hello, your Excellency," replied Father Weninger, as he kissed the Bishop's ring.

"How did everything go up by Rush Lake?"

"Not too good! I did hold a mission at St. Joseph's, after the dedication, and was able to persuade many of Albrecht's followers to repent and get in line, but Albrecht is still in charge of his little

utopia. He now even hears confessions."

"He what?"

"He hears confession. As if it weren't bad enough that he says

Mass."

"I will have to talk with Father Clemens Staub. We will have to write up a Bull of Excommunication. I was hoping it wouldn't go this far, but we have no choice. We must put a stop to this heresy. We must put a stop to this man. As soon as we get it written up, I'll send you back up there, and you and serve it to him, and make sure the people of St. Joseph's see it also."

"There are about 15 families that still follow Albrecht. I think I will write a letter to them, through 'The Wanderer'. Maybe they will realize the problem."

"Very well. I'm sure you are tired after this experience. You must rest now, for your job is not yet completed."

Back at Rush Lake, Father Joseph held a special meeting, in the church, with his three trustees, Anton, Bruno, and Frank, plus Christof Silbernagel.

"I didn't know if I was going to make it, or not," exclaimed Frank, as he entered, and took off his cap and coat. "It is really snowing out there."

"Yes, I know," replied Father Joseph, who was standing in front of the other men, who were already seated in the front pew. "I'll make this as short as possible," he continued, as he reached over the pew and picked up a large brown book.

After opening it up towards the front, he stated: "I've been paying close attention to who is paying their pew rent and who isn't. It looks like we have lost quite a few families. We are going to have to work hard to get them back into the fold. I expected to lose all of the

families over by the new church, but I was deeply saddened when I found out that some of the people, that live nearby, decided to leave. I went over to talk to the Doll's yesterday, but he wasn't home. I'd sure like to know what Weninger told them people."

"Christof," continued Father Joseph, as he directed his attention toward Mr. Silbernagel, "Why haven't I seen your brother-in-law in church?"

"I'm afraid that Sebastian has decided to attend St. Joe. I'll keep trying to convince him that you are right, though."

"Thank-you."

"Mr. Mohr stopped over yesterday," continued Father Joseph.

"He wanted to take his daughter home. She hasn't been here that long, but I think I can convince her to stay. She is old enough, so she can make up her own mind. Mr. Mohr went storming out of here, so we could expect some trouble from him."

"I think that if you continue on, just as you are, our friends and relatives, who went to St. Joe, will soon realize their mistake and return," stated Anton, as he tried to comfort Father Joseph. "We all know that you are older and wiser than the Bishop."

"Yes Father," added Bruno, "we know you speak the truth. You are, and always will be, our leader."

"Thank-you boys."

"Say Father," continued Bruno, "did you hear the results of that county vote?"

"No, I haven't."

"101 to zero, in Rush Lake township. The measure was soundly defeated county-wide. Ottertail will remain one county. Those who wanted to split us up into two, will have to forget about having a Holcomb County."

"That's good. It was a stupid idea anyway."

"Have you been up to Pine Lake, lately, Father?" asked Christof.

"No. Why?"

"Well, I was talking with several of the men that work for McCrea and Getchel, and they tell me about the work they are doing. I guess they have about 20 men, up there, cutting trees. It sounds like they are just going along and cutting everything in their path. It is quite a group!"

"Maybe I should go up there," noted Father Joseph. "Perhaps I can be of some assistance."

"Yes," continued Christof, "the men told me that they don't have a chance to do anything pertaining to religion."

Meanwhile outside, the cold Minnesota winter was making itself noticed. The heavy snow was falling, and the cold northwest wind was blowing the flakes in an almost-horizontal direction.

"It looks like we best be getting back home," stated Anton, as he looked out the window.

The other men got up, and Father Joseph led them to the door.

As they were about to head outside, he stated: "Thank-you for coming. You have made me feel much better."

The four men said good-bye and departed. Father Joseph then returned to the altar, where he knelt down on his kneeler. After making the sign of the cross, he placed his folded hands on his forehead, with his elbows resting on the top of the kneeler. After

several seconds of silent prayer, he began to cry.

Several weeks later, Father Weninger was, again, on his way back to Rush Lake. Upon his arrival at Perham, he was met by George Seifert and Balts Fuchs, who took him in their wagon to Rush Lake.

Father Joseph was walking with Big Joe and Cloister Tony (Anton Doll). They had just come from the stable and were on their way towards the church when the visitors arrived.

"What are you doing back here?" asked Father Joseph, as he watched Father Weninger get down from the wagon.

"I am sorry to inform you that I have a letter here, written by His Excellency, Bishop Grace," replied Father Weninger, as the two men entered the church. He took the letter out of his pocket, opened it up, and began to read aloud: "Thomas L. Grace, Miseratione divina et Sanctae Sedis Apostolicae Gratia, Sao Pauli Episcopies. To Whom it may concern — Salvation in the Lord! Since I, Thomas L. Grace, Bishop of St. Paul, in order to eradicate an evil, not once, but on two, three, and

four occasions admonished the priest, Joseph Albrecht, against performing priestly functions without authorization by the lawful Bishop. But he spurned these admonitions and continued to celebrate Mass and undertake other spiritual functions, although explicitly forbidden to do so. Yes, he even celebrated Mass in an interdicted church and dared to perform other official functions, and kept on doing so, and even attempted, sacrilegiously, to hear confessions, without the required faculties. Accordingly, we are compelled to break the obstinacy of this priest by invoking all the ecclesiastical power at our disposal and pronounce by this statement the 'great church ban' on Joseph Albrecht and declare him excommunicated, under the authority of God the Father, and the Son, and the Holy Spirit, the Apostles Peter and Paul, and all of the Saints. He is to be shunned until he betters himself and submits to the legitimate power of the Church, in order that on the day of judgement he may save his soul. Given at St. Paul, on November 23, 1871. Commissioned by the Most Reverend Bishop, Thomas L. Grace, of St. Paul. Father Clemens Staub, O.S.B., General-Vicar."

Father Weninger put down the letter and looked at Father Joseph, who was shaking very badly, and almost to the point of tears.

"Why?" Father Joseph asked, as he stared straight ahead.

"Why?"

"Until you straighten out, this ban will be in effect. That is all I have to say."

As he departed the church, he stopped by the church entrance, and posted a copy of the excommunication paper, on the door. Father Joseph, immediately, went over to the door, tore the paper off, looked at it for several seconds, and then ripped it up.

The next day, Father Weninger held Mass at St. Joseph.

"My people," he stated, "I have placed a notice on the door of your church, as well as on that of the church at Rush Lake. Heed these words. Have nothing to do with Albrecht. He has committed a grave sin and must repent.

"Remember, as Paul said to Timothy: Do not forget this: there will be terrible times in the last days. Men will be lovers of money and self, proud, arrogant, abusive, disobedient, ungrateful, inhuman, implacable, slanderous, licentious, brutal. They will be treacherous, reckless, pompous, lovers of pleasure, rather than God, as they make a pretense of religion, but negate its power. Stay clear of them. It is such as these who worm their way into homes and make captives of silly women burdened with sins and driven by desires of many kinds, always learning but never able to reach a knowledge of the truth. Just as Jannes and Jambres opposed Moses, so these men also oppose the truth; with perverted minds, they falsify the faith. But they will not get very far; as with those two men, the stupidity of this man, Albrecht, will be plain for all to see."

"Cursed be those who follow him," he continued. "Cursed the whole country and man and beast that liveth therein."

Joseph W. Doll, who was sitting near the front of the church, raised his hand.
"Yes?"

"What can we say to those who remained behind, so as to remove their blindfold and have them follow our example, so that the parish may be again fully united in heart and soul?"

"I have a letter here," replied Father Weninger, "which I plan on giving them."
After pulling the letter out of his pocket, and unfolding it, he began to read:

"It is not a question of what happened to Father Joseph Albrecht in the diocese of Cincinnati, where, as he maintains, that he was treated unjustly, but what he presumes to do now, here in Minnesota. Namely, he presumes to celebrate Holy Mass, to preach and perform other parochial functions, without having been accepted into the diocese of St. Paul. He tries to justify himself by maintaining that the jubilee empowers him. How naive! As a priest he should know that no jubilee in the world gives a priest the right to

overturn the entire ecclesiastical order. If the greatest saint enters a diocese, he must first be received by the Bishop and appointed as a pastor before he can conduct divine services and administer a parish. If injustice was done to Father Joseph Albrecht, in Ohio, that does not give him the right to act unjustly in Minnesota. He appeals to the Pope. Yet the Pope is the very first one who wants church laws observed and have everything proceed, according to order."

"Thus, when the Most Reverend Bishop heard that Father Joseph was conducting divine services and performing parochial duties, without having been accepted into the diocese, he immediately placed Father Joseph and the church, where he pleasured to hold divine services, under interdict. Father Joseph ignored the interdict. He cried: 'We stand under the Pope, and he is more than the Bishop.' But he was only throwing sand into the eyes of the people. It is the Pope who made the Bishop of St. Paul bishop and required him to uphold the church law. It is right and proper if he does not allow someone to enter the diocese as a priest, without first having been accepted by him. Who of you farmers, would permit another farmer, who says he was unjustly treated in Ohio, to come into his house in Minnesota, and run the farm, unless the owner accepted him and allowed him to do so? And where in the world have you farmers of Rush Lake ever seen a pastor admitting people to freely receive Holy Communion, without confession, as Father Joseph has done? And he does not care whether the people obey the commandment of the church regarding Easter, just as he does not keep the Easter law. He knows that he has no right to hear confession and validly absolve people. Every well-instructed schoolboy knows that the priest must first obtain authority from the Bishop before he can do so.

That was explained to the people in the mission. And then Father Joseph carried matters so far as to have the gall to hear confessions, thus making a farce out of the sacrament of Penance! What would you say if a farmer would don priestly clothes and sit down and pretend to hear people's confessions, absolve them, and thus make fools out of them? Should we not consider him to be a godless criminal, who wantonly commits sacrilege? But that is exactly what Father Joseph is doing in Rush Lake, and for that reason, the Bishop of St. Paul has excommunicated him and placed him under the great ecclesiastical ban. Therefore, shun him, all of you, who wish to remain Catholic and guiltless. Remember the three men in the Bible, Korah, Dathan, and Abram, who dared to perform

priestly functions to which they were not entitled. Moses spoke thus to the people of Israel: 'Stay away from these men, so that you may not fall into the abyss!' And so, I call to you in the name of Jesus and his holy Church. Turn away from this rebellious priest, who has been blinded by pride, and away from his adherents, so that you will not perish with them."

"The Reverend Father Ignatius Tomazin will now, occasionally, conduct divine services for you in this church, and by spring the Bishop will send you a regular priest, who will remain with you. And so, with God's assistance, Rush Lake will grow into a prosperous and happy parish. This, I wish from my heart and for this, I send you, my blessing."

As he put down the letter, and looked around at the crowd, he continued: "Remember, shun him. Have nothing to do with him. Have nothing to do with this sly fox. Convince your friends, relatives, and neighbors, to do the same. Pray that these fox Catholics will see the truth."

Assault On The Nunnery

CHAPTER XXIX

Life continued on at the Rush Lake settlement, with Father Joseph withdrawing more and more from the outside area, staying within the confines of the settlement, as much as possible. His followers had dwindled to 15 families, plus the brothers and sisters. These families were those of Bruno Boedigheimer, Anton Bender, Christof Silbernagel, Frank Staab, Victor Eifert, Ferdinand Eifert, Wendolin Fehrenbacher, Joseph A. Doll, Anton Doll, Louis Sarbacher, John Reinhart, Joseph Riesterer, John Doll, Joseph Weis, and Charley Foltz. Many people from St. Joe still respected him but had nothing to do with him in regard to religion. One morning, in the spring of '72, Father Joseph was in the church, with Brother Joseph. Father was standing beside the organ, while Brother Joseph was sitting on the organ bench.

"After religious instructions this morning, I will bring some of the children over here/" he stated.

"We'll see if we can find some new voices for the choir. Pick out some easy music for them."

Father Joseph then walked out of the church, and went directly over to the school, located over the stable. There were several boys playing out in front. When Father Joseph approached, he said:

"Come, my children, it is time for class." The three children, 13-year-old John Bender, 11-year-old Anton Staab, and 13-year-old Frank Boedigheimer, immediately headed for the outside stairs and ran up to the room, closely followed by Father Joseph.

As soon as Father Joseph entered the small room, the noisy group of children instantly became quiet. There were more children in the room than there was room for, with the boys all seated in the front rows, and the girls filling up the back.

"Good morning children," exclaimed Father Joseph, as he walked to the front of the room.

"Good morning, Father Joseph," replied the children. "Let's see if everyone is here this morning," continued Father Joseph. "As I read your name, please say here."

As the names were called off, the children did exactly as they were told. "John Eifert, Mary Ann Eifert, Irene Eifert, Matilda Eifert, Anton Sarbacher, Magdalena Sarbacher, Joseph Bender, John

Bender, Anna Bender, Maria Silbernagel, Christof Silbernagel, Mary Grismer, William Boedigheimer, Emma Boedigheimer, Simon Boedigheimer, Bruno Boedigheimer, Joseph Staab, Anton Staab, Adaline Staab, Theresa Staab, Charles Staab, Charles Weis, LeAnder Boedigheimer, Aurelia Boedigheimer, Rosa Foltz, Catharine Foltz, John Riesterer, Agnes Riesterer."

"Very good. This morning we are going to discuss the Sacraments. Can anyone tell me what they are?"

Several children raised their hands.

"Yes Maria?"

Ten-year-old Maria Silbernagel replied: "Baptism, Communion, Extreme Unction, Holy Orders, Matrimony, and Penance."

"Very good."

13-year-old Mary Ann Eifert raised her hand.

"Yes, Mary Ann, what is it?"

"My mother said that Confirmation is a Sacrament."

"Confirmation is of no interest to us," quickly shot back Father Joseph.

"A good Catholic will confirm his religion every day of the week."

Changing the subject, he continued: "What is the purpose of Penance?"

Again, several children raised their hands.

"Aurelia?"

"To ask God for forgiveness of your sins," answered the 12-year-old.

"That is correct. Of course, it is really unnecessary here. As long as you each lead a perfect Christian life, you should never have to go to confession. If you do something wrong, you can always talk to God and ask him for forgiveness."

"Matrimony," he continued, "is another of the Sacraments that we really should not have to study, either. Since the end of the world is fast approaching, we should not think about marriage, but rather, we should consider a life of continency, a life of religion. I would so

very much like to see all of you become priests, brothers, or sisters. In a letter from Paul to the Corinthians, he says: 'I tell you, brothers, the time is short. From now on, those with wives should live as though they had none. I should like you to be free of all your

worries. The unmarried man is busy with the Lord's affairs, concerned with pleasing the Lord; but the married man is busy with this world's demands and occupied with pleasing his wife. This means he is divided. Any unmarried woman is concerned with things of the Lord, in pursuit of holiness in body and spirit. The married woman, on the other hand, has the cares of this world to absorb

her and is concerned with pleasing her husband.'"

"For the next week, I want you to learn everything that you can about the sacraments of Baptism, Holy Orders, and Extreme Unction. I will quiz you on it then. Now, I want to take some of you down to the church, where Brother Joseph is waiting. We would like to see if any of you have a good voice, for our choir. Anyone under 12, may go home. The rest of you, walk single-file and follow me."

All of the younger children got up and rushed out the door, followed by Father Joseph, who led the other children over to the church.

Once everyone was inside, Father Joseph handed out several sheets of music, which he had picked off the organ, to the children.

"Now, Brother Joseph is going to accompany you on the organ. When he begins, I'll tell you when to start singing."

"Are you ready?" asked Father Joseph, as he looked at Big Joe. Brother Joseph nodded his head in the affirmative and began to play. Several seconds later, Father Joseph motioned to the children to start singing.

Brother Joseph was an excellent organist, but the singing of the children left much to be desired. However, Father Joseph did notice one beautiful voice. He continued to listen until he found out who that voice belonged to. Then he said: "Stop!"

He walked straight over to young Aurelia Boedigheimer, and stated: "Aurelia, your voice is excellent!"

Aurelia could say nothing. She only blushed. "Come with me," demanded Father Joseph, as he led her by the hand over to the organ.

"Brother Joseph, could you play this song? Here is the sheet."

Brother Joseph set the sheet of music on the organ stand while Aurelia looked at the sheet, and then exclaimed:

"But Father Joseph, I've never sung this before."

"That's alright. Just try and do your best."

Brother Joseph started to play and soon, Aurelia began singing. She sang very beautifully, and this pleased Father Joseph very much.

After the song was completed, Father Joseph remarked: "I would like for you to continue practicing with Brother Joseph, once a week. I will ask your parents if it is alright with them."

Turning towards the other children, Father Joseph commanded:

"Thank-you children, you may leave."

As the children departed, Father Joseph looked at Brother Joseph and said: "Well Brother Joseph, I think we found ourselves a singer."

On Tuesday, April 2, 1872, all was quiet on the church grounds at Rush Lake. Spring was in the air, and Father Joseph was outside, enjoying the peaceful surroundings. As he was slowly walking around, reading occasionally from his small black breviary, Sister Lucretia and Sister Afra were standing near the barn, feeding the cattle. Sister Cherubim was sitting on a stump nearby, sewing some Mass vestments, with Emma Bliley and Julia Boedigheimer patiently watching. Brother Joseph and Cloister Tony were near the barn, fixing a wheel on one of the wagons.

"Well Julia," stated Father Joseph, as he walked up beside the 13-year-old, "How do you like it at your new home?"

"Very well, thank-you," she shyly remarked.

"Good. Just learn from the sisters, and perhaps one day you will become just like them."

Just then, Father Joseph glanced to the west, and noticed a group of people approaching, in several sleighs.

"Sister Lucretia," he shouted, as he turned to the Mother Superior, "go to the nunnery and find Anna. Hide her in one of the rooms and lock the door. I think her father is coming."

Sister Lucretia and Sister Afra quickly ran over and entered the nunnery, while Father Joseph walked to the approaching group. Father Ignatius Tomazin was in the lead wagon, seated with Fred Mohr, George Seifert, Frank (Andy) Mutschler, and William Hassler. In the second sleigh was Wendolin Doll, Joseph W. Doll, Ignatz Steinbach, Michael Schmitz, and George Altstadt. In the third sleigh was Anton Friedsam, John Rock, Martin Fiedler, Adam Gerber, and Balts Fuchs. As they arrived in front of the church, Father Joseph stated:

"Good morning gentlemen. Is there something I can do for you?"

"Yes, there is," replied Father Tomazin. "Mr. Mohr here, tells me that he has been trying to get his daughter to come back home with him, and that you won't allow it. Is that true?"

"Of course not. Anna is old enough. She is 20 years old. She is here on her own free will."

"You have her brainwashed," shouted Fred, as he shook his hand at Father Joseph.

"That's nonsense. She can leave anytime she wants."

"Could you have her come over here, so I can talk to her?" requested Father Tomazin.

"I don't see where that would do any good," objected Father Joseph.

"I just want to find out for myself, what she really wants to do," shouted Father Tomzain, as he began to show signs of losing his patience.

Just then, Sister Lucretia came out of the nunnery, walked over to Father Joseph, and nodded her head.

"Noticing this, he turned to Father Tomazin, and stated with a smile: "If you can find her, you are welcome to talk to her."

While this conversation was being held, all of the other nuns had quietly congregated in front of the nunnery, each holding a broom in their hands.

Father Tomazin and Mr. Mohr walked straight over to the nunnery, while the other men remained by the sleighs. As the two men walked by the nuns, they noticed the angry look on their faces, but this did not stop them from entering.

Once inside, Mr. Mohr walked straight over to a small desk, and said:

"I'm sure they locked her up in one of those rooms. The keys are usually left in this desk."

After fumbling through the desk drawers for several seconds, he found the keys. "Here we are," he exclaimed, as he took the keys and headed for the nearby rooms.

He walked from door to door, unlocking each, and checking to see if his daughter was inside. On his third try he was successful. After opening the door, and seeing his scared daughter standing inside, he said: "Anna, come out of there. You are leaving this

place."

Anna just stood there, trembling, as her father and Father Tomazin entered the small room and grabbed her.

As the three of them came out of the nunnery, Anna was screaming and trying to get away. The other nuns began to kick at Father Tomazin, and gently hit him, and Mr. Mohr, with their broomsticks.

Several of the other men came running from the sleighs, to see if they could help.

"You'll never get away with this," shouted Father Joseph, as he shook his hand at the two men.

This threat did not stop the men. They continued to drag Anna to an awaiting sleigh. Once this was done, and the men were aboard, the group quickly left the church grounds.

Father Joseph was angry. As he watched them leave, he exclaimed:

"I will not let them kidnap her. They will not get away with this. Brother Joseph, get my wagon ready. I'm going to Ottertail City and press charges against those lawbreakers."

Brother Joseph quickly went over to the stable and did what he was told, while Father Joseph stormed into his house and made preparations to leave. Upon arrival in Ottertail City, he went directly to the courthouse. Once inside, he entered the sheriff's office.

"Sheriff," he stated, as he looked at Mr. Anderson, who was sitting behind his desk, "I want you to issue a warrant for the arrest of several criminals."

"What happened Father Joseph?"

"Father Tomazin and a group of his cohorts came by and kidnapped one of the girls from the nunnery."

As the sheriff handed Father Joseph a piece of paper and a quill pen, he stated: "Write down the names of those involved. What did you want to charge them with?"

"Assault and battery," quickly replied Father Joseph, as he began writing.

"Who is the girl?"

"Anna Mohr."

"Where is she now?"

"I suppose she was taken back to her father's place, over by Perham."

"How old is she?"

"Just about 20."

"Alright, I'll go over and check it out. Will Tomazin be over at St. Joe?"

"I don't know."

As the sheriff got up, he continued: "I'll bring Miss Mohr back to your place, but it probably won't be until tomorrow. I'll let you know what happens."

299

"Thank-you," replied Father Joseph, as he departed, and headed straight for the newspaper office, across the street.

"Mr. Ball," he stated, as he entered, "I need your help."

"Good afternoon, Father Joseph," replied the middle-aged man, who was standing by his press, "What is it?"

"I need a good lawyer, and since you are the best around, I would like your help. A group of men from the St. Joe area, led by Father Tomazin, came to my place, and literally kidnapped Anna Mohr. I just came from the sheriff's office, and Mr. Anderson is

going to arrest them."

"Alright Father. I'll need all of the particulars, and then I'll go see Judge Reynolds. We'll see what we can do."

The next day Sheriff Anderson arrived at the church grounds, with Anna Mohr.

Father Joseph, and the others, were overjoyed at the sight of her return.

"She'll be able to stay here," stated the sheriff, "until the trial. I've been ordered by Justice Henery, to go to Clitherall, and get 12 men, for jury duty, since your attorneys didn't think they could get a fair trial, with the people from around here. The trial is scheduled

for next Monday afternoon, in Ottertail City."

"Thank-you sheriff," stated Father Joseph, as he helped Anna down from the wagon.

"I'll see you then," he continued, as he watched the sheriff turn the wagon around and depart.

"Welcome back, Anna," stated Father Joseph, as he put his right hand on her shoulder. "You can return to the same bunk.

You'll find Sister Lucretia over by the barn. Go find out what she has for you to do."

"Yes Father," quietly replied Anna.

On Monday, April 8th, the trial began. The small courtroom was packed. On one side of the room were the followers of Father Joseph, while on the other side were the men and women from St. Joe. Anna was seated by a small table, near the front. Father Joseph, Mr. Ball, and Judge Reynolds were seated next to her. On the other side, at a small table, was seated Mr. E. E. Corliss, the county attorney. Behind him, were seated Father Tomazin, and the other men who partook in the raid. Nearby, were the 12 men that made up the jury. Justice Henery was seated behind a raised desk, at the front of the room. He was busily reading over several papers, which were on his desk.

"I have before me," he stated, "a complaint, filed by Lucretia Hog, stating that on Tuesday, April 2nd, a group of men illegally entered private property and took one Anna Mohr, from the premises, against her will. Mr. Corliss, how does the defense plead?"

"Not guilty, your honor."

"Very well. Whom would you like to call to the stand?"

"Mr. Fred Mohr," replied Mr. Corliss, as he stood up and approached the bench.

"Fred Mohr, would you please come forward," requested the Justice.

After Mr. Mohr came up and was sworn in and seated, Mr. Corliss stated: "Mr. Mohr, in your own words, would you please tell the court what exactly happened on the 2nd of April, and why you went to the nunnery?"

After several seconds of silence, the nervous, 55-year-old Mr. Mohr began: "Well, you see, it happened this way. Over the past few months, I have tried to get my daughter out of the nunnery, because I feel that she has been brainwashed by Father Joseph. He has been excommunicated from the Catholic Church, yet continues to practice his religion, and to perform his priestly functions. I do not feel that my daughter should have anything to do with him. Well, anyway, after the last time I was there, I decided to talk to Father

Tomazin, and see if he could help me. We got a group of men together and paid a visit to Father Joseph. When we got there, he refused to let us see my daughter, at first. Finally, he consented and we found her locked up in a room. We freed her and took her back to

my place. That's all."

"I see," noted Mr. Corliss. "You were allowed to enter the nunnery then. Is that correct?"

"Yes."

"Thank-you. That's all."

"Mr. Ball," stated Justice Henery, "do you wish to question the defendant?"

"No, Your Honor."

"Any more witnesses?" asked the Justice, as he looked at Mr. Corliss.

"I would like to call Father Joseph to the stand," replied Mr. Corliss.

"Father Joseph, would you please come forward?" asked the Justice.

Father Joseph looked at Mr. Ball, and then at Anna. He arose and approached the bench. After being sworn in, he sat down. Mr. Corliss walked up beside him, looked straight in his eyes, and asked: "Mr. Albrecht, what is your profession?"

"I am a Catholic priest."

"According to whom?"

"According to God and the Pope, whom I serve."

"Is it not true that Bishop Thomas L. Gace has excommunicated you from the Catholic Church?"

Father Joseph did not say a word. He looked down at his folded hands, for several seconds, and then continued: "Yes, he did, but he does not know what is happening. He does not understand. He was influenced by people who were jealous of me, including Father Tomazin, there."

"Is it true that you had Anna locked up, so that her father would not find her?"

"No. She was put in that room for her own protection."

"In a locked room?"

"Yes."

"No further questions, Your Honor."

"Mr. Ball," stated the Justice.

"No questions, Your Honor."

"Any more witnesses?" asked the Justice.

"No, Your Honor," replied Mr. Corliss.

"The prosecution would like to call Anna Mohr, to the stand," noted Mr. Ball.

Young Anna approached the bench, was sworn in, and sat down.

"How old are you?" asked Mr. Ball, as he walked up to her.

"Nineteen."

"Ah. Nineteen. That means you are old enough to decide for yourself what you want to do. Tell me, Miss Mohr, did you enter the nunnery at Rush Lake, on your own free will?"

"Yes. For many years I have expressed a desire to become a nun."

"When your father came, did you freely leave with him?"

"No, I did not want to leave."

"Thank-you Miss Mohr, that is all," stated Mr. Ball, as he walked back to his chair.

"Mr. Corliss," stated the Justice, "do you have any questions?"

"No, Your Honor."

"It seems to me," continued Justice Henery, "that we really don't have much of a case here. However, since we do have a jury, they are to decide if punishment should be dealt out. I have a list here of the gentlemen who went over to Rush Lake, on the 2nd of April, and reportedly committed the crime of assault and battery. Since there are no more witnesses in the case, I want you men to look at this list, and decide if they are guilty of any crime. You are to be shown to an adjoining room, and there to decide the verdict. When you have reached a decision, please return." The 12 men got up and left the room, in single file, while the Justice stated: "This court is in recess until the verdict has been

reached." With that said, he pounded the gavel, and got up. "What do you think our chances are?" asked Father Joseph, as he looked at Mr. Ball.

"From what I can gather, I think the men will be found innocent of any wrongdoing, and Anna will be given a choice of what she wants to do."

After a short recess, the jury returned to the courtroom. Moments later, the Justice returned, also. After pounding the gavel, and stating that the court was in session, he looked at the jury, and asked:

"Has the jury reached a decision?"

A tall, lanky, middle-aged man, in the front row, arose and said: "Yes we have, Your Honor."

The bailiff walked over to the man and grabbed the piece of paper and took it over to the Judge. Justice Henery opened the paper and read it to himself.

"Would the defendants arise?" requested the Justice.

"You have been charged with assault and battery. The jury finds you not

guilty."

A large roar was now heard in the courtroom. Shouts of joy were coming from the side of the defendants, while shouts of anger were heard on the other side.

The Justice pounded his gavel on the desk, and shouted:

"Order in the Court!"

After quiet returned, the Justice continued:

"Miss Mohr, since you are old enough to make up your own mind, the Court would like

to know if you want to return to Rush Lake or to the home of your father?"

"The nunnery," quickly replied Anna.

"Very well. Sheriff Anderson, you are hereby instructed to see to it that Miss Mohr is allowed to return to the nunnery."

As the Justice again pounded the gavel, he stated: "Court dismissed."

Father Joseph smiled, seemingly satisfied with the results of the trial. He gathered his group together and led them back to Rush Lake.

The scene now turns to the Rush Lake settlement on a warm summer day in 1872. The brothers, Joseph, Cornelius, and Anton were busy putting hay into the barn. The sisters were all gathered near the church entrance, talking with Father Joseph.

"Sister Theodilda has decided to return to Ohio," noted Father Joseph, her stay just did not work out for her. As you know, I have no objection since no one is bound by an oath to stay."

"Sister Lucretia. I need to have you send two of the girls over to clean the barn today. Send two others over to the nunnery, to clean, and have the rest go to the garden."

As Sister Lucretia took charge, Father Joseph walked over to the barn, where the men were busily putting up hay.

"Brother Cornelius," he stated, "would you get the horse and wagon ready, and take Sister Theodilda to Perham, this afternoon, so she can catch the train to St. Paul?"

"Of course, Father. What time?"

"You best leave here about 1."

"Sure."

"I'd like to get the rest of that field done today, if possible. Brother Joseph, do you think you and Brother Anton could do it yourselves?"

"No Father. We still have more than half left."

"Well, I promised Wendolin that you boys could go help him tomorrow. Maybe, I'll have to go and talk to him, and put it off for a day."

Just then, Father Joseph heard two of the sisters arguing, by the main barn door. He walked over to see what the problem was.

"No, I will not," shouted Sister Seraphim.

"But you must," replied Sister Cherubim.

"What is the problem?" interrupted Father Joseph.

"Ah, Father Joseph," stated Sister Cherubim. "Would you settle this? Sister Lucretica told us to clean the barn out, and the pig sty.

Well, I already did the pig sty. Sister Seraphim was supposed to clean the barn. When I came over here, she was sitting down, doing nothing. She says that she did enough in the barn, but I don't think it's clean. Would you tell her to finish her work?"

"If Sister Seraphim thinks the barn is clean enough, then let it be," replied Father Joseph. "You are not the one to give orders.

That is Sister Lucretia's job. Now you two know very well that I absolutely despise arguments. I feel a punishment is necessary. Sister Cherubim, I want you to go out to the large cross and pray three rosaries. Sister Seraphim, I want you to go to the pig sty and pray three rosaries. When you two are done, go to the chapel for adoration."

"Yes Father Joseph," humbly replied the two nuns, as they each went to their assigned places.

As Father Joseph stood there and watched them. Brother Joseph approached.

"Was that really necessary?" he queried.

Father Joseph turned and replied: "Never doubt my word,

Brother Joseph. You should know by now that I am always right and I do for my people what I think is best for them."

"We have all the hay put up from this wagon," continued Brother Joseph. "Do you want Brother Cornelius to go back out with us?"

"Yes, he has time. Before you go out though, hitch up my wagon. I'm going to take a trip over to a few of the neighbors."

As the two men walked into the stable, they noticed 82-year-old Joseph Bender busily putting a shoe on one of the horses.

"Ah Mr. Bender," stated Father Joseph, as he walked up beside him, "it makes me feel good to see a man of your age still leading a productive life. I hope that when I reach your age, I can still get around like that."

"Well, you're not too far off," replied Mr. Bender, with a smile.

"That's true. Say, are you just about done?"

"She's ready to go," replied Mr. Bender, as he stood up beside the horse. Brother Joseph took the horse and began hitching it up to a nearby wagon.

"This Minnesota climate has been quite good for you, hasn't it?" continued Father Joseph.

"Yes," replied Mr. Bender, "this is exactly like the weather my body was used to back in the old country."

"I'm going over to Kemper's. Is there anything I can get you?"

"No Father."

As Father Joseph mounted the wagon and began to leave, he waved to Mr. Bender and Brother Joseph. In a short time, Father Joseph pulled up in front of Kemper's store. After tying the reins to the wagon, he got down and walked inside.

"Good morning, Henry," he stated, as he walked over to Mr. Drahmann.

"Good morning, Father Joseph. Can I help you?"

"Yes. Do you have any mail for me?"

Mr. Drahmann looked through the mail bag. After several seconds, he replied: "No, I don't."

"Very well."

"Is there anything else?"

"How is everything over in that new town of Perham?"

"Fine. Henry is taking good care of the business. We've only been over there a couple of weeks, but I can notice the business picking up already. You should go over and see for yourself."

"I have no desire to go there."

"Jacob Berns and Victor Eifert did an excellent job on the building, which was the first wooden one in town."

"Victor mentioned that a while back," noted Father Joseph,

"that he was working in Perham. Tell me Henry, what is the going price for oats?"

"650 a bushel."

"Wheat?"

"$1.25."

"Good. I should have quite a bit to sell this year. Our crops seem to be progressing very well."

"Yes, with a little more rain, they'll be in excellent shape."

"Well, I should get going," continued Father Joseph, "I wanted to go see a few others yet today. Have a good day."

"Good day Father."

Father Joseph went outside, got aboard the wagon, and headed for the Wendolin Fehrenbacher home. As he approached the farmyard, he was met by 4-year-old Catharine. "Good morning, Father Joseph," she excitedly stated.

"Good morning my child. And how is my Catharine this fine morning?"

"Fine."

"Is your father and mother home?"

"Father is over by the barn, and mother is in the house."

"Thank-you," continued Father Joseph, as he rode over to the barn, where 30-year-old Wendolin was working on a fence.

"Good morning, Father Joseph," he stated, as he wiped his forehead. "What can I do for you?"

"Good morning Wendolin. I came to tell you that I won't be able to let you use the brothers until the day after tomorrow."

"That's alright. I'll just let the hay dry one more day."

"I knew you'd understand."

"How is everything going down at the church?"

"Nothing has changed. I still haven't heard anymore from the Bishop."

"Do you think he'll gradually give in?"

"Each day, I pray that he will."

"Well, you have nothing to worry about. You're in the right. It'll just take time, and everything will turn out right."

"I certainly hope so."

Meanwhile, back at the church grounds, Sister Lucretia had gathered all of the nuns and postulants, and was talking with them, near the nunnery. Those present were Sister Theresa, Sister Agamonti, Sister Lydia, Sister Afra, Sister Rustika, Sister Seraphim, Sister Cherubim, and the postulants: Emma Bliley, Julia Boedigheimer, Catharine Eifert, Barbara Eifert, and little 6-year-old Rosa Grismer.

Brother Joseph was over by the barn, talking with Cloister Tony and Brother Cornelius. They had just finished getting the wagon ready for Brother Cornelius.

"I don't know why you have to give her a ride to Perham," stated Brother Anton. "If she wants to leave, she should have to find

her own way."

"You know that's not the way Father Joseph is," objected

Brother Joseph. "He is not that kind of person."

As Brother Anton wiped the sweat from his forehead, he continued: "I sure wish Brother Martin would come back. With Joe Grismer going back to live with his father, that sure spreads the workload thin around here."

"Everything will work out," stated Brother Cornelius. "Father Joseph will see to it."

"Do you really think so?" asked Brother Anton. "I sometimes have my doubts."

"Have no fears, Brother," noted Big Joe. "Just have faith.

Leave the worrying to Father Joseph."

"Surely, you have seen all the changes that have taken place around here, since we first arrived?"

"Yes, that I have," noted Brother Joseph. "It used to be that everyone shared with everyone else. Now it seems that everyone is out fending for themselves. It is not turning out the way Father Joseph had wanted it. But, nevertheless, we should have enough faith in Father Joseph, to believe that he will take care of us in any time of need."

"I surely hope so," added Brother Cornelius.

A Hunting Accident

CHAPTER XXX

Very little of importance occurred at the settlement over the next several years. There were a few marriages, births, and deaths, but, on the whole, nothing spectacular occurred. In the fall of 1873, the completion of the new schoolhouse was taking place. District 13 was to have a new look. The new building, still located at the edge of the Wendolin Fehrenbacher farm, was replacing the old log house built several years earlier.

One morning, many of the men from the surrounding area, were seen working on the building, and the adjoining grounds. Henry Kemper was paid $460.00 to furnish materials for this project. He was standing in front of the building, watching the progress. Mr. John Weis was busily making new wooden seats. He had been paid $2.50 a piece and had to have 12 of them completed before the next school session was to begin. Joseph A. Doll was busy making a wooden fence around the schoolgrounds. Wendolin Fehrenbacher, who was paid $7.50 for rent of the land, was busy painting the outside of the school, being assisted by Anton, Bruno, and Charley. Father Joseph arrived on the scene.

"Good morning, Henry."

"Good morning, Father Joseph."

"I see you have been making good progress on the school," stated Father Joseph, as he looked at the building.

"Yes, it should be completed in time for the next session."

"Is there anything I can do?"

"No. We don't need your money here."

"I didn't mean financial help. I thought maybe there was something my brothers or sisters could do."

"No, I don't think so. The next session won't start until the 3rd of December, so we still have plenty of time."

Father Joseph shrugged his shoulder and walked over to the painters. "Bruno, Anton, you are doing fine work."

"Thank-you Father," replied Bruno.

"Who's going to be the teacher?"

"Young John Bishof."

"Good. He is a fine man. Sister Rustika's favorite brother."

Just then, 19-year-old John Staab approached the men. He was carrying a shotgun.

"Well Johnnie, where are you going?" asked Father Joseph.

"I'm going to see if I can find a deer," excitedly replied Johnnie.

"My dad said he saw several of them north of the Fehrenbacher woods, yesterday."

"If you get one, and need some help, come back to the church and get some of the brothers."

"Alright Father. I'll do that," replied Johnnie, as he began heading northward.

"That Johnnie is a fine young man," stated Father Joseph, to Bruno and Anton, as they watched him leave. "I'm afraid though, he won't be with us for very long."

"Why do you say that?" asked Bruno.

"I had a dream, and in that dream, I was saying a funeral Mass for him."

"I sure hope you're wrong," noted Bruno. "He sure has done a lot for his family. With Frank spending so much time drinking, Johnnie has had to help support that family."

"Yes. I thought I had Frank cured of his alcoholic problems, but I guess not. I'll have to work on that some more."

That evening, after Father Joseph had finished the evening prayer service, for the brothers and sisters, Frank Staab came running into the church. "Father! Father!" he shouted.

"Johnnie went hunting this morning, and he never came home. I'm afraid something has happened. He told me he would only be gone for a few hours."

"Well Frank," exclaimed Father Joseph. "There really isn't much we can do tonight. We'll have to wait till morning. If something did happen, we'd never be able to find him in the dark anyway. Come back at sun-up and we'll go look for him, if he hasn't come back by then."

"Then, it'll be too late. I'm going out now."

"If you insist. I'll go get the men and we'll go with you. Wait here."

Several minutes later, Father Joseph returned with Brother Joseph, Brother Anton, and Brother Cornelius. Each of them was holding a lantern.

"Let's go, Frank, stated Father Joseph, as they began heading in the direction of the Fehrenbacher farm.

"It's going to be difficult, but we'll try," noted Father Joseph.

"We'll head north from the school. That is where I saw him this morning. There is only 5 of us, so we're not going to be able to cover much ground."

When they reached the schoolyard, they turned northward, spreading out about 20 feet apart. There was a full moon out, with a clear sky, so it was somewhat possible to see. Father Joseph was in the center, with Frank and Cornelius off to his left, and Brother
Joseph and Cloister Tony, to his right. The group continued on, passing the home of Wendolin Fehrenbacher, and there still was no sign of Johnnie. A half hour passed, and then an hour. Still no sign.

"I think we better return," suggested Father Joseph. "We would probably have better luck in daylight. It's starting to cloud over now, and we're soon going to lose the moonlight.
Just then, Brother Cornelius hollered: "Father Joseph! Come
quick! I found him."

Everyone quickly raced over to where Brother Cornelius was. There, lying beside a fence, was the lifeless body of Johnnie Staab, with the shotgun lying close to his side.
Father Joseph got down on his knees and checked the body.

"He shot himself," stated Father Joseph. "Right through the heart. He must have tripped when he tried climbing over the fence. His body is very cold. I think he has been dead for quite some time."

Frank knelt down beside his son, put him in his arms, and began to cry.
"Why Father?" he yelled, in a frenzy.

"Why?"

"There, there now, Frank. Take it easy," consoled Father
Joseph.

"There is nothing we can do about it. His time had come.
We have no choice but to accept it."

"No Father," shot back Frank.

"We don't have to just accept it.

This could have been avoided. It's all my fault. I was the one that told him to come up here. Now, he's gone."

Brother Cornelius and Brother Anton tried to calm Frank down but met with little success. Father Joseph, quietly said a short prayer, and then picked the body up.

"Come! Let us take the body back to the church. We'll take your son home in one of my wagons."

The group began the return trip to the church. Frank, who was in tears all the way, was being led by Cloister Tony, on one side, and Brother Cornelius, on the other. Father Joseph, carrying Johnnie, led the way. Right behind him was Brother Joseph, who was carrying the gun.

Upon arrival back at the church, Brother Joseph went over to the stable, to hitch up a team, while the others remained near the church entrance.

"Do you want me to send someone ahead and tell your wife?" asked Father Joseph.

"No Father. I'll do it when we get there."

"Very well. Brother Cornelius, you and Brother Anton may as well go to bed. I'll have Brother Joseph go with me."

"Good night, Father," stated the two brothers, as they left.

"Good night."

When Brother Joseph arrived with the wagon, Father Joseph picked up the body and placed it in the back. He got on board and sat down next to it, while Frank sat down next to Brother Joseph.

"Alright!" stated Father Joseph. "Let's go!" The wagon slowly made its way over to the Staab farm. It was located only about a half mile from the church, but the trail was rough and difficult. Much care had to be taken as they crossed the river.

As they approached the farmhouse, they could see candles lit inside. "Your wife must still be up, waiting for you," exclaimed Father Joseph.

"Yes, I told her to."

As the wagon pulled up in front of the house, Mrs. Staab opened the door and came running out.

"Is everything alright?" she asked.

"No, it isn't," quickly replied Frank. "We found Johnnie. He's dead!"

Mrs. Staab stopped in her footsteps. "Oh no!" she gasped. She ran to the back of the wagon, where Father Joseph was beginning to unload the body.

"Oh my God! What happened?"

"He accidentally shot himself," replied Father Joseph.

"Oh Johnnie!" she screamed. "My Johnnie!" She could not hold back the tears any longer. Frank grabbed her and pulled her back, as Father Joseph carried the body into the small log cabin. He laid him down on the floor, near the fireplace.

"I'll have Anton bring over a coffin, in the morning," continued
Father Joseph, as he placed a blanket over the body. "I'll come back tomorrow morning and prepare the body. I'll also have Anton dig a grave up on the hill."

"Thank-you Father," replied Mrs. Staab, as she placed two lit candles beside the body.

"Good night, my dear friends," stated Father Joseph, as he departed, leaving Frank and his wife with their deceased son.

As he was getting back onto the wagon, it began to snow. It was the 7th of November and already it had been unusually cold. The biting north wind was beginning to increase, causing the trip back to the church to be very uncomfortable.

"This Minnesota weather sure can change rapidly," stated Father Joseph. "This morning it was nice enough to paint outside, and now it's snowing. It's about as predictable as some people around here. Perhaps, we should start thinking about a different place to live."

Brother Joseph looked at Father Joseph, with a surprised face. Although he did not say anything out loud, Brother Joseph began wondering how serious Father Joseph was. The wagon slowly made its way to the river. When they reached the banks, and stopped, Father Joseph got down and walked right up to the river. After checking the situation out, he walked back and hollered:
"Bring it across'"

Father Joseph stood by as Brother Joseph cautiously took the wagon across. Once that was done, he waded across to the other side.

By now, the snow was coming down very heavy. With the strong winds blowing, it was very difficult for the two men to see where they were going. Nevertheless, they finally arrived at the church. Father Joseph got off and hurried into his house, while Brother
Joseph had to take the wagon and horses over to the stable. Once inside, Father Joseph took off his black coat, and walked over to the fireplace, where he placed three logs on the grate and lit them. Once the fire got going, he backed up and sat down on a
nearby chair, staring at the flame.

"What am I doing wrong?" he wondered aloud.

"My dream is coming true. I will be burying Johnnie. Why didn't I take it seriously? Maybe this could've been avoided."

Just then, he broke out of his trance and exclaimed: "Nonsense!" He got up, went over to his make-shift bed, and laid down. When morning arrived, Father Joseph arose, walked over to the fireplace, and put several more logs on the fire. He then walked to the window and looked out. To his surprise, the snow was still falling.

"Huh," he exclaimed, "there must be over a foot out there already."

He hurriedly threw on his jacket and went outside. Trudging through the freshly fallen snow, with much difficulty, he made his way to the church, where the brothers and sisters, and several parishioners were patiently waiting.

"Sorry for being late," he exclaimed, as he entered. "I am surprised to see so many people here, what with this storm and all. I'll make it short today, so you all can get back home."

Outside the snow continued to fall. The winds were still blowing strongly from the north, causing the snow to drift. These blizzard conditions continued throughout the day. At the Staab home, Frank and Susan were beginning to wonder if Father Joseph would make it.

"Maybe we should put the body out in the shed, until it gets prepared for burial," suggested Frank.

"That's a good idea," agreed Susan.

As the other children watched, Frank and one of his sons, carried the body out into the snowstorm, gradually making their way to the storage shed, located a short distance from the house. Once inside, they placed the body on a small pile of loose hay. Mrs. Staab set the two candles down, on a nearby block of wood.

"I'll stay here for a while," she exclaimed, as she knelt down beside the body.

"Don't stay too long," suggested Frank. "It's too cold out here."

Frank and his son proceeded to return to the house. As they were about to enter, they noticed a horse-drawn wagon approaching. It was Anton Bender. On the back of the wagon was a pine-box coffin.

"Anton," greeted Frank, "I didn't expect to see you today."

"Father Joseph told me what happened, this morning. I would like to offer my condolences. I am sorry to hear of the tragedy."

"Thank-you Anton."

"I brought the coffin, as soon as I could," continued Anton, as he got down from the wagon. "Where do you want me to put it?"

"We just put the body in the storage shed. We might as well take it in there."

Frank and Anton carried the wooden box into the shed, set it near the body; and returned outside.

"Won't you come in and have a cup of coffee?"

"No, I don't think so. I really should get back home. I have to stop at Christof's on the way, and with this weather, I'd like to be back home as soon as possible. Thanks anyway."

"Thank-you Anton," replied Frank, as he watched his friend get back on the wagon.

As Mr. Bender was leaving, Frank noticed a man coming towards the house from the woods. As he got closer, Frank saw that it was Father Joseph.

"Joseph," hollered Frank, to his 15-year-old son, who was standing nearby, "go see if he needs any help."

Young Joe quickly ran over to Father Joseph.

"Are you alright, Father?"

"Yes, my son. I can still handle the elements."

"Can I help you?"

"No, that's alright. I'll make it."

The two of them slowly made their way to the log cabin.

"Father Joseph. Why did you come?" asked Frank.

"I knew that you needed help," replied Father Joseph, as he tried to warm himself up by the fire. "I didn't realize this 72-year-old body isn't what it used to be. When I started from the church, I thought the storm was just about over, so I decided to continue. And,
you know that when I start something, I always like to finish it.

Where's Johnnie?"

"We put him out in the shed. Susan is out there with him."

"Well, I better go out and get him prepared."

"Why don't you wait till you at least warm up?"

"I don't have time. I must get back to the church yet."

Father Joseph and Frank headed out to the shed. Father was carrying a small black bag, while Frank carried a suit. When they arrived, Father Joseph looked at Susan, and said:

"Hello, Mrs. Staab. I wish to offer my sympathy. The Lord works in mysterious ways. It was time for Johnnie to leave us and there is nothing we can do about it."

"Thank-you Father," sobbingly replied Mrs. Staab.

"Why don't you go back in the house, and warm up?" continued Father Joseph. "I'll take care of everything out here."

Mrs. Staab got up off her knees and was helped back into the house by her husband. Father Joseph proceeded to prepare the body for its final resting place. He walked over to the coffin and placed some loose straw in the bottom. He then took a white cloth and laid it on top of the straw. After this, he put the

black suit on Johnnie, and laid him in the coffin. He folded the boy's hands and placed a rosary in it. Within a short time, he had completed his task. He took out his small prayer book and began to quietly pray. After several minutes, he made the sign of the cross, arose, put the black prayer book back
in his pocket and went back to the house.

"As soon as the storm quits," he stated, as he entered, "bring the body back in the house. We shall have the funeral tomorrow if the weather allows it. I think it will quit any time now. I told Brother Joseph and Brother Anton to pass the word, so you may be receiving
company any time now. I shall send Brother Joseph over tomorrow morning, to bring the body over to the church."

Father Joseph now walked over to the doorway, opened it up slightly, and looked out. "There! It looks much better already," he stated.

He was right. The wind had stopped, and the heavy snows had slowed to a flurry. The sun was trying to peak through the clouds.

"I think I better return now. I shall see you in the morning."

It was still quite cold outside, but at least now the sun was shining, and the snow had ceased. It was a difficult trip back to the church, but he made it, without incident.

"Brother Cornelius," he noted, as he approached the barn,
"come with me."

Brother Cornelius, who had been busy removing the snow from in front of the barn, immediately set down his shovel and walked with Father Joseph over to the church.

"Prepare for the funeral Mass. We will be having it tomorrow morning. See if there are any flowers left and put them out. I am going to go over to see Mr. Bender and Mr. Boedigheimer before it gets too dark. Put a note for the sisters, telling them that there will be no services tonight."

Father Joseph returned to the barn, where he saddled his horse. Upon completion, he immediately, mounted and headed in the direction of Mr. Bender's farm.

When he arrived there, he noticed that Bruno and Christof were already there. He was greeted by young Frank Bender, who was standing out in front of the small one-room log house.

As he petted his dog, Frank stated: "Hello Father Joseph. My father, and Bruno, and Christof are already in the house waiting for you."

"Hello Frank," replied Father Joseph, as he got down from his horse, and tied it to the hitching post.

"Father," continued Frank, "before you go in, I would like to speak to you."

"Yes Frank, What is it?"

"I would like to ask you something. Could I get your blessing to be married? Mary Ann and I would like to be married next year."

"Frank, you know how I feel about marriage. I do not think it is a wise thing for anyone to do. Wouldn't you two rather spend the remainder of your lives sharing with the Lord?
I want so much for Mary to become a nun, and you, Frank, you would make an excellent priest."

"We have thought a lot about it, Father. I have talked with my mother and father, and they told me to do what I thought best. I have talked to Mary Ann's folks, and they say it's alright."

"But my son, you must remember that the end is near. What good is it if you got married and then something happens? Are you going to be able to save yourself? I have a feeling something very tragic is going to happen if you do marry."

Father Joseph stopped the conversation right there and proceeded into the house, where Bruno, Anton, and Christof were seated around a table.

Mrs. Bender, who was busy pouring coffee, stated: "Come in Father Joseph."

"Hello everyone," he greeted, as he entered, took off his hat, and sat down.

The three men returned the greeting.

"Well, did you hear what that Tomazin did now?" Father Joseph asked.

"No. What?" queried Bruno.

"He went to the Bishop and got permission to build a new church in Perham. Can you imagine that?"

"That won't affect us anyway," interrupted Anton.

"Yes, it will," continued Father Joseph. "How am I going to be able to get those people from around Perham to keep coming here for services?"

"We don't need them," argued Christof.

"We'll leave them alone, and hopefully, they'll leave us alone," added Bruno.

"It's something to keep in mind," continued Father Joseph.

"I'm afraid that Tomazin will be able to influence some of those families. So much for that! I needed to talk to you for several other reasons. I wanted to get your approval on the sale of some of our grain. We got more than we need, so we could just as well have the extra money. I wanted to take a few loads over to Craigies tomorrow, or the next day."

"It's alright with me," replied Anton.

"Me too," added Bruno.

"I have no objection," answered Christof.

"I also have something to tell you, Anton. I was just talking to Frank, and he tells me he wants to get married. Is that alright with you?"

"Yes Father. We talked about it."

"You know how I feel about that."

"Yes Father, I do," replied Anton, "but it is really up to him to decide what he wants to do. He is old enough to make up his own mind."

"Well, I'm definitely against it. I warn you now, something tragic will happen."

"Tomorrow morning, we will have the funeral for Johnnie," continued Father Joseph. "Anton, were you able to get that grave dug?"

"I sent Frank and several other boys over to do it. They had a few problems, but they were able to get it done."

As he rubbed his right knee, he continued: "I've been having trouble with this knee. Ever since that cow kicked me, it has been very sore."

"Let me see," requested Father Joseph, as he knelt down beside Anton, rolled up the pant leg and looked at the sore spot. He put both hands on it and said a short prayer, after which he got up, and said:

"There. Tomorrow it'll be better."

Life At Rush Lake
1874-1878

CHAPTER XXXI

A year later, on November 17, 1874, Frank Bender was married to Mary Ann Foltz. Father Joseph performed the marriage ceremony, even though he objected. During the ceremony, he took a break, and walked over to the podium and said:

"In the Acts of the Apostles, Joel, the prophet, stated: 'It shall come to pass in the last days, says God, that I will pour out a portion of my spirit on all mankind. Your sons and daughters shall prophesy, your young men shall see visions and your old men shall dream dreams. I will work wonders in the heavens above and signs on Earth below, blood, fire, and a cloud of smoke. The sun shall be turned to darkness and the moon to blood, before the coming of that great and glorious day of the Lord. Then shall everyone be saved who calls on the name of the Lord."

Father Joseph turned and looked at the bride and groom, and stated:

"Heed these words!"

The rest of the wedding went without incident, and the new married couple took up a homestead on a farm, given to them by Mr. Bender. All seemed to be going well.

TUESDAY, JUNE 15, 1875 —

The skies were clear as the sun began its slow journey across on this crisp morning. As Father Joseph awoke, he slowly got out of his bed, and prepared himself for Holy Mass. After straightening out his clothes, which he had worn to bed, he knelt down beside his bed and silently said a short prayer. After making the sign of the cross, he arose and headed for the doorway.

Once outside, he was greeted by Brother Joseph.

"Good morning," he quietly stated, as he patted Brother Joseph on the back.

"Good morning, Father."

"I understand there is going to be a baseball game in Perham today."

"Yes Father. The boys from Fergus Falls should be on their way. We were hoping to get your permission to go."

"Is the hay ready?"

"It can wait a few more days. Besides, that heavy hail we had last Monday, and the rain yesterday, really did some damage."

"Are any of the boys playing?"

"Not from our team, but Henry Kemper will be there."

"When is it?"

"This afternoon, around one o'clock."

Father Joseph stood and thought for several seconds, as he rubbed his chin. "I suppose the boys can go. I'm going to see how our poor friends are doing over at Pine Lake, then I'll meet you in Perham."

"Do you want one of us to go with you?"

"No, I think it'll be better if I went alone. Since that accident last week, they've been quite scared. Gustav was telling me that they're all dressed up in warpaint and just waiting for the Leech Lake Indians to attack."

"Do you think they will?"

"I'm not sure. That Mushshquette was very popular up there. It's hard telling what they'll do."

"What can you do about it?" inquired Brother Joseph, as he scratched his left arm.

"I don't know," bluntly answered Father Joseph. "Perhaps nothing."

The two men now began walking towards the church. As they approached the front entrance, they were greeted by several families, including the Boedigheimers, Benders, and Silbernagels.

"Good morning, my dear people," exclaimed Father Joseph, as he smiled and acknowledged their presence.

"Anton," he continued, as he turned directly toward Mr. Bender, "how are Frank and Mary doing?"

"As well as can be expected," replied Anton. "They are very excited about having a child. From what they can figure out she should have her baby sometime in October."

"Oh my!" exclaimed Father Joseph. "That's too soon! I'm so afraid for them. Something is going to happen. Be prepared Anton. Something is going to happen."

Anton looked at Father Joseph in amazement. Saying not a word, he turned, and entered the church while Father Joseph remained by the door and greeted the other parishioners as they entered.

A few hours later, Father Joseph was walking northward, along the river. He could hear the sound of voices ahead of him. It was the sound of lumberjacks, in the process of driving a large number of logs down the river.

As he approached the howling group, he recognized some of the men, and stood by the bank and waved to them, as they slowly made their way southward.

After watching for several minutes, he turned and continued on his journey. Soon he arrived at the Chippewa settlement, located on the shores of Big Pine Lake. The men and boys were all adorned with various colors of warpaint. As Father Joseph approached them, they encircled him, keeping a close watch on him, yet saying nothing. The women and children remained in the background.

Soon, the elderly chief came out of his teepee and walked directly up to Father Joseph.

"Greetings, my dear friend," stated the chief, as he raised his right arm, in friendship.

"Greetings," replied Father Joseph. "I come here in peace. I would like to know if there is anything I can do for you."

"You have already done much for my people. Your wisdom and charity will always be remembered, but this time there is nothing you can do."

"What happened to Mushshquette?"

"We buried him over there," replied the chief, as he pointed towards a small wooded hill, to his left.

"Were his people here?"

"Yes, but they have already departed, but we are expecting them to return."

"Is that why you have the paint on?"

"Yes, my friend. We do not trust them."

"Can I go over and see the grave?"

"Of course."

Father Joseph made his way over to the plot. As he walked up to the grave, he noticed that the four poles used in the burial ceremony were still standing. He knelt down beside the grave and said a short prayer, after which he got up and silently departed the camp, waving good-bye to his friend.

A short time later he arrived in the small village of Perham. As he walked down the muddy street to the baseball field, he noticed several new houses going up. He waved at the men working on them, but they did not return the greeting.

Nevertheless, Father Joseph merrily continued on his way, soon arriving at the hayfield, which had just recently been made into a baseball diamond. He walked over to where his fellow Rush Lakers were sitting.

"Hello Father Joseph," stated Christof Silbernagel, who was sitting on the ground between Bruno, Victor, and Brother Joseph.

"Hello," joyfully replied Father Joseph, as he sat down amongst them. "Whew!" he continued, "that was some walk. My aching feet are continuously reminding me."

"You should use the horse and buggy," suggested Bruno.

"I'll be alright," insisted Father Joseph, as he rubbed his feet with his hands. "Is this game about ready?"

"According to this watch, they should be starting shortly," replied Bruno, as he looked at his pocket watch.

"Christof, how is your wife?" continued Father Joseph, as he looked over at Mr. Silbernagel.

"She is never one to complain, Father, but I know she is having difficulty."

"I'll have Sister Theresa come over and help her. She should be due soon, right?"

"Within a couple of weeks."

"Perhaps, I should have her stay there until the birth."

"Thank-you, Father."

Father Joseph now turned his attention to the men out in the field. He could easily pick out the Perham players. They were wearing new uniforms, consisting of blue knee-breeches with a white stripe, flesh-colored tight shirts, with white stockings, and a new

black cap. The opponents, the Musculars, from Fergus Falls, were wearing plain gray pants and shirts.

The Perham boys were now on the diamond, warming up, while the Musculars were sitting on the ground, on the other side of the field, waiting to bat. Mr. Sam Nichols, a highly respected individual from Fergus Falls, was standing behind the plate.

"Are you ready gentlemen?" he shouted, as he glanced at each of the teams. "Play!"

The ballgame began.

"Where are the rest?" queried Father Joseph, as he looked directly at Brother Joseph.

"They're coming up with Mr. Bender. They had a few things to do yet, but they should be here soon."

Four - and one-half hours later, the game was completed. The final score was the Norwesters 64, the Musculars 48.

"That's a very interesting sport," remarked Father Joseph, as he got aboard Bruno's wagon. "However, we must make sure our people don't get overly enthused about it. It could easily get in the way of our work."

JUNE 28, 1875. The scene now turns to the Christof Silbernagel house. Sister Theresa is sitting beside the bed of Mary. Christof is by the kitchen table, having breakfast with the children, Christof, Cornelius, Matilda, and Lena. The baby, one-year old Joseph, is sitting next to Sister Theresa.

"Junior and I will be out cutting hay this morning, behind the barn," noted Christof, as he looked over at Sister Theresa. "If anything should happen, send one of the children out."

"Yes sir," replied Sister Theresa, as she turned her attention toward Mary, who has just beginning to awaken.

"Good morning," greeted Sister Theresa.

"Good morning. Oh my!" she exclaimed. "Why did you let me sleep so late?"

"You need all the rest you can get. Your family can manage for themselves for a few days."

"Won't you need help with the hay?" queried Mary, as she looked at Christof.

"Not today. Junior can help."

"Mr. Silbernagel," interrupted Sister Theresa, "don't you think it would be a good idea if we sent for the doctor?"

"We don't need no doctor. Besides, you know more about delivering babies than most of them doctors. I'll have Cornelius run over to the church and get Father Joseph. He is the only person we need."

"Very well," continued Sister Theresa, as she turned toward young Joseph, who was pulling on her habit.

"No Joseph, don't do that."

"I think he wants to show you something," suggested 5-year-old Matilda.

"What do you want, Joseph?" asked Sister Theresa, as she got up. Young Joseph immediately began to cry.

"Junior. Go change his diaper," demanded Christof, as he got up from the table and walked over to the nearby coat rack.

While putting on his cap, he continued: "Then, come out and help me hitch up the team."

Young Christof did as he was told. As Mr. Silbernagel and 6-year-old Cornelius were leaving the house, Matilda and Lena began clearing the table. Sister Theresa again sat down beside Mary.

"I think today is the day," Mary quietly stated, as she took Sister Theresa's hand. "The pains are starting to come."

"I have everything ready for you. I'll be right at your side." Mary smiled, as she took her other hand and grasped Sister

Theresa's hand. "Thank-you." It was not long, and Father Joseph arrived with Cornelius.

"How is everything?" he queried, as he walked up beside Mrs. Silbernagel.

"Fine," answered Mary.

"The pains are getting very close," noted Sister Theresa, as she took a damp cloth and wiped Mary's forehead. "Perhaps, Cornelius should go out and get his father."

Without saying a word, Cornelius turned and departed.

"Is there anything I can do?" queried Father Joseph.

"Pray," replied Mary, as she smiled and then, immediately began showing signs of anguish, as the contractions were becoming more unbearable.

"I'll wait outside," suggested Father Joseph, as he turned and headed toward the door.

Sister Theresa now arose and began preparations for the delivery.

Once outside, Father Joseph sat down near the entryway, with the children who had followed him out.

"Can you tell us a story?" queried Matilda.

"What kind?"

"Anything."

"Well, let's see," considered Father Joseph, as he rubbed his chin with his left hand.

Just then, Mr. Silbernagel and his two boys came running up to the house.

"Is Mary alright?"

"Sister Theresa is inside with her. There is nothing we can do but wait and pray."

As Christof began pacing back and forth in front of the door, Father Joseph turned back toward the children. "I think that instead of me telling you a story, we should all begin to pray the rosary."

Father Joseph pulled his rosary out from his pocket. As he began to pray, the loud cry of a baby was heard. Christof immediately stopped and looked at Father Joseph.

Father Joseph smiled back at Christof. A few minutes later, Sister Theresa came out the door. "Mary is fine, but I'm not sure about the baby."

"What do you mean?" queried Christof.

"I don't know," bluntly replied Sister Theresa. "I just don't know."

"Junior. Take the children down to the river," demanded Christof, as he headed toward the entryway.

The three adults now entered the house and walked over to Mary, and the new-born. They all looked at the baby, and then at Mary.

"Bring him down to the church tomorrow, and I'll baptize it," suggested Father Joseph.

"Perhaps, you should do it now," added Christof.

"No. I think it will be all right till tomorrow."

Christof now walked over to Mary and took her hand. "How are you feeling?"

"Very weak."

"Just rest now. Sister Theresa will take good care of you."

"I'm going back to the church," interrupted Father Joseph, as he grabbed his biretta, and placed it on his head. "Be there tomorrow, after Mass."

"Thank-you, Father," replied Christof, as he walked him to the door.

"Keep a close watch on that baby," continued Father Joseph, as he looked at Sister Theresa. "It doesn't seem to be breathing right."

"Yes, Father."

"Good-bye Father," noted Mary, as she waved.

"Good-bye, dear Mary."

The next morning came quickly. Father Joseph was on his way over to the church. As he was about to enter the side door, Mr. Silbernagel came riding up in his horse and carriage.

"Father! Father!" he shouted, as loud as he could. "My baby! My baby is dead!"

"There, there," noted Father Joseph, as he hugged Mr. Silbernagel, who had just gotten down from the wagon. "Everything will be alright. Perhaps, it was better this way. You can rest assured that he has entered the gates of Heaven and will be waiting for us."

"But Father," interrupted the crying Mr. Silbernagel. "That is easy for you to say, but it is difficult for us to understand."

"There is not much time left on this Earth for any of us," continued Father Joseph. "You must realize that our journey is soon to be over. This child is fortunate in that he does not have to travel that journey. He is already there. He'll never have to put up with the devil and all the evils in our society. Surely, you must see that."

"Yes, Father. I suppose you are right," noted Christof, as he wiped his eyes.

"Of course, I am."

On October 23, 1875, a daughter was born to Frank and Mary Ann Bender. She was baptized by Father Joseph and given the name of Mary Ann. On November 3, 1875, Bishop Rupert Seidenbusch, the first Bishop of the newly created St. Cloud diocese, came to Perham, to dedicate the small frame church of St. Henry's. Upon completion of the ceremony, on the 8th, he was driven by horse and wagon to the Rush Lake settlement, by Father J. H. Hilbert, the young priest who had just taken over at St. Joe, earlier that year.

As they approached the church grounds, Brother Joseph came out of the barn and greeted them.

"Hello," stated the Bishop. "Could you tell me where I can find Father Joseph Albrecht?"

"I'm sorry, but he's not here. Mrs. Staab had a baby this morning, and he went to see if she was alright."

"Oh!" exclaimed the Bishop. "That's too bad! I really wanted to talk to him. I was unable to see him several weeks ago when I was up here, so I thought I'd try this time. When he comes back, tell him that Bishop Seidenbusch was here to see him."

"Very well," replied Brother Joseph, as he stood and watched the Bishop, and his group, depart.

Once again, Father Joseph missed out on an encounter with a bishop. Only this time it had not been on purpose.

Bishop Rupert Seidenbusch, O.S.B.

On February 2, 1876, Father Joseph's dream about the Frank Bender family began to take form. Frank died that day, of consumption. Nine days later, the daughter, Mary Ann, likewise, died of consumption. At the funeral for the young child, Father Joseph took Mary Ann aside and talked to her.

"It is surely a sign from God," he stated.

"You must enter the convent. I believe you were meant to be a nun."

She consented, and from that day on, spent the rest of her time in the religious life. After the funeral, Father Joseph took a trip over to the farm of some newcomers, who had just recently taken over the John De Winter farm. It was located several miles northwest of the church, so, it did not take long for him to get there. Valentine Guck was standing in his front yard, when Father Joseph arrived.

"Hello Mr. Guck. I thought I'd come over and see how you are doing."

"Nice to see you, Father Joseph," replied Valentine. "Come in. I'll have Catharine make us some coffee."

Father Joseph got down from the wagon and handed a small package to Valentine. "Here is a little something that I thought might be of some use for you two."

"Well, thank-you."

"It's a small ham, but it should be big enough to provide you with a couple of meals."

"Catharine," shouted Valentine, as they entered the house.

"We have company. It's Father Joseph."

"Come in Father," exclaimed Catharine, as she put down a bowl, she was using for making bread.

"Here," continued Valentine, as he handed her the ham,

"Father brought this over for us."

"Thank-you," replied Catharine, as she took the package.

"I also brought over some wheat seed. All I ask is that you repay me this fall, with the same amount."

"Well, that would be fine," noted Valentine. "That is very generous."

"I haven't seen you come to my church," continued Father Joseph.

"Is there a special reason?"

"Our friends go to St. Henry's," replied Valentine.

"Well, you are more than welcome to come over to 'Our Lady of Miracles.'"

"We might do that some time." This was just another example of Father Joseph's good will towards his fellow man. Life at the convent in 1876 through 1878 was quite routine. Several of the sisters had decided to return to Ohio, having concluded that Father Joseph had done wrong. Sister Seraphim Hummel died at the age of 50, on April 28, 1876, and Sister Maria Theresa Doll, a daughter of Anton and Maria Doll, passed away of consumption on March 28, 1877.

On July 25, 1878, Father Joseph, now really beginning to show his age of 77, was visiting several of his parishioners. He rode into the yard of Christof Silbernagel.

"Hello Father," stated Christof, "I'm glad you could come. That sore on Matilda's forehead is still very bad."

"Let me take a look," requested Father Joseph, as the two men walked into the house.

After sitting down in a chair, beside the kitchen table, he closely examined the forehead of the 8-year-old girl.

"Huh," he exclaimed, "what have you been putting on it?"

"All of the remedies that I possibly could think of," replied Mrs. Silbernagel, who was standing beside him. "I'm sure that if you prayed for her, the sore would go away."

Father Joseph took out his prayer book, opened it, and began to quietly say a long prayer, after which he took some holy water out of a small jar that he had been carrying in his pocket, and blessed the child.

"I shall say a special prayer for her, for nine days in a row," stated Father Joseph. "By then, the sore should be healed."

"Thank-you Father," noted Mrs. Silbernagel, as her husband and Father Joseph went to the door. Upon his return to the church grounds, Father Joseph was met by 22-year-old Mary Ann Foltz, the widow of Frank Bender. "Father Joseph," she screamed, "my sister, Catharine, just came over and told me that our mother is very sick, and that I should go over and see her right away.

Would you like to come along?"

"Of course. Hop aboard."

"The Bishop was here again," continued Mary Ann. "He had confirmation over at St. Henry's a couple of days ago and was ready to return to St. Cloud. I told him where you were, but he said that he had to get back to Perham, to catch a train."

"Huh," dryly remarked Father Joseph.

"Did Catharine say what the problem was?"

"No," replied Mary Ann, as she began to cry, "only that when they got up this morning, she was having trouble breathing."

Father Joseph and Mary Ann quickly headed for the Charley Foltz farm.

Upon their arrival, they were met at the door by Charley.

"How is she?"

"Still the same. I don't know what to do." Father Joseph walked over to her bedside. "Mary Ann, can you hear me?"

Mrs. Foltz reached up for Father Joseph's hand, and softly said:

"Yes Father Joseph, I hear you. Please give me the Last Sacraments, Father. I don't think I have much time."

Father Joseph put Mary Ann's hand back down and walked over to Charley.

"She doesn't look very good. I better go out and get my bag. I'll be right back."

Several moments later, he returned with his bag. He walked over to Mary Ann and began to perform the Final Rites. As he was giving her a blessing, he noticed that she had passed away. With a saddened look, he walked over to Charley and the children, and said:

"I'm sorry."

Charley knelt down beside the bed and began to cry, while the children stood by, in utter disbelief.

Church Fire

CHAPTER XXXII

In May of 1879, activities at the church grounds were in a very high state. Spring planting was almost completed, and the gardens were taken care of. On the morning of May 12th, Father Joseph was seen walking with Brother Anton, in the church yard.

"I have my doubts about that Mr. Eek," noted Father Joseph.

"Many people have complained to me about the way he has been instructing."

"Yes," agreed Brother Anton,

"I don't think he has the right qualities to instruct us. Last week, in one of the classes, he was talking about how he was planning to go back to Ohio, someday, and

that he would have all kinds of money to do as he pleased."

"Young Gerhard has a lot to learn. He will find out in due time, that money isn't everything."

Just then, the men noticed smoke coming from the nunnery.

"Go sound the bells," shouted Father Joseph. "Get everyone over to the nunnery."

Brother Anton ran into the church and began ringing the bell, while Father Joseph went, as quickly as possible, to the sisters' house.

A huge billow of gray smoke was pouring out of one of the windows. As Father Joseph got near, several of the sisters, who had been nearby, were already coming with buckets of water. Soon, everyone was taking part in extinguishing the flames. After about 15 minutes, the fire had been put out and the smoke had cleared. Father Joseph and Sister Lucretia entered the small building, to inspect the damages. The firs had been contained to one corner, near the door, with very little destruction occurring.

"I wonder how this started," noted Father Joseph, as he checked over one of the destroyed beds.

"It looks like it started here," replied Sister Lucretia, as she pointed to a pile of half-burnt papers, lying on the floor.

"What would those papers have been doing there?" asked Father Joseph, as he rubbed his chin.

"I don't know," replied Sister Lucretia. "It almost looks like it was purposely set."

"Yes, it does, doesn't it? Well, have some of the sisters clean this mess up."

"Yes Father," replied Sister Lucretia, as the two departed. Father Joseph walked back to his room. As he was about to enter, he noticed Brother Joseph coming toward him. "Brother Joseph, would you come here?"

Brother Joseph followed Father Joseph into the house. "It looks like that fire was deliberately set," stated Father Joseph.

"Be on guard for any suspicious characters around the churchyard. Someone is not very happy here and we have to find out who it is, and why."

"Maybe it's someone from one of the neighboring parishes," suggested Brother Joseph.

"No, I don't think so. We surely would have noticed any strangers around."

Just then, there was a knock on the door.

"Come in," shouted Father Joseph.

The door opened, and in walked 13-year-old Charley Weis.

"Well Mr. Weis, what can I do for you?"

"Father, I need your help,"

pleaded Charley, as he walked over to where Father Joseph was seated.

"I've had this sore on my hand for about a month now. My mother and father have put various things on it, but it just won't heal."

Father Joseph grabbed Charley's hand and took a look at it. Placing his hands on it, he silently said a short prayer, after which he added:

"Charley, you can go home now. By the time you get there, it should be alright."

"Thank-you Father," replied Charley, as he left.

Brother Joseph, who was sitting nearby, watching the entire ordeal, looked at Father Joseph, and asked: "Do you really think it will be alright?"

"Of course. Don't you remember what happened to that sore on Matilda's forehead? After nine days it was cleared up. The same will happen here. God works wonders sometimes."

Brother Joseph sat there, in bewilderment. "Such faith!" he quietly exclaimed.

The next morning, as the sun was rising, the sisters and brothers were out on the convent grounds, beginning their daily chores. Father Joseph was busy doling out instructions for jobs that were to be done that day.

Just as he was about to finish, he looked over toward the barn.

"Fire!" he shouted. "The barn is on fire."

Everyone looked in amazement, and then, ran towards the barn, with water buckets in hand.

It only took a few minutes, and the barn was a raging furnace. "Try and pour some water on the church and the nunnery," shouted Father Joseph. "The wind could very well blow the fire onto them."

Soon, many of the parishioners began to arrive, intent on helping put out the fire. But the fight seemed to be futile. The fire soon spread across the driveway and began burning the wooden structures of the convent and the church.

Several people ran into the church, and convent, and brought out what they could, knowing that the chances of saving the buildings were very slim. Realizing the futility, the people moved back from the flames, knelt down and began to pray. Within several hours, all of the buildings were in ruin. The barn, which held all of the farm machinery, the wagons, and the buggies, was completely destroyed. The church, convent, and storage sheds were leveled to the ground. Once the last flame was put out, Father Joseph sat down under the shade of a tall oak tree. Along with him were Anton Bender, Bruno Boedigheimer, and Christof Silbernagel. Father Joseph, like the others, was dirty from head to foot. As he wiped the sweat off his forehead, he exclaimed: "What's the use!"

"We must rebuild immediately," insisted Anton.

"I suppose you are right, but it all seems so much in vain. Somebody does not want us to continue. It could be a sign from above."

"I'm sure that it is somebody from St. Henry or St. Joe," insisted Christof.

"We have no way of proving that," noted Bruno.

"We are really going to have to keep an eye out for any strangers or suspicious characters," continued Father Joseph. "We put out a fire yesterday in the convent, but we didn't find out who started that either."

"Father Joseph," stated Sister Lucretia, as she approached the men, "I saw a young man running into the bushes this morning, shortly before we noticed the fire."

"Could you tell who it was?"

"No, I was too far away, but he had a black coat and pants on, and I think he wore a beard."

"That doesn't tell us much," noted Anton. "Almost everyone around here wears black and has a beard."

"Well, make sure you tell that to Sheriff Bartelson, when' he comes," noted Father Joseph.

"It's getting too dark to do much of anything now," he continued. "We are going to have to find places for everyone to stay at, until we can get some kind of shelters put up. Do you men have any suggestions?"

"Well, Julia, Emma, and Aurelia can come back to my house," noted Bruno.

"Barbara can come home," added Christof.

"I can board a couple," noted Anton. "Maybe Sister Rustika and Anna."

"Sister Lucretia, how much room do you have in that house by the river?"

"Sister Afra, Sister Agamonti, and Sister Theresa can come," replied Sister Lucretia.

"Then, if Erana returns to the Riesterer's, and Mary Ann goes to her home, and Catharine to the Eiferts, all we need is a place for Anna Mohr."

"She can come to my place," spoke up Anton. "Good. The brothers and I can camp right here."

"That should take care of everyone then," noted Anton.

"Yes," replied Father Joseph. "Now go tell everyone that clean-up will start tomorrow morning. We have to see if we can salvage anything, and I would like to find out if we can find that money."

"You just reminded me of something," added Sister Lucretia. "A while back I was talking with Gerhard's mother, and I told her about the $6,000.00 that was hidden in the church. Maybe you should have a talk with her."

"You told her?" shouted back Father Joseph. "No one else was supposed to know about that."

"I'm sorry, Father," stated Sister Lucretia. "I didn't tell her were, though."

The next morning, shortly after Father Joseph and the Brothers awoke, the men of the parish began arriving, to initiate the task of clean-up. What a job it was! They, painstakingly, sifted through the ruble, in search of anything worth saving. As they continued this process, horses, and wagons were used to haul away the debris, not worth keeping.

"Look here, Father," shouted Charley Foltz, as he picked out one of the church bells. "Ouch!" he shouted, as he touched it. "It's still hot!"

"With the help of several other men, they were able to lift the bell out and carry it over to a clearing. Father Joseph knelt down on one knee, beside the bell, wiped off the side and noticed that part of the inscription had been melted away. "Her Sorrows penetrate the Hearts of all Men," he read. "Huh, the Blessed Virgin Mary has been melted away."

Father Joseph got up and walked back over to where the church had been. Several men, including Christof Silbernagel, Bruno Boedigheimer, and Joe Weis, continued looking through the debris.

'Have you found anything yet?" queried Father Joseph.

"No Father," replied Christof.

"It should be right in the area where you're standing."

"I'm beginning to think that Sister Lucretia is right," noted Christof.

"Then why is Mr. Eck helping?" asked Father Joseph, as he pointed over to Gerhard Eck, who was helping haul away the debris.

"I don't know Father, but I sure don't see any gold here."

"We probably will never know."

"Say Father," interrupted Joe Weis. "What did you do to my son's hand?"

"Why?"

"Well, when he came home, yesterday, it was completely healed."

Father Joseph did not say a word. He only smiled. Within several days, the job of clean-up was completed, and the construction of new buildings was underway. First to be started was the church. This building, located in the same spot, where the first log church had been, was to be much larger. The foundation was set, and the dimensions measured out to be 3O'x65'. To the rear of the building was to be located the sisters' refectory. Nearby, a new barn was being constructed, as well as several more storage sheds, a livery stable, and houses for the brothers and sisters. Needless to say, construction at Rush Lake was in a very busy state during the entire summer of 1879.By fall, activity on the convent grounds was back to normal. All of the sisters and students were back living on the grounds. The instructor, Gerhard Eck, remained for about a month after the fire,

and then he disappeared, never to be heard from again.

Father Joseph was quite pleased at the way things had progressed since the fire. Nevertheless, he did begin to spend more and more time on the grounds. He had come to the conclusion that even though it seemed that Mr. Eck had been the culprit in the church fire, there were still many enemies in the surrounding area. One day, Father Joseph was seen in his small house, sitting by the table, awaiting his dinner. Beside him was Brother Joseph.

"I received a message this morning," stated Father Joseph,

"that Father Schlachter was in Perham."

"What's he doing out here?"

"He has some relatives living nearby."

"Do you think he'll come out here?"

"I have a feeling that he will. I hope so. I always did like that man."

At that moment, young Catharine Fehrenbacher came into the room. She was carrying a plate of food. She set it in front of Father Joseph, and quietly left.

"Thank-you Catharine," stated Father Joseph, as he raised his right hand.

After returning from the room, Catharine heard a knock on the door. She walked over and opened it. Standing in the doorway was a tall man, dressed in the garb of a Precious Blood priest.

"Hello," he stated, in a strong voice. "Is Joseph in?"

"Yes, he is," shyly replied Catharine.

"My name is Father Schlachter," continued the priest. "What is a young girl like you doing here?"

"Whenever I get the chance, I like to come over and help the sisters. I consider it an honor to be useful to Father Joseph."

"Why?"

"He has been an inspiration to, not only me, but many of the people around here."

"Do you know the troubles that he is having?"

"Father Joseph leads an ideal Christian life," answered Catharine. "It is just that he is often misunderstood."

"I don't think you really know what is going on. I don't think you should ever come here again."

Catharine was very surprised at what she was told. She silently left the building and returned to the sisters' refectory, while Father Schlachter entered Father Joseph's room.

"Hello Godfrey," greeted Father Joseph, as he got up from the table. "Please, come in."

"Hello Joseph."

"Tell me, why do you honor me with your presence?"

"I came up to visit Jacob. I thought as long as I came this far, I should at least stop by and see you."

"As you can see, I have aged considerably since the last time we were together."

"Well, for 78, you don't look too bad."

"Come, sit down here," requested Father Joseph, as he pointed to a chair next to his.

As Father Schlachter sat down, Brother Joseph got up and silently left.

"Tell me Joseph," noted Father Schlachter, "have you been in contact with the Bishop?"

"No. I have no need to. Our community is doing fine."

"You mean that you haven't made peace with the Church yet?"

"I am at peace with the Church. My problem is the Bishop. I have really done nothing wrong. I am trying to lead a life just like Jesus wanted the apostles to lead. I try to set a good example for my people. My goal is to help them attain salvation. What is wrong with that?"

"I'm sure if you would bow to the wishes of the Bishop, you could get back into good standing with the Church."

"Ever since the fire, I have given it much thought. Maybe I did make a mistake or two over the years. Maybe I was wrong."

"I am taking the train to Minneapolis. Do you want me to stop and talk to Bishop Seidenbusch?"

Father Joseph thought for several seconds, and then replied:

"No Godfrey, I cannot. If I do, what will my people say? No, I cannot."

"You have always been a stubborn man," shot back Father Schlachter, as he got up from the chair. "I see that trait is still with you."

Father Schlachter grabbed his biretta and stormed out of the room, not saying another word. Father Joseph remained in his chair and stared. Soon, tears came to his eyes. He walked over to the window and watched Father Schlachter mount his horse and take off. "I just can't," he quietly said.

Tragedy was to continue to strike at Rush Lake, over the course of the next few years. On April 25, 1880, Father Joseph had just completed Mass, and was walking over to his house, from the church.

Walking alongside him was Sister Lucretia.

"I'm afraid for Sister Rustika," stated Father Joseph, in a very somber tone.

"I know," quietly replied Sister Lucretia. "She does not look very well."

"I only wish there was something I could do," continued Father Joseph, as he opened the door to his house, and followed Sister Lucretia in. "It just seems to be a hopeless case. I can't understand why God would do this to me. She is one of my best sisters, and here she is, lying on her death bed. It troubles me greatly to think that perhaps God is trying to tell me something."

"It is nothing that you did," assured Sister Lucretia. "This Minnesota weather could harm the purest of souls."

"We must continue to pray for her," interrupted Father Joseph.

"We can never give up hope. If we do, then we might as well all lay down, and die."

"Sister Theresa has been doing more than her share," continued Sister Lucretia. "She has spent many sleepless hours trying to comfort the poor sister."

"I realize that, and I'm sure she will be justly rewarded for her work, but I only wish there was something else that I could do." As Father Joseph sat down on a chair, near his table, he wiped his forehead with a dirty rag which he had just pulled out of his pocket. "I'm afraid this weather is getting to most of us. Perhaps we

should start thinking about moving to a more favorable climate."

"Is there such a place?"

"There must be. The winters here can be so miserably cold, and the summers so hot. I know that I'll never last here much longer."

Just then, there was a knock on the door.

"Come in," shouted Father Joseph. In walked Sister Theresa.

"Why sister, what are you doing here?" "There is no need for me to be with Sister Rustika. I think you should come with me right away and give her the Last Sacraments."

Father Joseph, hurriedly, arose and grabbed his small black book.

"Let's go," he shouted, as he headed towards the door. In a matter of seconds, the three were entering the small nunnery. Father Joseph walked up to the bedside of Sister Rustika.

The 28-year-old sister lay there, eyes open, and a smile on her face.

"Hello, Father Joseph," she weakly stated, as she attempted to sit up in bed.

"My dear Sister Rustika," stated Father Joseph, as he took her hand.

"Would you like to receive Holy Communion?"

"Oh yes," she pleaded, as she again began to cough.

Sister Theresa and Sister Lucretia approached the side of the bed and attempted to comfort her, but it did no good. The coughing persisted for several more minutes before she finally was able to lay back down.

Father Joseph opened up his black book, and quietly began to say a prayer, while the two sisters got down on their knees and made the sign of the cross. Sister Rustika looked at each of them, and finally looked upward, smiled, and closed her eyes forever.

Father Joseph proceeded to give her the Last Sacraments, pausing several times to wipe the tears from his eyes. On July 15,1880,15-year-old Frank Eifert, a son of Victor Eifert,

was killed in a logging accident. The scene now turns to the fall of 1880.

"Where's Christof?" queried Father Joseph, as he looked around at the group of men gathering in front of the church, this particular cool morning of August 22, 1880.

"He'll be a little late," replied Mr. Bender. "He had some trouble with one of his cows. He said he'd be over as soon as he could."

"I need him to go over to New York Mills," continued Father Joseph. "He is supposed to pick up the lumber that Mr. DeCurtains needs to finish the steeple."

"I can do that for you," suggested Victor Eifert, as he stepped forward.

"Thank-you Victor. Take a couple of men with you. Mr. Ott should have everything ready for you when you get there."

As Father Joseph and Victor walked towards a nearby horse and wagon, they were joined by Brother Joseph and Brother Anton.

"We'll go with you," offered Brother Joseph, as the two men boarded the rear end of the wagon.

"Mr. DeCurtains will be over this afternoon," continued Father Joseph, as he stood beside the wagon and watched Victor mount.

"He is just about done at St. Joe, so he'll be able to devote all his time here."

"We'll be back as soon as we can," noted Mr. Eifert, as he grabbed the reins, and began leaving.

Father Joseph waved as the wagon headed towards the river. He then turned and walked back to the other men.

"You can all go tend to your farms until this afternoon," stated Father Joseph.

"There's nothing to do until DeCurtains gets here."

As the men dispersed, Father Joseph walked over to the brother's quarters. Once inside, he approached the bed of 53-year-old Brother Michael Weber.

"How are you feeling today?" he queried, as he took a wet cloth and wiped Brother Michael's forehead.

"Not any better," weakly replied Brother Michael.

"You've been here three months. I thought this Minnesota weather would be good for you."

"I'm content, Father. I know I'm in good hands. You'll take care of me."

"Ah, Brother Michael. That is out of my hands. I can only pray for you every day. I pray that you will make the journey without pain. I pray that you are ready for heaven. You've been a good man, so I know you'll have no problems."

"That's all I need," slowly noted Brother Michael, as he reached out for Father Joseph's hand. "Could you give me Holy Communion one more time?"

"Why yes, of course," replied Father Joseph. "Let me go over and get my things, and I'll be right back."

Father Joseph put Brother Michael's hands back down in the praying position. He picked up a small rosary from the table, located next to the bed, and placed it in Brother Michael's hands.

"Use this until I return," suggested Father Joseph. He then turned and left the room, walking quickly to the church. He picked up the host from the tabernacle, grabbed his black prayer book and returned to Brother Michael.

When he entered, he immediately noticed that Brother Michael could not wait. There he lies on his bed, rosary in hand, eyes closed, and a smile on his face. Brother Michael had departed this world. Father Joseph stood there momentarily, as tears came to his eyes. He wiped them away and began to smile. He made the sign of the cross, as he got down on his knees, and quietly said a short prayer. Moments later, after again making the sign of the cross, he arose and continued to stare at the lifeless body of Brother Michael.

Just then, there was a knock at the door. Father Joseph turned and walked over to the entry. Opening the door, he saw two men, Brother Cornelius and Henry DeCurtains.

"Father Joseph," stated Brother Cornelius, "Here's Mr. DeCurtains."

"I thought you wouldn't be here till this afternoon," noted Father Joseph, as he walked outside.

"There was no need for me over at St. Joe, so I thought I'd get back over here and finish," answered the strong, well-built, middle-aged man. "Besides, I'd like to get back to Ohio before winter gets here."

"I don't blame you," added Father Joseph, as the three men began walking towards the front of the church.

"Some of my men are over at New York Mills, picking up the shingles right now. You are welcome to come in and have a bite to eat."

"You are doing a fine job," continued Father Joseph, as he stopped and looked up at the unfinished church steeple.

"Once the shingles are on, it should be done."

"I don't think it'll take more than a week," noted Mr. DeCurtains, as he scratched his beard, and looked upwards. "This has been one of my easier jobs."

"Brother Cornelius," noted Father Joseph, "would you go over to the garden and get Sister Lucretia and Sister Theresa? Have them come to my house right away. Brother Michael has just died."

"Really!" exclaimed Brother Cornelius, in disbelief. "Why, yes,

I'll go right away."

As Brother Cornelius turned and headed in the direction of the garden, Father Joseph, and Mr. DeCurtains entered Father Joseph's house.

"Please have a seat," offered Father Joseph, as he pointed to a chair next to the table. "I have to go back to the brother's quarters. I forgot to put some things away. It seems that I've been very forgetful lately."

"Thank-you Father," replied Henry, as he sat down in the chair and watched Father Joseph depart.

Outside, Father Joseph was met by Sister Lucretia, and Sister Theresa, and Brother Cornelius.

"Sister Lucretia, would you go in and make something to eat for Mr. DeCurtains?" queried Father Joseph.

"Brother Cornelius, go into Perham and get Mr. Schoeneberger. Tell him what happened. Sister Theresa, come with me."

Each person did their assigned task, without saying a word. Several days later, Brother Michael was buried in the cemetery on the hill.

It was not long, and the church steeple was completed. Mr. DeCurtains left for Ohio, and everything returned to normal at Rush Lake.

"Our Lady of Miracles" Church

Christmas Eve, 1882. The snow was gently falling on the small Rush Lake church as families were gathering for the celebration of Midnight Mass. In the poorly lit nunnery, Father Joseph was seated beside the bed of 27-year-old Julia Boedigheimer. Next to him was Sister Theresa, who was busy wiping Julia's forehead.

"I'm going to ask Bruno to take you home," stated Father Joseph.

"I have decided that you cannot become a sister. Your sickness has not improved since you caught that cold this summer. I believe it would be better if you were at home, rather than here."

After several coughs, Julia looked at Father Joseph, and pleaded:

"But Father Joseph, I've always wanted to become a Precious Blood sister."

"God has other plans for you, Julia," interrupted Father Joseph, as he got up and headed for the doorway.

"I must get over to the sacristy. Sister Theresa, prepare everything for her departure."

Julia had tears in her eyes. Between coughs, she attempted not to show her emotions, but the thought of leaving the nunnery upset her.

Sister Theresa got up and began putting several pieces of clothing together.

"I don't want to leave," begged Julia.

"This is my home. This is where I want to be."

"Hush, dear Julia," objected Sister Theresa.

"Father Joseph has made up his mind. He is our Superior, and whatever he decides, we must obey."

"Could you go get Emma?" queried Julia, as she again began to

cough.

"I'll tell her to stop over, after Mass," noted Sister Theresa.

"Now, you just lie here and try to get some sleep. I have to go over to the church. I hear them singing already."

After Sister Theresa left, Julia continued to lie in her bed, staring at the ceiling. She began to cry aloud, saying: "I don't want to go. I don't want to go."

Meanwhile, in the church, everyone was ready for Mass. Brother Joseph was sitting by the organ, leading the choir in playing, 'Silent Night.' Father Joseph was in the sacristy, making sure that everything was set. The small group of farmers were in a joyful mood, as Mass was begun. After Mass was completed, Father Joseph returned to the bedside of Julia. Along with him were Bruno and Mary Boedigheimer, and Emma Bliley.

"Come Julia, it is time to leave," noted Father Joseph. "Your parents are here, and they'll take care of you from now on." Bruno helped the dejected Julia out of the bed and put a heavy black coat around her.

Julia had difficulty holding the tears back. Emma walked up beside her.

"I'll come and see you whenever possible," stated Emma, as she took Julia's hand.

"You will always be in my prayers."

"Oh Emma," replied Julia, "please make them keep me here."

"Father Joseph thinks it's best for you to go home. You know that he is always right."

Julia began coughing as she gave a hug to Emma.

"Good-bye Julia," interrupted Father Joseph, as he helped lead her to the doorway. "I will stop over tomorrow afternoon."

"Here's your things," stated Emma, as she handed the items to her best friend. "God be with you."

"Good-bye Emma," continued Julia.

Bruno and Mary got aboard the wagon and the threesome departed.

"Good night, Father Joseph," stated Bruno, as he headed the wagon towards his home.

"Good night, my people," answered Father Joseph. Father Joseph and Emma continued to wave, as the wagon dis- appeared.

"It is only a matter of time," wryly noted Father Joseph. "She will not be with us much longer."

Emma just looked at Father Joseph. She then turned back towards the wagon and quietly began to sob.

On January 10, 1883, Julia died at the home of Bruno and Mary. One day Father Joseph was having a meeting with his trustees, Anton, Bruno, and Christof.

"My friends," he stated, "last night, I had a vision. I was directed to send two young men to Rome to be ordained to the priesthood by the Pope. I need $1000.00. How can we get the congregation to donate that much?"

"I'm sure if we go to each of them, we could raise that amount," noted Bruno.

"Who would we send?" asked Christof.

"I would like to send Brother Anton and Joseph Bender."

"Have you mentioned it to my son, yet?" asked Anton.

"No. I wanted to talk to you first. My time is soon to come to an end. My health is getting worse with each passing day. I'm not sure how much longer I will be here. One day, you will have to move from here. You will go to a place where there will be lots of long

timber and you will be able to build anything."

"Why do you say that?" asked Anton, in utter amazement. "Not one of us has even given the faintest thought about moving."

"Just mark my words, Anton. When I die, I will be buried on a little hill with a stream running by on the north side."

The three men were likewise surprised at these words. They thought to themselves, that the cemetery is located on a hill, but the stream is located to the east, not the north.

"We will go out and request donations from everyone, Father," noted Bruno.

"As soon as we get enough, we'll send the boys, just as you wish."

Within several days, the money was raised, and Anton and Joseph left on their long journey. From this time on, the health of Father Joseph began to really deteriorate. From the end of 1883, onward, he was confined to his makeshift bed. He would lie on this couch with his clothes on — even his big, worn boots, day, and night, with several parishioners taking turns serving him.

On the morning of February 11, 1884, while he was lying in his bed, Sister Lucretia, and young Catharine Fehrenbacher were cleaning the room.

"Sister Lucretia," he stated, "go get Sister Agamonti and bring her back here. I want you two to witness something for me."

"Yes Father," replied Sister Lucretia, as she departed the room, with Catharine.

Meanwhile, Father Joseph picked up a piece of paper and silently read it. Soon, Sister Lucretia and Sister Agamonti arrived.

"Please come here," stated Father Joseph, as he motioned for the two nuns to come by his bedside. "I have a codocil to my will, that I would like you to witness."

As the two nuns walked up to the side, he began reading: "I, Joseph M. Albrecht, of the county of Ottertail, and state of Minnesota, do make, publish, and declare this codocil to my last will and testament of Joseph M. Albrecht and I do hereby appoint the following named persons as trustees in execution of my last will and testament: Victor Eifert, Christopher Silbernagel, and Anthony Bender, who shall in all things faithfully execute all things to be done and performed in any said last will and testament. In witness whereof I have hereunto set my hand and seal this 11th day of February 1884."

After signing the document, he continued: "Signed and published and declared by the said testator to be a codocil to his last will and testament in the presence of us who have signed our names at his request and in the presence and of each other."

As Father Joseph set the paper down, he pointed toward the bottom of the sheet and said:

"Please sign your names here."

Sister Lucretia was the first to take the pen and sign her name. After which, Sister Agamonti Dietsche signed.

"Thank-you my dear sisters," stated Father Joseph, as he took
the piece of paper and folded it up.

"Now, I only have one more thing to do."

Death Of Father Joseph

CHAPTER XXXIII

The time on this Earth for Father Joseph was drawing close to an end, and he knew it. On the first of March 1884, he instructed Brother Joseph to have the three trustees come to his room. After they arrived and sat down, Father Joseph took several pieces of paper out from under the couch and showed them to Anton.

"I would like you gentlemen to read these papers. If I should die, I need you three to look after the welfare of the sisters. They really don't know what is going on here, and they will need your help. Also, I received a letter from Anton Doll. He said that they needed a paper from the local ordinary. I don't think we're going to be able to accomplish that task. We might as well bring the boys back home. I would like to have Father Ginther come and see me. He is supposed to be giving a mission nearby."

"Yes Father, we shall take care of everything," replied Anton, as he and the other two men got up and prepared to leave.

"I am counting on you," weakly noted Father Joseph, as he watched the men leave.

Outside the room, the three men paused to put on their coats and hats.

"I don't think he will be around much longer," noted Anton.

"We'll have to set up a schedule for us to keep an eye on him," suggested Christof. "I get the impression that he is beginning to be- come a little senile."

"Yes, I agree with you," added Victor. Just then, there was a knock at the door. Victor walked over and opened it. Standing by the entrance was Father Joseph Buh.

"What do you want?" asked Anton.

"My name is Father Buh. I would like to see Joseph."

"I'm sorry, but he is sleeping," noted Anton.

"How's he doing?"

"Fine," replied Christof. "He's just tired."

"I was hoping that he would want to see me."

"No, he has no need for you," shot back Anton.

"Very well," noted Father Buh, as he turned and left.

Father Joseph Buh

"We can't let any of those priests get to Father Joseph," bluntly stated Anton. "We must take care of him. Christof, you stay here now, and I'll come and relieve you in four hours. I'll have a talk with Bruno and Joe Riesterer and see if they will help."

During the day, the sisters would take care of the needs of Father Joseph. They would bring him food and water, even though he ate and drank very little. They would kneel beside his bed and pray the rosary, with Father Joseph quietly reciting along with them. At night, four men — Anton, Bruno, Christof, and Victor took turns standing guard duty, outside his door.

On the evening of March 2nd, just as Sister Lucretia and Sister Agamonti were leaving, Bruno Boedigheimer took up his post outside the room.

"Bruno," shouted Father Joseph. "Come in here!"

Bruno got up and walked over to Father Joseph.

"Tomorrow night, bring Charley and Joe with you. Bring a good team of horses. Father Ginther will be down at Clitherall. I want you to go get him and bring him up here. My time is near, and I want to talk to him."

"If that is what you want," replied Bruno.

"I remember the words in the Book of Job," continued Father Joseph, 'My spirit is broken, my lamp of life extinguished; my burial is at hand. I am indeed mocked, and, as their provocation mounts, my eyes grow dim. Grant me one to offer you a pledge on my behalf: who is there that will give surety for me? My lot is described as evil, and I am made a byword of the people! Their object lesson I have become. My eye has grown blind with anguish, and all my frame is shrunken to a shadow.'"

Father Joseph closed his eyes and went back to sleep. Bruno wiped Father Joseph's forehead with a towel and quietly walked back outside the door, and once again, sat down in his chair. The next day, Father Buh again arrived at Rush Lake. He got down from his carriage, and walked up to the door, and knocked. Sister Theresa opened the door.

"May I see Father Albrecht?"

"Wait a moment. I'll go get the Mother Superior." Sister Theresa closed the door and went into Father Joseph's room, where Sister Lucretia was busily caring for the sickly Father Joseph.

"Mother Superior," exclaimed Sister Theresa. "Father Buh is here again. He wants to talk to Father Joseph."

Sister Lucretia put down the towel and walked to the door. She opened it and looked at the visitor.

"You may come in," she stated,

"but we will have to be with you. He is a very sick man and must be watched at all times."

Father Buh entered. He set his biretta down on a nearby chair and walked directly to the side of Father Joseph, who was continually coughing. Father Buh knelt down beside Sister Agamonti and Sister Lydia, who were already in the room. He watched Father Joseph for several minutes, before he finally said: "Is there anything I can do for you?"

"No, everything is already set," weakly replied Father Joseph.

"I want you to know, that you have been in my prayers."

Father Joseph looked at Father Buh, and smiled, as he closed his eyes.

"Come Father," interrupted Sister Lucretia. "We must let him rest."

Father Buh arose and quietly departed the room. That evening, Bruno did exactly as he had been told. Charley Foltz, Joe Riesterer, and himself came to the church grounds. Without telling anyone else, Bruno sent Charley and Joe on their way, while he stood guard.

Several hours later, Anton arrived, with the intention of relieving Bruno.

"Ah Anton. You don't need to stay tonight. Charley will be coming very soon, so he can take my place."

"How has he been?"

"He seems very content. I've only had to go in a few times and help him. His coughing doesn't seem to be as bad."

"That's good. Has he had any visitors?"

"No. No one has been here."

"Very well," continued Anton, as he turned to depart. "Then, I guess I'll go back home."

"Have a good night sleep."

"Good night, Bruno."

Shortly after Anton departed, a horse-drawn wagon with Charley, Joe, and Father Ginther arrived. Bruno got up and walked out to meet them.

"Hello Father."

"Hello," replied Father Edward Ginther, a tall man of about 35 years of age. He had on a long Benedictine robe. He wore a full-length beard, which made him look much older than he really was.

"Come with me," commanded Bruno. "I'll take you to Father Joseph."

Father Ginther got down from the wagon, grabbed his small black bag and book, and followed Bruno into the house, where Father Joseph was asleep.

"You may leave now," stated Father Ginther, as he looked at Bruno.

Father Edward Ginther

Bruno turned around and went back outside, where Charley and Joe were still standing.

"You two might as well come into the entryway," stated Bruno.

"It's too cold out there to wait."

After the men got inside, Charley looked at Bruno, and asked:

"Do you think he is receiving the Last Sacraments?"

"I'm not sure. We probably will never know. All I know is that he really wanted to see Father Ginther. His health is worsening with each passing hour, so I don't think he will be around much longer. Perhaps, that is the way he also is thinking."

Time slowly went by that night. An hour passed, and then another. After three hours, the three men began to wonder what Father Ginther was up to.

"Christof will soon be here," stated Bruno, in an anxious tone, as he looked at his pocket watch. "I don't know what he'll do if he finds out Father Ginther came."

"I don't know why that should do any harm," replied Joe.

"You don't realize how he and Anton have been acting lately," continued Bruno.

Just then, Father Ginther came out. He was very tired, but he still had a big smile on his face. "He is quite a man," he stated,

"I shall always remember him."

"Is he alright?" asked Charley.

"Yes. He is in better shape now then he has been for many years."

"Is he awake?" queried Joe.

"No, he has gone back to sleep. Now, he can rest in peace."

The three men got back on the wagon and departed the grounds, just before the arrival of Christof. In the morning, at about six, several of the sisters arrived. It was Sister Lucretia, Sister Agamonti, and Sister Theresa. Young Catharine Fehrenbacher was also along with them. They entered the room, took up their places near Father Joseph, knelt down, and began to pray the rosary. Father Joseph was still sleeping, so Catharine stood in the background and waited for him to awake. After several minutes, Father Joseph awoke. He slowly looked around the room, pausing momentarily, to smile at each person.

Once he had done this, he looked upwards and said:

"Everything is alright." He closed his eyes and peacefully breathed his last.

Catharine, at seeing this, ran out of the room, in tears. "Mr. Silbernagel," she shouted, "Father Joseph has died."

"Oh my God!" exclaimed Christof, as he made the sign of the cross, and headed into the room. He walked up to the lifeless body, knelt down, and stared at the body. "Why?" he asked himself, as tears began to pour down his cheeks. The sisters were also now shedding tears. They continued to pray the rosary, but their minds seemed to be elsewhere. As Christof gazed over the serene, wrinkled face of his religious leader, he thought to himself:

"Now what are we going to do?"

Within minutes, more and more people came to see Father Joseph, but were stopped at the entryway, by Christof. "You cannot come in now," he would say. "I will see that the body is prepared and placed in the church, for viewing."

When Victor and Anton arrived, Christof told Brother Joseph to stand by the door, while the three men went inside to have a meeting. Once inside, the three went over by Father Joseph, and sat down.

"What are we going to do now?" asked Victor.

"Father Joseph wanted us to continue on," replied Anton.

"Yes, but how?"

"Brother Joseph can do the services."

"Brother Joseph?" objected Victor. "He's not a priest."

"That don't make no difference," answered Christof. "Father Joseph had been training him."

"What are we going to do about the body?" asked Anton.

"We're going to have to make a special coffin," suggested Christof. "We'll put it in a crypt in the church, under the side altar."

"Why a special coffin?" asked Victor.

"To preserve his body," quickly replied Anton. "To show to the non-believers that he was truly a saint."

"How are you going to do that?" continued Victor.

"Never mind," replied Anton. "Christof and I will take care of that. What I want you to do is to get several men and prepare a crypt in the church. Come, let's go over there and I'll show you."

The three men got up and headed over to the church. Once inside, they noticed several women, silently praying. They walked by them, over to the side altar of the Blessed Virgin Mary.

"Tear out part of this communion rail and erect a stone crypt here," pointed out Anton. "Make it so it is partially underground and build it up to about two feet above the floor. Build it so we will be able to walk alongside and view the body. Have it done within a
week."

"Very well. I'll get on it right away."

The three men now left the church. Christof and Anton headed for the Silbernagel farm, while Victor went to find several other men. As Anton and Christof were riding, they discussed their future plans.

"How are we going to preserve that body?" asked Anton.

"Well Anton, I'll have Martin Schoeneferger build an ordinary coffin, then line it with that lead sheeting that I have in my storage shed."

"What good will that do?"

"Then, we will fill the body with a preservative."

When the two men arrived at Christof's farm, they got off the wagon and went directly to the storage shed. Once inside, they immediately proceeded with their plan. They pulled out several sheets of lead material and carried them onto the wagon.

"There," stated Christof, "now we can go see Martin."

All that week, various parishioners would come in and pray for their fallen leader, who was placed in this long casket and set in front of the main altar of the church. While this constant adoration was being held, several men worked on the building of a stone crypt

near the side altar.

One morning, Father Buh, from the neighboring parish, entered the church. He walked up to the body, stood there, and began to weep. He glanced at the Holy Water sprinkler setting nearby but did not touch it. After several minutes, he turned and left. He glanced at the crypt, while leaving, but he made no comment. Christof and Anton, who were over by the crypt, had been watching the movements of the priest.

"Did you notice that?" queried Anton, as he looked at Christof.

"He didn't even bother blessing Father Joseph."

"Yes, I did."

On the next day, the funeral for Father Joseph was held. Brother Joseph was in charge of leading the services. He was preparing himself in the sacristy.

Many people from the surrounding parishes wanted to attend the services, but they were blocked at the entrance to the church, by several of Father Joseph's staunch followers.

The crowd that was allowed to enter, was a very somber group. All of them wore black. All of them wore very saddened faces, covered with tears. Father Joseph's casket lay in the middle aisle, near the main altar, on a catapult, with the feet of Father Joseph facing the entrance of the church. There were six candleholders set around the coffin, each containing a lit candle. The coffin was open for everyone to view. The extraordinarily emaciated and boney corpse was seen by all. It had dried up because of the cold northern air, but it was not decaying. Most of the people, having noticed this fact, were amazed, and seemed to have made their conviction much stronger that, surely, their former leader must have been a saint. White flowers were placed round the body. A rosary was in his

hands. The large cross, a symbol of his Precious Blood Society connection, lie on his chest. A new biretta had been placed upon his head. This picture of their leader was to remain in the minds of his followers for a long time to come. Brother Joseph began the solemn ceremony, as soon as the church bells stopped ringing. He was assisted in the services by Brother Cornelius. After genuflecting at the main altar, Brother Joseph went directly to the pulpit. The sisters were busily singing a hymn. Once they stopped, Brother Joseph began to speak.

"My fellow friends. It is truly a sad day for all of us. The man, whom we so loved and adored, has been taken from our midst. We have no choice but to let his soul leave us, but we must not let his ideals leave us. We must continue on the road to salvation, that he so, unselfishly, built for us. We must not let outsiders influence our thinking. We must continue our struggle. Surely, that is what he would want us to do. We have had pictures made of our beloved leader. Christof and Anton, who are in the back of the church, will

Father Joseph Albrecht

see to it that each family gets one. We want you to take this picture home with you. Place it on a small table between two candles. Keep flowers around it, and each day, pray to him, and never forget what he stands for. Pray that someday you too may join him in heaven."

After pausing for several seconds, Brother Joseph continued:

"Oh God, whose nature is always to have mercy and to spare, we humbly beseech you on behalf of the soul of your servant, Joseph, whom you have bidden this day to depart out of this world; that you would not deliver him into the hands of the enemy, nor forget him,
forever, but command him to be received by the holy angels, and taken to paradise, his home, that as he puts his faith and hope in you, he may not undergo the pains of hell, but possess everlasting joys. Through our Lord, Amen."

Brother Joseph now returned to the main altar. After genuflecting, he followed Brother Cornelius down to the bier. He then began to sing:

"Deliver me, Oh Lord, from everlasting death on that day of terror, when the heavens and the earth will be shaken. As you come to judge the worldly fire."

The choir responded: "I am in fear and trembling at the judgement and the wrath that is to come."

Outside the church, several men from the neighboring parishes were standing near their wagons.

"I can't believe they don't have a priest burying the old man," stated George Seifert.

"I suppose none of them could have done it anyway," replied Mike Schmitz.

Just then, Anton and Christof came out, and walked directly over to George and Mike.

"You guys get out of here," shouted Anton, as he pointed at the two men.

"You are trespassing, and we don't want you on our property."

"Who are you to tell us to leave?" asked George.

"We are the trustees," shouted back Anton. "Father Joseph willed this land to us."

George and Mike got back on their wagons and quietly left.

Meanwhile, Anton and Christof went back into the church, just in time to see the completion of the burial ceremony. The parishioners now had one final chance to file past the body and bless it, with the Holy Water sprinkler. After they did this, they
departed the church.

Once everyone was out of the church, several of the men: Anton, Bruno, Christof, Victor, Charley, and Joe took the coffin and slowly place it in the crypt. They then placed a large slab over the top and covered it with flowers.

"Rest in Peace, dear Father," stated Anton, as he placed his hands on the slab.

Preparations for Departure from Minnesota

CHAPTER XXXIV

After the funeral was completed, things seemed to have come to a standstill at the convent. The sisters continued to wait in seclusion, wondering what was going to happen to them. They did not know what to do. They had become restless, since no Holy Mass had been held at the church since the illness of Father Joseph had become too severe. Anton and Christof assured them that everything would be alright, but still, they had their doubts. At this time, there were three sisters who had taken the vow of fidelity at Himmelgarten, and 14 others, who had grown up at Rush Lake. This list included: Sister Lucretia Hog, Sister Afra Ruh, Sister Agamonti Engelberta Dietsche, Theresa Arnold, Barbara Foltz, Mary Ann Foltz, Emma Bliley, Anna Mohr, Aurelia Boedigheimer, Catharine Eifert, Anna Bender, Barbara Silbernagel, Matilda Silbernagel, Erana Riesterer, Martha Eifert, Elizabeth Eifert, and Sister Lydia Mahl, who had just returned from living at the home of Fridolin Zipfel, a close friend of Father Joseph's.

Sister Lucretia remained as the Mother Superior, living in her small one-room cabin, a short distance from the convent grounds, but now Mr. Bender seemed to be giving more and more of the orders.

One day as he was doling out instructions for the day, with Victor and Christof at his side, a visitor approached. He entered the church and walked directly up to Anton.

"Hello, I'm the Vicar-General of St. Cloud diocese," stated the priest. "I presume you are Mr. Bender?"

"Yes," replied Anton, "just a minute."

"Alright," he continued, "everyone else leave."

After the sisters and brothers had all departed, Mr. Bender turned his attention to the priest. "What can I do for you?"

"I have been instructed by Bishop Seidenbusch to take charge of the convent and get the position of these women rectified with the Holy Mother Church," replied the Vicar General. "We realize that they are not guilty of anything, so we would like to arrange a Mass to be said for them."

"Nonsense," replied Anton, "They have no need for you. We are taking care of them."

"Can I at least talk to them?"

"No, you must leave immediately," shouted Anton, as he pointed to the door.

"When will this ever end?" exclaimed Anton, in an angry tone, after the priest had left. "We are going to have to do something. We are continually being harrassed by these people."

"I read something the other day," noted Victor, "about Oregon. The article described a beautiful land of rich fertile soil, tall pine trees, clean clear rivers, and cheap land."

"Is that right?" asked Anton, in wonder. "Oregon. That's a long way from here."

"Yes, but the railroad is supposed to be completed sometime this summer."

"You mean we could get on the train and ride all the way out there?" queried Christof.

"Yes, that is quite possible," replied Victor.

"That is something we'll have to consider," noted Anton.

"Yes," continued Christof, "with that, and that county man coming and telling us that we have to place the remains of Father Joseph in the cemetery, I think it is time we seriously consider leaving."

After contemplating for several seconds, Anton continued: "Victor, would you like to go out there and see what you can find out?"

"When?"

"Right away. We could send you and your son John, and my son John."

"What about the spring planting?"

"We probably could wait till you got back. If it takes too long, we can always put your crop in."

"Very well," answered Victor, as he got up. "I'll start making the necessary preparations immediately."

Soon, everything for the trip was set. Victor and John Eifert, and John Bender were given a ride to Perham, where they boarded a train, heading west.

They slowly made their way towards Oregon. They went by train as far as it would take them, and then switched to stagecoach.

Upon arrival in Portland, they sought out the advice of Archbishop Seghers, at the Chancery Office. However, since the Archbishop was absent, Victor met with the Vicar-General, Father Blanchet.

"Please come in," requested Father Blanchet. As the three men entered, Victor said: "Hello Father. My name is Victor Eifert, and this is my son, John, and a friend, John Bender. We have just arrived here from Minnesota, having been sent out here on a scouting expedition."

"What would you like to find out?" queried Father Blanchet.

"We need to know if there is any good farmland available."

"There are many areas, that are still open. Perhaps, I should have you talk to Father Fierens, down the hall."

Father Blanchet got up from his chair and headed towards the door. "Come! Follow me! I'll take you to him."

He went out the door and down the long hallway, followed closely behind by the three men. At the end, they entered another large room, where seated behind a desk was a heavy-set priest.

"Father Fierens, I have some gentlemen here that would like to talk to you."

"Please be seated," offered Father Fierens, as he sat back and lit a cigar. "What can I do for you?"

Father Fierens

"Hello Father," began Victor, as he sat down beside the desk.

"As I was telling Father Blanchet, we represent a large group of people from Minnesota: several families of very good Catholic German farmers, plus a convent of nuns."

"A convent? What order?"

"Precious Blood. Their superior, Father Joseph Albrecht, died recently, and now the new leaders want to transfer the entire group out here."

"Who is their leader now?"

"Anton Bender."

"It sounds like an excellent idea. We have ample room out here and there are acres and acres of good farmland and the sisters would have plenty of work to do. We could definitely use the help out here. Yes, I think that would be nice. I know of some land down by the Jordan Valley. Perhaps, Father Blanchet could take you over there and you could see the place for yourselves."

"Excellent!" replied Victor, as he got up from the chair. "When could we expect to leave?"

"Let's see," continued Father Fierens. "Father Blanchet," he shouted, "could you come here?"

"Yes Father?" asked Father Blanchet, as he entered the room.

"Could you take these men down to the Jordan Valley, and show them some of the lands that are available?"

"Of course."

"How soon?"

"Right away, if they wish," answered Father Blanchet, as he looked at the three men.

"Good," stated Victor, "we are ready."

"Let me go down and get the wagon hitched up. I'll be ready in about 15 minutes."

"We'll meet you in front," stated Victor, as the four men began walking out of the room.

After shaking hands with Father Fierens, the four men went downstairs, and out into the street. While Father Blanchet was getting the wagon ready, the other three sat down on the front steps.

"Do you have that map of Oregon?" queried Victor, as he looked at John Bender.

"Yes, right here," replied John, as he reached into his pocket, and pulled out a large piece of paper.

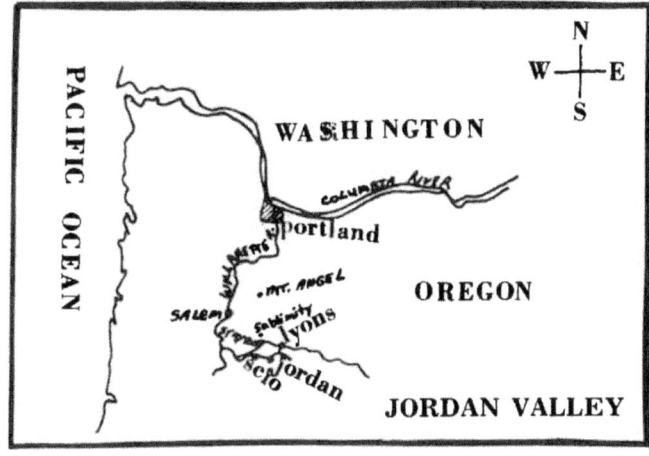

Victor took it from John and opened it up. He looked at it for several seconds, and then said: "That Jordan Valley is quite a distance from here. According to the map, it must be about 50 or 60 miles away."

As Victor began folding the map up again, he turned to his son, John, and said: "You better run back to the hotel and get our belongings. If we do find something down there, we'll have to send someone back to Minnesota from there."

"Yes father," obediently replied John, as he left.

Several minutes later, Father Blanchet appeared in front of the chancery office, aboard a horse-drawn carriage.

"Father," shouted Victor, "how long is this trip going to take?"

"Only a day or so."

"I sent my son back to the hotel, to get our things. He should be back shortly."

Father Blanchet got down from the carriage and walked over to the two men.

"Tell me, Father," continued Victor, "what is the possibility of having a priest down there?"

"There is a Benedictine monastery, not too far from there. I'm sure you could obtain the services of one of them."

As John Eifert returned, carrying several pieces of baggage, Victor looked at him and said: "Put them in the back, John."

Father Blanchet and Victor got in the front seat and the two others climbed aboard on the back. Meanwhile, back at Rush Lake, things were getting worse. Anton Bender was now spending all of his time down by the convent grounds, running the affairs of the church. It was he who would hand out the work assignments for the brothers and the sisters. It was he who would settle any arguments that arose. It was he who took care of the finances of the parish. On the morning of June 18th, as Mr. Bender arrived on the

church grounds, Sister Theresa Arnold came running up to him.

"What is it, Sister Theresa?"

"It's Sister Agamonti. She is really sick!"

"What's the matter?"

"She is all swollen up. She is having a very difficult time breathing."

The two hurriedly went into the convent, where Sister Agamonti was lying. They walked directly over to her. What a sight they saw!

The 40-year-old sister was in a very bad condition. Her face was swollen to twice its normal size. She was covered with a blanket from the neck down, but one could still notice that the swelling covered her whole body.

Anton and Sister Theresa approached her bedside. Sister Agamonti turned toward them. As she raised her right hand toward Anton, she said, in a very weak voice: "A priest. Please get me a priest."

"Nonsense, my dear Sister," replied Anton. "You don't need a priest. If you led a good life, like Father Joseph, you can rest assured that you will go to heaven."

Sister Agamonti could not believe her ears. She grabbed Anton's hand, and once again, begged, as tears came to her eyes. "Oh please!" After one final plea, she looked upwards, and died. Anton placed her hands on the rosary, which was lying on the bed. He closed her eyes, and quietly walked back outside, with Sister Theresa following.

"Now, she can join Father Joseph," stated Anton. "Ring the church bells forty times, and then go tell Sister Lucretia."

"Why did you object to getting a priest for her?" inquired Sister Theresa.

"Never mind. Just do as you were told."

As Sister Theresa walked toward the church entrance, Victor Eifert came riding up on a horse. As he dismounted, Anton came running over to him. "Victor," he shouted, "we have been patiently waiting to hear from you. Why didn't you write? What did you find

out?"

With the church bells ringing, in the background, Victor replied:

"We found an excellent spot."

"Where?" excitedly asked Anton.

"A place called the Jordan Valley. It's south of Portland. It has a delightful climate, beautiful flowers, lots of trees, rich soil. It's a real garden of Eden. There's enough room out there for all of us. I bought some land, and have notified the owners that there would

probably be many more coming. I left the boys out there."

"Good. I'll get everybody together, and we'll make plans, as soon as possible."

"Tell me, Anton," continued Victor, "what are the bells ringing for?"

"Sister Agamonti Dietsche died. I'll have to go talk with Brother Joseph, and set up a funeral."

The next day there was a special meeting held in the church. Those present were Anton, Bruno, Charley, Christof, Joe, and Brothers Joseph and Cornelius.

"As I'm sure you have heard by now," stated Anton, "Victor has found a new home for us, in Oregon. We must make plans to leave as soon as we can. Bruno and Christof, I need you to go to Perham and charter three railroad cars, one for us, one for the animals, and

one for our belongings. Get it for the end of July. By then, we should have everything else taken care of. I will hold an auction at my farm. Any of you are more than welcome to bring any of your machinery or personal belongings that you won't want to take with

you. As far as the sale of your farms goes, you probably will have to settle for what you can get, sell, rent, or whatever. Do what you have to as far as this year's crops go. We still have a bit of grain here at the convent, so we'll try and take that with us."

"Have you told Sister Lucretia?" queried Charley.

"No, not yet. But, I'm sure she will have no objections."

"What is the real purpose for our leaving?" asked Mr. Riesterer.

"Joseph, you know as well as I, that we cannot continue to be harrassed the way we have been. Just as Father Joseph led us out of Ohio to start a new beginning, so I shall lead you out of Minnesota to start a new beginning. We shall escape this religious persecution

and settle in a new land, a place where we can once again lead a true Christian life, without interference from outsiders."

"Do you really think that is possible?" objected Mr. Riesterer.

"If you do not want to come along, you can stay here,"

answered Anton. "After the funeral this afternoon, I'll be heading for Perham. If any of you would like to come along, just meet me outside the church, then."

The men arose from their seats, and departed, each heading for their prospective homes, to begin preparations for departure.

Trip To Oregon

CHAPTER XXXV

The next month was busily spent in preparation for the long journey to Oregon. All of the big farm machinery was put up for auction. The crops of the individual farmers, which were in storage, were sold, as well as most of the livestock. Each farmer kept only a few animals for shipment to the new destination. Some of the farmers sold their farms, while others rented them out.

On the evening of July 25th, Anton, Christof, and Victor met at the church.

"Did you bring the shovels?" asked Anton, as he looked at Christof.

"Yes," replied Christof, as he took out two spades from the back of his wagon.

"Remember, we must work quietly and fast,"

continued Anton, as the three men began walking toward the sisters' refectory, which joined directly to the rear wall of the church sanctuary.

The three men, upon entering, proceeded to remove the blocks from the inside wall. Once they had a hole of about three feet by three feet opened; Christof began burrowing a tunnel towards the resting place of Father Joseph. The dirt was piled up in the refectory.

The men took turns, shoveling, moving the dirt, and standing watch. Soon, they reached the coffin. Anton tied a rope around the box and brought the rope back to the refectory, where the three men pulled on it, until the coffin reached them. Once the coffin was inside, the men quickly filled the cavity with the dirt and replaced the blocks. As they were doing this, Anton said: "Victor, take that wreath of lilies and roses, that I have on the back of my wagon, and place them on the slab in the church. That way nobody will notice the body missing."

While Victor was outside, Christof looked over at Anton, and asked: "Did you get up to the cemetery last night, and get your father?"

"Yes," replied Anton, as he began to open the coffin. "He's over at my farm. We'll take Father Joseph over there too, and then leave for town, from there."

After lifting the lid up, both Anton and Christof were suprised at what they saw. The tall lean body of Father Joseph looked much like it had on the day of his death. There was a thin layer of mildew covering the serene face the black cassock, in which he was clothed.

The right ear was gone, but other than that, the body seemed incorrupt. The shriveled skin was yellowed, yet it did not look bad for having been kept in the damp earth for over four months. The two men took the body out of the coffin and laid it on the table. Christof went outside and got a pail of water. While he was gone, Anton took off the biretta, chasuble, and cassock, and threw them into a nearby wooden box. Christof came back in, with the water, grabbed a towel off the table and proceeded to wash down the body. As he was doing this, Victor returned, and after taking one look at the incorrupt body, quietly stated: "Surely, this man must have been a saint!"

Anton disappeared for several seconds. When he returned, he was carrying a fresh cassock and chasuble. When Christof completed his task, Anton began dressing the body.

"You guys, go out and get the new coffin," ordered Anton. "It's in my wagon."

While they were gone, Anton continued to dress up the body. When Victor and Christof returned, they placed Father Joseph into the new coffin. Anton placed the biretta on the head, and straightened the cross, which was lying on his chest. As he closed

the coffin, he stated: "There. Let's get out of here, before anyone notices us. Make sure we get all the tools."

After quickly checking over the room, and picking up the tools as they went, the three left the refectory, and headed for Mr. Bender's home.

Meanwhile, in Perham, Bruno and Charley were in charge of loading the train. They had brought their personal belongings and livestock in and began transferring them onto the three cars that were on a side track. In the front car was placed all of the personal items.

In the second, the furniture and farm machinery, and grains. In the third, they placed the cattle and other farm animals. The group of men, besides the train crew, included: Chris Silbernagel Jr. (age 18), Cornelius Silbernagel (age 15), Bruno Boedigheimer (age 17), John Boedigheimer (age 15), George Bender (age 28), and Anton Bender Jr. (age 13).

As they were finishing up with the Boedigheimer wagon, Anton and Christof arrived with their wagons.

"Chris," shouted Christof, as he looked at his son. "You and George take those nosey men over there and go buy them some drinks over at Schroeders. We don't need them snooping around here."

Young Chris looked over in the direction of the small crowd that had gathered near the tracks. He then looked back at his dad, who was still on the wagon, and said:

"Yes father."

He then walked over to George and said: "Come on. Let's go."

The two men went over to the group of onlookers. When they got near, Chris asked: "How would you men like to have some free beer?"

Since it was a very warm evening, the group decided to follow Chris and George over to the bar. With the onlookers, and the train crew gone, Christof got down from his wagon and walked back to Anton.

"Let's hurry up and get these boxes to the front of the car," exclaimed Anton.

Together, Christof and Anton lifted the two coffins, which now were in larger containers, onto the train. As Anton slid the boxes to the front, Christof went back to the wagon and began transferring large sacks of wheat to the car. After Anton had the large boxes in

place, he began piling the sacks over them. Once this was completed, they finished loading the boxcar with small items of furniture.

"Tomorrow morning," stated Anton, "I'll need you to stop at the church, and help bring the girls in, Christof. Riesterer is going to help. We should be down there by six, so we have enough time to get back here."

"How many people are going?" queried Christof.

"About 50 or so. I've jotted down a list of the people, here," he continued, as he reached into his pocket and pulled out a piece of paper.

"9 Silbernagels, 11 Boedigheimers, 8 Benders, 8 Eiferts, 11 Foltz's, and 7 other sisters. I come up with 54."

"Can that car accommodate that many people?"

"We'll just have to make the best of it."

As the two men walked back towards the middle car, Anton hollered:

"George, we need to keep watch over these cars tonight. You and Chris can do that, can't you? All you have to do is take turns.

We should be back by 6 in the morning."

The next morning, all went well. By sunrise, everyone had arrived in Perham, and they, hurriedly, boarded the sleeper car. This newly constructed car was comfortable and airy, and had plenty of room for movement, for the youngsters. There were berths above the seats, and these seats, which were on both sides of a narrow aisle, could easily be made into berths for the night. At one end was situated a heating stove, as well as a tank for holding ice water. At the other end was a small cook stove. Beside the stove, w&s a large wooden box and a large tank for water.

Several of the younger men were busy placing wood in the box, while others were filling the tanks, with water. It did not take long, and everyone had a seat. In the back, near the cook stove were the nuns and postulants. There was Sister Lucretia, sitting in a seat with Sister Lydia and Sister Afra. In the nearby seats were Sister Theresa, Erana Riesterer, Mary Ann Foltz, Anna Mohr, Emma Bliley, Catharine Eifert, Aurelia Boedigheimer, Barbara and Matilda Silbernagel, Anna and Elizabeth Bender, Elizabeth, Rose, Catharine, and Sophrona Foltz.

The other members of the group included: the Silbenagels, the Bruno Boedigheimers, with their children: Frank, Simon, Bruno, John, and Ignatius, Leander Boedigheimer and his wife of 2 years, the former Theresa Foltz, the Benders, the Victor Eiferts, and the

Charley Foltz family, and Ferdinand and Magdalene Boedigheimer. In the front seat were Big Joe and Brother Cornelius.

As friends and well-wishers came by to bid farewell, the boxcars were attached to the locomotive, and the train began to leave. The men, women, and children of Rush Lake stood alongside the tracks and waved at their friends and relatives, as they watched the big engine slowly build up speed, heading westward.

Inside the passenger car, everyone seemed to be excited and happy to be moving on to a new land. Anton and Christof were seated across the aisle from Brother Joseph and Brother Cornelius.

"Finally," stated Anton. "We are finally leaving this place."

"Have you heard from Edelbrock, yet?" queried Christof.

"No. I'm having Riesterer keep an eye on my mail. For now, we'll just have to make do with what we've got on that mortgage loan, plus our personal finances."

Anton reached into a small black bag, which was under his chair, and pulled out the beautiful golden monstrance, which he had taken from the church, the night before. "We should be able to get quite a bit for this, shouldn't we?"

"What did you take that for?" asked Christof.

"Why not? It's ours. Besides, we'll need it out in Oregon, anyway."

"What else did you take?"

"Everything that I thought was either ours or that we could use."

"What are the others going to use?"

"What? The people of Rush Lake? That's their problem."

"Uh," remarked Christof, as he turned and looked out the window.

"Just then, Victor came down the aisle and stopped by Anton.

"How long is this supposed to take?"

"We should be in Oregon in three or four days, five at the most," answered Anton. "According to the ticket agent, we are supposed to switch over at Marion, Dakota Territory. From then on, we go straight to Portland."

"You know Anton. It took us two weeks to get out there."

"Yes, but that was before the railroad was completed."

"What are your plans, once we get to this Jordan Valley?" asked Victor.

"First," replied Anton, "we'll have to set up homesteads, and get some crops planted. Then, we'll have to start building a church and a convent."

"Are you going to try and get a priest for us?"

"In due time, Victor. In due time."

"Did you get a letter off to Anton and Joseph?"

"Yes, I wrote to them several days ago, and sent them money to come to Oregon and forget about their plans in Rome."

As these men were talking, several of the ladies were busy in the back of the coach, preparing a meal. Rather than having the women cook for their individual families; it was decided that they should share the workload and food supplies and cook for everyone.

While the women were preparing the meal, and the sisters were praying the rosary, the children spent much of their time looking out the windows, at the scenery. For the first couple of hours, the scenery was splendid, with an abundance of trees and lakes. As the

train approached Dakota Territory; the trees gave way to prairie grass. It did not take long for the children to turn their attention from the windows to something else more interesting.

That evening, the train pulled into a small way station at Marion. It was getting quite late, and most of the people on the train were asleep. Anton, Christof, and Victor got up from their seat and went outside to see how long the delay would be.

Once they spotted the railroad foreman, the three men walked over to him.

"Sir, could you tell me how long we'll be here?" asked Anton.

The rough-looking man looked at him and replied: "About two or three hours. We have to transfer everything from the second car onto a different one. There are some problems we noticed with the wheels on that one."

"What?" exclaimed Anton. "You mean you have to move all of our personal possessions?"

"Don't worry. I got plenty of men to do the job. You guys could just as well stay inside and get some sleep."

"Oh my!" quietly exclaimed Anton.

After pausing for several seconds, he continued: "Well, I guess we might as well go back inside."

All three men returned to the passenger car. With a very worried look on their faces, they sat down, and nervously, watched out the window.

Several minutes later, the railroad foreman came aboard.

"Who's in charge?" he queried.

"I am," answered Anton, as he got up from his seat.

"Would you come outside?"

Anton, Christof, and Victor went outside to see what the problem was.

"We were transferring your goods and came across this box, with a very strong odor, so we opened it up," stated the foreman.

"Don't you know that it's illegal to transport corpses across state lines? I could have you arrested. I suggest that you take those two

bodies and bury them right away."

"But we can't do that," objected Anton.

"Why not?"

"The one has been our leader, and we must take him with us.

The other is my father, and I promised him that he would always be with our leader, Father Joseph."

"Well, I can't let you continue on this way."

"What's it worth to you?" queried Anton, as he reached into his pocket and pulled out a bundle of paper money.

"What do you mean?"

"I'll pay you to let us take the bodies with us to Oregon."

The foreman paused for several seconds, looked around to see if there was anyone else around, and then finally said: $2,000.00. You give me $2,000.00 and I'll see to it that the boxes are packed on the train."

"Very well," stated Anton, as he began counting out the money.

"Make sure you don't say a word to anyone."

As the foreman grabbed the money from Anton, he smiled and remarked: "Of course not."

Shortly after the three men returned to the car, the train began to leave.

The next afternoon, while the train was slowly making its way westward, a large group of cowboys, dressed up as Indians, came up on horseback. They had on warpaint, but one could tell that they were not real Indians. One of them lassoed the smokestack, in an attempt to stop the train, while several others broke windows in the passenger car. The yelping and shouting lasted for only several minutes. While this was occurring, the expression of fright was seen on everyone's face. As many of them got out their rosaries, they wondered why these men would be doing such a thing to hinder the first trip of the Northern Pacific train to Portland. The attack ended as quickly as it had started. The howling men gave some final yells and disappeared, off into the foothills.

On the following day, the immigrant train pulled into a small town in Montana Territory. They stopped over for two hours, in order to fill the coal car.

The group calmly waited in the car. After several minutes, a visitor came aboard. It was a Bishop — Bishop Martin Marti. He entered in the back of the car and walked straight to the sisters.

"Who's in charge here?" he queried, as he looked at the elderly sisters.

"I am," replied Sister Lucretia.

"What are you doing out here?"

"We want to start a convent in Oregon."

"Why Oregon? Why not stop here? I have a great need for sisters, like you."

As this conversation was being held, Anton finally noticed the stranger in their midst. He immediately went to the rear and walked right up to Bishop Marti.

"What are you doing here?" he asked.

"I'm having a nice talk with the sisters."

"I'm in charge of this group," shot back Anton. "If you want to talk to someone, you can talk to me. My name is Anton Bender. I am responsible for the well-being of the sisters."

As the Bishop turned away from the sisters, and looked directly at Anton, he continued: "I was just suggesting to them that it would

be nice if you all ended your journey here. I could use the sisters. There is a lot of work to be done."

As Christof and Victor walked up beside Anton, Anton continued: "I think you better come with us."

The three men led the Bishop off the car, and towards the rear of the train.

Sister Lucretia tried to watch the four men from the coach window, but her view was blocked.

"What do you suppose they are doing?" she quietly asked Sister Lydia, who was sitting next to her.

"I don't know," replied Sister Lydia, "but, I'm sure we'll never see him again."

How right she was, for several minutes later, the three trustees came back into the car. They were all smiling as they sat down. Seconds later, the train began to take off.

The slow treacherous trip across Montana Territory, Idaho, and Washington continued. On the morning of July 31st, the small immigrant train arrived in the bustling little town of Portland, Oregon.

As the train pulled up to the Union Depot, the tired travelers began to liven up. They curiously looked out the windows at the new sights that were before their eyes. It had been a long arduous journey, but they were finally coming to the end of the major part of it. While the elders were beginning to get their personal things together, Anton got up and said:

"Listen everyone, before we get off here, I need to talk to you. According to the train schedule, we won't be leaving here till this afternoon. We'll have about one to two hours. I need all the men to transfer everything from these cars to the next train. I want all the women and children to remain in the depot, and not to go wandering off."

As the people began to disembark, Sister Afra, who was walking beside Sister Lucretia, stated: "Surely, there must be a church nearby. We could do much more good there rather than a train station."

"That's a good idea," replied Sister Lucretia. "I'll go ask Mr. Eifert."

Sister Lucretia moved ahead of the others, and caught up with Victor, "Mr. Eifert," she shouted, as Victor turned around. "Could I speak to you?"

"Of course, Sister Lucretia."

"We were wondering if you knew if there was a church nearby. We would like to spend some time in prayer. If you don't know, could you find out for us?"

"Yes. I'll see what I can find out, but for now, you better go inside with the rest."

All of the women and children entered the large, newly constructed, stone building, and proceeded to find a bench to rest upon. There were many others inside, patiently waiting for their respective trains.

Several moments later, Mr. Eifert came in and walked over to Sister Lucretia. "I wasn't able to find the location of a church, but I believe this wild western town is too rough, and I don't want to see any harm done to any of you."

"I see," quietly replied Sister Lucretia, as Victor departed. While the women were patiently waiting, they had a visitor. He was a 28-year-old priest. He had been walking through the depot and had noticed all of the habits congregated together.

As he walked up to them, he said: "Greetings! My name is Father Dominic Faber. Who's in charge here?"

"I am," answered Sister Lucretia, as she prepared to get up.

"Oh please, don't get up on account of me. I was just wondering what you were doing here."

As Sister Lucretia sat down again, she stated: "We are on our way to the Jordan Valley. We just arrived here from Minnesota."

"Jordan Valley? What are you going to do down there?"

"We are traveling with a group of farmers. We want to start a new settlement and convent."

"Very interesting."

"Say Father, do you know if there is a church nearby?"

"Why yes. I am stationed at the Cathedral. It's only about three blocks from here, on Third Street."

"Huh," stated Sister Lucretia, as she turned and looked at Sister Lydia, "I wonder why Mr. Eifert wasn't able to find that out."

"Well Sisters," continued Father Faber. "I hope everything turns out fine for you. If I should get the chance, I would like to visit you sometime."

"That would be nice. We would like that very much," noted Sister Lucretia.

"I must go now. Hopefully, I shall see you again."

"Good-bye Father."

"Ah, it will truly be wonderful to have the services of a priest and confessor again," remarked Sister Lydia, as she looked at Sister

Lucretia. "It seems so long."

"Alright," interrupted Christof Silbernagel, as he came in,

"everyone get their things together and follow me."

The women and children hurriedly picked up their belongings and followed Mr. Silbernagel on to the railroad platform. He led them along the tracks for several blocks to the Jefferson Street station, and into a small awaiting passenger car. It was very crowded,

but the women and children were content with standing room. Soon, the narrow-gauge train departed Portland. The next stop was to be Scio.

The Oregonian Railway Company Limited train, which consisted of an engine, a wood car, two passenger coaches, and three freight cars, slowly made its way down the tracks, in a southerly direction.

Now it so happened that when this track was built from Silverton to Coburg, the small town of Scio was passed by. The line was built two miles to the west. So, when travelers pulled into West Scio, they either had the choice of transferring to 'Old Betsy,' a small

commuter train, or on to farm wagons.

Luckily for the newcomers, John Bender and John Eifert were waiting for them, with horses and wagons. Altogether, there were 7 wagons prepared to carry the travelers, and their personal belongings, to their new home.

The men quickly unloaded the boxcars, transferring everything to the wagons. While this was occurring, several other men let the livestock out of the rear car. Wherever possible, the women and children climbed aboard, and soon, the wagons slowly began to meander down the trail toward the Jordan Valley, with most of the men walking beside. The long journey for the wearied travelers was soon to be completed.

Life In Oregon

CHAPTER XXXVI

The scenery was just as Mr. Eifert had described it. The magnificently tall trees seemed to be everywhere. Abundant wildflowers were in full bloom and were seen all along the trail. To some of the older travelers, it reminded them of their trip from Ohio to Minnesota. To the younger ones, it was as if they were entering paradise. Little did they know that this so-called paradise was to change drastically and quite soon. Anton Bender and his son, John, were in the first wagon.

"I was able to get our house somewhat completed while I waited for you," stated John.

"I hope you'll like it. I tried to put it up, as you had instructed me. I staked a claim for our land, but you'll have to have the men take care of theirs."

"I'm sure I'll be satisfied. How much further is it?"

"Not too far. I would say about two or three miles. We should get there before dark."

After crossing a small creek, everyone was able to view their new lands.

"This is Thomas Creek," continued John. "Shortly, we will be entering the lands that are up for sale."

"It looks marvelous," exclaimed Anton, with a content look, as he glanced over the landscape. With little trouble, the caravan made it across the river and into a large open area, the Jordan Valley. This was to be their new home. This is where they hoped to find true peace and happiness, once again. Shortly, the group pulled up in front of an unfinished log cabin. It was the house that John built.

"Well, what do you think of it?" asked John.

"Splendid job, my son," replied Anton, as he got down from the wagon.

"I couldn't have done it better myself. This is where we will house the sisters, until we can get a convent built for them."

"But where will we stay?"

"We shall live outside for now. You and George, and a couple of the others, can take this large box," continued Anton, as he pointed at the coffin of Father Joseph, and put it in the house. Place it up in the beams, for safekeeping."

"Yes father. What about grandpa?"

"I'll take care of that, myself."

"Christof, Victor," shouted Anton, as he waved at his two friends, "I need to talk to you right away."

"We are going to have to do an awful lot of work here, before winter sets in," continued Anton.

"Tomorrow morning, we must check out the area and pick out the lands that we each want. We will set it up exactly as Father Joseph would have wanted it. We'll use the church money. Then, we'll decide what percentage should be given to the church. We'll also have to pick out a spot for a convent and church, and get that built, plus we'll have to build houses for our families. It's too late for crops this year, but I think we can make it on what we brought with us. For tonight, it looks like most of us are going to have to sleep outside, so I suggest getting a couple of the boys to go fetch some firewood."

As Anton was talking, Sister Lucretia approached. "Mr. Bender," she stated, "how far is it to the Benedictine Monastery from here? Do you think it's possible to send someone there to see if we could have a priest come?"

"No Sister. The nearest Catholic church, according to my son, is 36 miles away. Since it's so far, we are not obliged to hear Mass."

"I see," sadly replied Sister Lucretia, as she turned away, in disgust.

Everyone was kept very busy for the next several weeks. Farm sites were picked out and construction was begun on their homes.

The site for the new church was chosen and plans for its construction were developed.

The convent grounds were to consist of a church, convent, monastery, blacksmith shop, barn, pigsty, laundry building, chicken house, and several storage sheds.

While construction was being carried out one day, the group had a visitor. It was Father Dominic Faber.

"Hello Father," greeted Sister Lucretia, who was the first to notice him.

"Hello sister," replied Father Faber.

"Nice to see you."

As Father Faber looked around and saw all of the activity that was taking place, he said: "I see you people are really making progress."

"Yes Father, we want everything to be done before winter sets in," replied Sister Lucretia.

"Do you know what to expect when winter comes?"

"No, not really. I just heard that it rains a lot."

"Yes, the winters here are quite different than back in Minnesota."

"That's good news."

"They can be very damp and wet though."

"But not two feet of snow, right?"

"Probably the only snow you'll see is up on that mountain over there," continued Father Faber, as he pointed to the tall mountain range in the distance.

"Hello," interrupted Anton Bender, as he approached the visitor. "What brings you here?"

"The Vicar-General sent me down here to see how everything was, and to see if you needed any help."

"That's very kind, but we are doing fine."

"Have you gone over to see if you could get a priest?"

"No, not yet. We have too many other things to get done first."

"It must be costing you quite a bit of money to finance this project?" continued Father Faber, as he looked around.

"We are alright. Our community is self-sufficient. Victor, Christof, and I have full control of the monies and how they are to be spent."

"What?" queried Father Faber, in a very surprised tone. "You mean to tell me that three men are in control of the destiny of the entire community? Are you in charge of the sisters, too?"

"Why yes."

"That is not right. Laymen should never be in charge of religious."

"Wait a minute," shot back Anton. "Who are you to tell us that it's not right? Father Joseph willed it to us. We are simply carrying out the wishes of our beloved leader."

"Who is this, Father Joseph?"

"He is our spiritual leader."

"Where is he?"

"Gone to his just reward," answered Anton, as he looked upward.

"How can he be leading you, if he's dead?"

"He has been our priest for many years. He has helped us through many times of trouble and hardship, and he will help us here. His living body may not be with us, but he is still here."

"He can't help you now. He can't say Mass for you. He can't hear your confessions, nor baptize your children, nor bury your dead. You must get another."

"Nonsense. We don't need another. We still have Father Joseph. He will take care of us."

"You're speaking nonsense."

"That's enough."

"Christof, come here," shouted Anton.

As Christof approached, Anton continued: "Christof, would you kindly show this man the way back to Scio, and see that he gets on the train?"

"Why, of course," innocently replied Christof, as he turned and headed for his wagon.

"I advise you never to come here again," continued Anton, as he looked at Father Faber. "You are no longer welcome here."

In utter amazement and disgust, Father Faber turned and went with Mr. Silbernagel, and was never again seen at the settlement. Meanwhile, the men continued on their construction projects.

Once the outside of the L-shaped church was completed, they began to erect a small 12x15 foot building to the right of the church. Upon completion, Anton Bender stated: "There, now we can bring Father Joseph to his resting place. Boys, go get him."

The four boys went over to where the sisters were staying, got down the coffin, put it in the wagon, and returned to the shed, where Anton was waiting.

"Take the lid off," he requested. "I have a piece of glass here to place on the top."

The boys obediently did what they were told, and soon Anton had the glass covering in place. While the boys set the coffin on its small pedestal, Anton placed a small prie-dieu in front of it.

"There, now we can come and pray to him, whenever we want," happily stated Anton, as he placed a small vigil lamp beside the coffin.

When the men walked back outside, young Emma Bliley approached. "Mr. Bender," she began. "I need to talk to you."

"Yes Emma. What is it?"

"I realize that you trustees have been looking out for our welfare, but for a complete convent life, it is necessary to have the Holy Sacraments. Without them, we are lost."

"Nonsense," interrupted Victor. "We must make do the best we can, with what we have, and we still have Father Joseph. That is all we really need. He will continue to take care of us."

"My dear Emma," noted Anton, "obedience is your most necessary virtue. Let me remind you what Paul said to the Corinthians:

'You are not to live by the letter, but by the spirit, for the letter kills, but the spirit gives life.' Now, go back with the others. We have more important things to take care of."

As Emma left, Christof looked at Anton, and asked: "What are we going to do about a priest?"

"Nothing for the time being. Brother Joseph is very capable in leading us in the prayer services."

"Yes, but he can't say Mass."

"We don't need Mass for a while. I'm going to talk to them women right now, and let them know the situation we are in."

Anton noticed Sister Lucretia standing nearby, so he shouted:

"Lucretia, get all of the girls and sisters together and be over at your house. I need to talk to all of you."

Sister Lucretia did as she was told, and in a matter of minutes, all of them were at the house.

Anton was sitting by a table. As soon as he noticed that everyone was present, he began: "I have a piece of paper here that I need each of you to sign. It is merely a formality, but it is necessary for you, in order to be a member in good standing with the Society."

Anton laid a large white sheet on the table, next to a pen. The women obediently signed their names to it, without even reading what it said. When Sister Lucretia signed the letter, she looked at Anton, and said:

"I still think we should have a priest here, to hear our confessions."

"Why do you need a priest? I am here. I have been willed by Father Joseph to take care of you."

Sister Lucretia did not like what she heard, but she knew she had no choice in the matter.

"Now, my dear ladies," continued Anton.

"The church will soon be completed. When it is, I want you to set up a nightly vigil, just like before. Every evening we shall set aside one hour for meditations. I will direct them, just like Father Joseph did."

The women could hardly believe what they heard. How could he say such things? They knew that they could not object because they were helpless, so they went along with whatever he said.

"You are to do whatever I tell you, or Christof, or Victor, tell you. Believe me, it will be for the betterment of the community."

With those words, Anton departed the room. The lives of the sisters, over the course of the next 12 months, was very trying. They obediently listened to what the three trustees told them, without argument. They would work in the fields from sunrise to sunset, in their ragged clothing. At the end of the day, they would come in and have a scanty meal of potatoes and bread.

Then, they would be sent up into the nearby hills to pray the Way of the Cross. They then would return and spend time in meditation. The newly constructed convent, that they called home, left much to be desired. The outer shell had been finished, but very little had been done on the inside. Nevertheless, they did not give up hope. They carried on their duties faithfully, holding onto the hope that one day their desires would be answered. This way of living did not agree with others of the community either. One of them was Brother Joseph. Several months after their arrival, he decided to move out of the seminary. He found an old shack across the river and moved in there. One day, he had come down to the convent grounds. Young Emma Bliley was standing outside, pulling weeds from a small flower garden.

"Hello Emma."

"Well, Mr. Boedigheimer, hello."

"I am going over to find the monastery of the Benedictines. The situation around here is getting too ridiculous. When I find them, I'll try and get a priest to come back here and take charge."

"I wish you luck, Joseph," replied Emma. "Can you wait a few minutes? I wrote a letter that I would like for you to take to the prior. Let me go get it. I'll be right back. Wait here!"

Several minutes later, Emma returned, carrying a letter in her hand. "Here. Take this with you," she stated, as she handed him the letter.

"Do you know where to go?"

"I think so. I have a map, and according to that, the monastery is at Fillmore. That should be about 35 miles, or so, from here. It should only take me a couple of days."

"How are you going to get there?"

"I'm going to walk. Don't tell anyone what I'm doing though."

"Alright. Good luck!"

Joseph headed northward on his journey, across the less frequented fields, trying not to attract any attention. After two days, he finally arrived at the Benedictine monastery.

"Excuse me," he stated, as he walked up to one of the monks.

"Could you tell me where I can find the prior?"

The monk nodded his head in the affirmative and led Joseph to the office of Prior Adelhelm Oder matt.

Prior Adelhelm Odermatt

Joseph knocked on the door. Upon hearing a feint 'come in', he entered the room. There seated behind a desk was a short, elderly, heavy-set man with rimless glasses and a white beard and mustache.

"Can I help you?"

"My name is Joseph Boedigheimer, from Jordan. I was wondering if you could help me. About a year ago, there was a large group of us that arrived in the valley, from Minnesota. Among us were many women who belonged to the Precious Blood Society. Our leader, Father Joseph Albrecht died, and ever since, we've had problems. We have three laymen who give all the instructions. What we need is a priest."

"I see," answered the Prior, in a sympathetic voice.

"The sisters and postulants number 18. They would like to continue on as Sisters of the Most Precious Blood, but under the circumstances, it is very difficult."

Prior Adelhelm thought for several seconds and then said:

"I'll have Father Werner Ruttiman come down and visit you. He is presently the pastor at Sublimity, which isn't too far from Jordan. He covers many of the mission churches in Marion and Linn Counties. I'm sure he won't mind stopping by, to take care of your needs."

Father Werner Ruttiman

"Oh, thank-you," humbly replied Joseph.
"It would bring so much joy to the people."

As he pulled a letter from his pocket, he continued: "I have a short note here, that one of the sisters wrote. She wanted you to have it."

Prior Adelhelm took the letter, opened it, and began to read. When he was finished, he laid the letter down, took off his glasses, looked at Joseph, and said:

"Tell Emma that there will be a priest there within a week. I did not realize the situation was that bad."
As Joseph got up, he shook Prior Adelhelm's hand. With a smile, he said: "Good-bye."
Joseph quickly headed back for the Jordan settlement, with the good news.

On June 21st, 1885, joy came to the hearts of the people of the Jordan Valley. Father Werner Ruttiman had arrived that morning, to say Mass. The young priest was met near the church entrance by Anton, Christof, and Victor.

"Good morning," boldly stated Father Werner, as he got down from his horse.
"Good morning," replied Anton.
"Can we help you?"

"I'm hoping that I can help you. I am Father Werner Ruttiman, from the Benedictine Monastery, near Fillmore. I would like to celebrate Mass here this morning, if possible."
A smile came to Christof's face, as he heard those words.

"I have heard very much about your community," continued Father Werner,
"and I am very impressed with your Father Joseph. He must have been a very remarkable man."

"Why, yes, he is," replied Anton, as he turned to Christof and Victor, in bewilderment. "Surely, Father Joseph would like for his people to partake in the Holy Sacrifice."

"Yes. Yes, he would," answered Anton. "I'll have the men spread the word that you are here and are going to say Mass."

"Fine. Make it about an hour from now."

"Very well," stated Anton, as he departed.

"Father," stated Christof, as he extended his hand, "my name is Christof Silbernagel."

"Glad to meet you," replied Father Werner, as he shook hands.

"As you well know, we have had to struggle here. We've only been here for about a year, so this will be our first year of crops. I must admit that it looks like it'll be an excellent harvest, but that is mainly because of Father Joseph. He is still here, looking out after us."

"What do you mean, still here?"

"We built a shrine for him, next to the church. Would you like to go see it?"

"Why yes."

The three men walked into the small building and approached the coffin. Father Werner was amazed at what he saw. He was also quite surprised to notice that there was no bad odor in the room. He stood there as Christof knelt on the prie-dieu and said a silent prayer. Afterwards, the three men went back outside.

"When did he die?"

"March 4th, of last year," answered Victor.

"Why hasn't his body decayed?"

"Because he's a saint," bluntly replied Christof.

"How do you know that?"

"Well," continued Christof, "how else can you explain his body being the way it is?"

Father Werner was stumped. He had no answer to give. He had no idea as to what had been done to preserve the body. The three men now went into the church, and Christof showed Father Werner where everything was for the Mass. As the priest began making the necessary preparations, the church began to fill with men, women, and children. The first Holy Mass ever, in this church, was about to begin, on this feast day of St. Aloysius.

Everything went smoothly. What a joy it was for everybody to partake in the Holy Mass! What a heavy burden was taken off their shoulders! Once again, they were able to come up to the communion rail and receive the symbol of the body and blood of Christ. Surely, now everything would be alright! Earlier in the year, four more families had arrived in Jordan, from Minnesota. They were led by Joseph Riesterer. They brought with them, the slab monument of Father Joseph's, as well as a church bell. On this day, the bell was rung. As the people listened to its ringing, they were reminded of the good old days back at Rush Lake.

While Father Werner was saying Mass, Anton remained outside. He was walking along the convent grounds, in very deep thought. For some unknown reason, he did not seem to mind the idea of a strange priest offering Mass at his church. He now entered the
shrine of Father Joseph. After making the sign of the cross, he knelt down on the prie-dieu, and talked aloud to Father Joseph.

"What should I do?" he asked.

"You have given Christof, Victor, and I the control of these people. We have done what we thought you would like us to do. Anton and John have come back from Rome, and they are not priests. Joseph is no longer a brother. Surely, you do not mind seeing a priest here. He seems to be such nice young man."

While Anton was still in the shrine, Mass had been completed, and everyone was returning to their homes. All of the sisters and young girls remained in the church, at the request of Father Werner. After he had taken off his vestments, he came out of the sacristy
and walked over to where the women were sitting. In the front row were Sister Lucretia, Sister Lydia, Sister Afra, and Sister Theresa, with the others in the next several pews.

"Thank-you for giving me a chance to talk to you," stated Father Werner, as he approached the women. "I have talked with Prior Adelhelm Odermatt, and he has told me much about you people. You must realize that the Lord often works in mysterious ways. If you continue to put your full faith and trust in God and pray to him, asking for his help, surely, everything will come out alright."

"We have a new Bishop in Portland. He is Archbishop Gross. He has a very big need for sisters out here. I suggest that you get together and write a letter to him, telling him of your situation and of your desires to be religious nuns. Ask him what you should do. I'm
sure, he will be able to help you."

"I'm going back to the monastery in a few hours so, if you would like, I could take a letter back with me. I must go talk to Mr. Bender, before I leave, so why don't you draft a letter here and give it to me, when you're done."

"Father," shyly interrupted Sister Lucretia, "I have a question for you."
"Yes?"
"What about the Sacraments?"
"What about them?"
"Well, many of the people here have never been confirmed, and some of the children have never had the joy of First Communion."
"Really!" replied Father Werner, in an astonished tone.

"Why?"

"I don't think Father Joseph thought much of the idea of confirmation, as a Sacrament. He believed that each individual confirmed his religion every day of their life, by the way they lived."

"Huh. Perhaps I should set up a schedule and come down here, let's say, every other week for instructions, and prepare all of the candidates for Confirmation. I'll talk to Mr. Bender and see what he has to say." As he began to leave, he added: "Now, before I leave, I would like to have that letter from you."

Father Werner went outside and looked around until he spotted Mr. Bender, standing near the shrine, with Christof and Victor. "Thank-you for coming," stated Christof, as Father Werner approached.

"It was truly my pleasure. Say, I understand that there are quite a few here that have not been confirmed."

"That's correct," replied Anton.

"Would you mind if I came down every other week and gave them instructions?"

The question caught Anton off guard. "Why," he stuttered, "I guess it would be alright." He looked at the other men, to see if there was any objection. He then turned back to Father Werner, and continued: "But, doesn't that mean a Bishop will be coming?"

"Yes. Archbishop Gross of Portland would have to come down."

"I'm not sure about that. Father Joseph always warned us to be very cautious when it came to Bishops."

"Why was that?"

"You can't trust them."

"Archbishop Gross is a very fine man. He is truly a man of God. He is an exceptional person. I'm sure that if you meet him, you would like him."

The three men looked at each other for several seconds. Finally, Anton said:

"Alright Father, you can set up a schedule. We'll give him a chance."

"Fine. Have all the children come to the church a week from tomorrow, in the morning. I will instruct them and prepare them for confirmation and First Holy Communion."

"Very well," replied Anton, as he watched Father Werner mount his horse, which had been standing nearby. Upon getting on his horse, Father Werner continued:

"I shall return a week from tomorrow, for Mass and for instructions. Good day."

The three men said good-bye and waved as Father Werner left. As he rode past the front of the church, he was stopped by Sister Lucretia, who handed him a letter. With that in hand, Father Werner departed. Over the course of the next month, Father Werner spent much time at Jordan. He would stay for an entire week at a time. He said daily Mass, heard confessions, and instructed the children. July 31st was the day set for the visit of Archbishop Gross. Therefore, Father Werner didn't have much time to prepare his students. On July 30th, final preparations were made. Anton, Christof, Victor, and Bruno met the Archbishop at the train station in Scio, and led him to the church, by means of a special carriage, decorated in brightly colored flowers.

Archbishop Gross

When the carriage and the other wagons were about one mile from the church, they were met by a group of young boys, waving an assortment of banners. Eight of the older boys began playing music on their instruments. This brass band led the Archbishop, and his attendants, which included Prior Adelhelm and Father Werner, to the church grounds, where the women and children had been patiently waiting. It was a beautiful sight, as the church and the surrounding grounds were all decorated in garlands. The 48-year-old Archbishop was very pleased at what he saw.

Upon arrival in front of the church, the Archbishop and Prior Adelhelm got down from the carriage and disappeared for several minutes. When they reappeared, they were fully dressed for the Mass. The band stopped playing and the choir began to sing hymns. The church bells were ringing continuously, as the solemn procession entered the church. As the Archbishop approached the front, he noticed the large number of neatly dressed boys on the one side and the charming girls on the other. When he got to the altar, he genuflected, walked up the two steps and kissed the altar. After making the sign of the cross, he began Holy Mass.

About on hour later, with Mass and Confirmation completed, the Archbishop met with the three trustees, in the sacristy.

"Mr. Bender," stated Father Werner, "His Excellency and Prior Adelhelm would like to pay their respects to Father Joseph."

"Of course," replied Anton, as he looked at the Archbishop, "please come with me."

Mr. Bender, Prior Adelhelm, and the Archbishop walked around to the side of the church, and up to the small building.

"Here it is," stated Anton, as he opened the door. The Archbishop and Prior Adelhelm entered and walked up to the coffin.

"I can't believe this," stated the Archbishop. "It looks as if he died only yesterday. See if you can lift up the glass."

Prior Adelhelm lifted the glass covering off and set it beside the prie-dieu. He then pulled on Father Joseph's hair. "It won't come out," he stated in amazement.

The Archbishop stood there in disbelief. "Come Father, let's get out of here," he stated, as they turned and went back outside.

"Mr. Bender," stated the Archbishop, as they began to walk back to the front of the church,

"I must advise you that you should bury that body in the earth. Only the Pope, after long and tedious investigation and deliberation, can pronounce a man to be a saint. Only then can Catholics publicly venerate his relics. I am not saying that he is or is not a saint. I'm saying that it is not your decision, but that of the Pope."

The three trustees, who were walking with the group, did hot say a word, but one could see that they did not like what they were hearing.

"I was quite satisfied with the children today," continued the Archbishop. "I can see that they have been well-trained in the matter of religion. That tells me that the parents are also good Christians. This community can be very helpful to the Catholic cause in Oregon, but one thing you must do, is turn the deed of the church property over to the Archdiocese, to be held at the Chancery Office."

"But that is my private property," objected Mr. Bender.

"What better gift to give the Church than your own land," replied the Archbishop. "Now," he continued, "I would like to have a talk with the nuns and the postulants."

"They are all in the church, waiting for you," stated Father Werner.

As the Archbishop entered the church and noticed that the three trustees were intending to enter also, he stopped and said: "Please, I would like to talk to them by myself."

The three men waited outside with the Prior and Father Werner, as the Archbishop continued on in. After walking to the front, the Archbishop turned his attention to the women. "You must realize," he stated,

"that you people are really not religious, in the eyes of the Church, even though you do wear the habit. You have never been reinstated in your congregation. Now, I have a great need here in Oregon for nuns. I want to start an entirely new congregation, for the purpose of educating the Catholic children in my diocese."

"You younger girls," he continued, as he directed his attention to the children. "You have not entered a canonically erected novitiate and were never received by a legitimate superior. You have not been examined and invested by ecclesiastical authority. In other words, you never did belong to a true society. Now, my children, I can help you. Would you all like to join my new congregation? If so, I will do everything I can to get you in good standing with the Holy Mother Church. I can send you Father Werner, to instruct you, and train you for a new religious life."

Upon hearing these words, the group was overjoyed. Sister Lucretia got up, walked over to the Archbishop, knelt down at his feet, and said:

"I promise you, Your Excellency, that we will do whatever is necessary to correct our position in the Church."

"My child," stated the Archbishop, as he placed his hands on her head, "everything will turn out fine."

As Sister Lucretia arose and walked back to her seat, the Archbishop continued:
"I shall send Father Werner Ruttiman, to help you. I must leave now, but I shall return."

The Archbishop departed the church, and, along with Prior Adelhelm and Father Werner, walked to the awaiting carriage, which was to take them back to Scio. During the following week, Father Werner returned to the colony. He spent time preparing the large group of the younger children, for First Holy Communion. After instructing them for an hour, he would then go over to the convent, and begin instructing the women.

While this was going on, Anton came to the church.
"Ignatius," he shouted to the 12-year-old son of Bruno Boedigheimer,
"where is Father Werner?"
"He went over to the sister's house," politely replied young Ignatius, who was playing with Joe Foltz and Joe Silbernagel, in front of the church.

"I wonder what he's doing over there," stated Anton.

"He said he wanted to talk to them," replied Joe Foltz.

"Huh, it looks like we'll have to keep an eye on him."

The next week, Father Werner returned for Holy Mass. On August 15th, he distributed communion to his young class. After this Mass was completed, everyone met outside the church, for a picnic.

Father Werner was standing near the entrance, talking with several of the children, as Anton, Christof, and Victor approached.

"Say Father," stated Anton,
"we were wondering why you have been spending so much time with the nuns?"
"I have been preparing them for their vows."
"What?" shouted Anton, as he looked at Christof and Victor, who likewise, had the same expression of anger on their faces.
"The women are already religious," continued Anton.
"Father Joseph had made them sisters. We demand that you stop immediately."
"Yes, but the young women desire to receive this instruction, and I am only fulfilling the request of Archbishop Gross."

Those ignorant women don't know what they want," shot back Anton.
"Father Joseph had made us guardians of the sisters and we have no intention to abdicate our right nor to neglect our duty to our daughters. We demand that you leave this place and never return. You are no longer wanted here."

Father Werner was dumbfounded. Saying nothing, he walked over to his horse, mounted, and departed. The three men stood and watched as the priest disappeared into the distance. Life continued on at the settlement. Mr. Bender was now becoming more and more stringent in his demands. He was now in full control of the entire parish. Each morning he would hand out the daily tasks, to each of the sisters. He was in charge of the parish coffers and had final say in what was to be spent. He began to hold the services at church, in place of the priest. He did not attempt to say Mass, but he did give the sermons. It got so bad, that some of the parishioners stopped having anything to do with the church, altogether. Among these were the Bruno Boedigheimer family.

One evening, in late September, as the sun was setting, Joseph Boedigheimer came down to the church grounds. He quietly went over to the convent, and met Sister Lucretia, who was standing by a tree, nearby.

"Sister Lucretia," he stated, "I need to speak to Aurelia."
"I think she is over at the church," replied Sister Lucretia.
Joseph immediately turned and went to the church. After entering, he noticed Aurelia kneeling in the front pew. He walked up beside her, and quietly stated:

"Aurelia. Father Werner is going to offer Mass at your father's house, tomorrow morning. If you can, pass the word to the others. Make sure the men don't find out."

Aurelia smiled at Joseph, and nodded her head in approval, as Joseph silently left.

The next morning, before sunrise, Aurelia, Emma Bliley, Anna Mohr, and Erana Riesterer, quietly left the convent and headed for the Boedigheimer homestead, which was located a short distance away, across the river. They ran into somewhat of a problem when they arrived at the river.

In front of them stood a 10-foot-wide creek with a long stretch of low marshy soil on the other side. Not wasting any time, they took off their shoes and stockings and proceeded to cross. They were forced to crawl on their hands and knees over several logs, but finally, through sheer determination, they reached dry land. Once that was accomplished, they continued to carry their shoes and socks, for the last 50 yards to the small Boedigheimer house. A smile came to their faces, as they noticed Father Werner inside, preparing for Mass. The four wet girls, dressed in their worn black outfits, entered the house, and were greeted by Bruno and Mary.

"Glad to see that you could make it," remarked Bruno, as he grabbed a blanket and handed it to Aurelia. She took it and wiped herself off, and then handed it to Emma, who did the same.

"Did anyone see you leave?" asked Mary.

"No. I don't think so," replied Aurelia.

"Well," continued Mary, "come into the living room. I think Father is about ready."

Upon entering the small room, the girls noticed Father Werner, dressed in his Mass vestments, preparing an altar, which was a small table, covered with a white cloth. There was a two-foot cross located on the middle, with a Bible setting on the right side. There

was two candles on each side of the cross, which Joseph was in the process of lighting.

When Father Werner noticed the arrival of the four girls, he smiled and welcomed them to the Mass.

Meanwhile, back at the church grounds, Sister Theresa and Mary Ann Foltz were returning to the convent. After entering, they immediately noticed the missing girls.

"Where do you suppose they went?" asked Mary Ann, as she looked at Sister Theresa.

"I don't know, but we better see if we can find out, before Mr. Bender does."

"Sister Theresa," stated Sister Lydia, who was lying in her bed,

"they went over to Bruno Boedigheimer's, for Mass."

As Sister Theresa walked over to Sister Lydia's bedside, she

asked: "When?"

"About an hour ago," replied Sister Lydia, as she began to cough. "I think they thought everybody was asleep, but I heard them leave."

"I wonder why they didn't ask us if we wanted to go along," stated Mary Ann.

"I don't think they wanted the men to find out."

"How are you feeling today?" asked Sister Theresa, as she took a cloth and wiped Sister Lydia's forehead.

"The same. Would you or Sister Lucretia please ask Mr. Bender to find me a priest? I would so much like to go to confession and receive Holy Communion, and the Last Sacraments. I don't think I have too many more days left."

"You know how he's been," answered Sister Theresa. "I'm afraid neither of us would have much success."

"Well then, would you take me over to see Father Joseph today?"

"Yes, I can do that. I'll return after breakfast."

"Ah, thank-you," replied Sister Lydia, as she smiled, and went back to sleep.

The other sisters and girls were now awakening for another day. After dressing, they all headed for the church. Sister Theresa took Sister Afra by the hand and led her out of the room.

"I pray to God that he will take me from this place and send me up to heaven," Sister Afra exclaimed, as they were leaving.

"If Father Joseph were still alive, I'm sure he would cure my poor eyesight."

"Be patient, my dear," suggested Sister Lucretia, who was standing nearby. "Have faith, and everything will turn out for the best."

As the women were departing, they were met at the doorway by the four girls, who had just returned from the Boedigheimer farm.

"We were beginning to wonder if you were going to make it back in time, before the men noticed," stated Sister Theresa.

"Hurry up and get out of those wet clothes," ordered Sister Lucretia,

"we must get over to the church."

Just then, Mr. Bender arrived.

"Where have you been?" he shouted, as he looked at the four.

Aurelia looked at Sister Lucretia, and then at Mr. Bender. "We went to my father's house."

"Why?"

"Father Werner held Mass there, this morning."

"Who said you could do that?"

"No one. We did it on our own."

"This will not go unpunished," shouted Anton. "I want to speak to each of you after our meeting this morning. Now, get changed and get over to the church."

After Anton stormed out of the convent, the four girls changed into dry clothes.

"That is enough!" stated Anna. "I have just made up my mind. I am going back to Minnesota. There is absolutely no reason why we
should be punished for going to Mass. As soon as possible, I'm getting out of here."

"Why don't you wait?" noted Aurelia. "Some of my brothers have been talking about doing the same thing. Perhaps, you can go back to Perham with them."

The four girls finished changing their clothes and quickly headed for the church, leaving Sister Lydia all alone in the convent. She lay there, in her bed, with rosary in hand. For the past several weeks she had been quite sick, and unable to get out of bed. All she could do was lay there. When she was not coughing, she attempted to pray the rosary.

"Oh Father Joseph," she exclaimed, "how I long to be with you. Each day I pray that I will soon be with you in heaven. My time on Earth is short, just as you always said. I have tried to lead a good life, just the way you wanted it. I wish I could come and visit you now, but I will have to wait till the Good Lord decides that it is time. Please be waiting for me."

As she finished saying these words, she passed away. Conditions at the convent continued to worsen, as time went by. After the burial of Sister Lydia in the Jordan cemetery, Anna Mohr returned to Minnesota with several of the Boedigheimer boys. Sister Afra's health continued to worsen, to the point where she was totally blind. The remaining women were forced to work the farm, just like slaves, as well as make the meals, and do the laundry, and any other chores that the men deemed necessary.

In the spring of 1886, Prior Adelhelm and Father Werner reappeared at the church grounds. They had been sent by the Archbishop, with the goal of establishing peace, but the three trustees refused to concede.

The two men were met by Anton and Christof, near the church. As they got down from the wagon, Anton stated:

"What are you doing here?"

"We have been sent by Archbishop Gross to see if there is anything we can do to correct the situation that presently exists here,"
remarked Prior Adelhelm. "We would like to speak to the sisters."
"They are in the church," replied Anton. "But it won't do you any good."
Prior Adelhelm and Father Werner quickly walked into the church, while the two trustees remained outside.

"Sister Lucretia," shouted Father Werner, as he entered, "we need to speak to each of you. We must hurry, as we have very little time. We need to talk individually. We will be in the sacristy. Send one girl in at a time."

After Prior Adelhelm and Father Werner entered the sacristy, the first girl, 23-year-old Anna Bender came in."

"Tell me, Anna," began Father Werner, "how have things been around here?"

"Not too good, I'm afraid. I think my father has gone too far. None of us have said anything to him, nor to the others, but I think we all hold the same view. He is basically a very good man. He is pious and understanding. In many ways, he is like Father Joseph. I think that ever since the death of Father Joseph, he thinks he had a calling to take care of us. But who are we to try and tell him that he has erred?"

"Do you think everyone would be receptive to the idea of moving to a new convent?" interrupted Prior Adelhelm. After pausing for several seconds, Anna replied: "I think all of us older girls would like that. I don't know about the younger ones. I do know you would have a big argument with my father and the other men."

"We're not too worried about them. His Excellency wants us to remove you all from here, so we want to find out your feelings. Thank-you for letting us have this little talk. When you go out, send another in," noted Prior Adelhelm.

This process continued until the two men had talked to everyone. At that time, they came out, with Prior Adelhelm carrying a large white piece of paper.

"I have a statement here," noted the Prior, which I would like each of you to sign."

As Prior Adelhelm set the letter down on a small table, Father Werner placed a quill pen and a bottle of ink beside it. One by one, these valiant women came up and placed their signature on the paper. As this was going on, Prior Adelhelm turned to Father Werner, and said:

"Go outside and have the three trustees come in."

Father Werner obediently turned and walked outside, only reappearing several minutes later, with the three men. All three trustees came in with smiles on their faces. They were confident that the sisters had decided to side with them, since each of them had at least

two daughters of their own, in attendance. What a surprise they were in for!

Prior Adelhelm picked up the piece of paper, and began to read:
"We the undersigned, do solemnly swear to uphold our allegiance to the Roman Catholic Church, and to its representatives on Earth. We also promise to become members of a new religious congregation, subject to the Metropolitan of Oregon City, His Excellency, Archbishop Gross. No one has forced this statement upon us. With our own free will, we have signed it, and have now severed all connections with the trustees of Jordan. Signed: Lucretia Hog, Afra Ruh, Theresa Arnold, Emma Bliley, Mary Ann Foltz, Aurelia

Boedigheimer, Martha Eifert, Elizabeth Eifert, Theresa Foltz, Catharine Foltz, Elizabeth Foltz, Erana Riesterer, Matilda Silbernagel, Mary Barbara Silbernagel, Anna Bender, and Elizabeth Bender."

As Prior Adelhelm set the paper down on the table, he looked at the girls, seated in the pews, and said:

"Whoever desires to cooperate with Archbishop Gross, I would like for them to stand up."

To the great surprise of the trustees, all of the girls arose, as a single body.

"Sit down Anna," shouted Anton, in a very rough voice, as he ran toward her.
23-year-old Anna Bender had tears in her eyes, but she did not flinch.

"She is of age," shouted back the Prior. "She is old enough to make her own choice."

Just then, Christof went over to his two daughters, who were standing beside each other, and he said:
"Mary, I know you are old enough. You may do as you please, but Matilda, you are to come home with me."
16-year-old Matilda began to cry, but she did not move from her sister's side. Prior Adelhelm walked over to them and said:

"You gave her to God, and you may not take her back now."

Meanwhile, Victor stood and looked at his three daughters, Catharine, Martha, and Elizabeth. He smiled at Catharine and Martha, knowing that he could do nothing with them, but when he looked at Elizabeth, he motioned for her to follow him. 13-year-old Elizabeth looked at her two older sisters, and then at her father. After several seconds, without any emotion, she followed her father out of the church.

"I don't know what you're trying to do here," shouted Anton,

"but it won't work. Father Joseph will intervene."

Christof and Anton stomped out of the church. Once they were outside, Prior Adelhelm looked at the sisters, and said: "We can not take you along today, but we shall return as soon as possible. I'm not too sure of your safety, but I don't think they will harm you/'

"You must take Matilda with you now," suggested Sister Lucretia. "They won't harm the rest of us, but I'm sure Christof would take his daughter home, if he were given the chance. I know a good Catholic family not far from here, in the hills, that could take care of her for now."

"Who is that?" queried Father Werner.
"Bill Smith's."
"Ah yes. I know them."

Quickly, the two priests and Matilda Silbernagel went to the wagon and departed the church grounds, while the others went out in the front of the church, in order to distract the two trustees. On May 15th, more problems occurred at the convent. Early that morning, Anton, Christof, and Victor, came up in front of the nunnery. They got off the wagon. Christof and Victor entered the nunnery, while Anton went to the brother's quarters. Christof and Victor began taking supplies and loading them on to the wagon, as the sisters stood by, in utter disbelief, and watched. While this was going on, Anton entered the brother's quarters.

"Brother Cornelius," he stated, "I need your savings."

Brother Cornelius reached under his bed and pulled out a small box. As he handed it to Anton, he stated: "There is over $1,000.00 in there. I hope you need it for a good cause." "Of course," replied Anton, as he walked over to Brother Anton, who was sitting nearby.

"Brother Anton, what do you have for me?"

Brother Anton pulled out $600.00 from under his mattress, and gave it to Mr. Bender, without saying a word. By now Christof and Victor had completed their task and were awaiting for the return of Anton. "What's keeping him?" asked Christof, in a worried voice. Just then, Mr. Bender came running. He jumped into the wagon, and they departed.

Several moments later, two farm wagons from the Mt. Angel monastery arrived. Sister Lucretia quickly rounded up some of the girls and got them into the wagons. Emma Bliley walked over to the bedside of the elderly Sister Afra and said: "I know you would like to come with us now, but you are too sick. We will come back for you as soon as we can. Sister Theresa is coming along with us, but don't worry. We will keep you in our prayers."

Sister Afra wept sadly as she listened to the women make haste for the awaiting wagon. Altogether, nine women left the Jordan convent that day, taking nothing with them but the clothes on their backs. Tears came to their eyes as they looked back at the place they were leaving. Two weeks later, Sister Afra died and was buried beside Sister Lydia. At the same time, Catharine Foltz decided to leave. This left only four scared girls residing at the convent.

On June 12th, Father Werner returned, with the intention of rescuing the remaining girls. While entering the sisters' house, he noticed that many of the parishioners were arriving at the church. As Father Werner entered, he approached Elizabeth Foltz, who was kneeling by a table.

"Father Werner," she exclaimed, "I'm afraid! They have taken away our beds and left us to sleep on the floor. We haven't had a decent meal in days."

"Don't be afraid, child. It will all soon be over. Pack up everything you have. I have come to take you and the others away from here."

Elizabeth slowly arose and did as she was told.

"I am determined that you all cast off the shackles of this Benderian heresy," exclaimed Father Werner, as he turned and headed for the door.

At that moment, Charley Foltz came running into the room. "Father," he shouted, "be careful! There are men posted all over. I was supposed to tell you that if you were not gone by noon, the trustees would personally throw you out. They have a lot of parishoners worked up. It's hard telling what they'll do."

"Are you on my side?"

"Yes."

"Anyone else?"

"Bruno, Cornelius, Anton, and Joseph are outside."

"Good. Have them go in and guard the church."

"But Anton already has men by the doors," objected Charley.

"Never mind, just do as you are told. I'll be over there in a minute."

While Charley ran back outside, Father Werner returned to see if the girls were ready to leave.
Outside, in front of the church, Anton had the people very excited. The women and children were screaming. Men were fighting off those who were attempting to rescue the sacred vessels. Several of the ardent followers of Anton ran into the church. They went up to the altar, opened the tabernacle, and took out the monstrance, ciborium, and chalice, the three prized possessions of Father Joseph.

While this was occurring, another man ran into the sacristy and brought out a beautiful jewel-inlaid black cope.

"This is mine," he shouted, "in consideration for my donations for the bell."

Another man came up to him and grabbed at the cope. When it looked like they were going to tear it, Charley Foltz came in.

"Stop!" he shouted. "I'll give you my share of the bell, if you let me have this vestment."

The two men stopped, looked at Charley, and decided to let Charley have it. Mr. Foltz grabbed the cope and ran outside, over to Father Werner's wagon. Father Werner came out of the sisters' house, alone. He ran over to the wagon and got aboard. "The girls decided not to leave," he stated, as he grabbed the reins, and looked at Charley, who was standing beside the wagon. "I hope we have finally gotten rid of the last remnants of Benderism," he stated, as he turned and looked back. "I'm sure they all mean well. They have just been led astray on their journey of hope."

Epilogue

Later, Anton Bender lay on his deathbed. He had had nothing to do with the priests at the Jordan parish, during this time. Finally, the Archbishop was called, and Mr. Bender signed a letter of submission to the authority of the Church. Soon, the others signed the same letter, and all was well at the Jordan settlement.

As far as the sisters are concerned, several of them became charter members of a new religious order, in 1886. They were called: 'Sisters of the Precious Blood,' but in 1892, their name was changed to 'Sisters of St. Mary of Oregon.' Among them were Sister Lucretia, who became Sister Clara; Sister Theresa Arnold, Sister Mary Josephine Eifert, Sister Mary Rose Eifert, Sister Mary Cecelia Boedigheimer, Sister Mary Aloysius Bender, Sister Mary Wilhelmina Bliley, and Sister Mary Gertrude Silbernagel. Catharine Foltz became a Benedictine nun and was known as Sister Mary Barbara.

Concerning the will of Father Joseph, Abbot Edelbrock of St John's University, Collegeville, Minnesota, went to Germany and acquired quitclaim deeds from the heirs of Father Joseph. These were Rosina Schweitzer, Francis Joseph Schweitzer, Joseph Ernst, Philip Ernst, Philip Frey, Max Ernst, and Ferdinand Ernst. Abbot Edlebrock contested the will in court. The courts ruled that the will was not explicit enough and therefore, was invalidated. This placed the property in the hands of the Bishop of St. Cloud. In 1886, the small church at Rush Lake was taken over by the Benedictines, of St. Johns, with Father Lawrence Steinkogler in charge. It was blessed and renamed 'St. Lawrence.'

In 1902, a fire destroyed the shrine of Father Joseph. His charred bones were placed in a container and buried near the Pioneer cemetery. His grave, to this day, is marked by a simple white cross.

Bibliography

THE CHURCH IN THE NINETEENTH CENTURY
Raymond Corrigan, Milwaukee, 1938.

MEMOIRS, Sister Mary Wilhelmina, St. Mary of the Valley, Beaverton, OR, 1930.
THE DAWN, A Thesis by *Sister Mary Celestine Snider, SSMO.*

P. JOSEPH ALBRECHT, C.PP.S., F.G. Holweck, An Article in the Pastoral-Blatt, LIV (March 1920).

THE ATLANTIC BRIDGE TO GERMANY, Vol. 1, Baden-Wurtenberg
Charles M. Hall, Everton Publishers, 1974.

THE NAPOLEONIC WARS, AN ILLUSTRATED HISTORY, 1792-1815,
Michael Glover, Hippocrene Books, 1979.

HISTORY OF THE ARCHDIOCESE OF CINCINNATI 1821-1921,

Rev. John H. LaMott, S.T.D., Frederick Pustet Co. Inc., Cincinnati, 1921.

THE POLITICS OF HARMONY, Loyal E. Lee, Associated University Press, 1980.

THE AMERICAN PROVINCE OF THE C.PP.S., Vols. 1, 2,
Rev. Paul J. Knapke, C.PP.S., Messenger Press, 1958.

THE VOICE OF PRAISE, an Unpublished Book, by
Sister Adelaide Waltz, C.PP.S.

GERMAN HOMETOWNS, Mack Walker, Cornell Univ. Press, Ithaca, NY, 1971.

EARLY ECONOMIC CONDITIONS AND THE DEVELOPMENT OF AGRICULTURE IN MINNESOTA, *Edward VanDyke Robinson, Univ. of Minnesota, March 1915.*

A SOCIAL HISTORY OF GERMANY 1648-1914,
Eda Sagarra, Holmes & Meier Publishers, 1977.

THE SAINT JOSEPH DAILY MISSAL, Catholic Book Publishing Co., New York.

THE PARISH OF ST. JOSEPH MERCER CO., OHIO,
Rev. Dominic Gerlach, C.PP.S., 1961.

HISTORY OF ST. HENRY, OHIO, *Joyce Alig, Otto Zimmerman & Son, Newport, KY, 1972.*

NOT WITH SILVER OR GOLD, The Sisters of the Precious Blood, St. Anthony Guild Press, Paterson, NJ, 1945.

REFINING HIS SILVER, *Sister Teresita Kittell, O.S.F., Castle-Pierce Press, 1979.*

FOUR UNPUBLISHED BOOKS *Rev. Francis Brunner, C.PP.S*

www.ingramcontent.com/pod-product-compliance
Lightning Source LLC
LaVergne TN
LVHW010147070526
838199LV00062B/4282